Other *Leisure* books by Andrew Coburn:

ON THE LOOSE

GOLDILOCKS

ANDREW COBURN

LEISURE BOOKS NEW YORK CITY

*For my wife, Casey Coburn,
and our four daughters.
And to the city of Lawrence—
as it was and as it will be.*

A LEISURE BOOK®

January 2007

Published by

Dorchester Publishing Co., Inc.
200 Madison Avenue
New York, NY 10016

ISBN 0-8439-5707-7

The name "Leisure Books" and the stylized "L" with design are trademarks of Dorchester Publishing Co., Inc.

Printed in the United States of America.

Visit us on the web at www.dorchesterpub.com.

GOLDILOCKS

ONE

They met for a late lunch in a country restaurant noted for its gentility, New England charm, and chicken pot pies. Their window table, adorned with a slender vase of cut flowers, overlooked the springtime glitter of a pond and sparks from the flutter of redwing blackbirds. The man shifted his large feet. "I had a hard time finding this place," he complained, and the woman smiled lightly.

"But you succeeded."

She had ordered a garden salad. The man asked for the chicken pie and was visibly disappointed when served. He had anticipated a larger dish, which, the apologetic waiter explained, was available only with the evening fare.

"Don't make a thing of it, Henry," the woman said casually, endless patience and a certain wryness suggested in her cool manner. When the waiter moved off, she held her smile and went on in the same easy tone. "When you come to a place like this you should dress better."

He had on a denim jacket, a gray T-shirt, tight jeans, and orange construction shoes. He was in his mid-thirties, with appealing features and hair still the striking yellow of his youth. His eyes were bruised-blue, the kind the woman associated with hillbillies, Maine men, Southern crackers, and clamdiggers from the coastal communities of New Hampshire. His shoulders were powerful and his arms muscular. He ate well. Too well. He had the faint beginning of a gut.

"I don't see why we had to meet here," he grumbled with a glance that swept the celibate surroundings. The only other patrons were three elderly ladies puffed up in their finery at a corner table and two rotund businessmen just leaving. The restaurant was in the foothills of the Berkshires, fifteen miles outside the sedate Massachusetts town of Mallard Junction, where the woman lived in a gracious century-old fieldstone house occasionally photographed for local magazines. "I could've come to your place," he said with a full mouth.

"That's no longer convenient," she replied simply but in a tone that conveyed finality. She was at least five years older than he, a fact that would have surprised the two businessmen, who admired her in passing. She was gifted with exceptional looks and was marvelously put together, straight-backed and long-limbed. Her black hair, glossy and loose, fell to the fitted shoulders of her linen jacket. "I have something to tell you," she said, watching his face turn wise. "I hope you'll make it easy."

"Maybe I don't want to hear it."

"You have no choice."

"You're dumping me, aren't you?"

"I'm afraid it amounts to that," she answered without hesitation, and received a look sharply belligerent and accusing.

"You've got somebody else," he said, which faintly amused her. Digging into her salad, she harpooned a cherry tomato. He said, "What is it then? If I did something wrong, say so. I'll apologize."

"You're larger than life, Henry. Much too visible. Let's leave it at that."

"I don't know what you mean," he protested.

"It's not necessary that you do." She continued to eat, her shapely jaw moving slowly, her dark lashes lowered. He plunked his fork down.

"Now I'm not hungry."

"Come on," she chided. "You've had a good time. You haven't been hurt, have you? And you're a big boy, war vet and all that."

"You making fun of me?"

"No, I wouldn't do that." She stretched a slim arm past the flowers and briefly touched his hand, which was nearly twice the width of hers. Around his wrist was an identification bracelet acquired fourteen years ago at a sidewalk stall in Saigon, *Cpl Henry Witlo* engraved in the tarnished metal.

He said, "What if I told you I loved you?"

"I'd be touched. But it wouldn't change anything."

"You don't give a damn about me."

"If that were true, I wouldn't be here."

His voice tightened. "I don't like a woman leaving me."

Her expression sharpened in the instant. "I wouldn't want any trouble from you," she warned in an austere voice that chastened him. Gradually he relaxed, his face settling, as if everything in his brain were slowing down, clicking off. "Finish your lunch," she said, and he did, every bit of it, soaking up juices with a hunk of home-made bread he had overly buttered. At one point he flinched, as if somebody were giving him the evil eye, but

3

it was merely the elderly ladies glancing his way. When the time came for dessert, the woman said, "I recommend the apple pie." He chose custard instead and had it with ice cream while she sipped coffee. One of the ladies inadvertently caught his eye. Her mouth, pursed and painted, looked like a ruby planted in her face. At once he treated her to a smile. "Are you flirting with them, Henry?"

"I guess I got the right now. You don't want me."

"Don't make it sound tragic. We both know it isn't."

"You think you know me."

"No, Henry. Too much about you I don't know, and much I suspect I wouldn't want to know."

The check, delivered on a tray, was paid with her money but from his hand, a maneuver that did not embarrass him. He lived life as if back pay were owed and a bonus due. She put aside her cloth napkin. He said, "Two months, Lou. That's all we had."

"More than enough."

"You're being a bitch."

"It goes with the territory."

Outside the restaurant a warm breeze blew against them. Clouds of flowering azalea floated alongside the path to the car lot, where her shiny cream-colored Porsche rested beside his red Dodge Charger, in the grime of which someone had fingered graffiti, none of it original.

"It needs a wash, Henry."

"I'm waiting for rain," he said. The only hint of tension was in the straight set of his mouth. "What if I start wearing a shirt and tie, would that help?"

"No," she said gently.

"What if I get my old job back?"

"Henry."

"What?"

"It's over."

"Just like that?"

"Nothing lasts forever, does it?"

"Childhood," he said. "I used to think that did. Then I thought 'Nam would."

"Now you know otherwise," she said, lifting a hand against the glare of the May sun, which seemed to detonate the stones encrusted in her wedding band. He stood leaden, a thumb hooked in the tight waist of his jeans, and for a stunning moment he looked at her with the shallow unfilled eyes of an infant.

"I won't beg."

"Good," she said.

"But I'll miss you."

"Briefly."

Suddenly his shoulders swung forward, the breadth of him shadowed her, and his voice gushed into her hair. He wanted a good-bye kiss and went for her mouth, but she averted her head and pecked his cheek as she might have done to a close friend or a cousin. Always her public behavior bore a sharp edge of correctness, which matched the tasteful cut of her clothes and the aloof smile on her lips.

"Good-bye, Henry."

"That wasn't a good kiss."

"It'll have to do."

Harnessed inside the Porsche, she slipped on the dark glasses she had left on the dash, adjusted the rearview, and glanced over at him. He rendered a wave that was half a salute. They started their cars up in unison, but it was he who drove away first. And fast.

On the road she felt lifted, relieved of a weight, and she drove leisurely through countryside that seemed to stretch endlessly. The spring had been mostly warm and moist, and wildflowers flew up from the fields. Flooded with sunshine, the green of young pines appeared tender, more tentative than actual. Her window was open, and her alert ear picked up the scold of a jay and the anger of a squirrel but not the sound of the Dodge Charger until it was nearly upon her. Her lips parted in surprise, for he should have been not behind her but well in front of her and on the highway by now. In the rearview she glimpsed a snatch of his face, then her heart jumped because he gunned the Charger and abruptly appeared alongside her, his smile reckless. Sounding the horn, he mouthed words she could not hear and aimed a finger. Ahead was a meandering curve, a marsh on one side and opalescing foliage on the other. That was where he tried to run her off the road.

Her husband was in the garden when she returned home. He lifted himself from a surge of tulips, discarded his cotton gloves, and sauntered toward her with a smile wedded to his face. They met near the birdbath, where he gazed at her as if she touched his life at every point. "I missed you," he said.

"I wasn't gone that long, was I?"

"It seemed so," he said in a tone verging on a sulk, but he quickly collected himself. He had flat gray hair parted sharply, a trim mustache, and soft facial features. In his element—dinner parties, charity luncheons, bird walks—he exuded a gentle noblesse oblige, but in his puttering-around clothes he tended to dwindle in stature. "My first day home," he said, brightening his smile. "It seems odd—and exhilarating."

"You look wonderful," she said. What she meant was

6

that he seemed rested. He had spent the last two months in a private hospital just over the Connecticut line.

"But you look tired," he said with concern. "You work too hard."

"Nature of the business."

"I wish I had your energy, Lou. I wish I could keep up with you."

She slipped an arm around his slender waist. "Let's go in, Ben."

The rooms in the front of the house were of grand dimensions, the furniture a discriminating blend of the modern and the elegantly old. Many of the choice pieces had been in the family for generations. A forebear of his had served with Custer, luckily not at Little Big Horn, and another forebear, less lucky, had boarded the *Titanic*. Their ornately framed portraits, protected by blemished ovals of glass, hung over the marble fireplace in the sitting room.

He said, "I should take my medicine."

"Yes," she replied, glad that he did not need to be reminded and that Mrs. Mennick, their live-in housekeeper and cook and sometimes his nursemaid, arrived on cue with capsules and a tumbler of spring water. The capsules were of varying size and hue, and he washed down each with dedication and an uncontrolled and somewhat comical bob of his Adam's apple.

"I want to stay well," he said in a strong voice that restored his dignity. She took the tumbler from him and returned it to Mrs. Mennick, who stood heavily on skimpy legs. He looked at both women and announced cheerily, "I think I'll take a nap. I get drowsy after swallowing those things."

They watched him leave and then traded glances.

Mrs. Mennick said, "He'll sleep past dinner, that's for sure. What can I get for you, Mrs. Baker?"

"Nothing now," she said. "Maybe a sandwich later."

"In your room?"

"That would be fine."

There was a hesitation from Mrs. Mennick, who knew her place and when to step beyond it. "I hope you don't mind my asking, but did you get rid of the young man?"

"Yes."

"I'm so glad. I never trusted him."

"Nor I, Mrs. Mennick."

"I was always afraid he would cause trouble for you with Mr. Ben."

"Now you can rest easier."

The staircase was wide, with carved intricacies in the rungs of the banister. Her bedroom, which she did not share with her husband, was commodious and airy and at sunset commanded a fiery view of distant hills. A telephone was at her bedside, another on her writing table in the tall bow window where she conducted her business, and a third on the ledge of the tub of her private bathroom.

At the writing table she switched on the answering machine and listened to messages, none urgent enough to prompt an immediate response. She shed her linen jacket, which had gathered wrinkles, and glanced at herself in a mirror, the cords prominent in her neck, a sure sign of lingering tension.

In the bathroom she gave a half twist to the hot water tap in the tub, laid out a mammoth towel, and snatched up the phone. The first call was to Springfield, to a social club, Italo-American. She asked for Salvatore, who eventually came on the line and upon hearing her voice apologized for the delay. She spoke rapidly in a voice stripped of its husk, her words open and naked, as if displaced by something common. Her lacquered nails tapped on a tile. "Not tomorrow, today," she reiterated, the steel side of her character lengthening her face. "No need to see me. I'll leave the money in the mailbox, you hear?" He grunted. She said, "One other thing, Sal. Don't hurt him."

"You want I should kiss him?"

"You being smart?"

"Just making a joke."

"*I* make the jokes, Sal. You do the laughing."

Her next call was across the state to the florid little city of Lawrence, where she had been forged through fire and shaped to her own demanding specifications. The voice on the line belonged to Attorney Barney Cole's secretary, who put her on hold. Waiting, she kicked off her shoes. The tub, which was sunken and big, was not yet a quarter filled, and she turned the tap to full force. Attorney Cole came on the line and said, "This is a surprise. How are you?"

"I don't change, Barney. I'm a constant." Reaching under her skirt, she skinned off her panty hose and let her belly breathe. Her groin itched, and she scratched it. "How's the old crowd? How's Edith and Daisy?"

"Daisy's dying."

"Sorry to hear that. His liver?"

"I think it's everything."

"He's like Lawrence, isn't he, Barney? Burning up from within."

"I wouldn't go that far."

"Of course you wouldn't. You're too loyal to your beginnings. How's Chick? He still a cop?"

"He's a captain now."

"That was expected. How's my old buddy Arnold?"

"Hanging in."

"And you, Barney? Are you hanging in?"

"I like to think so."

"Are you still handsome?"

"I haven't looked lately."

"Still honest?"

"It's a struggle."

She smiled into the mouthpiece. "You'll never get rich."

"That's a given."

"Do you miss me?"

"That's another given," he said. "What's that sound I hear?"

"I'm running a bath." Her panty hose, diminished to a clot, clung to the outside of the hamper like an abandoned caterpillar nest. She tossed her blouse in that direction. "I need a favor," she said, and read resistance in his silence. "You owe me, Barney."

"Depends," he said. "Is it a big favor or a little one?"

"In between. His name is Henry."

It was the middle of the evening, heavy shadows draped over the Birdsong Motel, when Henry Witlo heard the rap of a knuckle too forceful to be friendly. He leaped off the bed, stood perfectly still on stocking feet, and said in a cracked voice, "Who is it?"

"Officers of the law, Henry. Mind if we come in?"

The door flipped open before he could answer, and two men in mufti were upon him before he could move. The more commanding one had a withered hairline and a pitted face, and the other was pug-nosed and slack-lipped, with skin too loosely fastened to his jaws. Henry regarded each with creeping fear and shuddered inwardly. He did not like the way they had flanked him, as if one might execute a sucker punch while the other had his attention.

The one with holes in his face said, "I'm Sal. That's John."

John, whose nose seemed too tightly screwed into his face, nodded. Henry gazed at each man with exacting scrutiny and came to a chill conclusion. "You guys aren't cops."

"Hear that, John? He says we're not cops. What are we, Henry?"

"You guys are wops."

"He's a smart fella, John."

"For a Polack," John said, scarcely moving his mouth inside the fleshy folds of his jaw. On the side of his neck was a puckered scar that could have come only from a gunshot wound. Henry's eyes ate it up.

Sal smiled at him. "Pretty guy like you oughta go to Hollywood. Tie a rag around your head and try out for Rambo."

"What d'you want from me?"

Sal shook his head. "That was a bad thing you did on the road to Mrs. Baker. She's got a nice car, don't look good with a dent. Me, I'd be plenty mad."

"It was an accident."

"You tell lies, your nose is gonna grow. Lucky for you Mrs. Baker don't hold grudges, but she don't want you around anymore. She says you should try the city of Lawrence, and she even mentioned the name of somebody there might help you find a job. I wrote the name down for you."

A folded slip of notepaper was forced into Henry's humid palm. He read the name, which meant nothing to him. His jeans were so tight he hurt his hand pushing the paper into a pocket. He said, "I've never been to Lawrence."

"You'll love it, won't he, John?"

"He won't ever want to leave."

Sal said, "Two-hour drive. Press your foot down, you can do it quicker. John and I will be behind you part of the way, make sure you don't get lost."

Henry put on a brave face, but his smile was lopsided. "What if I don't want to go?"

"Then you should take another look at John. Normal circumstances, he wouldn't hurt a fly. You cross him, you could say he's a rough mother."

"Some people say that about me."

"No, Henry. Nobody says that about you. You got my word."

They watched him put on his shoes and knot the leather laces and move agilely with buttocks in gear, as if he had strains of marching music in his head. He came out of the bathroom with toilet articles stuffed into a pouch and his hair slicked back. Clothes, mostly underwear and socks, he packed into a canvas gripsack that looked as if it had never been new. He hiked the collar of his denim jacket and rolled the cuffs just above his wrists.

Sal, looking at keys, coins, and a few crumpled dollar bills on the bedside table, said, "This is the extent of your wealth? Not exactly a winner, are you?" He suddenly tossed an envelope on the bed. "A few hundred bucks in there from Mrs. Baker. Don't blow it all at once."

"That a kiss-off?"

"You got it, Henry."

The sky was starlit, and the moon, a sizable chunk of

silver, had taken on the aspect of a weapon. Henry stashed his grip in the back of the Charger. They watched him while leaning against their car, which was long and sleek, the next thing to a limo. Sal smiled, the craters in his face brimming with shadow.

"What kinda car you got there, Henry?"

"It's a Dodge."

"Looks like a shitbox to me. What's it look like to you, John?"

"Don't matter," John said, "long as it gets him where he's going."

"You get there," Sal said, "stay out of trouble. You go to the joint, guys'll make use of you. Tell him, John."

"You'll come out with your asshole bigger than Callahan Tunnel."

Henry climbed into his car. He shut the door hard and locked it and peered out the half-open window. "You guys don't scare me."

"That's right, Henry. You keep thinking that all the way to Lawrence."

Two

Barney Cole sat in his closed inner office with Edith Shea, who was of deadly thinness, seemingly made of hot wires, too restless to stay in the worn red leather chair he had drawn for her. She sprang up and breezed by his cluttered desk to a window, where she spilled ash on the sill. "I should've divorced him long ago," she said, expelling smoke. "I shouldn't have listened to you. I blame you, Barney."

"I tried to do what was right for both of you."

"And failed miserably." The window faced a pack of scruffy pigeons on a ledge and overlooked the emptiness of an alley four stories below. The office was in the Bay State Building in the heart of Lawrence, a pint-sized tenement city oppressed by mammoth mill buildings no longer serving their original purpose, a shifting immigrant community evenly divided north and south by the abused Merrimack River and populated by too many priests and politicians and by far too many lawyers, most of whom, like Cole, lived in the surrounding suburbs.

"And what was right for the children," he added.

"That's a laugh." She stood like a streak of chalk in a white uniform pantsuit, and Cole could not remember whether she was working now as a waitress, hairdresser, or nurse's aide, all of which, between babies, she had been. She, not Daisy, was the sinew of the family, which had leveled off with the birth of her seventh child, a girl. The oldest, a boy, was a day student at nearby Merrimack College, a good portion of the tuition diminished by a scholarship that Cole, through a friend, had helped arrange.

"It's not too late, if that's what you want," he said, lowering his eyes as she lurched from the window.

"Of course it's too late. He's dying, for God's sake." She stubbed out her cigarette and lit another. "But he's taking his time. He farts around about everything."

Cole looked up from his desk and watched her fight off a small shivering fit.

"I didn't mean that, Barney. Well, I meant it, but not the way it sounded."

"I know," he said gently, wishing there was more he could say to show that he truly did understand. He had a bottle of Teacher's in the drawer of a file cabinet, but he did not want to offer her any, too early in the day for that. She ran a bony hand through her hair, which was dark and curly and shot with gray.

"There's no insurance. He cashed everything in. He's going to leave me nothing but debts. God knows how much he owes Arnold."

"Arnold won't dun you."

"I know that, but there are others. He owes everybody, Barney. How much does he owe you?"

"Nothing."

"That's because you're being sweet, one of your endearing qualities. I wish I were in the mood to appreciate it." She lurched to another window, this one overlooking downtown's midmorning traffic, unwieldy and unsteady, as if drunks were leading the way. "I know he's meeting you for lunch, Barney. Talk to him. Find out who else he owes. I wake up in a sweat at night thinking about it." The nervous quickness of a smile gave an odd twist to her mouth. "He'll tell you things he won't tell me. He might even be honest about himself."

Cole's secretary flashed him. He picked up the phone and murmured, "Later, Marge."

She pulled hard on her cigarette and continued to stare through the window, her face a wedge of bone. "No one in his family has lived a long life. That's the way it goes."

"Arnold would call it the luck of the draw," Cole said quietly, and she threw him a grudging look.

"We all came out of the same tenements. What did you do, stack the deck and draw aces?"

He arose from his desk, long and thin-bellied in a ten-year-old tailored suit, more muscular than most men of forty-four and fitter than many younger, his features unobtrusively handsome. He raised a hand to touch her, but she avoided it.

"What's in your eyes, Barney? Sympathy or pity?"

"Understanding, I hope."

"Is it free, or will you send me a bill?"

"Slow down, Edith. I'm not a shrink, I'm your lawyer."

"And my friend."

"Yes."

"But you're so fucking stuck-up." Her eyes, larger than most, glittered coldly. "Do you know you've never once,

16

all these years, made a pass at me? I've always resented that."

"I'm sure I did, one time or another, but you never picked up on it."

"Always the diplomat, aren't you?" She straightened her back, steadied herself, and prepared to leave. "Don't tell Daisy I was here. OK?"

"OK."

"I mean that."

"I know you do."

A heavy moment passed, and then suddenly she stepped into him. All at once, against his chest, he felt the hardness of her brow, the narrow length of her nose, and the sharp cut of her chin. "Hug me, damn it," she demanded and threw her rib cage and thin contraption of hips against him, producing almost a clinking sound, as if she could be easily taken apart and reassembled at a more appropriate time and perhaps to better advantage. The heat of her mouth and a rush of tears poured through his striped shirt. Her voice drilled into his skin. "Barney, I don't want to lose him."

Daisy Shea cut into his salad with a weighty knife and fork, broke a lettuce heart, and sliced a tomato wedge in half. Feigning an appetite, chewing deliberately, he got Russian dressing on a corner of his mouth and swiftly wiped it away with the napkin from his lap. He had the ruined face of a drinker, the cavalier eye of a sport, and the reckless air of a gambler reduced to bluff, all hopes pegged to serendipity. He was, like Cole, a lawyer, but with a negligible practice and an office above a used-furniture store, his rent in arrears, a horseplayer with a history of bum tips and a cardplayer whose big moments had passed, along with the red of his hair, which had wasted to white. He was Cole's age, almost to the day, but looked a generation older. He ate as much of his salad as he could stomach and pushed away the bowl.

Cole said, "How are you feeling?"

"I got a foot in the grave. How am I supposed to feel?"

They were in Bishop's, the most popular restaurant in the city, just beyond the post office and in sight of St. Mary's Church. The food was a mix of Arabic and American, and the lunch crowd, teeming with familiar downtown faces, was political, professional, mercantile. Here and there, in the semiprivacy of booths, developers discussed deals over skewered lamb, and at tables near the aisles bookmakers dressed like bankers exhibited their young second wives.

Playing with the menu, which never changed, Daisy appeared to take comfort in the babble around him. "A rough guess," he said, "off the top of your head, how many meals you figure I've eaten here?"

"I couldn't begin to imagine," Cole said. "What do you figure?"

"More here than at home."

"What's your point?"

"Who says I got to have one? A guy in my shape can say what he wants." He glanced about, craning his neck, which had begun to resemble drippings from a candle. In nearly every direction he glimpsed people he knew in one way or another, some since childhood. "In the old days everybody stopped by my table to talk to me. Now nobody does. They don't want to ask how I am. Scared I'll tell 'em."

"Maybe it's simpler than that."

"What d'you mean?"

"Maybe they're afraid you'll put the touch on them, or

maybe you already owe them so much they don't want to embarrass you."

"That's a low blow, Barney."

"Sorry."

"You should be."

The waiter, one of several who had been with the restaurant for years, removed their salad bowls and set down dishes, lamb on the stick for each, and a platter of French fries to share. The fries were a favorite of Daisy's, but now he merely picked at them. According to the strict diet laid out by his doctor, he should not have been eating them at all. When his napkin fluttered to the floor, he reached down and came up wheezing. He stretched his neck again, caught the waiter's busy eye, and ordered a Cutty on the rocks.

Cole said, "I thought you quit."

"I cheat."

They ate in silence, Daisy nibbling. When his drink arrived, he immediately reached for it with a tremulous hand that went steady as soon as the heat of the scotch touched his stomach, a part of which had been cut out a year ago. Color dribbled into his face, and he began eating with more energy, though with the same small bites, as if his teeth were tender.

"I heard from Louise," Cole said, and Daisy's head bobbed.

"What did she want?"

"A favor."

"You owe her one."

"She reminded me."

"Who loved her the most, Barney, you or me?"

"I think you had the edge."

His head dipped again, this time as if the rise of voices

in the restaurant were too loud, megaphonic, skull-hurting. Abruptly he drew up his chest and raised his chin. "She ask about me?"

"Yes."

"What did you tell her?"

"I said you were doing fine."

"Good. I wouldn't want the bitch feeling sorry for me." He rattled the ice in his drink and let the subject slide, as if at will he could excise certain essentials of reality from persons in his past. He quit picking at the French fries, which had gone cold, but he finished his lamb and the green beans that had come with it. Then, sucking on chips of ice, he glanced around again, at people leaving and some just arriving. "You haven't asked about Edith. Usually you ask right away."

"How is she?"

"Terrific. I go, she oughta have the wake here. Noon hour would be best. What d'you think?"

"You'd have a crowd, if that's what you want."

"No box. Why waste money, just lay me out on a table, nice cloth on it, kind they use here at Christmas to put people in the spirit. Later, if you're a real buddy, you could sling me over your shoulder and lug me up the street to St. Mary's for the mass. Priest—who is it now, Father Flaherty?—could prop me in a pew. I'd like that."

"What if someone comes in late and sits beside you, doesn't know you're dead?"

"I won't tell him. You want to, you can whisper to him I've risen. Jesus Junior."

Cole signaled for coffee.

"What's the matter, Barney, don't you go for that?"

"I wonder if we might be serious for a moment."

"About what?"

"Your debts."

"You putting the arm on me?"

"No."

"Then I don't want to talk about them. Not when I'm in such a good mood."

The coffee came. Daisy oversugared his and took a deep swallow, burning his throat. There was a time, high school, when he could bury flaming matches in his mouth and inhale Pall Mall cigarettes from the lit ends. The class cutup. The memory flashed bright in Cole's mind, succeeded by another image of Daisy, a second-stringer in the backfield, indestructible in helmet and pads, a sea of enemy jerseys parting as if by a miracle as he galloped fifty-five yards to score the winning touchdown over Lowell. Or was it Haverhill? At any rate, the Lawrence *Eagle-Tribune* published a page-one picture of him with a careless arm around the unlikeliest cheerleader, Edith Pratt, while his eyes sought the prettiest, Louise Leone, Cole's girl at the time.

"You gonna drink your water?"

Cole slid the tumbler toward him and with a faint twinge of nostalgia remembered the two of them commuting to Suffolk Law School in Boston, Daisy scrounging for tuition and struggling with his grades, graduating at the bottom of the class but passing the bar on the first try. With borrowed money and scavenged furniture, they rented and equipped dinky office space together in the Bay State Building, from which, for purposes of publicity, Daisy rang up restaurants during the busy hours and had himself paged: *Urgent telephone call for Attorney Francis J. Shea.*

Daisy's teeth lay apart in an odd smile.

"What's the matter?" Cole asked.

"I'm starting not to feel so good. God's punishing me in the stomach, what's left of it." He inched his chair back and rose carefully, which for a moment seemed a desperate undertaking. His first step, sideways, was shaky, but his next one straightened.

"Where are you going?"

"Men's room," he replied with a wink. "Don't want to embarrass you."

Alone, Cole sipped his coffee. Ten minutes later the waiter asked whether he wanted a refill, and he shook his head, somewhat disquieted over the time Daisy was taking. He paid the check with a Bishop's credit card and marked in a generous tip. On his way out of the dining room he paused to exchange pleasantries with two fellow lawyers, one of whom, despite dubious qualifications, was in line for a judgeship. He entered the lobby and descended switchback stairs to the lower level, where a woman with a small tidy face and beauty-parlor hair emerged from the ladies' room tugging at herself. A few years ago, quite successfully, he had represented her in a divorce libel, and he recalled everything about her except her name.

"It's all right," she said. "You can't expect to remember all of us." She spoke of herself, her remarriage, her daughter's graduation from Merrimack College, and then, with a long glance to her left, well past the cigarette machine, she whispered in a disturbed tone, "Isn't that your friend?"

"Yes," Cole said. "Please excuse me."

Daisy sat on a padded bench with his head tipped back against the hard wall, his eyes shut tight, and his hands limp in his lap. His legs were doubled in as if they had buckled, and the cuffs of his trousers had ridden up over his black anklet socks, exposing the chalk of his calves. Cole leaned forward.

"Excuse me, Daisy, but are you alive or dead?"

The eyelids fluttered open. "A little of each," he said and flashed a truculent little smile. "I'm gonna outlive all of 'em, Barney, even you. Wanna bet on it?"

Cole said, "What will you put up—an IOU?"

"I put him in the conference room," Marge said.

"Why did you put him there?" Cole asked with mild surprise, for the chairs in the narrow waiting area beyond her desk were unoccupied.

"I didn't like the way he looked at me," she said, and Cole did not question her judgment. She was efficient and intelligent, attractively plain in a wholesome way, with penny eyes and straight brown hair that fell just below her jawline. She had been with him for seven years, part-time for a while and then full-time when his regular secretary had left to get married, a step that did not appear imminent with Marge, who lived with and cared for her mother. Staring up over her IBM typewriter, she said, "He claims he had an appointment."

"In a manner of speaking."

"You should've told me."

"Yes, I should've."

"Is it personal?"

"More or less."

She lifted her appointment calendar. "You have Mrs. Goss at two. She's always prompt."

"I won't keep her waiting," he promised.

He opened the door of the conference room with scarcely a sound and shut it behind him with a noticeable one. The room, narrow and book-lined, austerely furnished with an old oak table and heavy chairs, had a cloistral atmosphere. His heels clicked over the carpetless floor. "Henry, isn't it?" he said, and watched the denim shape rise out of the farthest chair. A ham of a hand flew at him.

"Yes, sir, it is. Henry Witlo."

The handshake was firm but clumsy. Cole was Henry's height but was substantially outweighed. Henry's shoulders seemed to hover, and the blue eyes looked painted in beneath the shock of yellow hair.

"Sit down, Henry."

"Thank you, Mr. Cole."

Cole moved to the other side of the table, sat directly across from him, and for a cool moment studied him. The face, doughy enough to diminish lines, was not as young as it had first seemed, and the smile was looser than necessary. Cole said, "Mrs. Baker phoned to say you were coming to Lawrence and might be stopping by, but I didn't expect you so soon."

"What did she tell you about me, sir?"

"She said you were looking for work."

"I guess you and her are old friends."

"Yes, that's right." Cole drew a yellow legal-size pad close to him and produced a pen. "What kind of work do you do?"

"Anything with my hands, long as it's honest and proper. I'm into clean living. I like a few beers now and then, but I stay away from dope, don't want to ruin my head, and I don't fool with trashy women, don't want to worry about AIDS. I care about myself."

Cole scribbled on the pad, nothing legible. "How old are you?"

"Thirty-five. I won't lie, Mr. Cole, I've been around. Had my ups and downs."

"Ever been in jail?"

"No, sir."

"Where are you from? Originally?"

"Chicopee." He said it fast, making it sound like a birdcall. An apparent smile of innocence followed. "Polack capital of New England. I'm proud of my heritage."

"Have you ever done construction work?"

"Yes, sir. Plenty of it."

Cole tucked away the pen and spoke with his face forward. "I'll ask around, Henry, do what I can, but I can't promise anything. You understand that?"

"I'm staying at the Y, sir. Temporarily. You can call me there. How soon d'you think that'll be?"

"I just told you, no promises."

There was the smallest suggestion of a nod, then a slow lift of the jaw that was a shade challenging. "Were you in the army, sir?"

"Everybody was somewhere," Cole said, always alert to the unsaid.

"Nam?"

"No."

"Where?"

"I was in the reserve."

"Officer?"

"Yes."

"I was one of the last ones out of Saigon."

"You must've been pretty young."

"Sixteen when I joined. Big Polack kid, they were glad to take me. I had a phony birth certificate, wasn't hard to get. My girlfriend's mother worked in city hall and fixed one up for me. She was glad to do it, wanted me out of Chicopee, away from her daughter. Seems someone's always wanting me out of somewhere."

Cole found himself listening more to the voice than to the words, the tone suggesting a man who kept records of wrongs, real or otherwise, perpetrated against him. The telephone, which rested just out of reach, shrilled once and went silent—Marge's signal that she had seated Mrs. Goss in his office. Henry went on as if he had heard nothing.

"'Fore I went to Nam, my mother threw a party for me at Rutna's Bar & Grill, place where she worked. Never seen her looking so happy. She was thinking of the insurance." He lopped his arms over the sides of his chair. "You know who my best buddies were in Nam? Black guys."

Cole glanced at the scribbles he had made and then tore the sheet from the pad. He shifted his feet, ready to rise.

"You don't say much, Mr. Cole."

"I don't have to. I'm not the one looking for a job."

"No, but you owe me something," he said, his eyes cast implacably on Cole's face.'

"What makes you think that, Henry?"

"I figure I did your fighting for you—me and the niggers."

He apologized to Mrs. Goss for keeping her waiting, though he knew she never would have complained. Intensely shy and self-conscious, emotionally rootless since the death of her husband, she sat rigid and prim in the red leather chair, like a schoolgirl waiting to be called upon to recite in front of the class. She was fifty-nine, demurely dressed and inviolably proper. Her careful hair held the cinnamon tones of its original color, and her round face, smooth and childlike, resembled that of a plaster doll retrieved from an attic.

"I hope I'm doing the right thing," she said with a small catch.

She was in the throes of selling her house in Lawrence

and acquiring a condo in Andover, with Cole handling the legalities. The house, where she and her husband had lived most of their childless marriage, was in the city's Mount Vernon section, always vulnerable to random burglaries but in recent months afflicted with a rash of them, both in the nighttime and in broad daylight, horror stories attached to some. A woman whose frail mobility depended on a walker was pummeled by scruffy youths and hospitalized for a week. A family returning from vacation found their home looted, vandalized, and befouled.

"Nothing's cast in stone yet," Cole said. "There are always ways to get out of things."

"I've never made a decision like this before. I depended on Harold for everything." Her voice was hollow, as stark as Cole had ever heard it. "I feel so helpless. I've never even learned to drive a car."

"Perhaps you need more time to think."

"I miss him so much, Mr. Cole."

Her husband, a disciplined and puritanical sort, with a stale look of thrift about him, had died at his desk the month he was due to retire from the Public Works Department, City of Lawrence. That was last January, burial delayed until the ground thawed. Cole had met the man a dozen years ago when he came in with a supportive collar around his neck, an apparent victim of whiplash from a minor auto accident. He was pleased when Cole finagled an unexpectedly generous settlement but resentful when a third of it was deducted for the fee. To placate him, Cole undercharged him for drawing up a will.

Mrs. Goss said, "It's so lonesome with him gone. I try to think of people to talk to on the phone, but I never had many friends. Mildred Murphy was a good neighbor, but she moved to Florida when her husband died."

"Have you considered that?" Cole asked gently. "Moving to Florida?"

"I couldn't do that, Mr. Cole. My memories are here."

"It was just a thought," he said, wishing he had not offered it, for it seemed to have drawn a shudder, as if he had suggested an even deeper separation from her husband than death had brought. He straightened the papers on the pending sale of her house and returned them to the manila folder bearing her name in small block letters from Marge's neat hand.

"Please, Mr. Cole, what do you advise?"

He answered slowly, for he did not want to influence a decision he felt should be entirely hers, nor did he want to sound too much like her husband. "I think you'd feel safer in Andover," he said, aware her nights were often sleepless. Increased police checks of the neighborhood had not comforted her, and neither had the alarm system installed after her husband's passing. She feared that a burglar might circumvent it or that a squirrel or some other rodent might render it useless. "But you may not be happy there," he added.

"Yes," she said in a trance of wistfulness, "that's the hitch."

"You have to weigh advantages against disadvantages. In the condo, you'd have no maintenance worries. You'd be in walking distance of downtown. You'd have an opportunity to meet new people, make friends."

"Yes, I want to make friends, but I don't know how. I'm a private person, Mr. Cole. I wish it were otherwise, but it's not." Then she flushed suddenly and deeply, into the modest neck of her dress, as if she felt she were revealing too much about herself and, worse, taking up too much of his time. "I don't mean to be a nuisance."

"You're not."

"Thank you for being patient," she said, rising from the chair, her legs jelly.

He said, "It's not easy making a decision about a house you've lived in for so long." He lifted himself from his desk and edged around it. She seemed to stand in a daze of fatigue and uncertainty.

"So much of my world is gone, Mr. Cole."

With a hand under her elbow, his touch both friendly and formal, he escorted her out of his office and said, "Marge, would you please call a taxi for Mrs. Goss?" He opened the outer door, his name on the frosted glass, and together they made the journey down the dull corridor. Her steps were deliberate and cautious, as if inequalities existed in the floor, which had been washed many hours earlier but still smelled of the mop. At the elevator, he said, "You asked what I advise, I think we reach a point when what we want most from life is to be free from harm. Everything else is a gift."

The elevator door wheezed open, and he gripped the edge to keep it from closing too soon. A messenger boy with a bad complexion stepped out, followed by a young secretary with an unopened can of Pepsi in her hand. Mrs. Goss did not move. Tears stood in her eyes.

"But Mr. Cole, I don't want to leave my home."

Cole saw two more clients, rather quickly, and at a few minutes after four quit for the day, surprising Marge. "I have to drop my car off," he explained. "The starter's going." At the newsstand in the lobby he bought a roll of Lifesavers, a habit since he had stopped smoking, and scanned the front page of the *Eagle-Tribune*. On his way out, he gave a wave to the shoeshine man.

Essex Street was cleaner and quieter than in the old days. No bustle. No defiance. No mad rush of shoppers.

Little stores had failed first, then big ones. The Lawrence Redevelopment Authority, which had gutted much of downtown in the sixties, sterilized all of it in the seventies. Young trees, planted with federal funds, grew from neat circles on sidewalks widened to oblige crowds that had long vanished. Essex Street was made one-way for heavy traffic that, with hisses and fumes, was merely passing through. The biggest buildings now, stark in design, one no less formidable than another, were banks and insurance companies.

Once this mattered much to Cole, and now it seemed to matter not at all.

He ambled up Common Street, which ran parallel with Essex, and passed through the gates of Snelling's Car Park, where he got a greeting from the raised window of the brightly painted attendant's shack. Pausing, he smiled back at a slight young man with a corrupt little baby face and dumpling cheeks. "How are you, Snooks?"

"Fine, Mr. Cole. Tip-top. Keeping my nose clean like you told me."

Cole had defended him on charges of shoplifting in the big Sears store in the Methuen Mall and of assault and battery on the floorwalker who had seized his arm. Snooks was a scrapper. Cole stepped closer to the window. "I wonder if you might know who's been hitting on all those houses on Mount Vernon."

"Jeez, Mr. Cole, what are you doing now, working for the cops?"

"No, Snooks, but I though you might've heard something."

"Not me. I don't hang around the bad element anymore, but you want my opinion, it's gotta be spics. They do all the crime in the city."

"They do some of it," Cole said with less of a smile. "Not all of it."

His car was three rows away, a copper-colored Cutlass worn thin at the edges from long use, everything working well except for the starter, which fluttered and whined before triggering the motor. The sun was in his eyes, and he donned dark glasses as he maneuvered out of the lot. When Snooks came out of the shack and called after him, he braked sharply and shot his head out the window.

"If it's not the spics, Mr. Cole, it's gotta be the gooks."

The traffic on Common Street was heavy, and he took a right at the first set of lights, a rear tire grazing the curb. Everything in the city seemed squeezed together, but he knew where the cracks were, the shortcuts into Andover, North Andover, Methuen, spacious towns girding and dwarfing Lawrence, a hodgepodge of brick and wood, compressed tenement blocks, massive housing projects, commanding churches, dinosaurian mill buildings. Men and women who had worked in the mills claimed they could still hear the din. It was a city of immigrants but never a melting pot, always a mosaic, a patchwork of ethnic neighborhoods. It was a town before it was a city, and from the start, 1843, it was a business proposition for Yankees who hired cheap labor to dam the Merrimack, dig canals, and turn the tide for textiles. The British, mostly from Yorkshire, got the choice jobs in the mills, supervisory positions, and the Irish, Italians, and others took whatever was offered. Cole's grandfather, Scotch-Irish, survived the strike of 1912 but not the lint in his lungs. Cole's father entered Lawrence politics and made some serious money, much of which he was afraid to spend.

Cole wheeled the Cutlass down a short street and then

up a long one once famous for its speakeasies, "hidden tigers," they were called, situated in rear rooms of drugstores and ice-cream parlors. Cole had heard the stories. An alderman named Galvin had controlled the beer flow into the city, and those guzzling it had called it "Galvinized beer."

He stopped abruptly for a red light at the corner of a construction site where a building for the elderly was rising up, a murky slab seemingly inspired by some stone in a graveyard. He was on the Spicket River side of the city, and anyone born there was called a "Spicket Indian," which was not derogatory, merely informational. Cole was a Spicket Indian, and so was Edith Shea. And so, for that matter, was Louise Leone Baker.

The light flashed green as a young woman with an infant in her arms passed by the Cutlass—a dark madonna, Puerto Rican or possibly Dominican or Salvadoran. She and her child were the city's new blood, running rich through neighborhoods marked by arson and landlord neglect. With a horn tooting behind him, Cole watched her head toward a tenement house near the Spicket, little more than a crooked stream and a dumping site for abandoned supermarket carriages, bald tires, and, occasionally, human bodies that eventually flushed into the Merrimack.

A few minutes later he deposited his car behind the sturdy fences of West Street Motors, where the manager, hoping he would buy it, lent him a brand-new Oldsmobile Cutlass Supreme with all the extras. "It'll do everything for you," the manager said, an easy smile slung across his face, a man much at home with himself. "It'll talk to you and purr when you park it." He handed over the keys. "Drive it with love."

Instead, he drove it with slight recklessness through

the smell, blight, and racket of a bad neighborhood that carried a pervasive air of danger. He cut across downtown traffic by wedging in where he should not have, and when traffic snarled on South Broadway he weaved in the direction of South Union Street. Minutes later the tepid breath of the Merrimack blew against his cheek while the virgin tires of the car sang over the hard honeycomb surface of Duck Bridge, named after a mill that once made sails for America's Cup defenders. The street sloped into South Lawrence, past the ghost of Gilligan's, where Irishmen once stood at the bar, plotted politics, and grew old and sick but never seemed to die. Except Gilligan did, a massive coronary, and the club changed, faded, lost members, and fell to foreign hands.

Andover lay ahead. Always Cole approached the boundary with a feeling of escape and looked forward to the sudden welcome of trees, the lazy intervals of sun and shade, the muscular displays of rhododendron. Always he crossed the line with a soft surge of relief and sense of safety.

His house, shared with a woman named Kit, though lately he had seen little of her, nothing at all in the past week, lay across town. It was a split-level in the Wildwood section, snuggled in by flourishes of lilac, a spruce in front, apple trees in the rear, and blueberry bushes flanking the garage. He pulled into the drive, saw a car parked near one of the garage doors, and for a split second felt joy, for he thought the car was Kit's. Then he realized it looked nothing like hers. A man stepped out of bushes where he had just taken a leak, his gut sucked in as he closed the zipper of his jeans.

Cole stiffened and hollered, "What the hell are you doing here, Henry?"

THREE

"That your car, Mr. Cole? It's a beauty." Henry Witlo ran his large hand over the hood, metallic gray, his face reflected in the shine. "I like the color, suits a lawyer."

Cole stood with his feet planted unevenly on the hard surface of the drive, his dark glasses removed. His stare was severe. "I want to know what you're doing here."

"I came to apologize. I had no right saying what I did, no right at all. Hell, Mr. Cole, you don't owe me anything."

"I figured that out for myself. How did you know where I live?"

"I turned pages. You're in the book. A guy in Andover Square told me where Wildwood was. That's a nice house, Mr. Cole. You got a wife, kids, all that stuff?"

"No, none of that stuff," Cole said tightly, and continued to stare at him. "I don't get you, Henry."

"Lots of times I don't get myself, sir. I'm carrying too much around in my head. Not all of it's Nam, some's just me, the way I am. I guess I come off cocky, but inside I'm all chewed up."

"You sound like a country-western tune."

"In Chicopee we call 'em cryin' and hurtin' songs." He smiled lopsidedly as if straining to be understood. Tiny blackflies hovered near his head in a jittery formation. He batted the air. "I need someone like you, sir, to put me straight."

"That's not my business."

"You're a lawyer, aren't you?"

"If you have a legal problem I can give you advice. Anything else is out of my line."

Henry swiped at the air again. "That mean you're not going to help me get a job?"

"I didn't say that."

Insects thrummed from a tall tangle of hedgerose that bordered the lot line. From the thickest of the bramble a bird suddenly blossomed into flight and vanished over the house. Henry shoved his hands into the back pockets of his jeans. "Christ, it's pretty here," he said with a sigh. "I get depressed just looking at it. I'm thirty-five years old, Mr. Cole, and I got nothing. I've never owned a new car in my life, always somebody else's piece of junk, and I'll never have a house like yours." Through his teeth, cleanly and neatly, he spat on the grass. "I'm not blaming anybody, only myself. I try to face facts."

"You could've fooled me on that point."

"You don't trust me, do you, Mr. Cole? It's OK, trust has to be earned. I learned that in combat."

"What do you really want, Henry?"

"I wouldn't mind a beer, sir, if you got one."

Cole took him through the garage into the lower level of the house and seated him in the family room lit by a wall of windows. At the end of the room, covered by a sheet, was a pool table, seldom used. Dated magazines, mostly *Time*, were stacked into a corner, next to a rack of old reference books from Cole's schooldays.

Henry said, "Doesn't look like you spend much time down here. What's it look like upstairs?"

"I don't give tours. I'll be back in a minute."

Cole climbed one brief set of stairs and disappeared up another, his footsteps muffled in thick carpeting. Henry sat deep in an upholstered chair and stared at a fireplace that had not been used in years. Above the mantel was a brass clock whose hands gave out the wrong time. Cole returned with a tapered glass and a bottle of German beer that poured out as dark as chocolate.

"You buy the best, don't you, Mr. Cole?"

"You're not complaining, are you?"

"Not me. I'm grateful for everything I get."

"How well do you know Mrs. Baker?"

"I'm a gentleman. Some things I don't tell, but you could kinda say I grew on her."

"How did you meet her?"

Henry drank deeply of the beer. "Company I worked for, last September, did her driveway. Ever seen her house, Mr. Cole? Makes this place look like a shack. Her husband's a blueblood, did you know that?" He poured more beer into the glass. "I feel funny drinking alone."

"Don't let it worry you."

"I let everything worry me. Lucky I don't have an ulcer. Want to hear something rich, hard to believe? Only place I didn't worry was Nam. That's because in the army I mattered. I had two stripes said I did."

"Henry," Cole said quietly, "that was a lot of years ago."

"I know that better than you. Every morning I wake up, I got an exact count how long it was. I'm not brooding about it. Like I said before, I'm facing facts. Women like me now, five years from now they won't like me so much. Biggest thing I got going is I can pick up a shovel and hold my own with a road gang. Give me a hammer, I can pound a nail. Doesn't say much, does it?"

Without comment, Cole stepped to a window, gazed beyond apple trees in full flower to the darkening edges of the lawn, and had a vision of soldiers operating at high pitch during combat and going crackers with the silencing of the guns. He raised the window a few inches and admitted a mild breeze, his eye distracted by a wasp playing on the screen, his ear taken by the territorial anger of a robin.

"I got out of the army, Mr. Cole, I went back nights to school. Got my diploma in a year. I'm no dummy. Even went on to community college, but I didn't stick it out. I was still young then. Nobody told me I'd grow old so fast."

Cole spoke in a dry voice not entirely meant to be heard. "If you can name the people who didn't tell you, maybe we can sue."

Henry heard. "My mother, we can start with her. Except we'll have to dig her up. Chicopee cop did her in, Mr. Cole, but it got hushed up. Guys were always beating up on her."

"I'm sorry."

"Some people aren't meant to make it," he said with a shrug from the chair, his eyes blue studs beneath a careless fall of hair. "I could use another bottle of beer, if you can spare it."

"That's all she wrote," Cole said with a nod at the empty, a slow step removing him from the window. "Whatever you're leading up to, it's time you hit me with it."

"I want to go back to school."

"Commendable."

" 'Fore it's too late." His voice came from the depths, his whole life for a fleeting second distilled in his eyes. " 'Fore they find me in a ditch like they did my mum."

"There's a community college nearby," Cole said quickly.

"I still need a job."

"Yes, you've made that clear."

"I want to work for you, Mr. Cole. You got things need fixing on the house, I could do them. I saw right away you got a drainpipe needs replacing, probably the gutter too. I run out of chores here, I could do things at your office. Run errands, drive you places. I'm not talking full-time, just when you need me."

Cole felt a flicker in his stomach and a warning from a dark corner of his brain. He said nothing.

Henry cranked himself out of the chair, and his voice came out as a rush of water would to challenge a void. "Look me in the eyes, Mr. Cole, and tell me I'm asking too much."

Ben Baker was playing the piano in the drawing room, a romantic tune from the thirties that his mother had taught him. He played it badly. When he glimpsed the stout shape and skimpy legs of Mrs. Mennick, he gently lowered the lid over the keys as if putting the music to sleep. Mrs. Mennick approached with a caring smile, and he lifted his well-barbered head and viewed her with a degree of love, for she was a composite of his childhood nannies and tutors, none of whom his mother had found quite acceptable, though he had cherished them all. One nanny used to rumple his hair when talking to him, and another had cuddled him into her vast lap while reading to him. A sickly child, he had been educated at home until early adolescence, at which time he had been sent off to boarding school, the most miserable years of his life, his university ones only a scant improvement.

Mrs. Mennick said, "You certainly look rested."

"Well, I had a good night's sleep and a nice nap this afternoon." His nap had followed his medication, which he had taken early in order to be alert for the evening. His eyes shone, and his face had so much color that it seemed someone had slapped him on both cheeks.

"I'm so glad you're home, Mr. Ben. I prayed for you every day."

"That's why I'm better," he said to please her, and rose from the piano bench to breathe in the scent of cut grass from the open windows. Mrs. Mennick's brother, who operated a small landscaping business, had driven a mower over the lawns that morning.

"Dinner will be at eight," Mrs. Mennick said, "unless you'd like it earlier."

"Eight is fine." He gazed beyond her. "Is Mrs. Baker in her room?"

"Yes, she is. I just came from there."

"Then I think I might visit her."

"I'm sure she'd like that."

He left the room with a measured step and ascended the stairway, pausing to rest on the landing, for he knew that his stamina was limited. He paused again near his bedroom, his since childhood, some of his toys still in there, stashed in a closet. He peered in to see whether Mrs. Mennick had neatened up after his nap. She had.

His wife was in the master bedroom, his pleasure to have given it to her. She needed the space, the privacy, and he had wanted her to have the view from the bow window, where she sometimes struck a pose that had been his mother's. Her door was closed, and he placed an ear against it. If she was doing business on the phone, he did not want to infringe a rule by intruding. Hearing nothing, he rapped once and was answered immediately. He slipped in and clicked the door shut behind him. She came forward, slender and long-limbed, fluid in the way she filled a dress. His heart ached at the sight of her. His kiss was tenderly given and returned with enough life to make him heady.

"Such a long time," he murmured, exorbitant in his emotions, lips trembling, eyes almost filling. "I love you, Lou."

"I shouldn't want you to stop."

"I thought maybe . . ." He loathed his awkwardness. ". . . if you aren't too tired."

He marveled at the effortlessness of her movements and the dexterity of her fingers as she shed jewelry, then rustled out of her dress. Her beauty, to him, outmatched that of starlets, models, and centerfold maidens in *Playboy*, back issues of which a fellow patient had bestowed upon him at the hospital. Her lingering winter pallor added to his wonderment and made her seem pure and himself young. His blood ran quick. Yet in removing his own clothes he was shy and slow and stumbled over his shoes.

"Come," she said from the open bed. He felt special, lifted, extravagant, and responded with courage and daring. With an errant breeze on his backside, he absorbed her heat and scent, bruised his lips on a diamonded ear, and relished the rasp of her breath and the fire in his own. The telephone rang but scarcely disturbed him, and the answering machine soon silenced it.

Later he lay lulled, flattened, seemingly content, except for an arm thrown hard over his eyes. "What's the matter, Ben?" she asked from the prop of an elbow, and he smiled vaguely.

"The Romans had a catchphrase for it. *Post coitum triste*. The sadness that follows sexual fulfillment." His eyes were dim. "I don't want to lose you, Lou."

"Little chance of that."

"One never knows."

"Worry about real things, Ben. The rest is a waste."

The telephone rang again when he was back in his clothes and she was coming out of her bathroom, her black hair brushed back and her eyes liquid-bright. She answered it on the second ring, her voice brisk. Then her eyebrows shot up and she muffled the mouthpiece.

"It's business, dear. Would you excuse me?"

He moved with a jerk. At the door he turned tentatively, saw that her hand was still on the mouthpiece, and closed the door behind him.

Like her life, Emma Goss's supper was simple and solitary, a small plate of deli ham, leftover baked beans, and tomato wedges, with brown bread on the side. She drank her coffee black, with just a touch of sugar. She was, in actuality, quite accustomed to eating alone, for her husband used to manipulate his fork with one hand and turn the pages of the newspaper with the other. Of course the difference then was that she needed only to speak and he, eventually, would have replied.

She helped herself to an extra dollop of beans, conscious of the approach of evening, her loneliest hours. More easily managed was the daylight, and cherished were the errands that occupied her mornings. A taxi, often the same driver, toted her to the dry cleaner, the cobbler, the bank, the drugstore. Twice a week she went to the market on South Union Street, where the checkout clerk was especially pleasant and the manager, a bald man with a turtle face, never failed to wish her a good day. If the weather was suitable, gardening filled her afternoons.

She cleared the table, did the dishes, and took herself into the front room, where she sat erect in an armchair to thumb through magazines and glance out the window. The magazines were subscriptions that continued to arrive in her husband's name, as did utility bills and junk mail. His clothes and his shoes, including a pair of Florsheims he had never worn, remained in his closet, and his razor and heart pills were still in the medicine cabinet. The mattress on their bed harbored two hollows, the greater one his, which she sometimes slipped into as if an arm had drawn her. Sometimes, at her loneliest, she wished for the sleep of death.

She tried to believe in an afterlife but could not, perhaps because he had not. She did, however, believe in his ghost or, if not that, his leftover presence. Often, at odd moments, she felt she heard his footsteps in another room, and only last night, pausing near the china closet, she glimpsed herself mirrored in the glass and the shape of him looming up behind her. She was on the edge of fainting when she felt his hand touch her shoulder, familiar and firm enough to steady her but too intangible for her to grasp. That was when she knew she should not sell the house and leave him to strangers.

She put aside the magazines, which had failed to divert her thoughts, and gazed through the window at the trim bungalows across the street. Only from the stenciled markings on the mailboxes did she know the surnames of the occupants, busy people into whose lives she did not presume to intrude, not even when their children damaged her shrubs or chalked graffiti on the herringbone brick path leading to her front door. She might have spoken to the culprits herself but feared being sassed and making matters worse. She had little knowledge of children. Harold had opted to have none, and she was the only issue of late-married parents who had sheltered her from a world they had never much understood.

Suddenly, with no warning whatsoever, came a blast that made her heart flip. A youth on a motorcycle had detonated the engine and now was roaring past the house. Immediately she pressed her fingers against her ears to choke the sound and catch her breath.

A few minutes later she entered the spectral dim of the dining room, shades lowered to shield the furniture against the sinking sun, and stood before the china closet hoping to glimpse her husband, but the moment was not right. Even her own reflection was vague, as if she were more of his world, wherever that might be, than this one. "Harold," she said aloud to the dead air, which did not stir.

Her loneliness swelled when she stepped into the well-lighted den, where his long, dignified face of firm features pressed close to the bone peered back at her from a standup frame. It was one of the few photographs she had of him, for he had never been much for staring at a camera. The local paper used it when he was promoted to public works supervisor and reran it when he died. She gazed at it hauntedly while giving a little twist to her wedding band, the symbol of a marriage in which she had exerted little will of her own, instead snuggling herself into the comforting curve of his life and formulating her thoughts under the shadow of his. In return, he had given love, fidelity, and support. He had been close with money, but she had wanted for nothing, and their annual two weeks at a seaside cottage had been an adventure of sorts.

She sat at her husband's desk, switched on the flexible lamp, and took out a box of stationery. Her sole correspondent was Mildred Murphy, her old neighbor who had moved to Florida. Each week, in a small dainty hand, she wrote Mildred a letter filled with local news garnered from the *Eagle-Tribune* and frequently included clippings, which increased the postage. Mildred's reply was always prompt but never more than what fitted on the back of a picture postcard. With Harold's gold Parker pen, one of the gifts he got on retiring, she wrote *Dear Mildred* and then remembered she had written only two days ago.

In the kitchen a breeze gave her a chill. She shut the window and stood shivering near the telephone on the wall. When slipping into depression, she found it essential to hear the live voice of another human being. A few days ago she had rung up the reference desk at the Lawrence library and asked an amiable woman named Winnie Reusch for information on past mayors of the city ("When exactly did the Irish come into power?"), and another time she had spoken for several minutes to a Delta Airlines clerk about flights to Florida. This time, a question ready to roll off her tongue, she tapped out the home phone of attorney Cole.

His line was busy. And stayed busy.

A panic set in, but she fought it by returning to the desk in the den. She laid out a fresh sheet of stationery, picked up the pen, and began writing swiftly and fluently, her head tipping farther and farther to one side as if to let someone read the words over her shoulder.

The letter was to Harold. His eyes only.

Louise Baker had told her husband it was business, but that was true only in a general sense, for the caller was

Barney Cole and the subject was Henry Witlo. She said, "If he's too much for you, forget it, send him on his way."

"I just want to know what I'm letting myself in for," Cole said with a note of annoyance.

"What's the problem?"

"He barrels in. He twists and pushes, comes at me from every angle. I agreed to help him find a job, not adopt him."

"Is it that bad, Barney, really?"

"He's Goldilocks, for Christ's sake. I'm afraid I'll come home some night and find him sitting in my chair, eating off my plate. He's already taken a leak in my bushes."

Her laugh was grim and faint, perhaps not heard.

"You really pick 'em, Lou."

"No taste. That what you're telling me?"

"I simply don't understand, that's all."

"Let's say I had an itch and leave it at that." She spoke carelessly, and from his end of the line came a heavy sigh, as if something had been extracted from him, an illusion perhaps. She said, "We mellow, Barney, but we don't change. I'm still just a guinea girl from Lawrence."

His voice came slowly. "I heard through the grapevine you're doing well out there. You've got the best of all possible worlds."

"You heard correctly."

"You're gentry."

"I use the right fork."

"Must belong to a few clubs."

"I'm president of the Mallard Junction Improvement Society. We keep the town pristine."

"I've never met your husband."

"No reason you should have."

"Sickly fellow, I've heard."

She was silent, tolerating the tone of the conversation only because it suited her purposes.

Cole said, "I understand you're making money."

"That I don't talk about," she said coolly.

"We used to talk about everything."

"In bed, Barney, not on the phone." She shoved aside her hair and shifted the receiver to her other ear. "And in those days you were my lawyer."

"And those days are gone."

"Everything must end."

"I know that, but does Henry?"

She stared through the bow window. In the lowering light of day the lawns were fiercely green, as if paint had been applied, and the sky was at its bluest. "Now you have the nub of it," she said, watching crows sweep toward distant treetops. "You always did have a quick grasp."

"You want me to keep an eye on him, keep him occupied. You don't want him coming back on you and smudging what you have out there. Otherwise you'll have to deal with him in ways that might not be ladylike."

"Now you have it all," she said simply.

"Why didn't you tell me this in the first place?"

"I knew I didn't have to. But I've given you an out, haven't I? If he's too much of a chore, forget him, send him on his way."

"You know I won't do that. You know me too well."

"We know each other, Barney," she said with sudden softness, her mind reaching back to a time tender to them both, when the urgencies of youth put nonsense in their heads and his bulky class ring on her finger.

He said, "But how well do we know Henry?"

"He's only crazy around the edges, but everybody's jagged there. Comes from the bombardment of life."

A moment passed. "Will this settle my account?"

46

"Who knows, Barney, I might end up owing you."

"That's what worries me."

She was ready to ring off when the trace of a wistful smile crossed her face, and she turned from the window. "I have the same grapevine as you, darling. I hear you have a woman living in your house. Is it serious?"

"Only on my part."

"Does she have a name?"

"You wouldn't know her."

After she put the phone down, she stood for a few seconds in front of a mirror. Her general image satisfied her, but not the expression on her face, which she duly brightened. When she opened the bedroom door she saw her husband poised a few feet away, a quiet and emphatic presence. "Were you listening?" she asked, and his face heated.

"I wouldn't do that."

She moved quickly and pressed a propitiatory hand over his cheek. "I know you wouldn't."

"I love and respect you too much."

"And that cuts both ways, Ben."

He smiled shyly. "I was waiting to thank you."

"For what?"

He blushed again. "You know."

"You're welcome," she said as she might have to a child whose shirttail she had tucked in.

"Are you happy, Lou? Happy as I am?"

"I'm content," she said. "Happiness is something appreciated well after the fact, sometimes years."

"Were you ever happy?"

"Oh, yes. I was just talking to him."

His face fell, and his voice went weak. "Lover?"

"Friend." She fitted an arm around him. "You're my only lover."

47

* * *

Henry Witlo took a swim and a shower at the YMCA, across the street from Lawrence Common. He emerged sopping from the shower stall, squished his hair back, yanked in his stomach, and paused dramatically in a puddle like a hero ready to be cast in bronze and aggrandized on a pedestal. A voice sliced through the spongy air. "You have a great physique." A wiry man in gym shorts stood near an open locker, and Henry, who never shunned a compliment, offered a face of innocence, like a dinner plate licked clean. "You must've played football," the man said as Henry snatched up a towel.

"Not professional," he replied, perverting the truth, for neither had he played amateur, nor for that matter any team sport. At school and in the army he had been a bit of a loner and much of a posturer. He mopped his face and dug the towel into one wet underarm and then the other, his chest protruding, his private parts shaking. "But I had offers," he lied outright.

"You should've taken one."

"We all make mistakes."

A business suit hung in the open locker, and tasseled loafers were placed neatly together on the shelf. The man closed the locker and clicked and spun the combination lock. Then he moved obliquely closer with a bar of soap in his hand. He had a flattop cut of gray hair and comfortable crow's-feet at the edges of his narrow eyes. His voice was chummy. "First place you go soft is in the middle."

"You noticed, huh?"

"The rest of you is OK."

"I try to take care of myself."

"A man must." Each word came out quiet. "Lean men," he went on in the same deliberate way, "get less resistance in life and more of a lift from whatever breezes are blowing."

"That supposed to mean something?"

"No, but it sounds good."

Henry flipped the towel behind himself and whip-sawed the back of his shoulders. "You must be a fag. You can talk to me, just don't touch."

"You're quick to judge," the man said, nothing altering in his face.

Henry girded his middle with the towel. "I'm used to the attention. In the army I couldn't take a shower some guy wasn't looking at me." His clothes were heaped on a bench. Pawing aside his jacket to get at his jeans, he plucked out an Ace pocket comb and slicked it through his wet hair. "I was in Nam."

"Then you're older than I thought."

"You look exactly what you are. What are you, fifty?"

The man merely smiled. "I've been around the block."

"Yeah, so have I," Henry said with sudden bitterness and a slackening of stomach muscles that disturbed the whole of his posture, as if something had twitched and given. "What's your name? You got a business card? I ever need a job, I might look you up."

"Don't do me any favors," the man said lightly, which Henry did not take kindly. His mouth went sour.

"I don't want to hurt your feelings, but old guys like you are the sorriest in the world. You got nothing coming. Everything's going, you know what I mean? Up ahead, what d'you see? Not much, right?"

"That's the way the world works," the man said mildly, and, excusing himself, padded by on rubber thongs into the same stall Henry had occupied.

Henry marked time. He drew himself up and whipped the comb through his hair again. Moving to a mirror, he projected his jaw in the cloudy glass, studied his profile, and with a substantial breath regained a sense of worth. Moments later, as if being cued onto a stage, he sauntered into the cloying heat of the stall. The man's gym shorts drooped from a peg, the supporter hanging out, and the man stood dazzled in a cone of silver spray. His hair was soaped and his face sculpted into a perfect attitude of indifference.

"Thought I'd see you."

"It'll cost you," Henry said.

"Jesus bloody hell," said the bigger of the two uniformed policemen upon entering the stall. The grit from their heavy shoes made mud around the victim, who lay supine on the wet tiles, his face battered and discolored, his left eye swollen shut and his mouth bloody. The other officer crouched over him, and the big officer, dodging a drip from the shower nozzle, said, "Who spread the towel over him?"

"I did." The trembling voice came from the YMCA's assistant director, who stood shocked and frightened just outside the stall.

"Why didn't you tuck one under his head?"

"I was afraid to move him."

The big officer, whose eyes had a vague stinging effect, side-stepped another drip. "Was the water going?"

"Yes, sir. I turned it off."

"Then you're the one who found him."

"Yes, sir."

"See anybody?"

"No, sir."

"D'you know who this guy is?"

"I think it's Mr. Pothier, owns the furniture store off

Essex Street. He's been a member in good standing for years."

The big officer stepped around his partner and squatted on the other side of the victim, his leather accessories creaking and his holstered revolver riding up on his hip. His heavy face came forward. "Can you hear me, Mr. Pothier?"

"He can't talk," said the other officer.

"But he can move his head, can't you, Mr. Pothier?" There was a slight painful nod, and the big officer leaned closer. "Somebody did a job on you. You know who it was?" There was a long pause, then the barest of movements, negative, and the big officer grunted to his feet, his face pink from exertion and disgust. His partner looked up.

"What's the matter?"

"I don't think he wants to tell us."

Four

Barney Cole had a wearisome day, the morning spent in court trying to squeeze child support out of ex-husbands and the afternoon in the registry of deeds tracing disputed titles to the snarl of their nineteenth-century roots. His spirits lifted when he swerved into his driveway and saw Kit Fletcher's dusty car parked in her half of the garage. An excitement built when he entered the house and glimpsed the loaded briefcase dropped in an armchair and the navy-blue pumps discarded nearby. "In here," she called to him in a deep luxurious voice that was a natural extension of her beauty. His heart leaped.

"Where?"

She emerged from the sun room on bare legs strongly shaped by tennis, her tailored business clothes abandoned for a sloppy sweatshirt and loose shorts. Always his breath caught at her sudden presence. She was ten years his junior, blond and big-limbed, good-natured, eternally youthful, with the air and charm of an indifferent goddess.

"I've missed you," he said, staring into large eyes more gray than blue and at odd times, like now, more green than gray. He gave her no chance to speak. He kissed her. When he pressed against her, she did not mind, a good sign that everything was still right between them. They had a relationship he did not take for granted. It was, in her words, more of an arrangement, especially since she divided her time unequally between here and Boston, two semipermanent addresses. In Boston she had the glitter of Quincy Market, business breakfasts at the Ritz, evenings at the theater, and a harborside condo within walking distance of the esteemed law firm of Pullman & Gates, where her skill in litigation was growing. Here in Andover, a twenty-mile commute, she had the serenity of the Wildwood section and all of his attention. He whispered into her hair, "Rough two weeks?"

"No more than usual. I finished up that antitrust thing. Now I'm working on a libel." Her eyes flew up. "Has it really been two weeks?"

"Almost."

She liked living in two places, functioning in two worlds, a situation that only half pleased him. She liked her independence. He liked his too, but not so much of it. He would have proposed marriage by now, but he knew it was not on her mind. A brutal husband, whom she had shed after a single year, had left marks.

"Do you know what I want?" she said, and his eyes raced over her face.

"I hope it's the same thing I want."

"A drink," she said. "I need time to wind down." Which she could never do. Always there was a breeze about her, as if she had come out of the cradle with a sense of urgency.

In the kitchen, after stripping off his suit jacket and tie and hiking his sleeves, he measured out ice and poured from a bottle of Harvey's Bristol Cream. They carried their glasses out to the back lawn, for she wanted to breathe the air, smell the lilac, hear the birds, though the birds at that declining time of day were rather quiet. The neighborhood was an old apple orchard in which, some three decades ago, felling as few trees as possible, a developer had erected houses that sold for premium prices. Cole had bought this house fifteen years ago, the down payment a wedding gift from his father, who had furtively handed him the money in a shoe box, glad to be rid of it.

Kit dropped into a canvas lawn chair, extended her legs, tasted her drink, and watched him settle near her in the same kind of chair. "I met your pal."

Cole, puzzled only for a second, frowned. "What did you think of him?"

"Not the sort of handyman I'd hire. I was afraid he was going to fall off the ladder the way he was fiddling with the drainpipe. He was bare-chested and had a rag around his head. I thought he was Rambo."

"His name's Henry."

"Yes, he introduced himself. He's a talker, isn't he?"

"I wish you had called me."

"Why, is he dangerous?"

"Probably not, but I don't want him here again while you're home. Did he bother you?"

She smiled. "He asked if I was your lady."

Cole gazed off at small gouges in the lawn, the work of squirrels. In July and August the damage would be greater from larger animals snouting for grubs. He said, "What was your answer?"

"I didn't give him one."

"What would it have been if you had?"

She smiled again, the smile unreadable, and he rested his eyes on her lax and loose legs, her bare heels pressed into the grass, her shiny ankles perhaps a shade too thick, for him an endearing flaw that increased her appeal the way an error on a coin added value. A blister glistened on her little toe, left foot. The pumps she had sloughed off were new.

"How long will you be home?" he asked, implying that this was her real home and that her place in Boston was little more than a hotel room, though he was well aware that the bulk of her clothes were there, not here, and that all he knew about her life away from him was what she chose to tell, which sometimes was not much.

"I'm not sure," she said, holding her smile. "I never am, am I?" Her free hand reached out, and for a moment or so their fingers entwined. "For your information," she said, "I missed you too."

He believed she might have, but scarcely as much as he had missed her. She was too active, too driven, to moon over anybody, least of all a small-time lawyer content to strive for no more than a decent living and to keep the dark out of his soul. He had met her less than a year ago at an alumni function of Suffolk Law and had held on to her hand longer than was appropriate, forcing her to give him a second look. Their first date was dinner at Locke Ober's. He wanted to impress her, which fell flat when the waiter addressed her by name. A more serious date was in Lawrence, Bishop's, where he was proud to show her off and she relished the Arabic plate and said casually, "I know I'll never marry again." "That's silly, how can you know that?" he shot back, and she replied promptly, "The same way you know you'll never be president of the United States. Pass the salt, please." In his house for the first time she was a confident creature moving through rooms as if the light always tilted toward her. Later, in his bedroom, at ease with her nakedness despite ridges left by the pinching' parts of her underwear, she was a pink monument to health and beauty. Before slipping into the sheets, she placed something on the night table. He thought it was a book of matches she had taken from Bishop's for a souvenir. It was a condom in a discreet and dainty package. "I'm sure you understand," she said with a sigh. "We've reached a point in civilization where no one's word is good enough."

Now, rattling the ice in his drink and staring at the streaks in her blond hair, he said, "You could've phoned."

"Yes, I meant to a couple of times," she said. "Why didn't you call me?"

"That would have annoyed you."

"It's inconvenient only at the office," she said with an aloof sort of compassion. "You could've called in the evening."

"You take the phone off the hook."

"Not all the time, only when I bring work home." She looked him squarely in the face. "Tell me, Barney, are we arguing?"

"I hope not."

"I wouldn't want to."

Certain rules guided their relationship, and he had nearly broken some with his possessive eyes and insinuating tone. Sipping, he watched several blackbirds fly low over the lawn, the sound of their wings like the unwrapping of a package.

She said, "About this Henry. Where did you get hold of him? Is he a client working off your fee?"

"It's a long story not worth going into."

"I don't trust him."

"Neither does my secretary," he said, drawing himself up some. "Tell me about the libel case."

"No, not now. It would hurt my head."

"Mine too, I would think. Your cases are more complicated."

Her flawless face tightened. "I'm good, Barney, damn good, but they'll never make me a senior partner. They'll never give me one of the big offices, fresh flowers on my desk every day, private bar. That's only for the good old boys."

He smiled at her frankly, for she did not usually reveal her frustrations. She had graduated at the top of her class from Suffolk Law, a block of brick on Beacon Hill, and through dogged persistence had hooked on as an associate with Pullman & Gates, which normally drew only from Harvard and occasionally from Dartmouth. The raises in her salary had exceeded the rise in her status. He said, "Then why stay?"

"I like being with the best." Her wandering eyes returned to him circuitously. "I like the smell of old money."

"Then why are you bothering with me?"

"You're reality."

"No, I'm Barney Cole."

"Same thing."

"Are you sure?"

"Yes, I'm sure, and in the middle of the night I'm very sure."

The shadows had lengthened, and mosquitoes were beginning to bite. She slapped her thigh and he the back of his neck. They finished off their drinks. "Shall we go in?" he asked.

He followed her, aware of her gait, the swing of her hips, the straightness of her back. There were times, in an attempt to make his life simple, he tried to regard her only within a sexual context, but his feelings ran too deep. Never during her absences had he found a way to shut her out of his mind for an appreciable time. When the absences extended more than a week, his house filled with shadows out of which the likeness of his wife or the figure of his father sometimes crept, though never close enough to touch and never with words clear enough to catch.

In the kitchen he said, "Hungry?"

"I'm not sure." She opened the refrigerator and peered in for something to tempt her, but the selection was sparse. "You haven't been doing any shopping," she said over her shoulder. "That how you stay thin?"

"I've been eating out."

"I'll go to the market tomorrow," she said with the air of a housewife manipulating a busy schedule. She opened the freezer compartment and tilted her head. "For now, how about a pizza?"

He nodded as the telephone rang. He thought it might be Mrs. Goss with a shy and needless question painfully rehearsed, or perhaps Edith Shea with a grim report on Daisy. It rang again, a jolt to the ear. He was closer but made no move.

"Aren't you going to answer it?" she asked, and he shook his head. She made a face. "You'll wonder all night who it was."

"No, I won't."

Each ring seemed to sting her. "It might be for me. They know I'm here."

"They always know, don't they? Which one is it this time?"

"Chandler," she said.

He lifted the receiver and spoke. She was right, it was Chandler Gates, the sixty-year-old grandson of the firm's cofounder and the one to whom she owed the most gratitude. Cole knew the voice, sugar on the tongue, from past calls, knew the vulpine face behind it from pictures in the Boston papers. "Here," he said, dangling the receiver.

A breeze was blowing in, and he stepped directly into its path. She talked with her back to him, her voice cool and assured, and she turned and whispered, "It's about the libel." He half believed her, perhaps more than half. She placed her back to him again and said, "Yes, Chandler, I'm listening."

He made his way to the sun room. The real estate agent, a fashionable woman with the air of a prima donna, had alternately called it a sun room and a plant room. At the time it had been full of both ingredients, dazzling his wife. He sank into a wicker chair with the wish that he had poured himself another Harvey's. Insect sounds swirled through the screens. From time to time he rubbed the raw edge of his jaw where he had shaved too close that morning.

"It really was business," she said, and he felt his senses reach out. She stood just inside the rounded doorway with her face shaded in the diminishing light. "The *Globe* is hanging tough on us."

"That shouldn't bother you," he said.

"It doesn't. A settlement would flatten the fee, a trial could swell it."

"And give you a chance to shine. Do you have a good case?"

"Depends upon the purity of my client." She scratched

a knee. "Did you know I once interned at the *Globe* for three months?"

"No, you never mentioned it."

"Summer job. I worked with the court reporter. That's when Tom Winship was editor. The women in the newsroom called him Windshit, not to his face."

Her shaded smile was ambiguous, and one of her hands was loosely clenched. He knew he was being prepared for something and waited with patience, his eye stretching out to an apple tree where the last of the sun was burning between the leaves.

"Barney, I have to go."

"I thought that might be the case."

"I'm sorry."

"I know."

She opened her fist, leaned forward, and carefully tossed something into his lap. He retrieved it from between his knees. It was a condom.

"Do you have time?" he asked.

"I'll make time," she said.

It was late in the evening. He switched off the late news and rang up the police station in Lawrence. "Captain Ryan there?"

"No, he's not here," the desk sergeant replied. "That you, Barney?"

"Yes."

"Thought I recognized your voice. You wanna see Chick, try the dump."

"I should've guessed," said Cole. "It's a starry night."

"And there's a moon," the sergeant said. "Take your piece, have some fun."

When his clients had been mostly criminals, high on whatever they could get their hands on, he had occasionally carried a small revolver against the ribs, though always with the fear it would go off by itself and maim him for life. But he knew how to use it, at least well enough to stand next to police officers at the dump and fire fast at rats. Midnight contests with revolvers barking, a blood sport with rats erupting. The cops were good, especially Ryan, who was the best.

Cole drove through quiet Andover streets, windows wide open for the breeze, as the night had grown sultry. He took a back way into Lawrence. The dump was at the far side of the city near the Merrimack River, an illegal landfill used by building contractors and others, reachable through the grounds of a derelict tannery and then over a rough road through scrub pine and swamp maple. He drove slowly, the lights of the Cutlass bobbing and sinking. The potholes were deep. The smell of the river, which was low, was stronger than that from the dump. He parked between two police cars, one unmarked, and climbed out.

"Over here, Barney."

The voice came from a direction he had not expected, and he trod over gritty ground through intervals of shadow and moonlight. The moon was brilliant and gave Captain Ryan a silvery cast. Though clad in a custom suit from a Lawrence factory that cut cloth for Brooks Brothers, he was unmistakably a cop, from the staunch thrust of his jaw down to the sturdy tips of his shoes, which glittered like ink. His features were large and strenuous and his eyes deep-set. His wiry hair, which contained a clump of gray, charged out of his head. It was always on the rise, like the man himself. Commander of the early-night platoon, he fully intended to become chief.

"Aren't you shooting?" Cole asked.

"I don't have to prove myself," he said, and jerked his thumb. "They do."

Deeper into the dump, where anonymous objects lacked luster and definite shape, two young uniformed officers stood stark and still, one thin like a knife and the other somewhat stout. Each held a service revolver low against his leg. Cole guessed at a glance that they were rookies who did things for Ryan and liked to impress him.

Ryan's voice shot through the humid air. "This is my buddy Barney. You ever need a lawyer, he's the best." The officers nodded and then turned away as if something in his tone had told them to. Dropping his voice, he said to Cole, "I tried to call you earlier, line was busy."

"Sorry."

"What's the name of the guy again, the one you asked me to check on?"

"Witlo," Cole said, "Henry Witlo. Were you able to come up with anything?"

"Sure. You ask me a favor, you get it. That's the way it works with pals, right?"

They had known each other since childhood. Ryan had grown up in the same housing project as Daisy Shea, who was best man at Ryan's wedding and godfather to Ryan's first child, the mother a pretty raven-haired girl from Methuen, who was now totally gray and haggard, partly from bearing eight other children. Cole was godfather to the second.

They began walking toward the car. The towering pines, all their cluster at the top, seemed textured into the night sky, as if they had floated in like clouds to hover high. The ringing of peepers was shrill. Ryan stopped near his unmarked car and leaned a buttock against it. The radio was quiet now.

"I called the Chicopee PD. I got a friend there." He

patted himself down for his pocket notebook but could not find it. "It's all right, I remember the essentials. This Witlo guy's a bum. Works only when he has to, rest of the time lives off women."

"Was he in the army?"

"Yeah. Vietnam. He plays that up."

"Does he have a record?"

"Nothing much. Disorderly conduct, trespassing, malicious damage to property, crap like that. The older cops usually went easy on him. They knew his mother, if you know what I mean."

"No."

"She was a hot number. Cops used to pick her up to play with. Cop wasn't considered a cop till Wanda Witlo did French on him."

"Nice cops."

"It happens." Ryan grinned. "But not here. Not my boys."

Cole's head went to one side. "Is it true she was murdered?"

"If you want to call it that. She was found in a ditch, could've been hit by a car. That was some ten years ago."

"Henry thinks a cop did it."

"Who knows? More to the point, who cares?" Abruptly the radio crackled, and then the monotonous voice of the dispatcher cut through and directed a cruiser to a domestic disturbance on Newton Street, south side of the city. "I know the address," Ryan said with ruthless satisfaction. "White woman living with a spic. One of these nights he's going to slice her throat. Then he's ours."

Cole looked up at the stars. "Pretty world."

"We see the worst, Barney. The best is for other people." He stepped away from the car and called through a

63

cupped hand to the young officers, "How's it going, you guys?" There was no response. "They must see something," he said, his tough face pointed out. Then he swung it back to Cole. "Now let me ask you something. What the hell's Witlo doing in Lawrence? Don't we have enough bums?"

"He wants to better himself. Can't deny a man that."

"What's he to you?"

"Nothing. It's a favor to Louise."

Something subtle changed in Ryan's face, and his lips barely moved. "We talking Louise Leone?"

"It's Baker now."

"Yeah, I know. Only woman ever made me shit my pants. I'm not going to ask what Witlo is to her. I could guess, but I'm not going to. Don't tell me anything, I mean that."

Cole said, "We both owe her."

"Don't remind me."

Shots rang out, rapid and then paced, and Cole and Ryan looked at each other. They retraced their steps through the moonlight and quietly approached the rookie officers, who were holding their smoking revolvers skyward. The stench of cordite was killing. The knifelike officer stared at Ryan, his long face divided by a tentative smile. The stout officer stood stiff and square, waiting for praise.

"Not bad," Ryan said, stepping past them to inspect two messes strewn on the ground like bloody mechanic's rags. Only the pinkish-gray tails identified them. Ryan's gaze shifted to a much bigger mess, the large head whole, the eyes zeros. "But the cat don't count," he said.

"I'm here to work," Henry Witlo said to Cole's secretary with only half his usual smile. It was ten in the morning, and his face was puffy from a bad sleep, his stomach was not pulled in, and his hair was in need of a cut. The nap on the back of his neck fuzzed out at the sides like little feathers. "Did you hear me?" he said.

"Yes, I heard you," Marge said vaguely over her typewriter, a mug of coffee steaming beside her. Her penny eyes were on him in a way that did not entirely acknowledge him.

He said, "Mr. Cole called the Y, left word I was to come here 'stead of his house."

"Attorney Cole is busy. You'll have to wait."

"No problem," he said, stepping toward one of the chairs against the wall.

"There's coffee in the conference room," she said. "You can wait there."

"This is fine right here, if you don't mind."

She minded.

"Christ," he said, "I'm not going to bite you."

Twenty minutes later he was standing in Cole's office with his hands driven into his back pockets and his elbows winged out. He cocked his head. "I guess your lady doesn't want me around the house," he said, and Cole looked up from the clutter of his desk.

"There're things you can do here."

"I don't think your secretary likes me either. The problem is, Mr. Cole, people like me right off the bat or they don't like me at all, ever. They add me up too fast, total comes to nothing. Or comes to something I'm not. In Nam I pissed off a lieutenant just by the way I chewed gum."

Cole's expression softened. "You're hard to figure out, Henry. Maybe that's the problem."

"I got lots of problems, but I try to keep 'em to myself. Don't like to bother people. Worst thing in the world is to be a pain in the ass, I know that. All I want, Mr. Cole, is to make something of myself. I don't want to be a big shot, just want to amount to something. That's why I'm going to hit the books again." His smile suddenly was full-blown. "I might even become a lawyer like you. A guy at the Y thought I was one. What d'you think of that?"

Cole absently shifted documents from one part of his desk to another. "All you'll get working here is five bucks an hour. That's not much, and it's only part-time."

"I'll manage. I've had it tough before. There were times I lived on Twinkies. The sugar kept me going."

"Then if you're going to work out of this office, you should wear a real shirt. And you could use a haircut."

"I understand. I don't want to shame you." He pushed his hair back. "Truth is, Mr. Cole. I want you to be proud of me."

"You don't need me to be proud of you. I'm not your father."

"Hey, Mr. Cole, I'm not looking for a father. A mother was enough."

Despite the heat of the early June sun and the muggy air, Emma Goss was out among her flowers, weeding, thinning, and watering. Years ago around the flower beds her husband had laid a narrow stone path and nearby had anchored a birdbath. He had enjoyed puttering around on weekends, clad in the mended trousers of an old suit, a garden or lawn tool in his hand. Sometimes, when the sun slanted over the house at an obscure angle, she seemed to detect his footprints in the grass, a comforting illusion, for she was sure it meant he was still watching out for her, protecting her in a way no alarm system or passing police car could.

Through a break in the privet hedge she glimpsed her neighbor Mrs. Whipple shaking Japanese beetles off a rosebush. Mrs. Whipple, who was wearing a sundress, freckles dusting her shoulders, was in her early forties and had an adolescent daughter. Mrs. Goss wanted to give her a neighborly greeting but lacked the nerve to speak first to someone she did not know well, even though the family, distantly cordial, had lived next door for four years and had sent a note of condolence when Harold died. The opportunity to speak passed when the woman moved out of sight. Mrs. Goss returned to her flowers.

The sun was warm on her back, and she could feel herself perspiring. Her soft fingers were hot inside her gloves as she crouched low among the lilies, of which there were a variety, so that when some were losing their bloom others were gaining theirs, ensuring color from late May into the middle of August. Groping into the foliage to get at the weeds, she felt that the punishment of the sun was good for her constitution and the exercise vital to her health. Once she had flirted with the idea of yoga classes, but an image of herself in a bulging leotard had horrified her. She gave a start when her bare arm brushed a spiderweb and a bigger start when she heard a male voice behind her.

"Excuse me, ma'am."

She was on her feet in the instant.

"I didn't mean to scare you," he said as she pressed a hand over her heart, for the moment conscious only of his bleached blue eyes and his yellow hair neatly combed and parted. "I rang the front bell," he said, "but I guess you can't hear it out here."

"The windows are closed," she said, conscious now of her untidy appearance, especially of the sweat blotches

67

on her blouse and the grass stains on her knees, though her knees could not be seen. "To keep the house cool," she explained as he stepped closer with a polite smile. He had on a short-sleeved check shirt tucked tight into his jeans, and he smelled of a barbershop. In his hand was an envelope.

"Then you didn't hear the phone either. Someone was supposed to call you, tell you I was coming. You're Mrs. Goss, right?"

She nodded tentatively and removed her gloves, aware of a palpitation. She feared he was bearing bad news of a completely unexpected nature. Perhaps her payment to one of the utility companies had been lost in the mail and he was here to shut off the service . . . and all the neighbors would know.

He said, "I work for Mr. Cole. He's got something for you to sign. I don't know what it's about, but I guess you do."

She looked at him deadpan, for her mind had not yet moved ahead.

"Something about your house," he said helpfully, and gave her the envelope, which she opened with awkward fingers. Then, with a flood of relief, she saw that the document was a formal notification to the realtor that she no longer wanted to place her house on the market.

"Yes, of course, I'll sign it," she said eagerly.

They moved to the breezeway connecting the house and garage, where he produced a pen from the pocket of his new shirt. When she affixed her signature above her typewritten name, a wave of satisfaction passed through her, as if something vital had been restored. Tears formed in her eyes like a membrane over her emotions. She slipped the paper back into the envelope and returned it to him. Then, retracting the point, she gave back the pen and gazed at him with gratitude. She felt that in some way she should repay him.

"Would you like some ice tea? I could bring you out a glass."

"Thank you just the same, ma'am, but I got more things to do for Mr. Cole. My first day on the job, I don't want to mess up." He raised an arm and pointed. "I go that way, it takes me to South Broadway, right?"

"Yes," she said, happy to provide direction, to steer him on course.

"I'm still learning my way around. I'm new to Lawrence." His smile was big. "You got a nice house here, Mrs. Goss, the kind you see in the nicer parts of Chicopee. That's where I'm from. I'm Polish, you might've guessed."

She had not. She had thought Swedish. Birds clamored from high in a neighbor's tree that she had watched grow from a sapling. "I've lived here a long time," she said, and wondered how she could ever have considered moving.

He said, "I heard Mr. Cole's secretary mention you lost your husband not so long ago."

"Yes," she said in a voice she did not immediately recognize as her own. A robin flew to the neighbor's tree and dissolved in the leaves. "A heart attack took him away."

His voice also sounded different. "I know what it's like to lose somebody," he said and, in taking leave, patted her shoulder.

Barney Cole finished his business in district court and crossed the street to Dolce's Cafeteria, a deep hole-in-the-wall where denizens of the court and hangers-on gathered throughout the morning in numbers that diminished drastically by midafternoon. Now only a few tables were occupied. Cole carried his coffee away from the high counter, approached a table, and said, "Mind if I join you?"

"I'd be mad if you didn't."

The voice, hoarsened by the years, belonged to Arnold Ackerman, a retired bookmaker who had been a close friend of Cole's father and a bearer at the funeral. He was semibald and had moist eyes in a dry and strained face that looked pulled apart at the bottom, the mouth large and rubbery. His small hands encircled a cup of tea.

Cole, settling in, said, "How you doing?"

"Ten years ago I was doing better. Today I got pains that don't belong to me, someone must've wished me bad, put pins in a doll or something. Voodoo. You believe in that stuff, Barney?"

"I don't discount it."

"Also I don't sleep so hot. Happens, you get older. Dead of night you think you hear the phone ring, but it's just an echo in your skull. Could've been somebody calling you two days ago." He sipped his tea. "Few nights ago I dreamed your dad phoned me from heaven, but I wouldn't accept the call. It was collect. I regret that, Barney. I would dearly have liked to talk to him again."

"Think he's doing OK up there, Arnold?"

"Sure he is, and so will I, they let me in. To make sure, I'm touching all bases. I mail my envelope in to the temple, play bingo at St. Pat's, and tune in to Jimmy Swaggart. Ever watch that guy perform? His timing's perfect, and he sweats on cue. Say what you want about him, but those glands are God-given."

Cole smiled warmly. His father's old buddy, so many tales told about him. Could talk a dog off a meat wagon, a nun out of her habit. Never paid a dime for protection all his years booking. When cops tried to shake him down, he borrowed lunch money from them. Never lost an argument that counted. When it seemed he might, he mumbled, which made him incomprehensible and indisputable. Cole did not believe all the stories, only the implausible ones. He said, "I heard from Louise Leone."

"Did you?" The old face brightened. "Sweet girl. Smart. In high finance now. Bankrolls the big boys, that's what I hear."

"Yes, that's what I hear too."

"And she married blue blood. A guy, I bet, eats branny cereal for his bowels."

"His name's Baker," Cole said.

"Makes her an American now. She never did like being a wop. Long time ago we thought you two would marry. Surprised your dad you didn't."

Cole shrugged. He did not have an answer worth giving.

Arnold sipped his tea, which did not look hot. "Her father's sick. Something to do with his stomach. She mention it?"

"No," Cole said.

"Maybe she doesn't know." The glazed crumbs of a honeydip doughnut lay like flakes of ice on a plate Arnold had pushed aside. He gathered them up and ate them, his mouth moving loosely. "Lot of people are sick. I see your pal Daisy Shea. He sure as hell doesn't look tip-top."

"He's hanging in."

"So's Manny the tailor. Early last week he had a heart attack. I saw the ambulance guys wheel him out of his shop. They plunked his teeth on his chest, everybody to see. I visited him yesterday, Lawrence General. He looks pretty good now, especially with his choppers back in.

71

Guess who's in the same room with him. Buddy Pothier, owns the furniture store. Somebody beat up on him, left him with a detached retina and a few other unenjoyable things. Happened at the Y."

Cole's head came up. "Who did it to him?"

"He's not talking. Says it was a misunderstanding. There was always something peculiar about Buddy, you know that."

"When did it happen?" Cole's voice was toneless.

"Few days ago."

"I didn't see it in the paper."

"It was there. Little item that didn't say much in the tiny print they use under police reports. His name was buried in all the Spanish ones.

"Is he going to be all right?"

"He's going to live, that's what you mean. If you're asking about his eye, what do I know about detached retinas?"

Cole, distracted, looked away.

"I didn't know better," Arnold said, "I'd think you were taking it personal."

Emma Goss hung the gardening tools on sturdy hooks her husband had screwed into the far wall inside the garage, printed strips of adhesive tape indicating where each implement should hang, a precise place for everything. His green-and-white Plymouth, which he had coddled, stood almost as shiny as the day he had driven it home from Clark Motors. Only last week, using the same motions as he, she had run a rag over the hood and wiped the windows. She knew she would never learn to drive the car, but she could no more sell it than she could chuck his clothes or dispose of his toothbrush, which still shared a place next to hers. Hers was the pink, his the green.

She locked the garage and paused in the breezeway. The sun, which had given her a slight headache, remained relentlessly brilliant, but the texture of the air had changed, as if it had taken on another skin. Entering the cool and quiet of the house, the door locking behind her, she immediately looked for Harold in the glass front of the china closet, but it was only her own image that squinted back at her, somewhat disheveled from her day.

She took aspirin, ran a bath, and undressed. Always, when naked, chalk-white except for the color of her forearms and face, she suffered dismay. Too much unmitigated fullness, a legacy from her mother, which in her young married years had pleased Harold but had always embarrassed her, the reason that she had worn sundresses, never bathing suits, at their seaside vacations.

She bathed quickly, her headache still with her. When she rose from the soapy water, she felt dizzy and grasped the towel rack for support, holding on tight as a wave of nausea washed through her. Moments later, her heart thumping, she eased cautiously out of the tub on legs she did not trust. Gripping the edge of the sink cabinet, she stared into the mirror. "Please, let it be just a touch of the sun," she said aloud, her face full of fear. She feared not death but illness, the sort that would thrust her into the hands of strangers, nothing hidden from their anonymous eyes, her dignity and modesty violated.

A chill followed the nausea, and she shivered while drying herself. She also suffered barometric throbs in the joints of her knees. Rain was imminent. She struggled into a cotton nightshirt, wrapped herself in a robe, and took small steps into the kitchen, where she heated up chicken broth. Hunched over a steaming bowl at the table, she tried to remember the year of her last checkup and determined only that it was well before Nina Scarito redecorated her office. She dipped her spoon, but her stomach allowed no more than a few sips.

The rain came a half-hour later, not much more than a drizzle licking the windows, but it dragged the day into an early evening. Ensconced under an afghan on the living-room sofa, she lay listening to the coming-home traffic up and down Mount Vernon Street. The rush and squish was a comforting sound, narcotic enough to edge her into believing that Harold might be in it. She drifted off to sleep waiting for the hum of the Plymouth in the drive, for the scrape of his key in the door.

The real rain came later, the downpour sudden and clamorous, the winds impetuous. The thunderclaps could have come from cannons. She woke with the afghan on the floor and her nightshirt sopping with sweat under her robe. Her skin burned. She staggered up from the sofa and shed the robe. The room was dark except for a streak of streetlight that gave her a false color. An explosion of thunder, the loudest yet, gave her a fright.

In the bedroom, guided by the hall light, she scrapped the sodden nightshirt for a frail gown she hoped would let her body breathe better. She pulled back the bed-spread and blanket, a chore, for her arms had lost their strength, and then lay flat on her back, nothing over her, nothing wanted, for she was already sweating through the gown. She listened to the rain lash the windows. Half asleep, she heard a tree branch flogging the far side of the house and thought it was somebody moving furniture.

She slept for more than an hour and woke hot-eyed and dry-mouthed, her gown twisted under her. The house was in darkness, the electricity gone, which alarmed her until she forced her head up from the pillow and saw through the window the flashing yellow light of a utility truck prowling the street for damage. The rain had lessened. She lifted her head higher, her eyes investigating the dark of the room, failing to catch a movement in the depths. Then she heard a footfall, ever so familiar, and smelled rain in the room. A hand touched her, the fingers cool on her burning skin. "Harold," she said without surprise. She had known all along he would come.

"No," the voice said. "Henry."

FIVE

It was a little after ten in the morning. Attorney Cole, due in district court, quickly stuffed his briefcase and paused near Marge's desk as she was slipping a creamy sheet of bond paper into her typewriter. Without looking up, positive evidence that she was out of sorts, she said, "When are you getting me a word processor? It'd be like having an extra person."

"We have an extra person. Isn't he in yet?"

"He's no help to me. No, he's not in yet."

Cole grimaced. He had wanted Henry to deliver documents to probate court in Salem, but mostly he had wanted to see him for another reason. "Did you call the Y?"

"Yes. He's not there." She flicked back the hair from her jawline and raised her eyes, her face set in a recalcitrant frown. "Maybe we've seen the last of him."

Cole rested his briefcase on the edge of her desk. "You still don't like him, do you, Marge?"

"What's there to like? Even when he's ten feet away I feel he's breathing all over me. Maybe I'm being silly, but that's the way I am."

"Should I get rid of him?"

"That's your decision," she said, and returned her eyes to the typewriter. When he gripped his briefcase, she said, "Your lady friend from Boston called while you were on the other line."

"Kit?" He gave a fast look at his watch. "Does she want me to ring her back?"

"She won't be there. She just said to say hello and to keep the faith."

"That's all?"

"It sounds enough to me, but what do I know?" She pressed a button on the typewriter, and a red dot flashed above the massive keyboard. Her shoulders stiff, she began typing too aggressively.

Cole swept his briefcase up and stepped away, then looked back with an obscure sense of guilt. He knew her life was not easy at home. "How's your mother?" he asked.

She went on typing. "You don't want to hear."

"I wouldn't ask if I didn't want to. How is she?"

"Difficult," she said, and punched another button. A blue dot appeared.

Cole said, "It took you a month to learn to use that thing. How long would it take with a word processor?"

"A day."

"OK," he said, "I'll get one."

"When?"

"You order it." He moved to the door, looked back. "And I'll see about Henry."

Louise Baker and her husband lunched at the Mallard Junction Country Club. They had a choice table against the glass wall overlooking the flawless green of the links. Most of the patrons were women redolent of good breeding, fine schools, and scented late-morning baths. Some who had not known Ben was home from the hospital paused at the table on their way in or out. "Ben, you look wonderful." Most patted a shoulder of his apple-green blazer, the breast pocket of which bore the cachet of the club. "No, no, don't bother," he was told each time he started to rise, as if he were a precocious but sickly child, the illness unmentioned. An older woman, deeply tanned, president of the conservation commission, bent over him and pecked his cheek. "You're doing simply marvelously. Isn't he, Louise?"

Alone, he said, "People are grand, aren't they, Lou?" He smiled at her over his amber drink, an orange rind clipped to the glass. The drink contained just a touch of rum, not enough to interfere with his medication. He said, "Now I know why I've never wanted to live elsewhere. I'm so happy here. Are you as happy here as I am, Lou?"

"More," she said. She tore bread. "I have everything."

"You're the most beautiful woman here," he said.

She glanced around. "Yes," she said. "I am."

He ate sparingly until dessert, which was strawberries and peach slices with a dip dish of sour cream and brown sugar. Watching him manipulate his spoon, she felt him keenly. He seemed at once more alert and relaxed than ever, as if all the right spices had been added to the brew of chemicals simmering in his brain. His neat mustache glistened. His color was good. He said, "There's so much more to you than there was to Janet."

Janet was his first wife, glamorous but useless, with forebears nearly as prominent as his. She had demanded much of him and little of herself, and the result for each had been zero. She was now married to a New York stockbroker who had everything, including a clear mind. Louise said, "Don't think about her, Ben. Think only about me."

He finished dessert and patted his mouth with a napkin. Choosing his words carefully, he said, "I should start doing something useful. I shouldn't depend on you for everything."

She eyed him thoughtfully. "What would you do, Ben?"

"I thought perhaps I could help you with your investments, give you advice."

His voice was shy. Hers was firm.

"That's not where your strengths lie. That should be obvious to you."

"Where do my strengths lie, Lou?"

"In being Benjamin Baker."

"That's enough?"

"That's more than enough." She motioned to the waiter. "You were *somebody* the day you were born. For me, Ben, it took a while."

The waiter brought them coffee, regular for her, Jamaican for him, another treat. He sipped through a layer of whipped cream, the rim of the glass sugared. "Lou," he said.

"Yes, Ben."

"I'd rather be you."

Fifteen minutes later they left the clubhouse and walked onto the green, where three men in bright jerseys waited at the tee. Two were semiretired businessmen, and the other was the president of Mallard Junction Community Bank, where Ben had once been a trustee and Louise, shortly after marrying him, had negotiated his hopelessly outstanding loans while opening accounts of her own, the deposits substantial. The banker stepped forward with the flash of a smile for her.

"Always a pleasure," he said, his heavy hand swallowing her slender one. He was stocky and full-faced, with a prominent nose and genial eyes. Swiftly he turned to Ben. "Glad you could make it, Mr. Baker. Magnificent day."

"Certainly is," Ben said jauntily, and glanced toward one of two motorized golf carts where his bag of clubs awaited him, everything provided, including his studded shoes. Louise had seen to everything.

"You won't need this," she said, helping him off with his blazer and draping it neatly over her arm. Close to his ear, she said, "If you get tired, don't be embarrassed to quit."

"I won't," he promised, and sauntered off to the cart bearing his gear.

The banker shifted close to her, placing his back to the others, his hand dangling keys hooked to a leather tab, the extra set to her Porsche. "I put your money in the trunk," he said in a low voice. "All twenties make quite a bundle. If you could return the satchel this time . . ."

"Why not make it a gift from the bank," she said, taking the keys.

"Yes, of course." He glanced over his shoulder. "Your husband seems eager to play."

"Let him drive one of the carts. He enjoys that." She swished back her black hair. "And go easy on him. I want him to have fun."

"Yes, that's something people don't get nearly enough of." His genial eyes were suddenly narrow with insinuation, and his smile grew. "Don't you agree, Mrs. Baker?"

Her face took on the hard silence of stone. He started

to say something more but quickly changed his mind. As he stepped back with a shrinking smile, she called out to the others, "Have a good day, gentlemen."

In the Porsche, the windows open, she followed a back road away from the country club. The sky, swept clear of clouds, looked perfectly new, and for a while she drove slowly, savoring the smell of broom and timothy of a hayfield. Flowering dogwood flanked the entrance to a riding academy, where she had taken lessons a year ago. Then, with a glance at her watch, she speeded up.

She drove to the far edge of town, past the Birdsong Motel, and swung onto the highway to Springfield. A few miles later she veered into a tree-shrouded car stop and pulled up beside a sleek Lincoln Continental, two men in the front. She peeered out at the one on the passenger side. "How are you doing, Sal?"

"Pretty good, Mrs. Baker."

"Everything OK?"

He turned his head and looked back at the highway, his pitted face soaking up a stray scrap of sunlight. "I don't see a problem."

She struck a button under the dash, and the lid of the trunk popped up. Seconds later the trunk on the Lincoln sprang open, and the driver, John, climbed out and lumbered to the rear of the Porsche. She heard him grunt when he lifted out the bulky satchel.

Sal said, "Any more problems with the Polack?"

"None. What's our return?"

"Eighteen," he said.

"I thought we were going for twenty."

"They figure they got a track record with us. I didn't want to argue."

"You wouldn't shit me, would you, Sal?"

"I wouldn't dare."

John slipped back into the Lincoln and strapped himself in behind the wheel. She eyed them both and then said to Sal, "New York or Newark?"

"Newark," Sal said.

"Call me when you get back."

"I always do."

"Have a good trip," she said, shifting into gear and pulling away first.

After finishing up in district court and lunching alone at Bishop's, Barney Cole drove to Lawrence General Hospital, where a security guard let him park in a doctor's space. The guard, named Alfred, was a retired cop Cole had once represented in a claim for disability in the line of duty. Cole, squinting in the sun, said to him, "I understand Buddy Pothier's a patient."

"Yuh, that's what I heard," he said, pulling on a cigarette. "I'd've looked in on him, but I don't know him that well. Wife and I bought some dinette furniture from him years ago. Cheap stuff as I remember. Didn't last long."

"Hear anything about what happened to him?"

"Got beat up is all I know." He brought up an arm and let his hand dangle from the wrist. "Long time ago I heard he was this way, but I don't know that for a fact."

Each turned as an ambulance, roof lights flashing, swerved into the lot and headed toward the side entrance of the emergency room.

"Business here never falls off," Alfred said, snapping away his cigarette. "Always something doing."

"Take care," Cole said, stepping away.

"You too, Barney. I don't forget what you did for me."

The woman at the reception desk told Cole that Mr. Pothier had been moved to a private room and directed him to the new wing, which he had trouble finding at first. Checking room numbers and glancing in at beds, he heard a sigh much like the deep sound his grandmother had made when liberating herself from a corset. Farther down he glimpsed beyond an ill-drawn curtain a man perched on a bedpan, head bowed in apparent prayer for results. He forgot the number he was seeking, but an extra sense seemed to pilot him to the right room.

Buddy Pothier was sitting up, an enormous bandage taped over one eye, ugly-looking sutures in his upper lip, teeth obviously missing from a big part of his mouth. A nurse, who was pushing a pillow behind him, saw Cole out of the corner of her eye and said cheerily, "Ah, you have a visitor, Mr. Pothier." To Cole she chirped, "You should've seen him a few days ago before the swelling came down. You wouldn't have believed he could make such an improvement."

Cole moved self-consciously toward the foot of the bed. He had only a nodding acquaintance with Pothier and had never been a customer.

"Anything more I can do you for, Mr. Pothier?" the nurse asked and was answered with a shake of the head. She stepped past Cole with a smile and left with a swish.

"I hope I'm not disturbing you," Cole said, edging to the side of the bed. "I guess it's hard for you to talk, so I won't stay long. I'd just like to ask a couple of questions."

Pothier stared at him warily out of the good eye and then looked away as if from a commotion inside his head.

Cole waited a moment and then asked, "Do you have any idea who did this to you?"

The voice was small, the mouth barely opening. "None."

Cole remembered walking by Pothier's store as a child, when the father was alive and ran the business, the merchandise gothic-looking and indestructible. He said, "It's important to me, Mr. Pothier. Just between us, was it a big blond guy?"

The eye swung back at him. The voice, bigger, said, "It was nobody."

When Louise Baker returned home, Mrs. Mennick was waiting with an anxious air. There had been a telephone call from Lawrence. "Your sister wants you to call her right back," Mrs. Mennick said, and Louise nodded with no show of concern. Her sister, who usually rang up the private number and left desperate messages on the answering machine, was full of crises invariably involving money. "I wrote the number down," Mrs. Mennick said, "so you don't have to take time to look it up."

"Thank you," Louise said negligently, disappointing Mrs. Mennick, who enjoyed drama in the lives of others. Louise moved past her. "Would you get me coffee, please?"

At the hall table she picked through her mail, discarded everything with less than first-class postage, and left the rest, mostly bills, to open later. When her coffee was ready, she carried it upstairs to her bedroom office and rang up her sister's number. No one answered. She cradled the receiver with relief, for she had little patience with her sister and no regard for her deadbeat brother-in-law, who sold bad cars for a living, written-off wrecks doctored into some kind of usable condition for customers who could afford no better.

She sipped her coffee on the little balcony outside the door windows and surveyed the grounds and distant hills with a rich sense of proprietorship. A document in her desk, her prideful signature opposite Ben's biddable one, gave her clear title to the rousing beauty of the view. She placed cup and saucer on the rail and stood with her hands behind her back and her chest projected so that her breasts suggested birds about to fly away. Her head tossed back, she sniffed in the sweet air as if possessed of a wild animal's sense of smell. The ring of the telephone was a shrill intrusion and a taint on her mood.

She took her time stepping back into the bedroom and more time picking up the receiver. She expected her sister's voice and was prepared for a story, but the caller was Barney Cole. She was not prepared for his story and for a moment or so only half heard his words. "Hold on," she said. She put the receiver down and fetched her coffee from the balcony rail, though little remained in the cup. "What were you saying?"

"Is he violent? Does he use his fists?"

She drew in an irritable breath. "If there's a problem, Barney, tell me."

"Just answer my question."

"You're not in court, counselor. Spell it out better."

"I think he may have beaten up somebody."

"You think. Don't you know?"

"I wish I did."

"Easy solution, Barney. Why don't you just ask him?"

"He hasn't been around."

"Are the cops involved?"

"The victim's not talking."

She lifted her coffee cup and drained it. "Barney, you're wasting my time."

An hour later, when she was down in the sitting room reading the local weekly, her picture in it, she heard the sound of a car. The banker and his friends were dropping off Ben. A minute later she heard the front door open and lofted her voice. "In here, Ben." He appeared, flushed and smiling, strands of his flat hair hanging over his brow. He looked like an overheated and happy child, his mustache a smudge from hard play. "What's the grin for?" she asked.

"They cheated," he announced cheerily.

"You're not serious."

"I most certainly am. I won sixty-five dollars."

"You mean, they cheated in your favor."

His smile turned sheepish. "I pretended not to notice."

She put the paper to one side, rose from the chair, and spread her arms for the child in him to come to her. "Nothing much gets by you, does it, Ben?"

"I don't think so, Lou. I hope not."

She stood with her body to his. "Your mind is better than ever."

"I want to believe that," he said.

The air was soft and powdery when they took a stroll among the flower beds, which Mrs. Mennick's brother tended to weekly. The pansies circling the goldfish pool fluttered their petals like a swarm of butterflies and particularly pleased Louise. They reminded her of watercolors her third-grade teacher had tacked on the wall. The assertive orange of early-blooming day lilies arched high over their foliage. The sweet William had quickly passed its prime, and the red bloom had turned dark and velvety, which pleased Ben. It reminded him of a dress his mother had worn. As they moved closer to the side of the house, toward the roses, Louise said, "Mrs. Mennick's brother is picking her up soon to take her to the movies."

He nodded. "Yes, she told me this morning."

"That means you must take your medication yourself.'

"I will," he said.

They each heard the ring of the telephone.

"I'd better get that," she said. "I think it's my sister."

"Do you have to?" he said in mild protest, but she was already hurrying away. He waited near the roses. It was his favorite time of day, the sun firing low rays through the distant trees and creating immense patterns of light and shade. Mrs. Mennick, who had changed into a flowered dress and put on makeup, looked out at him through a window and smiled. Her crimson mouth was so big and bright that it appeared a painter had slapped her face with a brushful of madder. She vanished, but a few minutes later she returned and scratched on the screen for his attention.

"You'd better come in, Mr. Baker."

He entered through the front door. Louise was standing near the telephone in the study, her face a pale oval inside the neat fall of black hair. Her dark eyes gradually focused on him. "Come here, Ben."

He moved forward uneasily, as if on the edge of an experience sure to bear pain. She extended a hand.

"Take it, Ben. Squeeze it."

Her hand was dry and cool, almost cold. His hand was bigger, but her squeeze was greater. He said, "What's the matter, Lou?"

"My father died."

Henry Witlo spend the day familiarizing himself with the house. He inspected each room with an eye for detail and a thought for secrets, probing closets and dipping his hands into drawers. At the desk in the den he scanned letters, postcards, private papers, passbooks. In the attic, where he had to crouch, he pawed through a chocolate box of sepia snapshots of people in old-fashioned dress. In the basement he flipped through stacks of *Life* magazine dating back to the Truman years and carried one up to read on the toilet. The bathroom smelled of talcs and soaps. All the towels were pink. He showered with gusto, crushing shampoo into his hair, slapping soap into his

ANDREW COBURN

underarms and open legs, and using a brush on his back with particular vigor. He had a choice of two toothbrushes and used the green one. He whipped his hair back with a comb much cleaner than the one carried in his back pocket and admired himself in the mirror, his face full of light as if from some radiant purpose not yet fully revealed but becoming clearer by the moment.

He had made himself a big breakfast, had served himself an even bigger lunch, and now was thinking of supper. He walked softly through the dead silence and leaned into the haze of the bedroom, where the shades were three-quarters drawn and the bed was open and hot-looking, the pillows smashed. The fitted sheet, along with the mattress cover, had sprung loose from a top corner.

He said, "I'm going to make something to eat. You want something?"

No sound came from Emma Goss, who sat squeezed and immobile in a small rocker, as if time no longer moved for her. She was wrapped in a robe she had slunk into hours ago, the collar raised around her throat, the sash tied tight, every button buttoned. Her white feet seemed painted onto the floor.

"You oughta start talking to me," he said. "Makes it easier. And you should call me Henry. That makes it friendly."

Her eyes were on him, but not in a way that registered or even blinked, as if everything inside her head had clenched. Only the low catchy sound of her breathing gave a sign that she was functioning.

"You can't just sit there," he said. "Legs'll go, then everything else. You're not a spring chicken, Mrs. Goss."

All at once her face strained to speak, but nothing

88

came. Her mouth stayed a dry line. He angled closer, and she flinched.

"Good," he said. "Shows you're alive. Maybe you're worried about your kitchen. You don't have to. I clean up after myself. I got good habits."

Her chalk face colored, and her lips quivered. The words puffed out. "May I use the bathroom?"

"Sure you can. I don't know how you held it so long." His smile was broad. "You got a nice bathroom. Blue water in the toilet, I like that. What color's your toothbrush?"

"Pink," she said in a soft burst.

"Good. I used the other one," he said, and watched her grip the arms of the rocker and rise with a terrible effort that seemed to expend all her strength. Clutching the front of her robe, she gazed wildly about, as if she no longer knew where the bathroom was, and then murmured something he failed to catch. "What's that, Mrs. Goss?"

Her color deepened. "Can I shut the door?"

"Sure, you can even lock it. Have all the privacy you want. And while you're in there, do something to your hair."

She took a tentative step and then another, and he knew she was not going to make it. He reached out to help but drew back when she flinched again. Her third step was fatal. She softened, spread, and sagged in his arms. She was ice-cold beneath the robe.

In her ear he whispered, "You need me, Mrs. Goss. You just don't know it yet."

Six

Daisy Shea, feeling punk, locked up his little office and went home to an empty house in the middle of the day. In the bedroom he dropped his clothes where he stood and climbed into his unmade marriage bed, six of his seven children conceived there. The seeding of his first child had taken place on a blanket in a stretch of woods in Methuen that was now the site of a giant shopping mall. Pictures of all his children in identical frames stared at him from the walls.

He slept restlessly and dreamed that the medical examiner pronounced him dead but later, for a consideration, changed his mind. He dreamed that hospital attendants forced him out of bed and made him stand naked as if for inspection. Nurses scowled, visitors showed shock, and children, not his, tittered.

In another dream his wife seemed to be disseminating herself to a multitude of men, none of whom could get enough of her; so they stayed, waiting for more, arguing over rights once solely his.

In his final dream he was not dead but undergoing endless repairs.

He woke to the sound of voices in the kitchen. His younger children were home from school and arguing over their chores, with the youngest protesting the loudest. And his wife was home from work. He saw first the food stains on her white uniform and then her handsome bone of a face peering down at him as if from a great height. Concern tinctured her voice. "You OK?"

"Yes," he said, stirring under the covers. "I was a little tired, that's all."

"Louise Leone's father died," she said. "It's in the paper."

He pushed aside the covers and sat up, leaving the shape of his head stamped in sweat on the pillow. His bare upper body looked soft and gelatinous. "That means she'll be coming to Lawrence."

"Does that excite you?"

"Sure. She's a big shot now."

Edith stepped back to the door and closed it against the growing noise of the children. Daisy swung his legs out of the covers and sat on the bed's edge in his underpants. Memories tainted by the years thrashed through his mind.

"The old man never liked me," he said. "He had a thing against the Irish."

"As I remember, he didn't like any of Lou's friends, not even Barney."

He scratched an elbow. "When's the wake?"

"Tomorrow."

"How old was he?"

"In his seventies," she said.

"I can't be sad. He lived his life."

The room was stuffy. She raised a window, admitting the fat aroma of lilac, the bloom in its final burst of fragrance. The bush was the only color on the block. She stooped down, swept up his suit jacket, and hung it in the closet.

He said, "Do you have a boyfriend, Edith?"

She turned her head from the smell of mothballs. "When would I have time?"

"I wouldn't blame you."

"Yes, you would," she said, and tossed his trousers beside him on the bed as he scratched his other elbow.

"You know, Edie, there're things from a long time ago I never confessed. I wonder if it still matters."

"What things?"

"In law school, to make a few bucks, I peddled filthy funny books. Jane jerking off Tarzan, Blondie blowing Mr. Dithers, Batman abusing Robin. A couple of professors were my best customers."

She dropped his shirt beside him. "No, I don't think it matters now." She picked up his well-worn loafers and glanced at the heels. "You should take these to the cobbler soon."

"I cheated on you a few times, but I confessed that to Father Flaherty."

"That makes it all right then," she said out of an arid face, and deposited the loafers near his feet.

"The women didn't mean anything to me. That's the God's honest truth."

"I don't want to hear, Daisy. I want you to spare me."

"You don't care."

"As you said, it was a long time ago."

He rose with his face still squeezed from a sleep that

should have been longer and more peaceful. Glimpsing himself in the dresser mirror, he raced a hand through his white hair. "Remember when it was red, Edie?" Suddenly he felt like a slug and snatched up his shirt. Then he shivered, and his eyes glazed over as if an ancestral stirring were giving him a sense of chill Irish air with the smell of peat plugged into it. Quickly he worked his arms into his shirt and fumbled with the buttons. When she gripped his arm to steady him, he smiled into her face. "I was a handsome guy back then, no wonder women went for me."

"You're not going to spare me, are you?"

"And I was a spiffy dresser. Got my suits from Manny the tailor, God rest his soul."

"You got one suit from him, and you never paid him."

"Louise always had an eye for me," he went on with careless confidence, his shirttails dangling. "You must've guessed that."

"You're dreaming, Daisy. She never gave you a second look."

"That's how much you know," he said with a wink. "Why do yŏu think she went to bat for me the time I had the big trouble?"

"Because I asked her to."

He kept his smile as if unable to unglue it and squinted at her as if a harsh light had been thrown into his eyes. "You don't change, Edie. Doesn't matter whether I'm in the pink or sick as a dog, you treat me the same."

"It's the only way I know," she said. His shirt was buttoned wrong, and with quick rough fingers she fixed it and straightened the collar around the ruined flesh of his neck. The hair inside his ears looked like cigar ash, and for a moment it seemed she might try to blow it out. Instead she brought a hand to his face as if she could make it smooth and young again.

"I guess I'm just stuffing and wind," he said, and waited for her to deny it.

"All of us are some of that."

His eyes struggled to get into hers. "You love, me, don't you?"

"Yes, Daisy, I do."

The smell of lilac swelled around him and held him in place. "When they put me under the sod you'll miss me, won't you?"

"I already miss you," she said.

Barney Cole took Louise Baker's call in his office, and they met at a roadside restaurant on the outskirts. She arrived in her shiny Porsche and stood by it with her black hair blown back, her chino skirt stretched tight across her hips. He pulled up in his repaired Cutlass, which was giving him trouble again, this time the electrical system. He climbed out of the car slowly as if not to disturb its delicate condition. He had on a dark suit, one of his better ones. She looked at his tailored legs and said, "You take good care of yourself, don't you, Barney?"

They kissed.

"Not as well as you do," he said. "You're more beautiful than I remember."

"You're sweet to say that."

"It happens to be the truth."

In the lounge of the restaurant they sat at a small table with a bowl of nuts between them, an exotic mix that put salt on their fingers. A dozen or more customers sat at the circular bar, a few more at other tables. The decor was dark oak, with mammoth beams running across the ceiling. "Nice place," Louise said, her eyes roving. "New?"

"Relatively."

"Scampy would've had a piece of it."

Scampy, whom she had lived with for many years, had been a local loanshark, speculator, and string-puller, his influence having penetrated the police department, the district attorney's office, and city hall. Louise had been his straw in business ventures and his eyes and ears when he took sick. When he died his wealth went to her, including the money he had out on the street and in cash boxes stashed in his cellar, a considerable return well worth her years with him.

Over brandy she said, "Some people thought I put him in the grave. Did you?"

"No."

"You don't like me talking about him, do you?"

"Doesn't matter."

"Funny thing, Barney, I loved him, but I took his death in stride, buried him without a tear. I guess that's why people talked. My father I never loved, but his death has hit me hard. How the hell do you explain that?"

"Parents are the thread to your childhood. Nobody wants it broken."

"I think you're wrong, Barney. I hated my childhood." Her face seemed as much like ice as flesh could get, a small smile preserved in the permafrost. "You and I came from the same neighborhood, but your father could pay the rent. It's all right to be poor, but not willfully."

"You're still grieving for him."

"No, I don't think so. Maybe what I feel the most is a sense of waste. Not for him, for my mother. He never once went out of his way to make her happy."

Cole twisted the stem of his brandy glass. "How's your mother taking it?"

"My mother keeps everything inside. It's my sister

who's carrying on. That's why I had to get away for a while." She touched his hand and then squeezed it as if to extract strength. "Thanks for coming."

From the bar two men in business suits were shooting glances at her. He said, "You still draw attention."

"I see only you," she said, her dark eyes suddenly intent upon him.

"What are you doing?"

"Counting the lines in your face. Not too many. You've still got your college-boy look. You're a constant, Barney, thank God."

The bartender blew his nose, the noise like the note sounded by a hunting horn. The lighting inside the bar was a spray of tinsel. Cole said, "I was hoping to meet your husband."

"Ben has a health problem. I didn't want him making the trip."

"Yes, you mentioned once he has a delicate constitution."

"Blue bloods usually do."

"You're not ashamed of us, are you, Lou?"

"Not of you, Barney. You've always had class."

"You never did tell me how you met him."

"Didn't I? You sure?" She sighed. "It was a couple of winters after Scampy died. I booked a flight to Florida. I had Miami in mind but at the last moment chose West Palm Beach. I wanted elegance. Ben was down there with his housekeeper, who was acting as his nurse." Her voice, slurring, became sweet and mellow, sugar steeped in brandy. "He needed someone like me, and I wanted someone like him. The rest is history."

Cole smiled, feeling the wind of her words. "No regrets?" he asked.

"None," she answered. "I love him in a way totally reserved for a husband. What I mean is I'd never want to hurt him. I'd go to extremes to prevent it."

"Sounds serious."

"It is. I have exactly what I want in Mallard Junction and intend to keep it. You've never been there, have you, Barney? Beautiful place. And I have the oldest name in it. Ben's people founded the town, I forget the date. His name's on the library. Baker Memorial. It's on the town hall. It's in the park. You read the names on the old war memorials, you see a bunch of Bakers."

"You sound smug."

"I have the right. People with pedigrees kiss my ass because of his name and my money. You need both out there, and I've got 'em."

A man wearing a silver jacket and a glossy hairpiece that deceived nobody seated himself at the piano in the corner and began rippling out a vintage tune. Cole said, "But you get lonely."

"All of us have loneliness, doesn't matter where we are. It's a cold spot deep inside us. That's how my mother used to put it." Her face drew closer to the bone, and her voice acquired a husk. "Remember when your wife died? You couldn't stop shivering. You needed a warm arm. Remember when Scampy kicked off? I called you in the middle of the night. *I* needed a warm arm."

A shadow tumbled over the table.

"It's what you do in the face of death," she went on. "You reaffirm life by making love. That's what we did."

The waitress, her face glowing from an extravagance of makeup, whispered, "That's beautiful."

"I even wanted to get pregnant," Louise said, her hand again slipping over his. "But it didn't happen."

"A gentleman at the bar would like to buy you both a drink," the waitress said.

"Tell him to go screw himself," Louise replied without lifting her eyes.

The waitress smiled faintly. "I'll put it to him in a slightly different way if that's OK."

"Long as he gets the message."

The piano player was doing his best with another old tune, missing a note now and then. Cole said, "What have you got in mind, Lou?"

She looked at her watch, the face circled by diamonds, an old gift from Scampy. "Nothing, no time. I have to get back to my mother." Her eyes charged into his. "Anybody looking?"

"Somebody, I'm sure," he said as she leaned into his voice.

"Barney, kiss me the way you would in bed."

Emma Goss sat in an upholstered chair in the den with her eyes closed. Another night and much of a new day had passed. She heard Henry Witlo bumping about in the kitchen, but her mind refused to provide credence to his presence. Nothing about him tallied with reality, and she was not the woman sitting here in a robe but an unclean stranger she did not wish to know. The real Emma Goss, she was quite certain, was ensconced somewhere else, somewhere perfectly safe.

A few minutes later the doorbell rang.

His voice boomed in on her. "You sit right there, Mrs. Goss. I'll get it."

"I shall wake soon," she said to herself. "I shall be back from wherever I am."

Some vibration alerted her, and her eyelids flickered open. He was in the room, looming large but remaining unreal. He was yellow hair, blue eyes, an obtruding voice—nothing else.

"That was the paperboy," he said. "Collecting. I paid him out of my own pocket. Gave him a fifty-cent tip. Hope that won't spoil him." The blue eyes dwelt upon her. "I told him I was your nephew. We don't want the neighborhood thinking nothing dirty, telling jokes about lonely widows. You know how people talk."

Her face burned. She tasted sickness on her tongue and swallowed in an effort to eject it.

"If I'm your nephew, I should call you Auntie. Auntie. I like that, Mrs. Goss. How about you?"

"No." She answered the voice, not the man, who was now only a flash of hands.

"It's up to you," he said agreeably. He dipped down on one knee and placed his smile at her eye level. "But it's something you should think about."

Her robe was loose, but it did not matter. She felt she was safely elsewhere and functioning quite normally in a context of everyday banalities, the tutelary spirit of her husband watching over her.

"The thing is I worry about you," he said. "I've been doing all the cooking, which I don't mind, but you don't eat anything. That's not good for you."

Her stomach had tolerated a little toast, later some overly sweet coffee, that was all.

"You hear me, Mrs. Goss?"

Her mind stretched back to when her life was as fresh as roses, when a toy tea set and a cuddlesome doll were her prized possessions, when the shameless boy up the street made water behind a tree and her mother forbade her from ever talking to him again. Unlike other parents deprived of authority when their offspring reached adolescence, hers had retained their stature well beyond, and seldom, she recollected with pride, had she given them cause for displeasure.

"At least look at me, Mrs. Goss. That's only polite."

She gazed wistfully, not at him, but at the boy she had forever after shunned, whose obituary she had clipped from the paper only a few weeks ago, a life shriveled into a few dry paragraphs.

"That's better," he said in a pleased voice, and her head reared back as though a strong light had been thrust in her face. His hand swooped down where the broad line of her body broke through the robe. "Learn to relax, Mrs. Goss. People that don't, they get ulcers. Other things too. Their hair won't comb right. Their skin gets bad."

She palpitated. Her eyes blinked like those of a baby who had not yet learned to use them. Then his hand moved from here to there.

"You're lucky, a woman your age, you got nice skin."

Her face flamed. She felt hot down to her toes and wondered why her knee was not scalding his hand.

"And you got nice legs—just a little heavy."

She placed her hands on her head as if it had been hastily set on her shoulders and needed to be moved a little to the left or perhaps to the right. She seemed uncertain.

"That's kind of nasty," he observed, his fingers breezing over a small blueberry patch of burst capillaries. "But who's going to see it, huh?"

Her hands shot forward. Suddenly she needed help and tried to ask for it, but her tongue thickened over the words. Then it was too late. Her stomach turned and convulsed.

"Jesus!" he said, leaping to his feet.

Her eyes reeled in shame.

"It's all right," he said from his height. "I'll clean it up."

* * *

In the cloying floral smell of the funeral parlor, Louise Leone Baker stared down at her father's lifeless face, all the stress of the years rubbed out of it by the undertaker's ameliorating art, the inert mouth sealed forever. The hair on his head, darker than it had been in life, looked like stray bristles from a brush. The suit was from Kap's, her purchase, a pin from the Sons of Italy attached to a lapel. She whispered, "It's too hard to hate you, Dad, so I'm not going to try." Then she stepped back into a chorale of somber voices, a maze of distant family members whom earlier she had not immediately recognized.

A woman's voice said, "They did a wonderful job on him."

"Yes, they did," she answered automatically.

"Your mother's taking it well."

"My mother has always taken it well."

Another voice said, "People are starting to come."

The crowd grew into one of the largest at the funeral home in years, an endless line of arrivals bottling up in the foyer. Louise, tall and emotionless, stood beyond the overly ornate casket with her stiff-faced mother and sobbing sister and received a constant bobbing of faces. She was the draw, not the deceased. Lawyers redolent of aftershave offered condolences, and known liars and cheats from city hall took turns squeezing her hand too vigorously. "So nice of you to come," she said to each, pain creeping into her wrist. Old friends of Scampy's, short Italian men in alligator shoes, rose on their toes and planted arid kisses on her cheek. Cronies of her father's, men without neckties, gathered in front of her with filled eyes.

"Wonderful wake," said one. "Does honor to him."

"He's at peace," said another.

"Is that what you call it?" she said mostly to herself, tossing a concerned look at her mother, but her mother was doing fine and her sister was reveling through tears in the presence of so many mourners.

"Hello, Louise."

The avuncular voice warming her heart belonged to Arnold Ackerman, whom Scampy had called the only gentleman bookie in Lawrence, also the shrewdest, always knew when to lay off a bet. He viewed her with a concentrated eye.

"You're so beautiful."

"I know I'm beautiful," she said. "I've been beautiful all my life. I'm the Sophia Loren of Lawrence."

"You're more than that," he whispered out of his rubbery face. "You're bigger than Scampy ever was. He'd be jealous."

"No, Arnold. He'd be proud."

A downtown businessman she had once bailed out of trouble ventured a hand onto her shoulder and lingered too long until gently and subtly she prodded him on, a maneuver she repeated with a county commissioner whose debts to Scampy he had paid off with favors. A grizzled priest she had presumed long dead frowned at her with undeflectable Sicilian eyes and said in a gravel voice, "I understand you've strayed."

"I'm Episcopalian now, Father."

"I see. Are you also English, no more Italian?"

"Touché," she said, taking his arm and drawing close to his ear. "I remember the times you patted me on the bottom."

"I'm only flesh and blood."

"Yes, Father. So am I."

He started to pull away and then abruptly returned close to her. "Your father was not a bad man, you know, just a little one. Not everybody can be big."

"But we can try, Father."

GOLDILOCKS

"You've bought your position in life."

"It's what money can do," she said. "Bless me, Father, for I have prospered."

When the Sheas came upon her, she inwardly flinched at the sight of Daisy's florid face and neck of loose-fitting skin. Embracing him, she felt the breath come out of him. She smelled no liquor, only the wintery scent of a hard peppermint clicking against his teeth. He tried to say something but had no words, and she had none either. Then she hugged Edith and felt bones. Edith said, "I hope you'll be staying longenough for us to get together."

"I'll try," she said noncommittally.

"Have you seen Barney yet?"

"Yes."

Edith smiled with schoolgirlish insinuation. "I figured."

"You figured wrong, but that's OK."

Daisy found a voice. "I'm dying, Lou."

Edith said, "Let her handle this one first, all right, Daisy?"

"Is he?" Louise asked in a whisper.

"I don't think about it."

"As long as you care."

"I care."

Several elderly women from the old neighborhood converged upon her. They all looked like the embodiment of hymns. They were followed by members of the Sons of Italy. Voices boxed her in, and in time faces began to look alike. Then she saw one that did not. She saw first Chick Ryan's charging head of hair clumped with gray and then his full uniform of brass and braid. When he smiled at her, the lines in his face cut deep. His teeth became bigger.

"You haven't changed," he said as if he had expected deterioration and was mildly disappointed.

103

"I see you're a captain now," she said. "Congratulations."

He had a way of throwing his eyes out like darts. They shot into her. "This time I got the promotion by myself."

"That's why I'm congratulating you."

"But I don't forget," he said. "Anytime you want to call in the marker, I'm ready."

"I wouldn't worry about it, Chick."

"I'm not. I'm just telling you. Sorry about your father."

She glanced over at her mother's face but could not read it, everything held in tight. She looked at her sister, who, though younger, looked older because of extra weight from a sweet tooth. Her eyes raked the crowd for Barney Cole's face and finally glimpsed it near the entrance. He was a late arrival. Then the priest who in her mind had risen from the dead placed his hand on her elbow, which she started to shake off as if the fingers were ghostly.

"Your mother's asked me to say the rosary. That won't offend you, will it?"

"I'd be pleased," she said.

The priest took a place near the casket, and the room went quiet. His voice was a narcotic drone and evoked memories of her childhood and then a clear image of her father in an undershirt, his scrawny elbows on the table, pasta on his plate and sauce on his chin. It was no longer a provocative image, merely a durable one. Her sister tilted sideways and whispered, "I didn't know Dad had so many friends." Some minutes later, the ritual of the rosary over, she stepped to her mother's side and murmured that she would be right back.

"Don't be long," her mother said.

She needled through the shifting crowd, accepting quick condolences and compliments, and hooked on to

Barney Cole with a firmness that surprised him. "I need to breathe," she said, and bumped against him so that he would cut a path through the foyer, where more flowers had been placed, an overflow. An employee of the funeral home, his eyes the sort that swelled when he spoke, murmured a pleasantry and opened the front door for them. The evening air, touched with the smell of the city, rolled in on them. Outside on the small colonnaded porch, she said, "I had to get away from that casket. My sister picked it out with my money. Such elaborate packaging for a corpse."

"You sound hard," Cole said.

"It's an act."

Somebody was standing on the bottom step, a gray-haired man with a handkerchief in his grasp. He had a small trivial-looking nose, almost not worth blowing, but he blew it anyway and then hopped apologetically out of their way. They stepped down onto the sidewalk and immediately moved out of the streetlight to avoid people who were leaving. Across the street a woman squawked Spanish at a man who looked no good. Figures loomed in the large lit windows of a four-family house. A siren wailed from the direction of downtown. Once again Louise snuggled her arm inside Cole's, and they moved along, avoiding the seams in the sidewalk. Her stride was stiffer than his.

"Something feels wrong," she said.

"What?"

"I don't know."

"What makes you think it?"

"I don't know that either." A car flashed by, painting them. "Maybe it's being back in Lawrence. I hate it, Barney. I have no good memories, except maybe of you."

"You're forgetting Scampy."

"That wasn't all roses," she said without explanation.

They strolled to the corner, where the vast concrete Masonic temple hovered like the hulk of an abandoned ship, distress lights burning from the bridge. Across the way, buried in darkness, lay Campagnone Common, out of which ricocheted the rapid fire of youthful Spanish voices. She listened, and then turned away.

"No spics in Mallard Junction, Barney, and except for the guy that runs the Texaco station I'm the only wop."

"Makes you a novelty."

"Except I won't wear off." Abruptly she pulled herself erect and retook his arm. "I think I'd better get back, give my mother a break from my sister."

They retraced their steps to the front of the funeral home, where reluctantly she released her hold. She could tell from his expression that he did not intend to go back inside with her.

"You don't mind, do you?" he said. "I have somebody waiting for me."

"Your friend?"

"Yes."

"Lucky woman," she said. "Or maybe you're a lucky man. I'll see you at the funeral tomorrow, won't I?"

"Yes," he promised.

"I'm not as tough as I seem."

"I know that."

"You more than anyone else," she said with a blank stare, as if someone had put out the light in her eyes. "When I go back in there, maybe the old man will be sitting up enjoying himself. He always did like attention."

"We all want that," Cole said.

"My sister kissed him, but I didn't want to touch him. I didn't want to make him more dead." She smiled over the chill of her jewelry. "Go, Barney. I'm talking foolish." They embraced, and then she watched him edge away into the gap between two parked cars, one a limousine insolent in its size and glitter and tinted glass. He was halfway across the street when, surprising herself, she called out, "Barney—don't leave me."

She saw him turn around, but the scrape of the shoe she heard was not his. It was quicker and closer, either behind or beside her. She moved reflexively but vaguely as if she were not quite with her body. She glimpsed the face, a sheen of sweat, and then the pistol, which seemed to make no more noise than the double crackling of a banknote.

"I don't believe it," she said more in anger than in panic. Then she looked for Cole.

His arms swept around her and kept her on her feet. At the same time she exercised a strength of her own, which brought her to the threshold of an imbecilic calm. The bug-eyed man from the funeral home rushed toward him. Cole said, "Get an ambulance."

SEVEN

Henry Witlo came into the den and threw her a look of impatience. She had rid herself of the robe for a dress and had done something with her hair, but she had buried herself again in the upholstered chair and, as if to ward him off, had tilted her husband's picture toward the doorway. "I brought in your mail," he said, sorting pieces. "You got bills to pay. I'll leave them here." He dropped them on the desk near her husband's photograph. "Who's the person sending you a postcard from Florida? I can't read the writing."

"It's none of your business," she said with courage, and he smiled.

"That's better, Mrs. Goss. About time you showed a little life."

She sank deeper into the chair, the shock of her own voice pushing her there. She wanted to say something else, but her thoughts were too loose to collect. Then, quite suddenly, her eyes were drawn to his feet, and she experienced another shock. "Take them off," she said.

"Why?" he asked amiably. "They fit fine. My first pair of Florsheims."

"They're not yours."

"They're not anybody's. Your husband's gone, Mrs. Goss, won't be back, so what's the harm? Unless you're afraid you'll hear me and think it's him."

Again, desperately, she wanted to add something vital but could generate nothing. She felt that her head was no more than the pulp of a peach adhering to its stone. Henry moved closer.

"Time you got up again, Mrs. Goss, did some walking around." With what seemed an amazing lack of effort, he gripped her under the arms, lifted her to her feet, and tilted her toward the light as if to examine her for freshness. "We've got to make some rules," he said. "From now on you eat at the table with me, no more stuff about not being hungry. And you talk more. I want real conversations."

She imagined herself dying the death of a thousand cuts from the bite of his voice. He had steadied her and was maneuvering her out of the den, her shoulder brushing the frame of the door. Her slippered feet were clumsy on the carpet. "Easy," he told her. The bathroom door was open. She saw her husband's toothbrush, razor, and metal comb laid out neatly on a folded towel beside the sink. "You got to go in there?" he asked, and she shook her head fast. He guided her into the kitchen, where everything looked spick-and-span, not a dirty dish in sight, no stains on the floor, though she had heard things spill. "When I was a kid, Mrs. Goss, my mother never cleaned anything. I did it all."

She wanted a drink of water and edged to the sink, which appeared perfectly clean until she gagged over the exhalation from a rancid sponge. "I've always taken care of people, Mrs. Goss. Nobody's ever taken care of me. The army did a little, but that wasn't personal, and then they stopped caring when I got to Nam."

She deposited the sponge in the wastebasket under the sink and then turned on the tap and watched the water glove her hand. When the water was cold enough, she filled a tumbler.

"Only one who really did something for me was God. He gave me looks. Bet you think I dye my hair, Mrs. Goss. I don't. It's my natural color. Women, that's the first thing they see, my hair. Then my eyes."

She drank too much water, and it stung her stomach.

"We both got nice eyes," he said. "Yours are kind of like violet."

"Please," she said. She did not want to be touched, but his hands were already on her, propelling her in a direction that seemed dictated by drafts of air from windows not normally open. There was something he wanted to show her, he told her, angling her into the dining room, where he had placed a mass of cut flowers in one of her larger vases.

"Got 'em from your garden," he announced proudly. "Figured they'd look good on the table in case we start eating in here. Kitchen's OK, I don't mind it, but this would be nice and fancy."

More than ever she felt the shape of her world bending in, leaking precious air, deflating around her. Staring at the china closet, she cried her husband's name, the cry inward.

Henry said, "While I was getting the flowers I saw your neighbor, Mrs. Whipple she said she was. I told her I was

110

your nephew, just to keep the story straight. I said I've come to look after you for a while, you not being all that emotionally well since your loss."

For a number of seconds she had no feeling in her face, none in her neck, and only a little in her arms, which she could not raise.

"Why are you staring at the china closet?" he asked. "You think I took a dish."

She imagined herself on her hands and knees at Bellevue Cemetery, tearing at the sod, as if it were possible to yank her husband from the grave and make him see what his death had done to her.

"Those are your best dishes, Mrs. Goss. I wouldn't use them unless we were eating fancy."

"When?" she said. "When are you leaving?"

He moved close to her, breathed her air. "You really want to live here alone, Mrs. Goss? You're no spring chicken. What happens if you have a stroke or something on the toilet, who's going to pick you up, make you decent? Cops come, see you that way, they wouldn't even bother to pull your dress down."

Her gaze was frozen, her arms stiff, her feet planted.

"Ambulance attendants, they're no better. Nobody looking, they grab a feel."

Her wrists twitched. There was life in her forearms all the way to her elbows. Cautiously she lifted them.

"I'm here, you think I'd let that happen? No way, Mrs. Goss. I haven't known you very long, but already you're special to me. What do you think of that?"

She spread her fingers and with the nails went for his face.

Dr. Stein, who was in his early forties but had the small puckish face of an old man, looked Barney Cole up and down and said, "You look pretty fit, I'll say that for you, but of course I don't know how you are inside. You could be rotten."

"From the neck up I'm perfect," Cole said, "every thought pure."

The doctor laughed. He was still in his scrubs and had blood on his knee. "I've never had you under my knife, have I? Lucky you."

Each stepped aside as an attendant pushed by with a steam trolley of food. Cole said, "Maybe not me, but you had my uncle."

"God, yes, I did a gastrectomy on him. Years ago, but I remember it well. I thought his intestines were going to spring out at me. That happened just as the head scrub nurse sliced herself on a scalpel. And I had a miserable headache all through it. How's he doing?"

"He's fine. Living in Florida."

"Glad to hear some of my patients survive."

A nurse came out of Louise Baker's room and said to Cole, "You may go in now."

"You going in too, Doctor?"

"I've seen her. She's doing OK. Lucky for her the weapon was small-caliber, otherwise the nerve damage would've been greater."

"There were two shots," Cole said.

The doctor held up a single finger. "That's all she took."

There were no flowers in the room. Cole had expected to see many, but she had allowed none. He had expected to find her flat on her back, but she was sitting erect in the high cranked-up bed. Her black hair was swept back, giving her pallid face a stark emphasis. Cole's eyes traveled curiously over her.

"This what you're looking for?" she said, and widened

the top of her johnny. The bandage embraced her left shoulder and ran tightly taped down to the rise of her breast, which was black and blue. Awkwardly she tipped her face, and Cole kissed her dry cheek.

"You look uncomfortable," he said.

"I'm in pain, but they give me stuff. The worst of it was I lost blood and got transfused. That scares the hell out of me."

"The blood was mine."

"Good. I didn't know that. You're in my veins, Barney." She patted the bed. "Sit here. Just don't do it hard."

He sat gently on the edge. "I called your housekeeper. She made the decision not to tell your husband just yet."

"That was wise. I'll call him later." She shifted slightly against the raised pillow and winced. Her voice went flat. "You know what it was, don't you, Barney? It was a hit."

"No," he said, "I don't know that."

"You know I'm connected."

"I prefer not to know. None of my business."

"You knew Scampy was."

"That was the suspicion."

She tugged at the covers with a hand bleached of its color. Her face was gloomy. "Am I in all the papers?"

"The *Eagle-Tribune* ran an inside story, no picture. I doubt any other papers picked it up."

Her eyes flashed at him. "I don't get it."

"The police are treating it as a shooting during an attempted mugging. I told them a man tried to snatch your jewelry, you resisted."

Her eyes filled. "I thought everything I worked for in Mallard Junction would be gone. I'd be too notorious. Thank you, Barney."

"Thank Chick Ryan. He went along with it."

Her eyes fluttered shut and reopened grudgingly, as if

whatever sensations were running through her were unpleasant. "I saw his face, Barney. No one I know."

"Can you describe him?"

She shook her head. "That close, he should've got me. I lucked out, didn't I?" Her mouth parted in a slow unnatural smile. "You didn't set me up, did you Barney?"

Cole did not bother to answer. There was a picture on the wall, a pastoral scene in watercolor. He stared at it.

"I'm sorry," she said. "But it's a funny feeling to come that close. You're not the same after." She picked up a water glass and drank from it, her long throat pulsing as the water went down. Then she clenched the glass and said, "I need your help."

"I'm not a bodyguard."

"I need answers, Barney. For my own safety I need them fast."

"I wouldn't know where to begin."

"No," she said, "but Chick would. Scampy died leaving a lot of money on the street. Me in charge, people thought it was uncollectable until I used muscle. That made me enemies. Tell Chick to start there. I've got to know if this thing was local."

For several seconds Cole was silent, his gaze back on the watercolor, the name of the artist etched childishly in a corner. "Chick was your muscle, wasn't he?"

She turned her head slightly as if the lighting were defining her face more than she wanted it to. Her jaw was set.

Cole said, "Why don't you deal with him directly?"

"I want to do it through you. You're the one I trust."

"Few moments ago you didn't."

Her eyes were half closed. "Remember when we were kids, Barney? I mean, little kids. We played cops and robbers, and Chick was always the cop. He pat-searched me."

"Till you got wise."

"You put me wise. Do this for me, Barney."

Cole stood up. He pried the empty glass from her hand and placed it on the bedside cabinet. "What makes you think I will?"

"Because I'm scared, and you know it."

The hour was late. Cole, awake, lay with his head high in the propped pillow. A nightlamp burned vaguely from the top of the dresser, for Kit Fletcher did not like sleeping in the dark. Her silken underthings had been left errantly about, tossed here and there in languid abandon. She lay sprawled beside him on her stomach, a large exemplary leg thrown clear of the covers. He thought her sound asleep, but her voice curved up at him. "Are you thinking about her?"

"I'm not thinking of anything," he said.

"That's humanly impossible." She turned over on her back, much more of her coming out of the covers, and lay pink and vivid, her contours unsparingly feminine and heroically proportioned. She made a dish of her belly. "I want to know more about her."

There was nothing he wanted to add to the little he had already told her, and he bided his time by staying quiet. She shifted closer, her body blissfully cool and clean against him.

"So far she sounds fascinating."

"She's dangerous," he said, "if that's what you mean."

"In her business she has to be."

"I didn't say what kind of business she's in."

"You didn't have to." She pushed the covers from him and passed a hand over his chest. "You love me, Barney?"

"Yes," he replied.

"More than her?"

115

He raised his head higher. In the half-light the mirror over the dresser looked like water on the wall. "I can't believe you're jealous."

"I can't either, but I am." Her smile was frugal. "A side of me you haven't seen before. Drink it in, Barney, I don't show it often."

He felt the faint chill in her voice and the cool give of her leg against him, as if the jealousy were some ill-begotten child coming to rest between them. She drew her knees up.

"When is she getting out of the hospital?"

"Tomorrow," he said, conscious of a drumroll. He was not sure whether it came from his stomach or hers.

"What kind of help does she want from you? Legal?"

"Personal."

"That's what I thought."

"You're making too much of it."

"I was an only child, Barney. I'm not used to sharing."

Her raised knees were gleaming and taut. The heel of her left foot bore the ghost of a blister, from which he drew an image of her forging through Boston crowds with a high sense of purpose. She said, "If you had to choose between her and me, I wouldn't be automatic."

"How do you know that?"

"The way you talk about her. She has deep roots in you, mine are shallow." She lifted her face, one cheek carrying the phantom pattern of the pillow. "You probably think I take you for granted, but I don't. Never have. Everything's an act, Barney, just like in the courtroom. The best of us lawyers deserve Oscars."

He touched her. "What are you afraid of?"

"You."

"That's silly."

"Then of the future."

"Why should you be afraid of the future?"

"Half of life is sadness. The second half."

He spoke slowly. "Then maybe you should marry me."

"I've had enough of marriage."

He stared, his eyes alive to the unswerving beauty of her face. "Then I don't know what to say."

"Sometimes nothing is best."

She rose from the bed, and as always he was taken with the sight of her calm wholesome shape. After she vanished into the little bathroom, he lay listening to the rush of tap water and the flush of the john. He heard her blow her nose. When she reappeared he was moved by the ever-newness of her, the soap-and-water freshness that made her bright and immediate.

"Barney."

"Yes."

"I don't want you to be asleep."

"I'm not. Can't you tell?"

A knee pressed down beside him, and the other one swung over him. She sat astride him, a warm and wide weight below his chest. "Barney."

He gazed straight up. "What?"

"I'd never hurt you. Don't ever hurt me."

"We're running out of everything," Henry Witlo muttered as he rummaged through the refrigerator, clinking bottles and bowls. Finally he said, "We'll have pancakes, that OK with you?" Emma Goss said nothing, and he forced her to set the table while he broke eggs and made the batter. Dishes rattled. "Will you calm down, for God's sake? Will you do that much for me?"

She was shivering and shaking, and her wrists still ached from where he had fended her off, gripped her hard, and brought her to her knees. Her breathing was labored. She poured maple syrup into a small pitcher, spilling some.

"What's the matter with your hand?" he asked.

Her thumb hurt. For the first time she noticed it was hot and swollen.

"You did that to yourself," he said. "Not my fault."

She transferred flatware to the table, dropping a spoon.

Seconds later she found herself with a knife in her hand, the sharpest in the house, and she stared at the blade.

He had eyes in the back of his head. "What are you going to do, stick me with it?"

He made a heap of pancakes, placing some in the oven to keep them hot. The rest he forked onto their plates and drenched them with syrup, emptying the pitcher, though she protested with her eyes. She sat with her chair not fully drawn in, as if at any moment she might leap out of it. She took little bites until hunger urged her on to greater ones, and she began swallowing almost without chewing. Henry, jaws stuffed, grinned from across the table.

"Guess I'm not such a bad cook."

She rendered the smallest kind of answer with her eyes, distrusting what was going on behind his.

"Use your napkin, Mrs. Goss." He touched a corner of his mouth with his little finger. "You've got something here."

Her face changed color. A part of it puckered.

"Jesus Christ," he said. "Don't cry."

Later he left her alone to clean up, and she was glad to busy herself, to be away from his face, the grip of his eyes. Her stomach heaved from what she had eaten, but she ignored it, along with the throb of her thumb. Then too soon she heard his heavy tread. He reappeared with eyelashes wet and yellow hair slicked back at the sides. He had on one of her husband's white dress shirts tucked tightly into his jeans, the collar open, the cuffs turned back at the wrists. Something was in his grasp. Sharply she turned away.

"Don't be afraid."

She stood like a child while he brushed her hair and yanked the back of her dress to straighten the seam. Then he jingled something in his free hand. A pouch with two keys falling loose. She stared at them. They were to Harold's Plymouth.

"Guess what," he said. "I'm going to take you for ice cream."

She tried to lock her feet to the floor, to hook her hand under the table, but his strength would allow none of it. The white of her husband's shirt blinded her. Her feet slid forward when he pushed open the side door. She was about to say, "Leave the light on," but it no longer mattered as she pictured her death in dark woods or behind a derelict building, with a policeman beaming a light over her body. She floated out onto the breezeway, where the evening air gushed hot from the street against her face.

"You don't even need a sweater," he said cheerfully.

Inside the garage the darkness swelled around her, and she thought she heard voices: her parents calling to her, her teacher correcting her, her husband scolding her. The garage door rose with a clatter, and streetlight plunged in on her. Henry nudged her into the car and within seconds was sitting beside her. As soon as he turned the key the radio came on with the cracked voice of the aged Sinatra, Harold's station, the only one he had tuned in on the push buttons. She shuddered. The motor purred as if brand-new.

ANDREW COBURN

"I've checked everything, Mrs. Goss. All it needs is a little air in the tires."

He backed swiftly out of the garage, past his Dodge Charger, which was crushing the lawn, and swung smoothly onto the street. Her heart leaped when the headlights picked up Mrs. Whipple talking to a neighbor, and her face flamed when Henry tooted and waved. Farther down the street, he switched from Sinatra to rock.

"Please," she said, pressing an ear.

He turned it off and stuck an elbow out the window. "Where's the best place for ice cream, Mrs. Goss?"

She could have mentioned Sid White's in Andover or Benson's in Boxford, places Harold had liked, but she said nothing. He drove into the thick of Lawrence, the traffic fretful and full of fumes. When he stopped at a signal, she stared at the glow of brake lights on the car ahead of them. When he sped over the bridge to the north side of the city, she prayed for a collision, a stupendous crash with a rain of glass and metal, in which he would die and she would rise up to walk away whole.

"I'm not sure where I'm going," he said. "You want to help, I'll listen."

"I don't want an ice cream," she said.

"We get there, you'll change your mind." He smiled over at here. "You wait, you'll see."

On Broadway, where the traffic was sluggish, forbidding steel shutters locked in stores for the night. Companionless men hung around outside the Wonder Bar. She felt conspicuous, certain that their reaching eyes would hit upon her. In front of a novelty shop a whiskered scavenger, whose chesty cough she could hear, was dismantling a pyramid of empty crates. Hispanic youths moved as if to a rhumba beat against the savage

120

glare of a sub shop. At any moment she expected them to launch an assault.

"You're safe, Mrs. Goss." Henry continued to smile. "You got me beside you."

She sat with her head driven back, her nose clogged from diesel exhaust from an old Mercedes that had cut in front of them.

"Still don't know where I'm going, Mrs. Goss. Hold on."

He cut through a crossfire of lights, took a sharp turn down a sidestreet of narrow alleys, and presently emerged in a section of the city where rickety tenement houses had been razed for the construction of apartment buildings, which had risen up without rhythm or thought. It was a gray area that suggested neither comfort nor need, only neutrality. Here, staring at Henry's hands held lightly on the wheel, she expected to be strangled.

Many minutes later he said, "Open your eyes, Mrs. Goss."

She saw a row of yellow lights and large illuminated windows, behind which families crowded tables, children frolicked in the aisles, and teen-age waitresses floated like angels. Through a loudspeaker a man announcing numbers for take-out orders strove to put thunder in his voice. He sounded like God.

Henry, turning off the ignition, said, "I'm going to guess vanilla, am I right?"

Left alone, she continued to stare out at the windows, now with a fear that the faces inside were real only while she looked at them and would fade the instant she faltered. It all seemed less an image of reality than a play upon her imagination. She dropped a hand tentatively on the door release and shifted her weight. Her dress, mysteriously wet, clung to the seat.

Henry smiled at her from the side of the building, then leaned his head into the take-out window. A kitchen worker with his heavy hair trussed in a net emptied trash into a dumpster. Girls wrapped in the attention of their boyfriends huddled near a shiny car with racing numerals on its side. She considered a cry for help but was racked with questions. Would they think her crazy? Would they answer with giggles? Would they turn their backs in distaste? She pressed at the door, but it stayed shut.

Henry returned with two sugar cones, which he carried like candles. His was chocolate, a large scoop, and he was already licking it, tapering it. Hers came with a napkin through the open window. Immediately it began to drip on her fingers. Settling in, he said, "Careful, Mrs. Goss, you're getting it on your dress." He plucked the napkin from her and wiped the front of her. "You're worse than a kid, you know that?"

Her bottom lip quivered. "They're going to put you in prison," she said.

"Me?" His eyes rolled. "Not me, Mrs. Goss. You'd better worry about yourself. You write letters to your husband. He's dead. They could put you in an institution for that."

"I'm going to tell the police," she said.

"Sure, you do that, Mrs. Goss. Cops come, see me in your husband's clothes, driving his car, sleeping in his bed, what do you think they're going to believe? They're guys, men of the world, they know what widows do. And Mrs. Whipple, what do you think she'll tell them?"

A kind of loneliness washed over her, as if till now she

had lived her life a thousand miles out at sea and this was her first time ashore, a stranger.

"You don't have to eat that, you don't want to." He lifted the ice cream cone from her sopping hand and tossed it out of the car.

EIGHT

Barney Cole parked his Cutlass in the uphill drive. Chick Ryan's house was a large venerable Victorian, the best in the neighborhood. Chick's wife opened the front door and smiled with eyes of a melancholy turn. "Such a stranger," she said, letting him in. The carpet was thick, the hall furniture solid mahogany. The chandelier was enormous. "You can kiss my cheek," she said. "I won't mind."

He kissed her with a sense of loss. He remembered her as a tall, high-waisted brunette with a long mane. Now her hair was short and gray, and her height seemed diminished. "How are the kids?" he asked.

"Wish they were all married. Then I wouldn't worry so much." She laughed faintly. "Chick's out at the pool."

"I didn't know you had one."

"That's how long it's been since you've been here."

"The house looks lovely."

"We've recently redecorated." With gentle ceremony,

she led him through the large living room and through the dining room to the kitchen. At the back door she said, "Would you like to bring a beer out with you?"

He shook his head. "Thanks anyway."

A stockade fence concealed the pool. Cole stepped through a narrow gateway and shielded his eyes. The pool was almost Olympic size. Chick, wearing red trunks, was flopped in a deck chair, a sprung-open can of Budweiser in his hand. His body hair was black, a pelt that made him part bear. He grinned under dark glasses. "Where's your beer?"

Cole made a negative gesture with his hand. "Nice pool."

"I got extra trunks, you want to go for a dip. No? Then sit down and live the life."

Cole pulled up an aluminum chair almost weightless to the touch. "The house looks great. New furniture?"

"I'm a dirty cop, Barney. Can't help it. It's the way I am." He grinned again under the glasses. "Sure you don't want to take a dip? Wife and I used to go skinny-dipping till she lost her shape."

Cole said, "What have you got for Louise? She's anxious."

"I was her, I'd be anxious too. What I've come up with is zero, depending on how you look at it. I've checked everybody. It wasn't local."

"You're sure?"

"Sure as I can be on something like this. Hey, would I shit Louise? How's she doing?"

"She's out of the hospital. Staying at her mother's place."

"She really must be big-time, somebody wants to hit her. Tell her she wants a bodyguard, I might be able to round somebody up."

"I'd hope she ~~has her~~ own resources."

"Comes down to a matter of who you can trust." Chick took a swig from the can. "By the way, I had coffee at Dolce's with Arnold Ackerman. He says Buddy Pothier's losing the eye. It got infected, doctors can't save it. The other one's OK. I guess that's why we got two of everything. *Most* everything. I was Buddy, I'd get the guy who did it and cut off what he's only got one of."

"He's still not talking?"

"He wants to talk, all he's got to do is come see me. That's what I told Arnold."

Cole rose from his chair. "All that hair, Chick, how do you expect to get a tan?"

"I don't. Sun's not good for the skin."

"I'll pass on your information to Lou."

"You do that."

Cole headed for the gate with the sun hot on his neck and the queasy feeling that he was a bit player in a drama for which he had no script, only cues.

"Barney."

He turned.

"When you say g'bye to my wife, give her a squeeze. I ain't got the desire anymore."

After a bout of dark thoughts, some that took the breath out of him, Daisy Shea shivered up from his desk, took the phone off the hook, and, as had become habit, quit early for the day. He descended the narrow stairs, the wood worn smooth, and poked his head into the furniture store below. "Anybody comes looking for me," he said in a loud voice, "take their name."

"I'm not your secretary," an old man called back. "And where's my rent?"

With dignity, Daisy stepped onto the sidewalk and

loosened his tie. The afternoon hung hot. Next door was Patty's Pet Shop, where mongrel dogs lolled in the window and a stink hung out the open door from a filthy monkey in a cage. Patty, fat of face and thick of torso, sat on a kitchen chair outside the store with a cigar in his mouth. His heavy eyes blinked. "Going home?" he asked.

"Yes," said Daisy, "I'm going *home* home."

"Home home? What's that?"

"Where I was somebody, Patty. Where nothing was so bad a good night's sleep couldn't take care of it."

He cut through an alley to a back lot, where his car stood baking in the sun. Soon he drove onto Broadway with a hand in his wavy white hair, the feel and fall of it a clue to his health. Passing a construction site, he envied the vigor of men in work helmets tipped at belligerent angles. Cruising over the O'Leary Bridge, he breathed in the rank odor of the Merrimack and held it in his lungs as if it were medicinal. With a tremor of anticipation he turned left at the lights on Essex Street and penetrated an area where he had once known every smell and sound, every scar on the sidewalk, every face on the block. With a trace of fear he watched the street deteriorate, and with an interlace of soft feelings he parked against a bleak backdrop of public housing.

"I'm here," he announced to himself, his tone uncertain.

The outline of the Essex Street Housing Project was there, the sheer bulk of the architecture, but the essentials were blunted, the details effaced, the grass gone, along with the trees he had seen planted and had watched grow. The only brightness came from the graffiti smeared on the brick buildings. He could not read the graffiti. It was in Spanish.

He got out of the car with a brave smile and an unsteady step, as if someone were dangling a noose over his head. A dirt bag from a vacuum cleaner and leavings from a McDonald's take-out lay in the gutter. The whole place was strangely quiet, the time of day, he supposed. Nothing looked familiar, let along friendly, which ate at his courage but not his resolve. He stepped onto the sidewalk as a Hispanic woman was passing by. He smiled at her and pointed a finger.

"I used to live there," he said as she quickened her step. "That building in back. Second floor."

A breeze guided him along an asphalt pathway much narrower than he remembered. Underfoot were skins from an orange, the tongue from a shoe, the chain from a bicycle. A bread wrapper lifted itself up and fluttered away. From an open window protected by steel mesh came the dull bark of a dog. A dark-skinned woman, full-bosomed in a sleeveless top, peered down at him from a doorstep, where the metal rail listed on loose stanchions. "You selling?" she said. "We don't buy."

"No, no," he said without breaking stride. "I belong here."

He made his way to the courtyard and beheld swings, sandboxes, and seesaws where there was only the carcass of a burnt-out Pontiac GTO and the debris of marginal lives. His head jerking this way and that, he looked for his mother who enjoyed chatting with neighbors, for Casey the cop who distributed candy from his pockets, for Riley the maintenance man whose breath was telltale of alcohol, for old Mrs. Madigan who at odd times of the day appeared pleasantly out of her mind. Glimpsing none of them, he strained an ear for their voices and heard only the rapid Spanish of young toughs wearing felt hats and goatees. He knew they were talking about him and smiled.

"Guy gotta be crazy," said one in English.

He moved quickly but clumsily, overcharged and over-anxious, to the building where he had lived. NO ES COSA was spray-painted on the battered door, and he wondered what it meant. The urinous odor of the hall-way dismayed him without deterring him. He heard the wail of a baby from the bottom apartment and wondered whether Mrs. Flanagan had added to her brood of seven, but when the door suddenly opened it was a squat duck-legged woman with black skin who peered out at him.

"It's all right," he said. "I'm visiting."

She did not understand. "You a reporter? You come to write about us?"

"I'm not a reporter."

"You come to look at us?"

"No, no, I belong here," he said, and toiled up con-crete stairs. Out of breath, he paused on the second-floor landing and with a flush of pleasure gazed up at the door ahead of him. At any moment he expected it to fly open and one of his sisters to pop out. He could almost hear the fragments of their voices. What he did not hear was the footfall behind him. The man wore beads, bangles, a scarlet undershirt, black pants. A Zapata mustache sprang out of his small muscular face. The force of his voice was chilling.

"Give me your wallet."

Daisy obliged without thought, without fear. Pictures of his children fluttered to the floor.

"You got no money." The man could not believe his eyes. "You got no credit cards."

Daisy said, "I got a quarter in my pocket."

"Empty 'em."

Daisy obliged, and the quarter tinkled onto the con-crete and rolled down the stairs.

"You got to have something. Maybe you hiding a hundred-dollar bill up your ass. Take off your clothes."

Daisy knew men who could look strong simply by standing still, and he tried to be one. "I won't do that," he said.

"I cut your belly, you don't." A knife appeared in the man's hand. A Bic lighter was in the other. A flame shot high. "Then I burn you up."

Daisy closed his eyes and in his mind already felt the kiss of the blade, which relieved him of the anticipation.

"You want to die, that what you want?"

"No, I want to live," Daisy said. "I want to see grand-children. I want to see my wife with white hair. I'd like very much to see the year 2020."

The man shivered with anger, then opened his pants. "Get on your knees."

Daisy opened his eyes. "No, I won't do that either."

The man looked injured and deceived, as if he had been stripped of his weapons, robbed of his worth, what little it was. "Give me something!"

Daisy wet a thumb and anointed the man. Pretending it was Latin, he whispered, *"No es cosa."*

Barney Cole had climbed out of his car and was walking toward his house when a green-and-white Plymouth pulled into the drive. As soon as the driver hopped out, Cole recognized the yellow hair and blue eyes but not the solid gray suit. The necktie was maroon, the shirt white. Henry Witlo approached with a loose gait.

"You like my car, Mr. Cole? It's not new, but it's nice. I try to trade up." He shot a look at Cole's automobile. "You're the only guy I know trades down. What happened to that nice new Cutlass Supreme?"

"That was a lend," Cole said.

"You should've kept it. People rate you by your wheels, also what you wear. Like my suit?"

"You in the chips, Henry?"

"Just bettering myself," Henry said with nonchalance. "Man's got a duty to do that, else he's garbage."

"Why am I never sure of your meaning? Where have you been?"

"Staying out of your hair. That's what you wanted, isn't it?"

The dustheads of dandelions glinted on the lawn, as if the dying sun were singling out coins. A mockingbird was busy in the hedgerose. A curtain twitched from a front window of the house, and Cole knew that Kit Fletcher had peeked out.

Henry said, "I've got a position now, so I don't need your help anymore. But I appreciate what you did do. That's what I come to tell you."

"What's the position?"

"Kind of a caretaker. Guess I can do anything, I put my mind to it."

"Something I want to ask you," Cole said mildly. "It has to do with a fellow named Pothier. Do you know him?"

Henry knitted his brow. "Pothier. French guy, huh? No, never heard of him. Should I of?"

"Somebody beat him up bad enough to cost him an eye. It happened at the Y, just before you quit staying there."

"You're not accusing me of something, are you, Mr. Cole?"

"Simply asking."

"I don't mind you asking long as you know the truth when you hear it. I haven't beat up anybody."

Cole suspected a greater depth in those blue eyes than he cared to think about. They would have suited, he was

131

sure, the angelic expression of a child who had just tortured a cat. "Have you read the papers lately?" he asked.

"No. Why? Something I missed?"

Cole considered telling him about Louise Baker but instead gazed across the way at slender birch trees that seemed poised to spring out of the ground. "Nothing important," he murmured.

"Anyway, Mr. Cole, that's what I came to tell you. I'm doing OK for myself, and you don't have to bother about me." He lifted his shoulders and gave a straightening pull to his necktie. "I won't keep you standing here. I know you got your woman waiting."

Cole watched him turn away, his eye drawn to the jacket of the suit. "You're ripping a seam."

Henry paused and lifted an arm. "That's funny. It was made for me."

Daisy Shea entered Wild Bill's Tavern in the belly of South Union Street and groped through a dimness that suggested purgatory. At the bar he sat with men who salted their beer and peppered their pickled eggs. The pepper came out of a baby-food jar with a punctured cap. The movie on the television above the bar was *The Great Escape* with Steve McQueen. Everyone seemed to have seen it before, some several times, which perhaps was the reason they were watching it again. No surprises. Everything comforting and reassuring. Daisy cadged a drink from Plug Brown, a retired janitor who looked like a dead man, but later he ran into abuse when he tried to borrow five dollars from Sugar O'Toole, a widower devoted to the memory of his wife and to the quiet violence of his drinking.

"Get away from me. You're a deadbeat."

"Maybe you think I won't be around long enough to

pay you back," Daisy said with Christlike calm. "Not to worry one little bit. I've been to hell and back. Nothing can touch me now."

Sugar sank a shot of rye in a glass of beer. "You got a hole in your brain."

The bartender said, "Don't bother the customers, Daisy."

Sugar said, "You want the hard facts, Daisy, you and Plug over there, they're going to bury you together, put the two of you in the same box."

Plug Brown turned a pepless face and gave them the watery stare of a sockeye salmon. The bartender, clinking bottles, said, "Watch the movie, Sugar."

"Who asked you?"

"I don't have to be asked. It's my bar."

Available, besides pickled eggs, were precooked hamburgers and hot dogs. Daisy had forgotten how hungry he was until he ambled midway down the bar and saw Frank Flanagan bite into the greasy bun of a hamburger and seconds later bring up a brimmer of beer and blow at the foam. Sidling up, Daisy said, "Your mother's had another kid, huh?"

Frank Flanagan's bald head swung turtlelike out of an angular collar. "What the hell you talking about?"

"I heard the baby cry," Daisy said.

"You been on the sauce too long. My mom's in the old folks' home."

"I know what I know," Daisy said adamantly.

"You alive—or you dead and none of us know it yet? Maybe you're up in heaven somewhere. That the story?"

"I went back to the project, Frank. I heard."

Frank Flanagan pulled a bill from a roomy pocket of his work pants and slapped it on the bar. "Give him a double. He needs it."

The bartender said, "Your night, Daisy."

Daisy moved away from the bar with a large Cutty on the rocks firmly in his grip and one sock slipping into his shoe. The only woman in the place was returning from the ladies' room to a chrome-stemmed table in the dim of a corner. She had a blast of blond hair, snow on fire, and was wearing a tight cream dress, a streak of lightning. "Pearl, can I join you?" he said, and got a look that should have withered him.

"I'm with somebody," she said, dropping into a chair, her elbows slamming onto the table, where her mixed drink shimmered next to a bottle of beer and an unused glass. She was the ex-wife of a fireman and had been a classmate of Daisy's in grade school, where a male teacher had likened her to a sugar cookie and lost his position for acting on his impulses.

Daisy sat down anyway. "Your friend doesn't like me, I'll leave. Where is he?"

"Little boys' room."

"Who is he?"

"Don't know, just met. Daisy, you got some stinking nerve."

Her tablemate returned shortly, a younger man than Daisy was expecting, and bigger. The man seemed to be climbing out of his suit, which did not look right at the shoulders. His eyes were blue studs, and at that moment his face was inscrutable, as if some sort of ticket might be needed to enter his privacy. Then he smiled and, rocking the table, plopped down next to Pearl. "This your father?"

"His name's Daisy. Daisy, this is Henry."

"Daisy?"

"He was a kid, he used to pick 'em. Give 'em to the girls. G'bye, Daisy."

"Let him stay."

Henry's attention, along with a strong swallow of Cutty, warmed his heart and pushed his face to a higher shade under the white waves of his hair. He took another swallow, which stabbed his throat and burned his chest, and let his mind reach back to his single stellar performance on the football field when Jesus Christ Almighty clamped a hand to the seat of his pants and gave him nowhere to go but forward. He remembered the first time he saw Edith wearing a chemise over no underwear, and he remembered the day his oldest daughter graduated from St. Mary's High, third in her class, braces still on her teeth. He turned to Henry and said with a surfeit of feeling, "This is decent of you."

"I do what I can for people, way I'm made."

He started to reply, but a pain bent him in two, which gave Pearl a start. Her nylons hissed as she uncrossed her legs.

"What are you doing?"

"Fixing my sock," he wheezed, and then came up in his chair sweating, his face heated, his hands cold. Tension gripped his chest.

"You look lousy," she said, and frowned at Henry. "He's sick, you know. They took his stomach out. Christ, don't drop on us!"

"He's all right, aren't you, buddy?" Henry picked up money from the table. "Here, get yourself another drink."

He rose too fast to his feet and saw double. He stood stiff and heavy, ill in a frozen way except for his eyes, slits of fire. He took a tentative step, and Pearl said, "He's not going to make it."

"Yes, I am."

He hobbled to the bar as if he had a pebble in his shoe

and a bit of a load in his pants. Steve McQueen's tight-lipped face burned bright on the television. Sugar O'Toole looked away from the screen and with a yawn showed a cavern of a mouth and a flab of a tongue. Plug Brown was eating an egg, sharing the pepper with the man next to him. The bartender leaned toward Daisy and said in a confidential tone, "Why don't you let Pearl and the guy alone? She's looking to get laid."

"I'm not stopping her." He dropped money down. "The fella's buying me a drink. They want me there."

"You got enough here for another double. That what you want?"

"Yes."

He returned to the table with slightly less of a hobble and smiled at the two of them as if he held the key to their happiness. As he sat down, his necktie got in the way of his hand. He sloshed Cutty and licked his fingers. Pearl said to Henry, "You win. He made it."

Henry drank beer from the bottle. "There was never any doubt. Right, champ?"

Daisy answered with a smile. "Someone's looking over me. I know that now for a fact. Do you believe in God, Henry?"

"Let's not get into that crap," Pearl said.

Henry said, "I was six years old, a priest and I went into the woods looking for God and ended up taking a leak together."

"So you've never seen him?"

"Sure I have, in Nam. He was wearing a V.C. uniform. He shot at me point-blank and missed. You see, he knew it wasn't my time and jerked the trigger."

Daisy's chest billowed like a pigeon's. "Do you believe that, Henry?"

"For Christ's sake, Daisy, he's putting you on."

"She's right," Henry said. "What I told you was bull-shit. It was me fired point-blank and missed. That's how jittery I was. See, I didn't dope up that day. My black buddies told me to, but I didn't listen. They knew something I didn't. Know what that was?"

Daisy shook his busy head.

"The army didn't give a shit about us, white or black, no difference. Painted us all orange."

"You got sprayed?"

"How do I know I didn't? Think the army's going to tell me? I wake up at night, feel something funny in my gut, maybe I got cancer. I could be dying this minute and don't know it."

"I'm sorry for you, Henry."

"For the love of God," said Pearl, "I came in here looking for a happy conversation, not two guys dying."

Henry stretched an arm around her. "You want happiness, I'll give you happiness."

"He's a saint," Daisy said. "Second one I've met today."

"He's a saint, I'm the fucking Queen Mum."

Daisy lifted his glass. "They come in strange packages, Pearl. You have to have the eyes to see them. First one I met had a mustache and was bilingual."

She rattled ice. "Go buy me another drink."

"I've lost my wallet."

"Hear that, Henry? He's lost his wallet."

"God knows where it's gone," Daisy said, and closed his eyes, for the pain that had bent him in half hit him again, deeper down. This time he took it like a soldier. The body protested the pain, the muscles flexed against the outrage. Through fluttering lids he glimpsed Pearl's hand curling around Henry's neck and pictured her as a pillow caving in wherever someone's head might hit. He loosed gas and felt better.

"You pig," Pearl said a moment later.

"Time you went home, champ."

He did not want to go home. He did not want to lie wide awake in the dark of the bedroom and pray for dawn. For the sound of a single bird. For the rumble of the first car on the street. For the first sign of life-sustaining routine.

Pearl said, "You won't, we will."

"Don't go," he said, and heard the scrape of their chairs and the scuff of Pearl's high heels. In another moment he would hate her, so he turned his head.

"I don't see you again, champ, you take care, you hear?"

He nodded, he almost smiled. Their voices clung to the air, Henry's the hardest, and then faded. A few minutes later he rose uncertainly from the chair with an empty glass in his hand. At the bar Frank Flanagan stuffed relish into a cold roll and shoved in a frank, which he overpainted with mustard. He glanced at Daisy and said, "No more," His voice rose. "I mean it."

Daisy placed his empty glass on the bar. The bartender said, "You're shut off."

He drifted away through layers of cigarette smoke, with a need for relief. For a moment or so he forgot the way to the men's room, but then he smelled it as if it were some unwashed secret. The light inside, though not bright, hurt his eyes. He stood at the urinal as if he had been about to walk into the wall and had frozen in his tracks. Blinking, emptying his bladder, he enjoyed a moment of unrestrained flatulence, and in the deepest memory part of his brain a trumpet blared. As a boy he had briefly and badly tried to play one, expecting a bolt from above to give him the skill. From the dim of the doorless stall behind him, a voice said, "Sugar says he's sorry."

He turned slowly, zipping up and shaking his head at the shadow on the toilet. "Sugar never said that."

"I'm saying it for him." Plug Brown rose with his trousers in hand. He lifted a leg and hit the flushing lever with his shoe. The roar of the flush—splintered chokings and savage gurglings—sounded as if it came from the depths of Hades. "Enough shit in this world without Sugar adding to it," he said, stepping out.

Daisy stood stalwart. "I thank you, Plug."

"It's little enough."

"It's more than you know."

"It always is, Daisy. That's why I do it." Plug went to the little stainless steel sink and turned on the tap. "I always wash up afterwards. I shake hands with somebody, I don't want him wondering where mine's been."

"You've got good habits, Plug."

"We gotta take care of ourselves. That's prime."

Daisy waited, his eyes whiskey-soaked and his nose burning, and then washed his hands too.

A short time later he stepped out of the side door of the tavern and rubbed his hot face against the night air flowing through the narrow lot. Before slinking away, a dog bared its teeth and growled. Cars glittered as they sped by on South Union Street. He moved toward his car with high floating steps as if someone were reeling him in through unsettled waters. His car was a two-door, the driver's side ajar, the inside dome light dropping a dull glow. Without surprise, he said, "Where's Henry?"

"Gone."

"Was it good, Pearl?"

"It was adequate." She sat rigidly, her hair somewhat

wild, her lipstick smeared, which seemed to relocate her mouth. "Can you give me a ride home?"

"Can you drive?" He dangled keys. "I'm not sure I can see."

"I'm not sure I can move."

He opened the door wide. "Maybe I can help."

"Don't touch me." She struggled, favoring a leg, and squeezed out backwards with her wrinkled dress riding up. Her bottom blossomed through floral underpants like a mushroom springing through leafmold. She stood crookedly. "Get a good look, Daisy?"

"Nothing I haven't seen before. Remember the eighth grade, Pearl?"

She began to cry. "The son of a bitch hurt me."

Awkwardly, with obvious pain, she slid in behind the wheel, and Daisy, with pain of his own, crept in from the other side. The car bucked when she started it, but then smoothed out as she steered it onto South Union, where she ran a red light. Her expression was sour.

"What was the problem, Pearl?"

"I reminded him of his mother."

Emma Goss was asleep, a sheet drawn over her, her shape like a piece of furniture shrouded away during the owner's absence. The sleep was unnatural, the fault of pills she had purchased after Harold's funeral and had never used until Henry discovered them and made her swallow several because of shadows under her eyes and a slur in her speech. That was ten hours ago, when sunshine was flooding the room. Now, from another window, there was moonlight.

Twice, briefly, she had come out of the sleep, the first time with the fear that someone was tracing a tightly clenched fist over her body and at any second would strike a vital spot. The second time she woke with only a vague sense of identity, as if her life had lost its distinguishing contours and were rounding in on her, dull and anonymous. Now she stirred again, this time from a voice in the room.

"I'm home."

She heard a heavy tread near the bed, but remained impassive, incurious, her eyes only half open. When an arm swung over her, she smelled perfume on the sleeve.

"Look at me."

It was a man's voice, beer on his breath, but his face was only a ball of wax. Half of him was on the bed.

"Do you know who I am? Look at the suit."

Her eyes worked to see. Her hand touched the scented sleeve.

"I'm Harold," he said.

NINE

"Rita?"

"Yes."

"Louise Leone here."

"That's not your name now."

"Baker."

"Yeah, I knew it was something like that. Tough about your father. I know what it's like to lose people."

"Rita, I had a close one."

"Yeah, I heard. How are you?"

"Healing. I wonder if I might drop over."

"Where are you?"

"Ten minutes away."

"Sure, why not? It's been a while."

"I'll leave now."

"Come around the back. That's where I'll be. I'm a woman likes to take it easy now."

Louise racked the receiver. She was in her mother's bedroom, where the crucified Christ hung over the bed and religious pictures adorned the opposing wall. A photograph of her father, idealized beyond belief, stood on the dresser beside a smaller picture of her and her sister in Easter dresses. She glanced into the mirror, touched her hair, and then left the room.

Her mother, sitting at the kitchen table with an untouched cup of tea, did not look up, not even when Louise dropped a hand on her mother's frail shoulder, which felt like the back of an arthritic cat. Leaning over, she kissed the top of her mother's head and said, "Love me, Ma?"

"I love both my children."

"Me best?" she asked, playing her sister's game.

"Both the same."

She kissed her mother's head again and straightened up with a sharp twinge. "I'm going out for a while."

"You should stay off your feet."

"Too much to do," she said, and moved toward the door. Her mother looked up.

"Am I going to lose you too?"

"No, Ma, I'm too tough."

Her mother dropped her eyes and touched the teacup. "Maybe you only think you are."

A few minutes later she was cruising along Route 125 under a bright sky bearing a distant fleet of little clouds. The road edged Harold Parker State Forest, where pines sprang to heroic heights. She soon crossed the line into Andover and, at the state police barracks, took a left onto Gould Road and then another left into the Farrwood Drive area, which lay on the fringe of the forest.

Rita Gardella O'Dea's house was a sprawling contemporary, much of it glass, and stood on the top of a graded rise, where pines had been toppled to make way for birches. Lousie left her Porsche at the foot of the drive and hiked up a wide walkway partly overrun by creeping ground ivy. In the oblique sunlight, beds of border flowers glimmered like displays of old jewelry. At the top, winded, she rested for a few seconds and then followed a narrow footpath to the rear of the house, where the green of the lawn looked hard and healthy, full of the strength of early summer.

"Here I am," Rita said, as if she could be missed. She stood on the patio, an explosively overweight woman in a sleeveless frock that exposed the heft of her arms and the voluminous cups of a bra that barely restrained her fullness. Her black hair fell long and straight down her back, and her dark-eyed face was disarmingly pretty, more that of a plump schoolgirl than a widow in her forties. She was the sister of a slain Mafia leader, whose money she had inherited, along with remnants of his power. "You thirsty?" she said. "I got lemonade here."

A pitcher stood on a round table, hornets drawn to it. Beside the pitcher was a plate of puff pastry.

"You want to eat? Go ahead, take something."

"No thank you."

Rita slumped into a chaise longue and gestured. "Go ahead, sit."

Louise sat in a padded chair, grateful to be off her feet. She crossed her legs and placed her hands demurely in her lap as Rita scrutinized her.

"You look OK, for what you been through. A little pale, that's all."

"I was lucky."

"Tell me about it."

"A man approached me outside the funeral home. I didn't see him until he was on me, no one I knew. He fired twice and was gone. He only hit me once. He must've been nervous."

"What does that tell you?"

"He came cheap."

A small butterfly gently worked its way through the air and ventured first toward Louise and then toward Rita before flitting away. Rita said, "So all you got to do is figure out where he was coming from."

"Yes, that's the problem."

"Somebody turns on you, it's usually this," Rita said, and rubbed a thumb against two fingers. A hornet flew close, and she swatted the air. "You've built yourself a sweet operation. The big people are happy with you."

"When Scampy died, they thought I'd fall on my face. I surprised them."

"You didn't surprise me."

"But maybe I've surprised them too much."

Rita's eyes were smudges of darkness, the line of her mouth an unspoken irony. She reached down and scratched the heft of her calf, leaving chalk marks. "You scared?"

"Only of them."

"Relax. If they wanted your operation, they'd have sent a real shooter. Your head tells you that."

Louise nodded. "I guess I needed to hear you say it."

"Knowing who it wasn't pretty much tells you who it was. My brother used to say that. You didn't know Tony, did you?"

"Only from a distance," Louise said, remembering a silver head of hair and an expensive suit of clothes. She remembered his face from a photograph in a Boston paper and a framed one perched on his closed casket, the North End funeral home filled with so many flowers the air hung sick. She said, "I drove Scampy in twice a year to meet with him. I always waited in the car."

"Scampy never introduced you?"

"No."

"Smart of him. My brother could do things to women with just a look. Remember the actor Cesar Romero? That was Tony." Rita's large eyes filled. "I got tough skin, but I'm all lonely underneath. Most people wouldn't guess it, but you know it, don't you?"

"I'm a woman."

"It's more than that. I wasn't so heavy, you and I could pass for sisters."

Louise smiled, and Rita suddenly shifted her weight, swung out a round arm, and reached into the plate of pastry.

"Tell me about your operation."

"I bankroll only the biggest buys. I don't look for business, it comes to me now. I give a reasonable rate, and I've never been burned."

"Far as you know." Nibbling, Rita got powder on her chin and wiped it off with the padded heel of her hand. "Right now, this particular time, you got a lot of money out?"

"Yes."

"More than usual?"

Louise nodded.

"Who's your legman?"

"Sal Botello from Springfield. John Rozzi rides shotgun, also from Springfield. When Scampy was dying, he recommended Sal in case I ever needed help. Their mothers were cousins or something. I took him on when I decided to expand the business."

Rita licked her fingers. "No man, no matter how much he kisses your ass, likes working for a woman."

"Sal doesn't kiss my ass, but you're right."

"He watched you grow, probably thinks he made it happen."

"Yes, I've suspected that at times."

"What else do you suspect?"

"He thinks he could be me."

Rita's eyes absorbed her. "You had it figured before you came here. Only thing you didn't know was if the son of a bitch was acting on his own. Now you know."

Louise closed her fingers into her palms, pressing the nails. Her eyes focused on the pitcher of lemonade, prismatic in the sunlight. Rita smiled at her.

"Go ahead, have some. It's not from a mix. I made it with real lemons."

Louise rose, fearlessly fought away hornets, and poured from the pitcher, the ice cubes gushing forward, then clogging. She filled one glass and partially filled another. She offered the full one to Rita, whose hand flew up like a pigeon, wings spread.

"Thank you, dear."

Louise gazed off at the far reaches of the property, where the top branches of towering swamp pines examined the sky. "I know what I have to do," she said. "All I need is permission."

Rita drank deeply, the right armhole of her dress gaping wide and revealing a neglected underarm and the vast motions of her torso. She smacked her lips. "That was good."

"Do I have it?"

Rita deposited the empty glass beside the chaise longue. "Do what you have to do."

Louise immediately leaned over her and kissed her cheek. "Thank you."

Rita said, "Try the pastry."

Barney Cole crossed the street to city hall, which was topped with a clock that had not worked for decades and a bell that had never rung, no tongue. It was a pigeon-stained fortress where questionable politicians were kept in office by ancient machinery and the remains of ethnic voting blocs, of which Cole's father had been a member in good standing. The double doors suggested portals into the lobby of a secret society. Inside, a rotunda shot up three flights to a leaded-glass skylight. At one time the welfare offices were on the top floor but were shifted when a morose recipient humiliated by a clerk went haywire, hurled herself over the rail, and was dead upon impact, her head laid open on the marble floor like pottery pieces. Cole's father had been among the witnesses, and Cole still remembered the pallor of his father's face when he had returned home that night.

Cole approached the snack stand, which was operated by a blind man who recognized customers by the sound of their footsteps and detected their moods by the depth of their voices. His name was Al. "You must be a ghost," he said.

"Not quite," Cole replied.

"You're right. Your dad's step was a shade quicker. Same fall, though. You in a gloomy mood, Barney?"

"Not that I know of."

"Must be my imagination," he said, smiling under inkblot glasses. "You've been a stranger. Watcha doin' here?"

"Killing time," Cole said with a glance at his watch. He picked up a candy bar and paid for it with a bill he pressed deep into the man's dry hard palm, which seemed no bigger than a baby's. "That's a single, Al."

"What kinda candy?"

"Mars bar."

"Your dad went for Milky Way." Al made change and

spoke with a sigh. "The best of 'em are gone, Barney. Your dad, Vin Foley, Phil DiAdamo, Eddie Fallon, Gerry Guilmette. When it gets slow here, I can still hear their steps."

Cole unwrapped the candy bar. He took a small bite and then immediately closed the wrapper and slipped the bar into a pocket.

"They were the cream, Barney. Hard to bury guys like that. They rise to the surface."

Cole glanced around the lobby. Many faces were unfamiliar. A woman stopped in midstride to sort the documents she was carrying, her lean legs quivering on high heels. A few fellows were talking near the elevator, which was disgorging visitors, mostly Hispanic women whose somber expressions contrasted with the exuberant colors of their clothes.

"I never believed those stories about your dad. All bullshit as far as I was concerned."

In Cole's memory his father had had a head of majestic shape; in photographs it was ordinary and balding, which gave Cole a jolt whenever he opened the album. "Even if they were true, Al, what does it matter now?"

"That's not the point, Barney. It mattered *then*."

The woman with the documents suddenly sprinted across the lobby as if somebody had laid a whip across her bottom. A man with shirtsleeves rolled high stuffed letters down the mail chute next to the elevator. Cole rechecked his watch.

"You seem nervous, Barney, or is that my imagination again?"

Cole looked to his left. A scrawny man in the dull uniform of a deputy sheriff had entered the lobby by a side door and was standing near the city clerk's office. The shabby braid and tarnished buttons of the uniform gave him the look of a stray from a Memorial Day parade. Cole said, "Al, it was good talking to you."

"You didn't say much, Barney."

Cole strolled over to the deputy, a trusted flunky of District Attorney Chugger Doogan, who had offices next door in superior court. Earlier the district attorney had telephoned Cole, an uncomfortable conversation that had cramped Doogan's voice and altered the color in Cole's face.

"You're ten minutes late," the deputy said. "D.A.'s waiting for you."

"How'd you know I was here?"

"I saw you go in."

"Nothing personal," Cole said, "but I don't like you coming after me."

"Just doing what I'm told, Barney. I've been doing that since I was a kid."

The courthouse exuded its age, its grime, its intricate and irreplaceable architecture of a dead era. Police officers and bondsmen, lawyers with their clients, assistant district attorneys floated in hazes of dust through wide corridors and up expansive stairways. Gray-haired clerks filtered through the dim, the women indistinguishable from the men, as if age had made them androgynous, especially in that part of the building that seemed like a mausoleum. "Where the hell are we going?" Cole asked, for they had passed the district attorney's offices and were descending stairs into the pit of the building, where the fluorescent lighting hung low.

"D.A.'s interested in privacy," the deputy said over the hum of a dehumidifier stirring up ancient odors. Each door they passed bore the legend *Records*. Finally the deputy halted at one and opened it while giving a quick rap. "I'll leave you now," he said, and vanished.

The room, lined with fireproof file cabinets, looked into an inner chamber, where the district attorney was sitting at a table with two men who looked like high-powered insurance salesmen and sure winners of company achievement awards. The district attorney struggled to his feet, and his feedbag of a body moved slowly toward Cole, no strength of purpose in the short stout legs. The smile on his face seemed an aberration.

"I don't like this," Cole said in a low voice.

"I don't either, Barney, but what can I do? They're feds."

Mrs. Whipple's polo shirt was bright yellow, her red shorts even brighter. Whenever she moved to rake or dig or pull up weeds, Henry Witlo glimpsed the colors. They flashed between the low-hanging branches of a tree and through the boundary of shrubs. Moving closer, he saw the movement of her arms and the spring of her legs. He cut through the foliage, smiled boyishly, and said, "Excuse me, ma'am."

She turned with a bamboo rake in her hands and gave him a quick inquiring look. "Yes, Henry?"

He was pleased she remembered his name, though he had been reasonably sure she would, mostly from a glimpse he had once gotten of her husband, unsparingly bland, which gave him a clue to the tempo of the marriage. "I don't mean to bother you."

"It's OK," she said. "What is it?"

He liked the way the sun iced the gray cracks in her blond hair, and he liked the sound of her voice, though it reminded him of an elementary school teacher who had

151

jacked him out of a chair and boxed his ears. "I don't mean to cause trouble," he said.

"Don't keep me in suspense."

"It's the stereo. Sometimes you're not home, your daughter plays it loud. I don't mind, but it kinda gets on my aunt's nerves. You know how old ladies are."

"Tell Mrs. Goss I'm sorry. I'll try to make sure it doesn't happen again."

"I didn't want to mention it."

Mrs. Whipple tipped her head. "You're very good to her."

"She's a nice lady, only family I got."

"What do you do for work, Henry?"

"I draw disability. I got banged up pretty bad in Vietnam."

"That was a terrible war. My husband missed it, thank God."

"I was proud to serve."

"And your aunt must've been proud of you."

"She wrote me twice a week, and she sent me a lot of packages."

Mrs. Whipple wound the leather loop of the rake handle around a finger. "Are you married, Henry?"

"No, but I've come close a few times," he said. He liked the way her eyes played upon him, some sort of promise implicit in the playfulness, which was no less than what he had expected. "Long as my aunt needs me," he said, "I've got no plans."

"She's lucky to have such a nephew."

"We're both lucky."

Mrs. Whipple smiled. "May I tell you something, you won't get mad?"

He smiled back. "I won't get mad."

"You promise?"

"Sure."

All of a sudden a mask slipped away. Mrs. Whipple's face was bald and shiny. She said, "I think you're bullshit shoveled high."

He needed a telltale second to look his most innocent. "I don't follow."

"Whose idea you call her Auntie? Hers or yours?" Mrs. Whipple's smile was as smug as it could get, which brought out the creases beneath her eyes, the dimples in her cheeks. "I never would have suspected the old girl, so prim and proper, but the old cliché about the quiet ones is usually true."

Henry kept his mouth shut, deferring to her smile. Everything inside him that had gone tight now relaxed.

"The time she was in the car with you, I never saw anybody looking so guilty."

Henry hung his head forward, somewhat contritely. "I guess something like this, you don't fool anybody."

"Not for long, Henry, not the way you two do it."

"Just because her husband's gone doesn't mean she has to rot." Henry rose on his toes. "She's got a right to a life same as the rest of us."

"More power to her," Mrs. Whipple said with amused condescension.

"I respect her, ma'am. Don't say anything against her."

Beginning to turn away, Mrs. Whipple smiled her sweetest. "I wouldn't dream of it."

The district attorney introduced Barney Cole to the two men seated at the far side of the table, agents Cruickshank and Blue, each clad in a pinstripe suit that would have pleased a Boston banker. Cruickshank, who looked a little like Max Headroom with less of a smile, gripped Cole's hand. Blue, a slender black man in gold-rimmed glasses, half rose and immediately sank back, indicating that his function was merely to monitor. The district attorney quickly removed himself to a distant chair, which he sat in tentatively, as if his presence were provisional and his departure imminent. Cole sat directly across from Cruickshank, whose demeanor was placid and poised.

"Relax, Mr. Cole. Nobody's going to bite you."

"I hope not," Cole said. "This is the age of infection."

Without a smile, Cruickshank drew his chair closer to the table. His fair hair seemed molded to his tall head. A deep note crept into his voice, which resonated. "Do you know what this is about?"

"No," Cole lied.

"The district attorney didn't tell you?"

From his outpost, the district attorney also lied. "I was vague."

"The assault on Louise Leone Baker," Cruickshank said. "Apparently you were the only eyewitness."

"Yes, apparently," Cole said.

"You said it was an attempted mugging."

Cole seemed to nod, and Cruickshank opened a vinyl folder and extracted a sheet of paper, which he did not look at. "According to the police report, you said a man tried to rip jewelry from Mrs. Baker's neck."

"Yes, that's what it looked like."

"You seem to be hedging."

"It was dark."

"She was in the light, no?"

"It happened fast."

"Bang, bang. Two shots."

"That's what it sounded like."

"That part rings right, Mr. Cole, but I'll tell you my problem. It's like I'm doing a puzzle and I have pieces that don't belong. I hate it when that happens. What do you think, Blue?"

Cole was suddenly aware that the other agent had been observing him with excruciating care, scrutinizing each movement in his face. "If you have pieces that don't belong," Blue said, "you should throw them out."

"Yes," said Cruickshank. "My theory, Mr. Cole, is that it was an attempted assassination that was botched."

Cole shrugged. "It's possible, anything's possible, but that's not the way I saw it."

"You could be wrong. You're aware that Mrs. Baker has Mafia connections."

"I've heard people say that."

"You're an old friend of hers."

"Yes, but I don't see much of her. She lives across the state."

"But she's been sticking around here now, recuperating, I guess. Or else biding her time. What do you think, Blue?"

Blue kneaded his chin with fingers extraordinarily long and tapered. "Perhaps Mr. Cole knows."

"I'm sure you know much more than I do," Cole said. "I don't make her my business."

"We'd like you to make her your business," Cruickshank said flatly, with the vestige of a smile. "We're not asking you to wear a wire or anything dramatic like that. We merely want you to glean as much information from her as you can. We know something's going to happen, Mr. Cole, surely as all of us are sitting here. We'd like to be on top of it."

Cole, in a frozen pose of amiability, said, "I'm a lawyer, gentlemen, not an informer."

"We're all officers of the court," Cruickshank said, "which is why we find it so easy to talk to you. By the way, you'd be compensated for your time."

"Mrs. Baker doesn't confide in me, and if she did it would probably be privileged."

Blue suddenly placed his well-sculpted hands on the table, the fingers fascinating both Cole and the district attorney. He spoke with cold formality. "We don't want you to answer now. We want you to think about it."

Cruickshank returned the sheet of paper to the vinyl folder, and both agents got to their feet, vividly aloof, sartorially correct. Blue gazed down with sphinx eyes through the gold glasses. Cruickshank, slipping the folder under an arm, said, "No need to tell you this is confidential."

Blue, moving gracefully past Cole, said, "We'll be in touch."

Left alone, neither Cole nor the district attorney spoke for several seconds. The district attorney was absorbed with his fingernails and then with the front of a thumb. Finally he said, "I want you to know I'm not a part of this."

"A piece of the puzzle that doesn't belong," Cole said without spirit. "Is that it?"

"Feds are funny guys, Barney. All my life I've never known 'em to play fair. Christ, they even throw a black guy at you. Did you see his fucking fingers?"

"They must be expecting something from you, Chugger."

"They expect everything. You know why? Because they know everything, all the right and wrong stuff on everybody. True or false, doesn't matter, it all goes into the files. Christ, they must have bigger computers than the Pentagon."

"What do they know about me?"

"Nothing bad, Barney. Considering you were born and bred in Lawrence, you're an angel. No, it's your father and me. They know I went to bat for him. They know I went to bat for a lot of people." He gave out a harsh laugh. "Christ, if I had gone after those indictments there'd have been nobody left to run the city."

"Do they know Scampy was your friend?"

"Course they know. I told you, they know everything, half of it wrong."

"Can they get you on any of it?" Cole asked gently.

"Naw." He tugged at the purse of skin under his chin. "But they could throw shit at me come election time."

Cole stared off at a row of file cabinets, at the bars and bolts securing them. "I'm sorry, Chugger."

"Not your fault, for Christ's sake. None of it's your fault."

"What do they want you to tell me?"

"That it would suit everybody, including yourself, if you cooperated."

"That's all?"

"They don't threaten, Barney. They insinuate."

Cole lifted himself from the chair, tugged at his suit jacket, and smiled distantly. "What's your advice, Chugger?"

"Fuck the feds. We take care of our own."

"When are you coming home, Lou?" The voice was plaintive. It could have belonged to a six-year-old, and for a quicksilvery moment she thought it did.

"Soon as I can, Ben. I promise."

"How soon?"

"Soon. My mother's still not herself. You wouldn't want me to leave her that way, would you?"

"You could bring her here. Then we'd both have you."

"She wouldn't do that, Ben. Too far from my father's grave." She shifted the receiver to her other ear and glanced over her shoulder. A woman was waiting to use the phone. "I'm going to be a while," she said with a hand over the mouthpiece, and the woman turned away.

"Where are you, Lou?"

"In the lobby of a bank, downtown Lawrence. I needed to cash a check, and they know me here. In fact, I still have an account."

"You're really coming back, aren't you?"

"Ben," she said in a disappointed tone.

"I need you to tell me. Just tell me."

"You have my word," she said forcefully. They continued to talk, she in reassuring tones, but an undercurrent of doubt remained in his voice, along with a suggestion of weariness. "Let me speak to Mrs. Mennick now," she said.

Waiting, she gazed over at a man tapping the buttons on a money machine, his posture tense, as if he feared the machine might not accommodate him. The building was old, the lobby floor marble, the walls megalithic, the windows vaulted. She cast her gaze over the expanse to the teller's window where her father had once cashed checks that did not belong to him and avoided prosecution only because of Scampy's intervention.

Mrs. Mennick came on the line.

"Can you talk?" Louise asked.

"Yes. He's gone to the bathroom."

"How's he doing?"

"He refused his medication yesterday, but I managed to get it into him today. I have my tricks."

A worried expression took hold of Louise's face. "So does he. Are you going to be able to control him?"

"I'm doing my best, Mrs. Baker, but it's you he needs. I'm his nanny, but you're his mommy."

Louise stiffened and did not respond, fearful of what she might say.

"I'm sorry," Mrs. Mennick said. "I didn't mean to say it exactly like that. It's just that I see how much he misses you."

"I'm aware of that," Louise said evenly. "But I know you can handle the situation. I'll be home as soon as I possibly can."

"I don't mean to trouble you," Mrs. Mennick said quickly. "You've been through a lot yourself. And you sound so tired."

"Worry about him, Mrs. Mennick, not me."

"I worry about you both."

"I know you do," Louise said, lowering her voice, relenting. "I don't mean to be harsh."

"I understand."

"You always do."

A few minutes later Louise stepped out of the bank into a balmy breeze on Essex Street, where, despite millions of federal dollars spent to prettify it, many buildings stood in varying phases of decay and abandonment. Too many gaps, blank façades, and clouded windows; too many lengths of loneliness, which hollowed her step. Gone were the big stores like Sears and Sutherland's and the charming ones like Peter's Sweet Shop and Ritzy's Diner. Gone were the gimcrack goods of the Racquet Store, where her mother had once bought a toaster her father later hocked for fifty cents. The hockshop was gone too, swallowed by a block of elderly housing.

Her car was parked around the corner, mere steps away, but her strength ebbed while the discomfort from her wound grew as if she still carried the bullet. She took instant refuge on a sidewalk bench, whose last occupant had left behind a crushed Royal Crown Cola can, which she tossed into the gutter. Collecting herself with measured breaths, she watched the unloading of a senior citizens' minibus, the progress slow, a jolt forward now and then. An old man spryer than the rest scuttled across the street with no mind to the cars and was nearly struck.

"Louise."

She skewed her head around and saw the narrow figure of Edith Shea in the soiled uniform of a waitress, a hip nearly slicing through the thin nylon where loose change sagged a pocket. Edith smiled. Teeth and gums showed no matter how small the smile. She sat down with a jingle.

"Terrible what happened to you. I can't imagine being shot."

Louise said, "I still can't."

"I called when you were in the hospital, but they wouldn't put me through."

"I know. I'm sorry."

"I can't believe you're waiting for a bus. You're not, are you?"

"No."

Edith lit a cigarette and held it at shoulder level, her bone of a hand bent back. Her curly hair, salt and pepper, was cropped close to the skull. She touched it with the hand holding the cigarette. "I had it cut yesterday. What d'you think of it?"

"Nice."

"No matter what I do, I still come out the same." She drew carelessly on the cigarette. "You, on the other hand, you've been through hell, you're pale as a ghost, and you sit there looking more beautiful than ever. Not fair."

Louise watched a pigeon marbled in greasy colors alight nearby and billow its breast. "I don't feel beautiful."

"God, I used to hate you. So sickeningly gorgeous. In

the back seat of the car Daisy used to forget himself and say 'Lou' in my ear. Drove me nuts."

Louise smiled, watching the pigeon peck at curbside debris. "I think you're making that up."

"Take my word for it. Daisy's always had a thing for you, and I've always had something, more or less, for Barney Cole. How come you didn't marry Barney?"

"He wasn't going anywhere. Scampy was."

"But you didn't marry him either."

"It was like a marriage."

"Now you've got a real one."

"Yes."

Edith flipped the cigarette away. "We used to be such damn good friends, Lou, but we're not anymore. I mean, how can we be? Different worlds now. I'd hate to ask how much that dress you're wearing cost."

"You'd be surprised," Louise said tonelessly. "I still look for bargains. Some things don't rub off."

Edith nodded with a smile. "Yes, in some ways we're still on the same level. We both married weak men, didn't we? We've both got sickies for husbands."

Louise looked at her with fresh interest and, surprising herself, with no anger. "What makes you think that?"

"Talk I've heard. Jesus, Lou, you might live clear across the state now, but you're a legend here. And why shouldn't you be, the things you've done for people? The time Daisy dipped his fingers into that senile lady's trust fund, he could've been disbarred, gone to prison, if it hadn't been for you. You're like a little godmother."

"Is that what you think, Edith?"

"I talk too much, don't I?"

"You really do resent me."

"No, Lou, not *you*." Edith's voice stretched thin, as if some fine filament connected their deeper thoughts. "Just the dress you've got on. The life you've got. I just want a little of it."

"There's a price. Always a price."

Edith said, "I've paid it."

Louise glanced around. A fat man paused on the sidewalk to pant. An old woman appeared with bread for the pigeon. Louise said, "I have to go."

"Yeah, me too."

Both women rose and stood at exactly the same height. Louise heard the scuff of a shoe behind her and felt someone had looked at her intently, hungrily, and then moved on.

Edith said, "I'm not supposed to know it's there, but Daisy's got a list hidden in his socks drawer. It's the people he wants at his funeral. You're on it."

"I'd be hurt if I wasn't," Louise said.

Edith abruptly stepped into her and kissed her cheek. "I'll tell him."

Emma Goss shuddered as Henry Witlo gripped the back of her shoulders with both of his hands. Always he seemed to be pushing her somewhere, directing her feet, moving her to his music. The mirror in the bedroom flashed bright. "Look at yourself," he said, forcing her almost against the glass. "Look at those dark circles. Trouble is you're not getting enough natural sleep." His voice was dark, full of reprimand. "And look at your hair. You're letting yourself go again."

She screwed her head to one side and protested, not to him, but to the picture of her husband, which he had moved from the den and placed on the dresser. A kind of static cruised through her brain, as if Harold were trying to communicate back to her through too dense a darkness. Suddenly Henry's hands slid off her shoulders.

"Come on, we're going to bed."

"It's too early," she said.

"All the better," he said, tossing off his shoes, Harold's.

"I want to sleep alone."

"We've been through that."

He undressed quickly, his chest bursting our of his shirt, his knees stabbing free of his jeans. It was always the same. She did not know where to put her eyes. He padded to a window and lowered the shade. When he turned around she held Harold's picture high in front of her.

"What are you doing with that?"

He moved toward her with his genitals suspended in exaggerated isolation and stripped the picture from her hands. A terrible inertia, like a final defense, came over her. She watched him perch the picture on the bedside table, Harold's side.

"There," he said. "He wants, he can watch us." He turned to her. "Come on. You don't want me to do it for you, do you?"

She picked at her dress with a grim unnaturalness as if guns were pointed at her, but her fingers were too clumsy for results. Nor could she keep the tears out of her eyes when a commotion of hands fell upon her, as if Henry were more than one person. Racing through her mind when he unlatched her bra was the horrible thought that Harold was helping him.

"You got nothing to be ashamed of," he said. "Plenty of women half your age don't look as good."

Her wraith of hair topped her round loose nakedness. A chill in her spine plummeted into her knees, which knocked against each other as he walked her to the bed. She shivered, and his arms girded her.

"Don't worry, Mrs. Goss, I'll warm you."

He angled her athwart the bed, where she was startled by the white of her own legs. She wanted a sheet on her, but he pushed it away. She tried to knock her husband's picture over, but he would not let her. "I don't want him to see us," she protested, distorting her mouth as if to disguise her face.

"He wants, he can close his eyes."

She accepted the queen-size pillow beneath her but rejected the grip of his hand, her breast still sore from the last time. From his knees, he gave her a grand look that turned painstaking and made her feel that he was writing his name on the soles of her feet, on the lazy parts of her thighs, on the soft mass of her stomach. "Please," she said, jiggling a half-clenched fist, "let me do this."

He floated over her. "Trust me."

With no slickness to ease his entry, he delivered nothing but a bolt of pain, another bolt when, with his full width upon her, he pried her up for a tighter fit. His breath fell hard between them. He tried to rouse life from her, but she closed her eyes to him, then her mind. He mouthed things into her ear, but she was conscious only of the essence of his underarms and a sepulchral wail from the picture.

She knew it was over when his breath collapsed against her throat.

A while later he drew the sheet up and tucked it around her. She lay with her back to him, stiff and straight, on Harold's side of the bed. He said, "Know what, Mrs. Goss? It's getting better each time."

"You bastard," she said quietly.

"*Me*, Mrs. Goss?" he said in a playful tone.

"The both of you."

TEN

Kit Fletcher woke with a start to Barney Cole's alarm, snugged her legs into the warmth of his, and whispered her sudden decision to take some days off, a bunch due her. Cole killed the alarm and overslept an hour. She rose when he did and made the coffee. When he came into the kitchen after a quick shave and a shower, he said, "I don't get it. What about the *Globe* case?"

She poured coffee. "It's on hold."

"I still don't get it."

"I want to protect my interest."

"That's in Boston, isn't it? Pullman and Gates."

"It's here too," she said. She placed the cups on a tray and added cream. He knotted his necktie.

"I don't know whether to be flattered or suspicious."

"Be neither. Feel loved." She lifted the tray. "Shall we?"

He looked at his watch.

"Please," she insisted.

They settled in the sun room. It was a watery-looking

165

morning, glassy and green, with the whole notion of summer laced into the moist restless air flowing through the wide screens. Spiders abounded, especially daddy-longlegs, which scaled the screens, some making their way inside. Kit sat in a wicker chair with her legs thrown under her. Seated in an identical chair, Cole said, "You look solemn."

"I had a bad dream."

"What was it?"

"I dreamed I was still married. I did something my husband hated, and he was about to throw a punch."

Cole gazed at her over his coffee cup. "That was a nightmare."

"Yes."

"Do you have many?"

"No." She gave out a loose careless smile that seemed to spill out her words. "The beatings were bad, but worse was the way he could shake every vital thought out of my head. For such a stupidly long time I never considered divorce. The world was all male, all my professors at Suffolk were, and I pictured all judges as men who would pick me apart like sections of an orange."

"You've come a long way."

"Do you want to hear the irony of it?" Again she smiled carelessly. "I went to a male shrink. That's something I haven't told you. It was like stretching out on an anvil and being hammered back into shape, and afterwards he'd place his hand on the back of my neck and try to knead courage into me. Yes, we had sex. He had no qualms, no apologies. Everybody's a user. He was using me, he said, and I should use anybody and everybody, especially men. It's how the world works."

"Nice guy," Cole said tightly, crowded by his own thoughts.

"He did his job well, and I did mine better. I hit him with a lawsuit on the sex thing and got a big settlement. That's how I bought my condo."

"Why don't I want to congratulate you?"

"Because you're a man."

He nodded. "That's probably the answer."

"I *have* come a long way, Barney. I work harder than anybody else at Pullman and Gates, and I'm probably brighter than most of them. I impress my clients, and I invest a third of my salary. If I had to, *really* had to, I could live alone the rest of my life. I could die alone. Death doesn't scare me." Her eyes turned playful and droll. "I figure heaven is Boston without crime. No gobs of spit on the sidewalk and no homeless people. Everybody has a dreamy apartment and theater tickets."

Cole was listening hard for false notes, but each word she uttered seemed to have its own irrepressible truth, its own unstinting way of revealing her. He said, "How do you use me?"

"Always with care. Haven't you noticed?"

"Now that you mention it."

"I don't want to marry you, Barney, but I don't want to lose you. You're good with a woman, and I don't mean just with your hands."

He swallowed the last of his coffee and, rising, put the cup aside. "I'll try to figure most of that out on my way to work."

She put her cup down. "I trust you, Barney, or I want to trust you, the reason being I love you, or I think I love you, which often amounts to the same thing."

He smiled. "I think I love you too."

"Do you trust me?"

"You make it damn hard and too easy at the same time." He looked at his watch. "I have to go."

Her eyes were on the carpet. A daddy-longlegs was sprinting in a silly fashion into his path. "Don't step on it," she said, getting out of her chair.

"I never do," he said and kissed her.

Court was in session, a full docket of divorce libels, mostly uncontested. Lawyers sat in a line inside the rail, and nearly every seat in the back of the court was filled. The demurely dressed young woman nervously stepping to the stand looked drained, as if she had pulled her own plug. She avoided looking at the bench, where the judge sat godlike in his robes. In a low-pitched voice she swore to tell the truth and, questioned by Attorney Cole, testified that two weeks after her marriage her husband went to jail for having brutally assaulted his best friend at the wedding reception. When a tremor tripped into her voice, Cole smiled encouragingly.

"Would you like a chair, Mary Jane?"

She shook her head, standing wide-eyed, flimsy, reduced. Only her bright lipstick added to her.

"Why did your husband assault his friend?"

"I don't know," she said hoarsely. "Tommy had been drinking."

"Tommy's your husband."

She nodded.

"Did Tommy serve his sentence, the full year, at the Lawrence House of Correction?"

"Yes," she whispered.

Cole retreated a number of steps to make her raise her voice, though the judge did not seem to mind one way or the other. His drooping ears looked worn out from too many years of listening, and his eyes were closed. Cole said, "Did you visit him there?"

"Yes, sir. As often as I was allowed. And I always brought packages."

"Things you baked?"

"Yes, sir. And personal articles. And one time I brought him a sweater."

"One you knitted?"

"No, sir. I bought it at Marshall's."

Cole smiled, more at himself than at her. "Did you write letters to him?"

"Yes, sir. Long ones."

"And what did you add at the end of every letter?"

"'You are never absent.'"

"That's poetic. Is it something you read?"

"No, sir." Her eyes dimmed. "It was how I felt."

Cole moved to the table where he had deposited his briefcase. "Did anything unusual occur the day your husband was released?"

"Yes, sir."

Cole extracted a paper from his briefcase. "Please tell the court what happened."

"Tommy hit me. He punched me hard in the stomach."

"Why?"

"He said it was in case I was pregnant."

"Were you?"

She raised her chin. "No, sir."

"Did he have reason to think you were?" Cole glanced at the judge, who rubbed an ear and opened an eye.

"He had no reason at all," she said with sudden force.

"Did you require medical attention?"

"Yes, sir. At Lawrence General Hospital."

Cole passed a copy of the hospital report to the clerk to give to the judge, who accepted it without scrutiny. "And are you still under a doctor's care, Mary Jane?"

169

"Yes, sir."

"Where are you living now?"

She pointed. "With my mother."

The mother, too old for her blond tresses, later approached the stand with the same depleted look as her daughter and gave corroborating testimony in an identical low voice. Afterward Cole thanked the court, drew a nod from the judge, and escorted the two women out of the building and into the sunshine. They crossed the street cautiously and entered the common, where the sun enriched what was left of the grass, bathed trampled flower beds, and increased the value of shade trees. The trees whispered. The three of them sat on a bench, and Cole, placing his briefcase between his feet, glanced past the mother to the daughter.

"How do you feel, Mary Jane?"

Her smile was paltry. "I'm glad it's over."

"Is it?" the mother said suspiciously, as if she had put money down on something that might not be received. "The judge took it under advisement."

"That's a formality," Cole said, watching two men come into the common and sit on a nearby bench.

"I wasn't sure he was listening."

"That's his way."

"Do you think Mary Jane wore too much lipstick?"

"She looked fine," Cole said, nodding to the two men.

"More lawyers?" the mother asked.

"Sort of," he said, and switched his eyes over to Mary Jane. "Everything's fresh now," he said to her. "A different life ahead of you."

"I just wish I hadn't lied."

"Hush," her mother said.

Cole, surprised, said, "What did you lie about?"

170

Her voice receded. "Those words I wrote at the end of the letters. I got them from *Reader's Digest*."

"God understands," her mother said. "Don't you think so, Mr. Cole?"

"I'm sure She does," Cole said with a wink.

They all rose, the mother brushing off the seat of her dress. Cole offered to take them for coffee, but the mother, with a shake of her head, said she thought Mary Jane had had enough excitement. Cole kissed the young woman on the cheek and said, "Good luck."

"Don't I get one?"

"Of course," he said, and kissed the mother.

He watched them plod across the grass and was amazed how quickly they faded into the shade of the trees. Then he loosened his necktie, ran a finger inside his collar, and picked up his briefcase. He ambled over to the two men. Agent Cruickshank said, "We watched you in court. My wife ever wants to divorce me, I'll tell her who to see."

"I didn't realize you guys were there."

Agent Blue, adjusting his gold-rimmed glasses, said, "How did you miss me?"

Louise Baker sipped a Pepsi from the can and said, "Why did you pick this place?"

"You said you wanted a quiet place," Chick Ryan said. "Nothing quieter than this. Besides, I own it."

"You're kidding," she said.

"Nothing's on paper, but it's mine."

It was a tawdry little sandwich shop, pinchbeck with its walls of coated plastic paneling and paper brick. A ceiling fan worked sluggishly, each lugubrious whirl seemingly its last. Louise and Chick sat at a corner table, the only customers except for a shabby man with a cough who was seated at the counter. The woman who ran the place lifted the protective dome from a cake and gave the man a slice.

Chick said, "I also own the empty store next door. Valuable properties. The whole block's going to be taken for public housing." He stretched a leg. He was in mufti except for his heavy-duty police shoes, which had once broken a suspect's ribs and injured his spleen. "People look at Lawrence," he said, "they think it's been plucked clean. No way. Plenty of stuff going on here."

"I'm glad you're doing well," Louise said.

"The bookies still take care of me."

"I'm happy for you."

"Then you got spic dealers wearing ruts in the road driving to New York and back. Crack's the thing. That's what they're all pushing."

"You getting anything from it?" she asked.

"Not as much as I should."

"You ought to learn to speak Spanish."

"Yeah, that's what one of the spics told me, knowing I wouldn't." An awful cough racked the man at the counter. It almost jerked him off the stool. Chick rose in the instant and flailed an arm. "Get him out of here." The woman, broad and bandy-legged, hurried around the counter to the man, who had averted his head and was using a napkin. There did not appear to be much of him inside his clothes. The woman whispered to him and then swung around.

"He wants to know if he can finish his cake."

"Tell him to take it with him. And put up the Closed sign. Lady and I want to talk." Chick sank back into his chair. "I'd shut this place up for good, but I'll get more if the property's an operating business."

Louise watched the man shamble out of the shop, holding the tattered piece of cake in his hand like a hurt canary. The woman latched the door and hung up the sign, a hand-printed square of cardboard that read AIN'T OPEN, the drollery of the previous owner, a bookmaker now deceased. "I'll be back later to clean up," the woman said, and left by the back way.

Louise said, "You should've let the man eat his cake."

"Life's hard." He grinned. "When I helped you out a long time ago I thought you were going to take me along, let me grow with you."

She played with the Pepsi can. "That was never a promise, not even a consideration. It was strictly a business deal, and your promotions weren't part of it. They were personal favors. Those were big strings I pulled."

"I'm not complaining. I've done all right, and I'm glad I could help again in this trouble you've got. Why didn't you come to me direct? You didn't have to go through Barney." His eyes confronted her. "I could've told you straight out nobody local would dare take a pop at you."

"Sometimes I need a filter."

"I did Barney a favor, you know. Well, I guess it was really for you. I checked up on that Polack from Chicopee. Nothing but a punk. Not even big enough to have a real record. Only thing going for him is he's a stud."

She gazed at him with noticeable reserve.

"I guess I should shut up. Maybe Barney wasn't supposed to mention it was for you. Comes down to who you can trust, Lou. Me, you always know where you stand."

"Yes," she said. "You always tip your hand."

"Because I got nothing to hide. That's the best thing about me."

She let her head fall back for a second, then spoke

lightly. "Something about you I've never liked, Chick. It probably goes back to childhood."

"Probably. That's when you didn't know shit from your underpants. Lucky for you I didn't have pubic hairs then." He grinned. "You want another Pepsi?"

"No, thank you." Her neck and shoulder hurt her. Smiling thinly out of a face of warm moisture, she pushed her chair back and sat sideways for comfort.

"Goddamn nice legs," he said.

"You're OK yourself," she replied in a tone too subtle for interpretation. "Except for that clump of gray, you haven't changed all that much since we graduated from high school."

He watched her dent the soda can with her thumb. "We're talking around something, Lou. You want to tell me what?"

"Business."

"What kind?"

"Big business."

He drew his smile wide. "Something's changed, Lou. You ought to know that right off the bat."

"What is it?"

"I don't come cheap anymore. Those days are gone."

While Emma Goss watched from the kitchen window, Henry Witlo did business in the driveway with a man wearing a necktie and a short-sleeved shirt that had come untucked in back. The man inspected the outside of Henry's Dodge Charger, ran a finger through the grime, squatted to examine the tread of a tire, and yanked up the hood with a signal to Henry to start the engine. Later, the hood closed, the engine off, Henry and the man stood in the sunshine and talked some more. Through the screen Emma listened to the plangency of their somber male voices without hearing a single word. She closed her eyes when the man stooped to attach a dealer's plate to the car and opened them when she heard him slam a door and drive off. Henry thumped in with a check in his hand.

Her voice quivered. "Why did you do that?"

"No sense having two," he said.

"You can have the Plymouth," she said. "Take it and go."

He wrinkled his brow. "What would Harold say?"

"He's in hell . . . in heaven." She was confused, bedeviled. "Harold's gone."

"No, he's not." Henry pointed. "He's standing there!"

Her head snapped around.

"No, *there!*" He pointed in another direction.

She staggered against the table, unstrung by the spin and play of his voice. It was like the time she was a child and an older boy full of moods pushed her higher and higher on a schoolyard swing, not to please her but to terrify her.

An arm squeezed her. "I was only fooling," he said. His finger came at her, took a tear away. He fluttered the check and tried to make her read the figures, but she averted her eyes. "It's for us, Mrs. Goss. I want to pay my keep."

"Are you never going to leave?"

He did not answer right away. His hand was fixing her hair, the palm smoothing it as she stood quite still and composed, faintly breathing and screaming to herself. "If I left, who would take care of you?" he said. His jaw came closer. "Who does the cooking? Not you, Mrs. Goss. You burn things. Cut yourself. Look at your fingers."

Worse were her nails, chewed as if in a kind of ritual mutilation. She felt dog-eared and overly thumbed, like the pulp pages of lurid magazines boys in her class had passed around.

"Who makes sure you shower?" he said. "Look at your dress. It's not clean." His hands passed over her. "You've got to change it," he said. "And your breath is a little bad. You've got to brush your teeth."

She had no choice, no stamina, no will to resist the direction in which he was pushing her. For a second she feared they might bump into Harold.

"Watch your step, Mrs. Goss."

In the bathroom she used a damp pink towel to ease the heat in her face. A warm breeze blew in on her. She picked up a toothbrush, not the green one, which was his, or Harold's. She was not sure. The Colgate tube lacked a cap and was squeezed in the middle. She brushed her teeth vigorously, almost savagely.

From the doorway he said, "Gargle good."

In the bedroom he chose the dress he wanted her to wear, but when she put it on he stepped back and grimaced. He did not like the fall of it. He selected another and said, "Thought we might go to the movies tonight." When she looked away, he said, "Or maybe just for a ride." He did not like the second dress either. Patterned with roses, it made her look like a floral offering, and he told her to take it off. Pawing through the closet, more of Harold's clothes in there than hers, he said, "You don't have a hell of a lot to pick from. We got to do some shopping sometime."

She stood in a partial state of insensibility, with a ladder in her pantyhose. He had another dress in his hand, but he soon tossed it aside and slowly circled her with critical eyes. A smile emerged, and his voice lifted. "It's not the dress, Mrs. Goss, it's you. You've lost weight." His eyes danced. "Everything about you is better, I'm not kidding.

More shape to you now. Nicer titties, honest." He swallowed hard. "Even the dark circles make you different."

"Pig," she murmured.

"Beg pardon?"

Her voice was arid. "You're going to do it again, aren't you?"

"It's on my mind, Mrs. Goss."

"Then get it over with," she said coldly.

Barney Cole got home a little before three and changed into casual clothes while Kit Fletcher, wearing a white shirt and chino shorts, stuck a chilled bottle of wine and hastily wrapped sandwiches into a basket. While she was poking into a cupboard for paper cups, Cole lifted her hair and kissed the back of her neck. When his arms started to go around her, she pushed him back with the point of an elbow. "If you start that," she said, "we'll never leave."

A short time later they drove down Wildwood Road to Route 125 and within minutes penetrated Harold Parker State Forest. Cole parked the Cutlass off the road near Field's Pond, where a number of Hispanic women from Lawrence were fishing off the bank, some sitting on boulders and dangling their feet in the limpid water. Their bare-chested children dawdled nearby. Kit climbed out of the car and stretched her legs. Looking at the women, she said, "What do they hope to catch?"

"Bass, perch, I'm not sure," Cole said, joining her. "The pond's man-made. The state stocks it."

"I can see they're not doing it for sport," Kit said, her eye gradually shifting from the women to the children, scrawny little beauties.

Cole took the basket from her and they followed a footpath into pinewoods lit only by the sun's ability to hurl knives through the thick branches. The air was spicy and green and without grit from the road. The path meandered but never far from the pond's jagged edge, where skeletal stumps lurked in the water and blueberry bushes grew mammoth with the promise of fruit. Cole, who led the way, soon strayed from the path.

"Don't get us lost," she said.

"I don't think it's possible," he replied, for he had too often walked the woods with his wife to lose his bearings.

They wended their way through brush and fern, stepped over fallen branches, avoided trampling wildflowers almost too small to see, and came upon a clearing where a cardinal flared up and disappeared. Kit said, "You've been here before, haven't you?"

"It seemed fitting," he said.

They sat near a scaly rock on a sunburnt patch of ground, the basket between them. Kit poured the wine as Cole held the paper cups. The sandwiches were salami on rye. Cole ate the pickle slice in his and tasted the wine.

"What exactly do you want to know?" he asked.

"How did your wife die?"

"Slippery road. She always drove too fast. It was in her blood."

"You make her sound fated."

"Perhaps she was," Cole said. "She wasn't the sort to let time drag. She wanted oomph in every hour. I was consumed in building a practice, and she was into causes, the kind I gave lip service. She donated all her energy. She worked her head off for politicians she liked, state and national. She was a good organizer with no patience with people who complained they had only two hands. Busy, busy, that's how she lived. When she went to sleep at night she wanted big bright dreams. Otherwise sleep was a waste, she said." He smiled. "That was my wife, Sandra, a kind of breathless person."

"Pretty name." Kit drew her knees up and hugged them. "What did she look like?"

"She had red hair."

"I can't picture you with a redhead. My mother used to say redheads have different dispositions from the rest of us. Was she thin, fat? Did she have freckles?"

"Some freckles, and she was well-built."

"A full bottle like me?"

"In a way."

"Attractive, I take it."

"Not ravishing, but she stood out."

"Most women do if they manage their weight and their makeup." Kit slipped off her sneakers and flexed her toes. Then she picked up a sandwich as Cole bit into his. The warmth of the afternoon sun curved around them. "Were you good to each other?"

"We tried to be. We were each other's second choice, which we joked about, not often because it could turn touchy. A couple of times we nearly broke up over things that never should have mattered."

"Did you love each other?"

"Yes, in our spare moments."

"Was that something else you joked about?"

"At times. Sundays we tried to make ours. We took walks here. Sometimes we put a canoe on the pond."

"Why didn't you have children?"

"We were waiting. We waited too long."

Kit poured more wine. Together they watched the shadow of a low-flying bird streak through the growing grass. "Regrets, Barney?"

"I wouldn't be human without them. The trick is not to let them deepen with the years."

"Any guilt?"

He shook his head. "More the case of a few haunting images. The night she was killed we had met at Bishop's, arrived in the rain in separate cars. Both of us were on edge. I'd had a lousy day in court, and Sandra had a headache from a state senatorial campaign that was falling apart, some bad stuff coming out about the candidate. Halfway through dinner we got into a stupid argument and said things we shouldn't have. She went down to the ladies' room and didn't come back. The waitress brought me two words scribbled on a toilet tissue. *I'm leaving.* I didn't know whether she meant she was leaving the restaurant or leaving me forever. I remember thinking about that very hard when I paid the check and said good night to the hostess. As it turned out, it was forever."

"I'm sorry, Barney."

"Me too."

"What I mean is, I'm sorry for making you dredge this up. I'm not jealous of her, but I have to know the competition."

He looked at her with an intimate widening of his eyes. "For God's sake, she's dead."

"No," Kit said. "As long as you live, she's alive."

Clouds strayed in front of the sun, but the air stayed warm. The Spanish voices of children drifted in from a distance and dissipated. Kit lay back and closed her eyes, letting dry grass grip her hair. Her bare toes worked up a cloudlet of dust. A bird was whistling from a tall pine and receiving no answer. Kit half opened her eyes.

"I was going to ask about your friend," she said, "but there's no need." Her lips parted in a dry smile. "There's a joke on somebody here. I hope it's not on me."

"What's the joke?" he asked.

"We tend to be alike."

"You and I?"

"No," she said. "Your women."

He sloshed the wine in his cup and drank it. "If that's the joke, why do you think it might be on you?"

"Call it female intuition, but I think you'd do things for your friend you'd never do for anybody else." Her eyes were fully open now, and she gazed at him as if charting his thoughts and understanding them all. "Am I right?"

He said, "You may be."

"If she's Mafia, it could be the ruin of you."

"You may be right about that too," he said, and looked at his watch and then up at the sky. The sun broke through the clouds and fired a beam straight in his eyes.

She said, "I have a good future at Pullman and Gates. I wouldn't want to be touched by any scandal."

"I'd never let that happen."

"Your word?"

"My word," he said.

She hoisted herself up on one arm and slung the other around him. She kissed him with a passion she allowed to surface and with a trust she had long held in reserve. When he sank back, she plunged both hands into his shirt, popping a button and then another, drawn to him as if on a rope. A light plane appeared against the sky and began smoking out a commercial message, but neither noticed it. Moments later a spider's thread of semen glittered across her spread fingers.

"Damn it, I do love you, Barney."

At nine in the evening Cole drove into Lawrence, to a large beige house off South Union Street, where the district attorney lived with his wife and his spinster sister, who many years ago had come for a visit and had never left. It was the sister who opened the door for Cole, shyly escorted him to the door of the district attorney's study, and silently vanished. Cole stepped into the room and said, "Good of you to see me, Chugger, this late hour."

The district attorney, seated in a deep chair, had obviously been dozing. He was in shirtsleeves and slippers and had a newspaper in his lap. "Sit down," he said. "Watch out for the cat hair." A cat was sleeping on the sill of an open window, its body stretched against the screen. "There are four more roaming around somewhere. My wife and sister collect them, God bless their simple souls. What's the problem, Barney?"

"Cruickshank and the other guy followed me onto the common this morning. I thought you might've been watching from your office window."

The district attorney shifted his feedbag body. "I got better things to do than that. You want coffee or something? No? Just as well, it'd probably have a hair in it."

Cole said, "They put the squeeze on me."

"You knew they would."

"I didn't like them throwing my father in my face."

"You must've expected that too."

"And Daisy Shea. They know about the time he transferred money out of that old lady's trust. Cruickshank insinuated I was in on it."

"What was his reasoning?"

"The old lady was originally my client," Cole said. "I let Daisy have the account when we busted up our partnership."

"Some people you should never do favors for. The art of politics—the art of anything—is knowing who you do for and who you don't. Always figure out who's going to make you bigger for the favor. Otherwise, forget it."

"I've never operated that way."

"That's why you're a good fella and a rinky-dink lawyer. Your only assets are your office furniture, your house in Andover, and a couple of CDs. I know, because Cruickshank showed me a financial statement on you and asked where you were hiding it."

Cole laughed.

"Yeah, I laughed too," the district attorney said, "but they don't know you like I do. They figure you do business in Lawrence, you must be dirty. That's why they're tossing shit at you and staying on your ass like a diaper."

"Sounds like it's *me* they're after."

"No, they just want to get to you."

Cole gazed at the cat, which was stretching its front legs to the fullest, the claws tearing against the screen. "They must want Louise awfully bad."

"My guess, Barney, is they want to spin her around. The truth is, I think they're after bigger fish."

"They don't know her very well."

"I don't think we do either."

Cole sat silent for a while. The cat, which had orange fur and yellow eyes, stood up and humped its back. Then it leaped from the window and clawed the carpet. "It's a funny world, Chugger."

"It's a changing one, Barney. Far as I know, women aren't supposed to do what Louise does. Perverse, you ask me."

Cole set himself to evacuate his chair. "I'm keeping you up."

"No, you're not. I wait for my wife and sister to go to bed so I can do what I want in the house. My sister's going soft, you know. Alzheimer's probably. God help me."

"I'd better be going anyway," Cole said, and rose. The district attorney also pulled himself up, the throes of the effort in his face. They moved into the passage to the front door, where the district attorney stooped to adjust a slipper. Another cat appeared, this one fat and fluffy, with erratic markings. It rubbed against Cole, leaving hair on his trousers.

"Kick him, Barney. It won't bother me a bit." The district attorney stooped to fix the other slipper. "If I come back in another life, it's going to be as a goddamn cat. Then I'll just eat, sleep, and let people do for me."

Cole opened the door, and the cat scampered out and vanished beyond the spray of the light.

"Don't worry about it. Maybe he'll get run over."

"I don't really know why I came here tonight, Chugger. Maybe it was just to kill time."

"A little warning to you. Cruickshank does the talking, but I think it's the black guy that calls the plays. That's my impression."

"Mine too," Cole said. "The clue was his fingers. I could imagine them around my neck."

The district attorney followed Cole outside to the top step and inhaled the moist dark air. "I'll give you some advice while I'm at it. Don't do Louise any harm, but by the same token don't do her any favors. You could get caught in a crossfire."

Cole consulted his watch. "I'm meeting her in twenty minutes."

"I don't want to know."

Cole smiled. "At this moment I think I'd rather be in your slippers than my shoes."

The voice of the district attorney's wife sounded from a deep part of the house. "Don't leave the door open. Bugs."

"No, you don't, Barney."

Cole drove to the north side of the city. Downtown was mostly in shadow and deserted except for loitering bands of boys, the faces Hispanic. Cole turned onto Amesbury Street, cruised through a green light, and pulled into a shadowy parking lot. A cream-white car was waiting in the middle of one of the lanes. Cole drifted alongside it and braked. Louise Baker smiled over at him, her oval face perfectly framed in the open window of the Porsche.

"What's all this secret stuff for, Barney? You trying to hide me from your girlfriend?"

"Nothing like that. How are you?"

"I'm fine. What's up?"

"I think you should be careful."

Her voice went hard. "What are you telling me?"

His foot was poised lightly on the gas pedal because the motor was idling hard. Suddenly it coughed and stalled.

"If you know something," she said, "tell me."

"I'll say one word, Lou, all right? Feds."

Something significant changed in her face. Her voice softened. "They been talking to you?"

He held up two fingers. "A pair of them. For both our sakes, don't tell me anything. Ever."

"You've never let me," she reminded him.

"Aren't you glad?" he said, and tried to restart the motor, but it failed to catch. He tried again, unsuccessfully, and looked over at her.

"You're driving a junk, Barney. If you had devoted your professional energies to me, you'd be in a Cadillac now."

"Wasn't meant to be."

"That's what I tell myself when I'm alone at night." She slipped the Porsche into gear. "Will you be able to start that?" He nodded, and she smiled. "Thanks for your information, Barney. I was just a little bit afraid of coming here."

"Why?"

"You never know." She gave him a sudden affectionate look and blew him a kiss. "Forgive me."

"What for?"

He did not get an answer. He watched the Porsche drift away with the silence of a fish, and seconds later, in the rearview, he saw it float out of the lot. He was about to give the motor another turn when he heard a sound from about twelve feet away and froze in his seat. Poised between two carelessly parked cars was the partly shadowed figure of a man with a shotgun held downward, laid against the leg. Under the bill of a baseball cap a smile was perceptible one instant and not the next, as if the man were clicking it on and off. Then he swept forward.

"Hello, Barney."

"Damn you," Cole said, coming out of his freeze.

Chick Ryan leaned forward while keeping the weapon pressed against his leg, concealed from anyone who might enter the lot. He was in civilian clothes, a protective vest under his jacket. With chilling nonchalance, he said, "Louise was nervous. She was scared someone might try to blow her away."

"Then damn her too."

Chick tugged at his cap. "She's not herself. You wouldn't be either, somebody was gunning for you."

"Did she think I would set her up?"

"You never know what you might do unwittingly."

Cole's face was stark, and so was his voice. "Would you have shot me, Chick?"

"Not you, Barney. Whoever else it might've been."

Cole turned the ignition key. The motor caught at once, held, and purred as if new. "I'm leaving, Chick."

"I know how you feel, and I don't blame you. Let's forget this even happened. Matter of fact, nothing happened. Right?"

Cole slapped the gearshift into Drive. "Good-bye, Chick."

"Keep the faith, Barney."

"I'm not Catholic."

"God bless you anyway."

Cole wanted time to collect himself and drove through Lawrence in a roundabout way. The night mist gave fleecy contours to tenement buildings and to grand old houses that had been whittled into apartments, and moonlight gave an aura of mystery to an unoccupied store and the bushy vacant lot beside it. On a side street, where cars were parked bumper to bumper for the night, a bad smell flooded the air, as if a pipe had burst.

On Mount Vernon Street the air blew clean, and Cole drove slowly past single-family houses, trying to remember which one belonged to Emma Goss. He had been there once when Harold Goss was alive and once or twice after his death. Then he spotted it, bathed in streetlight, small and neat. Visible in a window was the flickering glow of a televison screen. For a fraction of a second he considered stopping to see how she was doing, but then he remembered the hour and drove on. A minute later he crossed into Andover, where the air was even cleaner.

Shortly after midnight a light rain began to fall, and Emma Goss, wide awake, listened to it from her pillow. She lay straight and immobile under the covers and felt quite at odds, neither here nor there, and utterly without energy. Henry Witlo moved and mumbled beside her but, to her relief, did not wake. Soon he breathed deeply, reconfirming his sleep. The shadows of leaves twitched in the rain as if the tree outside the window had hundreds of heartbeats.

The rain stopped a half hour later, and she fantasized stealing away into the night and forever leaving behind her degradation and shame. She easily imagined herself boarding a bus to Boston but trembled at the thought of peregrinating a hotel lobby and facing the desk clerk's cold eye. An image rose up of the clerk taking one look at her and immediately shooing her out or, at best, simply ignoring her while others jostled her aside. When she placed a forearm across her eyes, Henry suddenly tossed in his sleep and gouged her with a toenail.

Sometime after one-thirty she woke from a dream that vanished, leaving her only with the sensation that the dream had been vivid and perhaps pleasant. Unexpectedly she thought of her friend Mildred Murphy in Florida, and an idea burned in her head. It soothed and sustained her, it took the kink out of her neck and eased the knot in her stomach, and it almost put a smile on her mouth. Within minutes she dozed off.

It might have been three o'clock when she woke again, her eyes leaping open as if someone had touched her. The silence was too profound to be peaceful, void even of Henry's breathing, and her first thought was that he had left the bed. Then she heard the end of a snore flutter off his lips, and through the gloom she made out the broad line of his body and the naked curve of his shoulder, from which the covers had slipped. She would have felt better were the alarm system working, but he had long ago disconnected it with the boast that his presence was more than enough protection. She lay with her arms outside the covers, filled with a premonition that something was dreadfully wrong.

She was still awake and fully alert when she heard the first sounds, a kind of ticking or tapping from the kitchen, followed by the chime and tinkle of falling glass. She reached over and firmly shook Henry's shoulder. He came awake slowly, unwillingly, with his eyes cut small.

"What's the matter?"

"Somebody's in the house," she whispered.

He pushed his head deeper into his pillow. "Probably Harold."

"No," she said, "it's not his step."

ELEVEN

Lying still, his ears pricked, Henry whispered, "He's in the kitchen." In the dusk of the room, her voice failing, Emma Goss silhouetted two fingers to indicate a second intruder, for her ears had picked up nuances his had not. She knew from the smell of him that he was sweating. "It's like Nam," he murmured in a ragged breath. "You don't know where they are. You don't know how many." His damp hand touched her. "Don't move," he told her. "Don't breathe." She waited for him to do something, but he stayed anchored under the covers. In a moment of giddiness, as if infection were the only threat, she concentrated on the throb in her ankle where his toe had torn the flesh. His hand stayed with her. "I don't want to die, Mrs. Goss."

"I don't either," she said, though she had no problem imagining her death. Even a violent one was within the realm of her eye. She would merely think of other things, and it would be done with.

"We lie low, maybe they'll miss us," Henry said. His arm bumped against hers. His flesh had gone cold, and the smell of him was dank as if he had lain a long time in wet leaves. She, on the other hand, lay hot and welcomed the cooling lick of breeze that carried the taste of the rain that had fallen earlier. Henry said, "They could be gone."

She knew they had just begun, for her ear detected drawers being opened in the den. Harold's desk. She had no sense of violation, for she felt that too little remained that could be touched. "They're not gone," she said. "You should do something."

"Why me?" His tone was strange and remote, as if he were talking to others, not to her. His leg, cold as ice, stiffened against her. "Why should I get killed?"

She tried to shift away, but an acute indifference came over her. How could everything and nothing be real at the same time? It made no sense, and she could not recall the last time anything had. "I think you should cut your toenails," she said. "At least one of them."

"We're gonna be all right," he whispered.

She heard the linen-closet door breathe open and then close as if by the soft kick of a heel, ear-searing to her. "No, we're not," she said, her uncanny eyes piercing the gloom. Two figures floated into the room, the first with a mincing little step that was like a dance. The other had less of a lilt and hung back. Each was pygmy in height. She thought they might be children, but they were youths with dirty mouths that proved to be mustaches.

"Move, mother, I cut you."

"I won't," she said, for she thought he was talking to her. Then she saw that the tip of the knife was at Henry's throat and that the hand gripping the hilt was as slender as a girl's, the kind she imagined a mother kissing. The

ANDREW COBURN

youth wielded a flashlight in the other hand and flicked it on. The light tore up her face, then Henry's. The youth laughed.

"What you doing sleeping with an old lady?"

"Gooks," Henry murmured, blinded.

"Spics," the youth corrected him.

"He has money," Emma said in a voice so definite her head rang. "He sold his car, but you can have Harold's."

The light flew back and forth over their faces. "Who the fuck's Harold?"

"Her husband," Henry said with sudden muscle in his voice as if he had swallowed spinach. "He'll be home in a minute."

"He don't care 'bout you?" The youth, much amused, shot a glance at his friend. "Hear that?" Then he played the point of the knife against Henry's throat and traced it up to the chin. "You fuck Harold too?"

Henry's eyes fought the light and lost. Emma said, "The money's in his jeans. On the floor."

"You being good to me, mama. You must like me, huh?" A brilliantly toothed smile lit the youth's face, and he fired another look at his friend, who had not moved. "What you think?"

The friend said, "Do him, keep her."

Henry's hand leaped up. He was not quick enough to escape the kiss of the blade across his palm, but he was strong enough to wrench the youth's arm nearly out of its socket. When the knife spun against the wall, Henry bent as many fingers back as he could grab and broke them. The youth screamed. Henry hit him.

Emma put her fists to her face. The other youth was gone. She heard him bang through the kitchen and burst through a screen in the breezeway. She could not see Henry. She could only hear what he was doing. The slaps

192

sounded like gunshots, and she rammed her fists against her ears to enjoy the crush of silence.

She did not know how much time passed after Henry dragged the youth away by his hair and threw him out of the house. She knew only that she was struggling toward the bathroom when he reappeared, stained and bruised, naked except for Harold's boxer shorts, which were nearly falling off his hips. She tried to avoid him, but he threw his arms around her and bloodied her with his wound. "I didn't let them hurt you, did I, Mrs. Goss?" He was shaking, shifting his feet for balance, and squeezing her too hard. "They won't be back, you can take my word for it."

"Let me go," she said.

He followed her into the bathroom and hung by her as she waited by the sink to be sick. When nothing happened, she wet a cloth and moistened her face. He said, "I saved us, Mrs. Goss. I did a brave thing."

"Please don't stand so close."

"Why couldn't I do that in 'Nam, Mrs. Goss? In 'Nam I let guys die. Do you know why?"

She scarcely heard him. She was not interested.

"Because I didn't have you," he said.

She tossed the cloth aside. "You'd better run your hand under water."

"It's pretty bad, Mrs. Goss. Will you fix it for me?"

"No," she said.

He stayed in the bathroom, and she sat in a chair near the front window in the living room and listened to birds heralding the dawn. Once he called to her, but she did not answer. She rested her back and watched a police cruiser proceed slowly along the street, its headlights cutting through the gray mist. It hesitated near the house but did not stop.

* * *

"Stupid Russians, you'd think they'd learn from our mistakes." Arnold Ackerman, a shaving cut on his chin, rustled his newspaper. "I don't know, Barney, can you believe what you read?"

Barney Cole stirred his coffee. "What are you talking about?"

"Afghanistan. You ever been there?"

"Never."

"I think it's made up, meaning I don't think it's there. Pentagon propaganda."

Cole said, "You ever been to Vegas?"

"You know I have."

"That's made up too, but it's there."

Arnold dumped his doughnut in his tea. He and Cole shared a table in Dolce's, full of shuffle and chatter from the morning crowd. The retired judge at the next table whistled under his breath over an article in the local paper and flipped pages to read the runover. A young policeman with a face not yet fully awake punched a pill into his mouth and washed it down with grapefruit juice. Arnold said casually to Cole, "Federal boys been talking to you?"

Cole's surprise was immediate and revealing. "How did you know?"

"Two of them, salt and pepper, came to the house last night. Thank God the place was picked up, but they caught me eating out of a frying pan. Big smirk came over the white guy's face. He said he didn't know bigshot bookies ate that way. I told him it's how I get my iron. My age, you got to watch out for your blood. It's not just women, you know."

"What did they want, Arnold?"

"Dirt."

"On Louise?"

"You. I told them they should be so clean."

"They buy it?"

"What's there to buy? It's the truth, isn't it?"

"Truth doesn't always wash."

"That's their problem, right?" Arnold stuffed the remainder of the doughnut in his mouth and licked the glaze off his fingers. "I told them I was flattered they came to see me, being retired and out of circulation, and I asked the black guy how he liked working for the government. He smiled and asked me how I liked banking at the Arlington Trust. Then he took a list out of his pocket and read off a bunch of other banks I got accounts at. I asked him why he was trying to scare a poor old buck like me, and he said the last time anybody scared me was back in 1948 when a shark from Lowell was going to break my legs because I owed him money. Christ, I'd forgotten all about that. Then I remembered and told him he was wrong. The shark was from Dracut, a Greek."

Cole, after a moment of quiet, said, "Can they hurt you?"

"Naw, I pay my taxes, always have." Arnold looked over at the judge, who had finished with his breakfast and his paper. "How you doing, Your Honor?" he said in a loud voice, for the judge was hard of hearing and had been all his years on the bench. Rather than admit it, he had made defendants and witnesses feel at fault by shouting at them to speak up.

He scowled and said, "You behaving yourself, Arnold?"

"My age I have to, but Barney here, I don't know about him."

The judge may not have heard. He said, "What did you do to your chin?"

ANDREW COBURN

"Cut it shaving, Your Honor. A man retires, he's got to make himself shave every damn day, otherwise people think he's a bum."

The judge picked up his paper and, despite obvious protests from his arthritis, got to his feet. His Irish eyes went from Arnold's dry rubbery face to Cole's lean angular one. "Don't let him corrupt you, Barney. He can do it."

Cole watched the judge leave with a gait that belied the arthritis. "How old is he now?"

"Got to be past eighty. Good man, Barney. I went before him a few times. He always found a way to let me off."

Cole checked the clock. He had to be in district court in a few minutes. He said, "Do you know why the feds want something on me?"

"Sure." Arnold finished his tea. "Leverage."

"Then you can surmise the rest."

Arnold's head rocked. "God, I'm proud of her. The feds never came after me."

"That's a peculiar way of looking at it."

"I'm putting it into perspective, that's all."

Cole reached down for his briefcase. "I have to go."

"Me, I got no place to go. I'll sit in the back of the court with the rest of the old folks got nothing better to do."

The traffic on Common Street was heavy. Kid music—earsplitting rock, a song howled as if by a maniac—surged out of a slowly passing car. Cole and Arnold crossed the street cautiously and then in a rush, which took away Arnold's breath. He had to stop on the sidewalk. Cole waited, casting an impatient glance at the courthouse, where the sun was wincing off the windows.

"Look, Arnold, do you mind if I run?"

"Sure, forget the old man."

The young policeman, also on his way to the courthouse, was behind them. "You mind?" Cole said, and thrust his briefcase into the officer's surprised hands. Then he gave Arnold a quick perplexed look. "You asked for it."

"What are you doing?"

Cole swept Arnold Ackerman off the ground and, scarcely aware of the weight, carried him up the courthouse steps.

Mrs. Mennick served Ben Baker an egg, soft-boiled, scooped from its shell and lightly salted. She worked a spoon delicately into the egg and brought a small portion to his mouth. "In it goes," she said.

"I can do it myself."

"But you won't," she said, and in it went. They were at the trestle table in the kitchen's big bright bow window, which overlooked the lushness of the morning.

"No more," he said. "I'm not hungry."

"You're not eating enough to fill a mouse. What's Mrs. Baker going to say when she comes home and hears about it?" She forced the spoon upon him again. "You're not taking your medication either. What's she going to say about that?"

"Why isn't she here now?" he asked gloomily.

"She's still tending to her poor mother. You can't begrudge her that. And I imagine she has business to attend to as well."

He spoke shakily. "Is it possible she's left me?"

"I don't think that's at all possible."

"She's the best wife I've ever had."

"You've only had one other, Mr. Ben."

"Janet was a bitch."

Mrs. Mennick wiped egg off his mustache and said, "Maybe she just didn't understand the care you need."

Later, standing over him, she made him take his medication, though he managed to hold one of the capsules in his mouth. He removed his tassled loafers and slipped on sturdy shoes for his customary walk on the grounds. Mrs. Mennick looped a silk ascot under his chin, fluffed it into his shirt, and placed a flat plaid cap upon his head. Then, top-heavy on her skimpy legs, she stepped back to admire him.

"You're a real country gentleman, Mr. Ben."

He gazed into the mirror. "Yes, I am, thanks to Mrs. Baker and you."

"No," she said incisively. "It's your bloodline. Never forget that, Mr. Ben."

Something nostalgic touched him deep, for in that moment Mrs. Mennick's manner reminded him more of his mother than of his old nanny. She opened the door for him, and he stepped outside and waded into the morning sunlight washing a sparkling aura of fantasy over flowers and shrubs. Bees bundled themselves into the trellised roses, and jays bobbed on the outer branches of the berry bushes, attacking the fruit at will. A man in khaki was down on one knee repairing the nozzle of an endless lawn hose. Ben said, "Fine morning, Howard."

"Yes, sir." Mrs. Mennick's brother had a large bold head topped with thinning hair and smelled strongly of processed fertilizer.

"I don't suppose it'll rain."

"No, sir."

Ben would not have minded some idle conversation but knew that Howard lacked the skill. "Well, I guess I'll start my walk. I try to go a little farther each day."

Howard, surprising him, said, "Don't overdo it, sir."

He trod silently over immaculate grass, all Howard's work, and could not imagine a dandelion daring to defile it. With lightly swinging arms, he set out to perambulate the rear lawns, which had the look of a golf course but in his grandfather's day were fields flush with wildflowers. With reverence, he remembered his grandfather's breakfast of oatmeal and oranges, the peels of the oranges later tossed on the mulch pile. Halfway across the green the sun breathed more heat into the air. He looked back and could make out Howard lifting something out of his pickup truck. When he reached the end of the green he looked back again, but the sun blinded him.

He followed a path into a woodlot, where the darker smells of summer wrapped around him and moisture dripped from the trees, some so leafy no slivers of sunlight fell through. At one point, where insects shot through the air, the ground threw up a damp smell of a vulgar quality, as if animals used it for a pisshole. Breezes in the high branches of an evergreen funneled down a music he did not appreciate. It was too much like a hymn. When he came upon a crushed cigarette package, he suffered anxiety over the possibility of being challenged on his own land.

The path took him to the narrow back road that marked his property line. Here the sun burst full upon him again. He tramped along the shoulder and admired roadside lilies of an orange so intense they looked fake, waxed, glued to their stalks. Two cars ghostly in the sun drifted by, one after the other. Neither driver knew him, which mildly disappointed him. He would have welcomed a wave from either. Presently a white car traveling too fast for the road came up behind him in a rush and nearly percussed him off his feet in passing. It was too big and old and not at all clean enough to be Louise's Porsche, but slowly he convinced himself that it might have been. That was when his heart began to act funny.

He did not hear the crash. It was too far away and the

day too sublime to concede tragedy, but many minutes later when he paused to rest he heard distant sirens. He was hustling along, a quarter of the way up a lazy rise in the road, when the rattle of a pickup truck startled him. At first he thought it was Howard, but Howard's truck was red, this was not. A door swung open.

"Get in, Mr. Baker."

Who was it? Without really looking, he sensed it was Sam, who raised chickens and whose wife sold the eggs, delivering weekly. He climbed into the cab, hesitantly, like a child warned against accepting rides, and saw claws gripping the steering wheel.

"I heard the sirens, Mr. Baker, must be an accident."

"Not my wife," Ben said. "Please, not my wife."

The pickup was a rattletrap and rode hard, jolting over lumps in the road and forcing Ben to prop an arm against the dash. They passed excited children clustered in front of a house whose original tenants Ben remembered well, an ever-growing family. His mother had dismissed them as low-breeds and half-breeds, nomenclatures that had stuck forever in his head. They passed another house, then a shack where a man was peering out his door.

"It's up ahead, Mr. Baker. I can smell the gasoline from here."

Ben looked at him. Yes, it was Sam. Then he stared through the windshield, which was sticky with the resin of trees. Sam abruptly aimed a talon over the steering wheel.

"There it is!"

They pulled up behind the flashes of the town's only police cruiser. More lights whirled from an ambulance, which was owned and hired out by the local undertaker, whose great-grandfather had abandoned barbering to start the business. A van and a ranch wagon were backed up in the opposite direction, their owners standing at the roadside.

Sam climbed out of the cab first, and after a mustering of will Ben followed. The air stood shocked, tingling with phantom echoes. Sam said, "That don't look like your wife's automobile."

The white car had apparently sideswiped a concrete post before crashing into a stone wall with such force that the motor lay in a drainage ditch like a monster that had fallen from the sky. A woman's body lay near it.

"You're wrong," Ben said, standing still with tears in his eyes. "It's her way of going for good."

Beyond the cruiser two ambulance attendants were talking with a burly policeman, who was the youngest member of the town's three-man force. Sam left Ben and joined them. Ben looked at the blue of the sky and wondered whether she was up there yet. He saw three crows winging across a field and imagined they were spreading the news. Then he closed his eyes.

"Mr. Baker."

The voice, which belonged to the young policeman, chilled him. His mind was too jagged for questions, and he hoped he would not be asked many.

"That's not your wife, sir. It's Bonnie Snell."

Bonnie Snell, he knew, was the weekend waitress at the Town Grill, a plain young woman with a luckless figure and peroxided hair that gave her a loud look. Not so many weeks ago she had come to the house to help Mrs. Mennick with the spring cleaning. Reluctantly he opened his eyes to the policeman's smooth face, which seemed as big as a beach ball.

"Everybody lies to me."

"If you don't believe me, sir, go see for yourself."

The invitation seemed monstrous, and he sharply turned away to watch more cars pulling up alongside the road. He saw some faces he knew and called out, "My wife."

"Don't worry about it. I'll take him home."

That was Sam's voice, and it was Sam who touched his shoulder. He recognized the claw. "No, you won't," he said, and strode away.

Emma Goss surprised her friend Mildred Murphy with a telephone call. "How wonderful to hear your voice," Mildred said, warming Emma. "You haven't written lately. I was beginning to worry."

With a flush of pleasure, Emma said, "I've been busy, but you're never far from my thoughts."

They chatted at length. Mildred spoke of Lawrence people living in Florida, so many former city officials and workers, retired police officers and businessmen. She was always running into someone she knew, almost like a high school reunion or an endless retirement party. Then with a note of sadness she mentioned the passing of some, in particular Phil DiAdamo, a former police captain and, when Lawrence was under an archaic form of government, commissioner of public safety. "Such a handsome figure of a man. I always had a crush on him, Emma, do you remember?"

"Yes," said Emma, remembering that Mildred had clipped pictures of him from the *Eagle-Tribune* and preserved them in a scrapbook doomed to the flames when her husband, Michael, discovered it by chance the month before his death. Emma said, "I never met him, but I know Harold had great respect for him."

"I danced with him once, Emma, that big victory dinner when he first got into office. Michael was jealous. Do you remember?"

"I never went to those things."

"That's right, Harold never took you. Are you still a stay-at-home?"

"That's why I'm calling," Emma said with cheer in her voice. "You're always mentioning in your cards I should come down to see you, and I've been thinking I'd like that very much. Just for a little visit, Mildred, if you don't mind."

After a barely perceptible pause, Mildred said, "What a perfectly grand idea, but I don't think you'd like it at this time of year. It's awfully hot. Right this minute I'm sitting here sweating bullets. I mean, even with the air conditioner. Can you imagine!"

"The heat's never bothered me," Emma went on happily. "It always made Harold irritable, but I've always rather liked it."

"It's just a little trailer, Emma, nothing much. Did I ever tell you how narrow the bathroom door is? You have to squeeze in sideways." Mildred laughed. "Picture that, if you will."

Emma got the message but preferred to believe she was misreading it. "I'd pay you something, of course."

"That's not the point," Mildred said with a slight hint of exasperation. "It wouldn't be comfortable for three."

"Three?"

"I have a gentleman friend, Emma."

Emma flushed with embarrassment for having failed to foresee such a circumstance, and she suffered a rush of depression from the collapse of a good idea. She mumbled something apologetic, and Mildred said she should have mentioned her friend long ago, a pleasant Armenian fellow widowed twice, who could not do enough for her. Emma, feeling her head moving with the rise and fall of Mildred's voice, broke in and said, "Well, I won't keep you."

Mildred said, "You ought to find yourself a man, Emma."

Emma hung up the receiver and moved unfeelingly from one room to another. The shades were drawn, and the house was cool, quiet, and untidy. Unwashed dishes cluttered the kitchen sink. The bathroom mirror had scum on it, the floor dried traces of blood from Henry's hand. In the den some of the drawers from Harold's desk lay dumped out on the floor. The bedroom smelled stale. On the bed was the open suitcase she had planned to pack a few things in.

Henry, who had been sitting in the breezeway under torn screens, came into the house looking for her. "Where are you, Mrs. Goss?"

She moved back into the den, and he came in nursing his mutilated hand, which he had bandaged himself, a bad job. The strips of cloth had fallen off, and only the gauze pad sticking to the wound remained. He appeared pale and frightened.

"It keeps throbbing, Mrs. Goss. It's got all swollen too." He wanted her to look at it, but she would not. He said, "I think I ought to see a doctor. Who's yours? Will you call him for me?"

"It's a woman," she said flatly.

"OK, call *her*."

"Call her yourself."

He looked at her with dismay. "What's her name?"

She was silent.

He said, "I guess I could go the hospital instead."

"You can do anything you want," she said.

He went into the living room and lay down on the

sofa, his good hand over his brow and the bad one over his heart.

Henry slept for less than an hour, a sick sleep fraught with bad dreams. In one dream, men mauled his mother and abused him. In another, a slender black soldier struck out ahead of him through thick foliage and vanished in a pop of light, leaving behind a shirt laden with gore and a boot empty except for a single chocolate-brown toe with a pink nail in need of a clip.

He woke feverish and ugly, and for a few seconds he was disoriented. He thought the sofa was the one he had sometimes slept on as a child, and for a terrible moment he thought he was that kid. The pain in his hand had spread into his arm, which he was unable to lift.

"Where are you, Mrs. Goss?"

He stumbled into the dining room and gave a start when he thought somebody was staring at him out of the china closet. In the kitchen he ran cold water from the faucet over his aching hand, which he avoided looking at. The gauze pad had become a part of the wound and had taken on its color.

"Damn it, answer me!"

The house echoed empty.

Sal Botello lived a few miles outside of Springfield in a lakeside cottage previously the property of an inveterate gambler who had borrowed money from Sal and had hopelessly fallen behind in interest payments. The furniture had also belonged to the gambler. "Nice place you got here, Sal," Louise Baker said, stepping to the glass slider leading to the deck. "Nice view."

"It suits me," Sal said. "Can I get you a beer, maybe something harder?"

"Nothing," she said, surprisingly fresh after her long drive from Lawrence. She stood long-limbed in a beige suit, the skirt stylishly short. Her dark eyes were clear and alert.

Sal said, "We were worried about you, weren't we, John?"

John Rozzi was ensconced in a low cushioned chair, the weight of his face sunk between his shoulders, the skin gathered in pleats under his chins. He had a can of Canadian beer in his hand. "We didn't know what to do," he said.

"Nothing," she said.

"That's what we did."

"I did something," Sal said. "I checked around, see who might've put the hit on you, but I drew a blank."

"I did some checking too," she said easily. "I didn't do any better."

"John and me, we didn't want you to get any wrong ideas about us."

Louise's smile was gracious. "It crossed my mind, Sal, but I dismissed it."

"That's a relief. We were concerned, weren't we, John?"

"I wasn't concerned," John said. "You know me good enough, don't you, Mrs. Baker?"

"I know you both," she said, stepping away from the deck door and glancing at a framed photograph of three children on the television set. "Your kids, Sal?"

"Belongs to the guy used to own the house." Sal was watching her closely. "The way I see it, Mrs. Baker, somebody in Lawrence must hate you a lot."

"That's more than possible, Sal. The problem is I don't know who. That's why I've got myself a bodyguard now."

"You should've asked John. He'd have done it for you, wouldn't you, John?"

John said, "I'd do anything for you, Mrs. Baker."

"I'm using Chick Ryan," she said. "You remember him, don't you, Sal?"

Sal visibly relaxed. "Sure I do. He was a help to you after Scampy kicked."

"You were a help too."

Sal grinned. "I knew a winner when I saw one. Your brains, Mrs. Baker, we've done well."

"I needed someone like you."

"I'm glad I fit the bill." Sal ran a hand over his pitted jawline. "So where's Ryan now?"

"I don't need him everywhere I go," she said, and smiled down at John. "I'd like to talk to Sal alone for a while, you don't mind, do you?"

John was on his feet, and Sal said to him, "Go take a walk around the lake. Listen to the birds." John deposited his beer can on the top shelf of the room divider and left through the kitchen. Sal called after him, "You see Mrs. Reynolds, say hello for me."

Louise dipped her fingers into the half pockets of her jacket. "Who's Mrs. Reynolds?"

"Woman lives across the lake. Her husband travels. It's warm enough, she and I go swimming late at night. She says she never knew a guy like me."

"Sounds like you have it nice here."

His eyes embraced her. "I'd give my heart and soul it was you I was going swimming with."

"I'm a married woman, but thanks just the same."

He drew near. "That Polack I got rid of for you, I'm ten of him."

"I don't doubt it." The heel of her hand pushed him back. "Let's talk business."

"Everything's on hold."

"For now, that's the best place for it. I've got word the

government's interested in me. It doesn't surprise me. One thing follows another."

"What's it mean to us?" he asked.

"It means I'm going to fade into the background for a while and you're going to take a more active role, make a few decisions. Think you're up to it?"

His eyes glittered, and his color rose. "Sure I can do it. I can do anything you want. Maybe in time I can call you Louise instead of Mrs. Baker."

"First things first, Sal." She lowered her head for a moment. "You know I've made a lot of money."

"I got a small idea, Mrs. Baker, but it probably doesn't come anywhere close. I don't want to be nosy but if you want to tell me I'll listen."

"It's enough, Sal, so that maybe I might retire, who knows?"

He shook his head. "I never thought I hear you say that."

"Somebody shoots you, it changes your whole way of looking at life. You understand."

"Nobody's ever shot me."

"You're lucky." She stepped back to the sliding door and peered through the glass. "If I look hard, can I see Mrs. Reynolds's house?"

"Naw, it's hidden."

"Maybe I'll have that beer now.

He grinned and moved past the room divider into the little kitchen, where he pulled two barroom glasses out of a cabinet and yanked open the refrigerator. Bending, he said, "O'Keefe, Stroh's Light, or Bud? You got your choice."

"Let me think," she said slowly. Her expectant eye picked up Chick Ryan slipping into the kitchen on the quietest of feet. Glimpsing her, he signaled with his free hand, a gesture that had the intimacy of a whisper laid against her ear. In a strong voice she said to Sal, "I'll have what John was drinking."

Sal reached deep into the refrigerator.

She turned her head. She did not want to see it happen and tried to occupy herself with a broken nail. It was over in one shot from a nine-millimeter semiautomatic pistol, point-blank, base of the skull. Sal went down as if someone had pulled his feet from under him. Louise waited for the coup de grace, but it did not come. Her head still averted, she forced a quaver out of her voice and said, "Make sure."

Chick, looking down, said, "I don't have to."

Staring through the glass, she watched John charge up the rise from the lake as if someone had strong reins on him and were whipping him up a rough road. Minutes later the front door flew open with a bang, and John pushed into the kitchen and pulled up short. For an extended moment the silence was acute and critical. Chick smiled, and Louise, remaining in impeccable profile, said, "What's it going to be, John?"

"I'm with you, Mrs. Baker," he said.

Sun poured through the slider and lay in her hair. "You know why this was done, don't you?

"Yes, ma'am, I do."

Chick, in a voice marked with doubt and disappointment, said to her, "I hope you know what you're doing."

"Do I, John?"

"Yes, ma'am. You'll never have to worry about me."

She opened the slider for air. "Some cleaning up to do here, John. Also a disposal problem. May we leave it in your hands?"

"I'll take care of everything," he said flatly.

Chick ejected the clip from the pistol and wiped the

weapon with a paper towel. "While you're at it, John, get rid of this.."

"See you back in Lawrence," Chick said with a glance at Louise.

"Yes, eventually," she said.

Chick left by the front door, and she departed by way of the deck, beneath which she paused to let a sickness pass.

Ben Baker stood as if catatonic on the edge of an interstate highway, where the traffic could deafen a person, and was nearly swept away by a fifty-thousand-pound rig that roared by at a fantastic speed. Youths in an open car swerved into the breakdown lane and threw empty beer bottles at him. None hit him, but some shattered nearby. A priest in a car bearing New York plates offered him a ride, but something in the clergyman's manner alerted him.

He began walking again, unsure whether he was going west or east, toward Mallard Junction or away from it. His silk ascot had loosened and fluttered outside his shirt like a little bird under his chin. He was tramping over grass now, ignoring the vibrations from the highway, the chaos in his head, the weariness in his legs. He concentrated only on forging ahead while cursing the greatest injustice in life: loss. When his feet refused another step, he took deep breaths and stared at the river of traffic as if waiting for the strength and the proper moment to plunge into it.

He did not see the red pickup truck gliding toward him, half on the grass, two faces swimming in the sun-struck windshield. Not until the truck pulled alongside him in a small fluster of dust did his eyes fly up. Mrs. Mennick's face poured out the passenger window.

"Thank God we found you, Mr. Ben."

The door winged open, and Mrs. Mennick's reedy legs

dangled free, then the rest of her, like a large ball ready to bounce at him. He stood stationary, the greater part of him paralyzed by fatigue. "Lou's gone," he said simply.

Mrs. Mennick approached him with arms ready to reach out, as if she thought he might bolt. "No, Mr. Ben. We heard all about it. It was Bonnie Snell got killed. You remember her."

The name Bonnie Snell no longer meant anything to him. He watched Mrs. Mennick's brother climb out of the other side of the truck and stand motionless with a face totally bare of expression, which he found vaguely unsettling.

Mrs. Mennick said, "How did you get here, all this way?"

Walked. How else could he have got here? He had walked and walked. When she asked whether he had planned to do anything foolish, he did not reply, as if he were beyond explanation. When she reached for his hand, he recoiled.

"Don't you want to go home, Mr. Ben?"

"No," he said.

She looked around. "I need your help, Howard."

Together they forced him into the cab of the truck, where he sat scrunched between them, his nostrils filled with the fertilizer smell of Howard's clothes. He took an elbow in the stomach when Howard shoved the gearshift into drive with unnecessary force, and he nearly fell into Mrs. Mennick's arms when the truck lurched onto the highway. It sped from one lane into another.

"Take it easy," Mrs. Mennick said, and Howard flipped her a look of disgust.

"You care more about him than you do your own," he said.

"We both live pretty well off them, remember that," she countered easily.

He hunched over the wheel. "It's more than that with you."

"Think what you like, Howard, but where would your business be without Mrs. Baker?"

Ben, listening, said, "I know what you two are saying."

"No, you don't," Mrs. Mennick said, stroking his head. "That's the problem, Mr. Ben. You really don't."

Emma Goss walked the length of Mount Vernon Street, something she had not done in years. She avoided the voices of children, but with a boldness that sent a chill into her ankles she nodded to the man watering his patch of lawn and went out of her way to speak to the woman checking her mailbox. The woman, who twice a year knocked on doors for local charities, responded perfunctorily, "And how are you, Mrs. Foss?"

Emma did not correct her.

Wind chimes sounded from a front porch, though she was unaware of a breeze. Two boys oblivious of her drifted by on bicycles, their language foul, which did not bother her. She felt there was nothing she could not push out of her mind. The only real bother was her body, for no matter how many times she bathed she did not feel clean.

At the end of Mount Vernon, corner of South Broadway, she entered the drugstore, where early in their marriage Harold had bought condoms, a month's supply at a time, which would last a year, not because he had lacked ardor, but because he had been a pinchpenny and washed them out after use. When she had learned where he was buying them, she stayed away out of embarrassment, despite her craving for the sweets at the soda fountain. Now, surely, it was safe.

But nothing was the same. She remembered space, and there was none. Instead she found herself poking claustrophobically between tall displays of brightly packaged products that had a tinselly smell. Gone, or at least hidden from view, was the mammoth penny scale on which she had weighed herself, always with anxiety immediately justified by the reading. She lifted her nose. Gone was the intoxicating scent of chocolate.

"May I help you, ma'am?"

The voice was a boy's, so handsome he was, with glossy black ringlets fringing his forehead and eyelashes so long she imagined herself brushstroked in his gaze. He stood in a vanilla jacket behind a glass counter, innocence in his early adolescent eyes. Moving toward him, she saw herself in the mirror behind him and wished she had done something with her hair, which was a fright, and had worn a different dress. The one she had on looked as if it had been passed on to her.

"I don't see the fountain," she said, and the boy screwed up his Byronic face.

"Ma'am?"

"The soda fountain," she said, her eyes shooting here and there, but she could not remember where it had been situated. Everything had been rearranged and juggled, and too much was in the way.

The boy said, "No soda fountain here."

She pointed. "There. I think it was there."

The proprietor peeked out from the back room. He had cropped silver hair, a crimped forehead, and a warm voice. "Twenty-five years ago at least," he said, "I had it taken out."

"It seems only yesterday I—" she murmured, and stopped.

"That's the way it goes," he said, smiling. "When

213

you're young time floats. Then it flies." He paused. "Sorry about your husband."

He recognized her, remembered her after all these years, and she flushed, half with pleasure and half with embarrassment, and remembered she had never been totally indifferent to his smile. Turning quickly to the boy, she said, "I'd like some aspirin, please."

The proprietor said, "Good to see you again."

Trees were dropping their shadows when she trekked up Mount Vernon Street with a lighter lift to her step and with her mind reaching far back to better days, though for the first time in her life she questioned whether they had been that good. Had her parents not been so protective, she might have had choices beyond Harold, and had Harold not feared the expense of fatherhood she might have had a daughter to warm these late years. Had things been different she might even have learned to drive an automobile. As she neared the Whipples' house, she heard the clip of high heels in the driveway and then, plainly Mrs. Whipple's voice.

"Good to see you out and about, Mrs. Goss."

She immediately felt shabby and humble against the gloss of Mrs. Whipple, whose gray-blond hair had just been done and whose summery dress was conspicuously expensive. Her sense of uncleanliness intensified from a whiff of Mrs. Whipple's scent. Silver car keys dangled from Mrs. Whipple's hand.

"I'm out to do a little shopping. Then I'm meeting my husband for dinner at Bishop's. Have you eaten there, Mrs. Goss?"

She shook her head. She had never set foot in the place, but she knew that Harold had occasionally lunched there with men from his department and brought leftovers home in a distinctive doggy bag. Mrs.

Whipple seemed to be circling her, floating around her in a scent of Estee Lauder and viewing her from all angles with curiosity and amusement.

"The food's fabulous. You ought to get that handsome nephew of yours to take you."

Emma recoiled as if a pin had been pressed into her face. It was not the tone of Mrs. Whipple's voice, but something in the eyes, an insinuation, as if she, Emma, had a taste for the shameful.

Mrs. Whipple said quickly, "Was there a ruckus around here late last night? Something woke my daughter."

Emma stood utterly motionless, with no feeling in her face, and chose ambiguity over a lie. She watched Mrs. Whipple bounce a hand over her hair.

"The whole neighborhood's getting noisier. I suppose it can't be helped. It's getting younger, have you noticed?"

"Yes, it's inevitable," Emma said in a rush of breath, glad to have said something, proving that she had a voice, a thought, an opinion. That she was more than a widow and a victim. "I must be going," she said.

"Yes," said Mrs. Whipple, gazing over at Emma's house. Henry was in a window, his good hand pressed against a pane as if he meant to push it out. "Your nephew looks impatient."

With no fear in her face but with a drag to her step, she entered the house through the breezeway and averted her eyes from the mess in the kitchen. Henry confronted her near the bathroom.

"You could have at least told me you were going out."

"I don't have to tell you anything," she said.

"I'm burning up, Mrs. Goss." His voice was a whine. "Feel me," he pleaded, and she clamped a hand over his brow and felt the heat.

"Good," she said with her first smile in a long time.

* * *

Louise Baker, cruising up the drive, was glad to be home, and she breathed deeply of the air, her eyes soaking up the colors of the flowers and the green of the lawn. "This is where I belong," she murmured aloud. "No other place." Her hands, which had been trembling on the wheel, were now steady and firm upon it. She steered toward the khaki figure of Mrs. Mennick's brother, who was stacking landscaping equipment into the back of his truck. He did not stop his work until she climbed out of the Porsche and declared herself with a bright smile. "Everything looks grand," she said with a thrilling sense of proprietorship. "You do a good job, Howard."

"I do my best," he said in his buttoned-up way.

Louise looked toward the house, manorial in its size and setting. "I should've been born to it, Howard. It would've been easier."

"Yes, ma'am," he said with a slight change of tone that made her glance quickly at him.

"Anything wrong, Howard?"

"I'll let my sister tell you," he said.

She entered the house, cool with its clean smells of polish and care, rich in heirlooms that would stir the genitals of any antique dealer. The Persian carpet softened her step. She called her husband's name and was answered by Mrs. Mennick from the west side of the house, where the late sun was flooding the windows. Mrs. Mennick and Ben were in the room that Ben's mother had assigned exclusively to herself for writing letters, perusing the better magazines, and taking to the sofa under a goose-down throw during her time of the month. Louise walked by the open door.

"In here," Mrs. Mennick said.

Louise turned back and looked in. Ben was sitting on the sofa, wrapped in the folds of the throw that might have still borne his mother's scent. His eyes were squeezed closed as if he were afraid to open them. Mrs. Mennick had her arms around him.

"He's all right, Mrs. Baker. His teeth were chattering for no reason, but he's better now. Open your eyes, Mr. Ben."

He opened them with a grimace as Louise entered the room. Then his face swelled in a wave of emotion, and he gazed at her as he always did, as if she were a flower in a slender vase. "Are you alive, Lou?" Are you really alive?"

"There was an accident on the highway," Mrs. Mennick explained swiftly. "He thought it was you."

"I'm quite alive, Ben. Let him be, Mrs. Mennick."

Mrs. Mennick loosened her embrace and, careful not to disturb him, pulled herself to her feet. "I was afraid to give him a sedative on top of his medication, and I didn't want to call the doctor either. Only you can make him right, Mrs. Baker."

"You've done fine," Louise said, a bit short. "You can leave us alone now."

Mrs. Mennick lingered. "The man from the chicken farm told me and Howard about the accident. It was terrible, terrible. Would you like to hear?"

Louise tossed up a deferring hand. "Is it something that affects my life?"

"No," Mrs. Mennick said, slightly put out. "Not your life."

"Then tell me about it later."

Left alone with him, Louise stared at her husband with a critical eye. He was waiting for a kiss, but she could not bring herself to give him one. Her stomach was churning too emphatically, and her head was hot.

"Do you have to have that thing around you?" she said.

"I'm cold," he said, his eyes verging on tears. "You shouldn't have stayed away so long. You know how I get."

Her eye turned harder. "Was this your mother's room, Ben?"

"Yes."

"I'm not your mother, am I?"

"No," he said. "You're not. You're my wife."

"How old are you?"

He smiled. "You know."

"I want you to tell me. Say it out loud."

"I'm fifty-one."

"How many feet do you have?"

He smiled. "Two."

"Good," she said. "Stand on them!"

Later he followed her upstairs to her bedroom, but she shut him out. She took a long hot bath in the luxury of the sunken tub, her head thrown back, her legs stretched to the limit. With a prodigious effort of will, she cleared her mind of the day's events and thought only of distant things. The times she and Barney Cole had made out in the back row of the Central Theater, their mouths sore at the movie's end. The week she had labored to teach him to dance so that he could take her to the senior prom. The Sunday evenings spent watching television in his living room, his father treating her like a princess. She remembered elevating his father to a man of means despite the inevitable hole in the heel of his sock.

The gauze pad taped below her collarbone tore loose in the water and floated up in front of her. She plucked it from the suds and flung it over the side, then traced an exploratory finger over the wound, no more than a round puckering, ugly in its colors and intriguing in its symmetry.

Clad in a gown of thin flannel, she propped king-size

pillows and slipped under the covers to await supper in bed. Mrs. Mennick came in presently with a tray bearing lentil soup, crackers, a slice of buttered French bread, and a pot of herbal tea. "Are you sure that'll be enough?" Mrs. Mennick asked, her feelings still bruised.

"Plenty," Louise said, glancing up. "I'm sorry I was short with you, but I've had a hard day."

"Not just you, Mrs. Baker. I've had a hard time too. All the while you were away he was needing constant care. I even had to have Howard help me."

"I said I was sorry."

"You don't know what he's like when you're gone."

Louise looked at her sharply. "Who do you think keeps this ship afloat?"

"Truth be known, Mrs. Baker? We both do."

As Mrs. Mennick left with the air of someone vastly unappreciated, Louise made a mental note to amend matters later. She rearranged the tray closer to her and crushed crackers into the soup. With no appetite, she ate for the nourishment. Chewing on bread, she felt a coolness in the air and then heard the light fall of rain, which she thought was fitting. A cleansing. She was drinking her tea when Ben looked in.

"May I?" he asked, and advanced into the room like a puppy that had been punished and partially forgiven. His hair was wet-combed, and she suspected Mrs. Mennick had done it. His expression was contrite.

"You were right to talk to me that way."

"I'm glad you understand," she said, and patted the bed for him to sit, not too close because of the tray. "You'll never be a complete person unless you understand a lot of things, especially about yourself."

He sat on the bed's edge and looked at her full in the face. "I'm never going to be right, Lou. I know that. It's my chemistry. Nothing to do with my mother or anybody else. I know that too."

"With medication you can function. Do you also know *that*?"

He nodded, his eyes humid but clear. His neat mustache was darker, the probability strong that Mrs. Mennick had applied eye shadow.

"Then why don't you take it like you should?"

"I try, Lou, honest, but it drains the strength out of me. It makes me feel less, like somebody else is in charge, and I don't have any say in my life."

"What happens if you don't take it?"

He glanced away. "I do silly things."

"So you have to take it. You have no choice." She put her teacup down and used a napkin. "I'm tired, Ben. Would you take the tray away?"

"You want me to go," he said, springing up. The tray rattled in his grip. "Have a good night's sleep, Lou. I won't bother you."

When he shut the door behind him, she closed her eyes and sank deep under the covers. Fatigue took hold of every part of her body except her brain, which stayed lit, leaving her with little confidence that she would fall asleep easily. More than an hour later, the room dark, she was still awake. She groped for the phone and rang up Barney Cole's number. Within moments, he was on the line. She had caught him at a bad time, which she disregarded. Dropping her head back, she said, "Just talk to me."

"I'm not alone," he said.

"Say something sweet, please."

"There's an outside chance the feds have bugged my line."

"I don't give a damn. Say something sweet!"

For the first time ever, he hung up on her.

TWELVE

"You shouldn't have done that," Kit Fletcher said after he clamped the receiver down. "Maybe it was a matter of life and death."

"You have no idea what the conversation was about."

"I know it was from your friend. That's all I need to know."

"Sometimes she's too much."

"Never, Barney, not if she's a real friend." Kit's hand glided over the stereo. The telephone had rung during a Simon and Garfunkel song, and she had lowered the sound. Now she turned it off. "Your mother and father are both dead, aren't they? They were the only people on earth who would've forgiven you anything, who would've kept on loving you no matter what horrid thing you might've done. Who do you have now? Me? Would I be that forgiving?"

"I wouldn't think so," Cole said.

"You're right, Barney, not me. I'm not put together

that way. But how about her, your friend? That's something to think about, isn't it?"

Cole looked at her askance. "You send mixed signals."

"Granted, I'm jealous, but that doesn't fuddle my thinking."

"It fuddles mine. Louise is trouble, and you've made it clear you don't want any."

"I wouldn't expect you to involve me," she said, moving to a window and gazing out at the dark. She had on a green blouse and denim skirt that made her look more Andover than Boston, more Indian Ridge Country Club than the Ritz. "Loads of fireflies out there, Barney."

"Little taillights," Cole said. "Like traffic."

"But no pollution."

"None."

She turned with a half smile. "What was that business about your line being bugged?"

"I was joking."

"No, I can tell when you're joking and when you're not. Should I be concerned about calling out?"

"I'd use discretion."

"How much?"

"All you've got." He smiled. "I really am joking."

"No, you're not."

A little later they undressed for bed and read together under twin flexible reading lamps, their feet casually tangling and untangling far under the covers. Without her telling him, he knew she was leaving in the morning, and he asked when she thought she might be back. "The weekend," she replied without looking up from the page of the Joan Didion novel she had plucked from a bargain table at Barnes & Noble. She turned the page. "In the interval, maybe you could zip in and take me to dinner."

"It's a possibility," he said, doubtful that she expected or wanted him to take her up on it. Near the house trees shifted their shadows and sent in drafts of cool air. He put aside his magazine and switched off his lamp. "Do you want me to stay?"

"For a bit," she said, closing her book. When he stretched past her to extinguish the light on her side, she traced her fingertips along his rib cage, and produced a shiver. "Those are my fingers," she whispered, "not your friend's."

"Glad you told me."

"Some other things I'd like to tell you, but I don't think you'd understand."

"Try me."

"Another time," she said and settled into his arms.

It was nearly midnight when he eased his legs over the side of the bed, slipped on his undershorts, and stood listening to the depth of her breathing and the nighttime chorus of peepers. He made his way by touch through the dark to the kitchen, where he put on the stove light and looked up Louise Baker's number in his private phone book. She was obviously asleep, for several rings went unanswered. When she finally came on the line she sounded drugged. "What?" she said. "Who?"

"Barney," he repeated.

Her voice came awake. "Some nerve, Barney, you hang up on me and then call back at this hour. How did you know my husband and I sleep in separate rooms?"

"Guessed."

"Have you forgiven me about that little thing in the parking lot? It wasn't that I didn't trust you, you surely know that."

"It's forgotten," he said. "Have you forgiven me for hanging up?"

"Nothing to forgive. I knew you'd call back. I know what's in you."

He stood silently looking down at his bare toes and listening to June bugs bashing their brains out against the lit screen in the window over the sink.

"Still there, Barney?"

"Yes."

"I needed you tonight, it would've been better if you were here, but this will do." She sighed happily. "I'm so glad we didn't marry. We never would have stayed this close."

"I don't know if that's such a good thing, do you?"

"I'll let you answer that," she said, "so that I can go back to sleep. Good night, baby."

"I haven't said anything sweet yet."

"Another time."

Cole hung up, left the stove light on, and made his way back to the master bedroom. Leaning over the bed, he could just barely make out Kit's face. Her eyes were open.

"You were listening in, weren't you?"

"Yes," she said.

He turned away, started for the door, knowing her voice would stop him.

"Barney."

He placed a hand on the door frame and with his other hand hitched up his undershorts. "What?"

"I'd love to meet her."

Henry Witlo soaked his hot hand in a pan of water at the kitchen table. On the table was the small black-and-white Magnavox that Harold Goss had kept in the garage for company while puttering around. Henry watched the Red Sox game and after each inning changed the water, for his hand heated it. He was hungry, but little in the refrigerator appealed to him. He ate a tomato and two plain slices of granola bread. After the game he watched the late news, all of Johnny Carson, and most of David Letterman, whose humor was too slapstick for him. It hurt his head. After dumping out the water for the final time, he shuddered. The soaking had bleached his hand and withered the ends of his fingers while leaving the wound black.

Emma Goss was asleep, her face turned to the wall. He tried to creep into bed without waking her and fell slowly into Harold's hollow. Drained of strength, he soon dropped off, but his sleep was fitful, without sustenance. Soon Emma woke him for good.

"I can't sleep with you in the bed," she said. "You toss and turn. You groan."

"It's not my fault," he said as if talking to his mother or to a superior officer.

"You gnash your teeth."

"I can't help it."

Her white face waxed in the dark. "And I can't sleep!"

He went into the front room and rolled up in a blanket on the sofa, where he dozed off and on for what little remained of the night. He heard the first birds, the clatter of a rubbish truck, and the slap of a newspaper on the Whipples' walk. With the blanket wrapped around him, he stumbled to the bathroom, rummaged in the medicine cabinet, and came across a plastic cylinder bearing an old prescription label, Harold Goss's name typed on it. The pills were penicillin. He took two.

His right hand bore the wound, which made it awkward for him to shave. He nicked himself several times. Showering was no problem, but drying himself was. Then he switched to a face towel, which made it easier. He dressed with a lack of patience and skill, leaving his shirt unbuttoned and Harold's shoes untied. With less patience he waited for Emma to get up.

She slept until eight-thirty, not at all like her, and appeared muffled in a bulky bathrobe, which made her bare feet seem tiny. He had returned to the bathroom and peered at her from the mirror. She said, "Will you be long?"

He went to her immediately, extending his bad hand. "I don't like the look of it, Mrs. Goss. I should've gone to the doctor's like I wanted."

"Nobody stopped you."

"I got it saving you."

"Saving yourself, not me. Are you through in here?"

She stayed a long time in the bathroom, the door locked, and a couple of times he put his mouth to the crack and called in to her, "What are you doing?" He was too fidgety to sit, and he went out onto the breezeway, where the sight of the shattered screens depressed him. He spat through one of them. "I shouldn't have let the little bastard crawl away," he whispered to himself.

When he returned to the kitchen, Emma was in a neat housedress, her hair drying from a wash. He stared at her with disbelief and outrage. She was making herself breakfast, nothing for him. He struck the countertop with his left hand. "What am I, black?" She ignored him. He slapped a plate on the table and threw down cutlery. "I want something too!"

"I don't care what you want," she said, and he verged on striking her, holding back at the last instant. Her eyes were calm. "What's stopping you?" she asked.

"I never hit my mother, I won't hit you." His face was a patina of sweat. "But if you don't make me something, I'll break every window in the house. I don't care if the cops come. You think I'm kidding, watch me!"

226

All she was having was toast. She dropped a slice on his plate. He held it in place with the pained fingers of his right hand and buttered it with his left. She poured herself coffee.

"I want some too."

There was no cup for him on the table. She waited for him to get one, which he did with an expression of deprivation and injustice and then reseated himself with such force that the back of the chair gave way a little. He watched her pour.

"Thank you," he said in a voice pitched higher than normal. He ate his toast with his mouth open to annoy her. "See, I can play the same game."

She did not respond, not even with a grimace, her natural reaction now. She spread jam over her toast and ate quietly. A silence grew, which she seemed to relish. He sullied it with a cough and glared at her through a dazzle of sweat.

"You wouldn't care if I died, would you, Mrs. Goss? You'd just go right on with your business. Fuck Henry."

She looked away.

"I want something more," he said. "I'm sick, I've got to eat." He leaped up. He shook cornflakes into a bowl, the last in the box, and added milk, the last in the carton. Back at the table, he had trouble manipulating the spoon with his left hand, grew impatient, and began eating with his fingers.

Emma left the table.

He left soon after. Unsettled in the stomach and wobbly in the knees, he groped to the bedroom and flopped down on the unmade bed, sinking into Emma's hollow instead of Harold's. He did not expect to sleep, he felt too sick, but he slipped off at once and dreamed he was chewing a salt pill against the jungle heat and slogging through muck. There was too much of everything. Too much sun beating a fever into him, too much uncertainty in his step. Too many black guys were laughing at him, for he had rolled his sleeves up, a fool thing to do. Leeches laddered his bare arms. He tried to pick one off, but it was blubber, like a lip, and fastened to him as in a kiss. His arms pulsing with kisses, he sank to the warm wet of the jungle floor, a heady way to go, as irresistible as freezing to death. It was a religious experience of a vulgar variety, not unlike the time a Pentecostal preacher came to Chicopee, talked in tongues, and brought people to their knees, including his mother, who did it for the giggle.

He did not want to wake. He cherished where he was, but he felt pressure from above and a renewed throb in his hand. His eyes fluttering open, he saw the same blade that had raced so swiftly across his palm that he had failed to feel it and now could feel nothing else. Now the tip of the blade was tickling his throat, with Emma's violet eyes pressing down into his.

"I wish I could do it," she said. "I wish to God I had the nerve."

"Do it," he said.

Marge raised her penny eyes from her IBM typewriter and said, "Can I get you something, Mrs. Shea? A cup of coffee maybe?"

Edith Shea said no. She was sitting in one of the hard waiting-room chairs, her knifelike legs crossed. "I drink too much coffee as it is. I got coffee nerves, that's one of my problems. I won't tell you the others. How long do you think he'll be?"

"Not long. He knows you're out here."

"I don't have an appointment."

"He knows that too."

Edith wiggled a foot. "Is he a good guy to work for, Marge?"

"We get along well."

"I bet he couldn't do without you."

"He lets me think that."

"Yes, Barney's a charmer." Edith lit a cigarette. A *Thanks for Not Smoking* sign stood on Marge's desk. "You don't mind, do you, Marge?"

"There's an ashtray under the magazines."

"Hiding it, huh?" Edith pulled apart old copies of *Life* to find it and then settled back in her chair. She was not in her waitress uniform but in a peaceful shade of blue, with a polka-dot scarf round her neck. "You're not married, are you, Marge?"

"Not yet, Mrs. Shea."

"Christ, call me Edith. I'm not that much older than you. Or am I? Yeah, I guess I am." She spread her fingers out when she brought her cigarette to her mouth. She inhaled hard and blew out fast. "Any boyfriends?"

"Not really."

"Don't you get lonely?"

"I live with my mother. I don't know what I'd do without her."

"Someday you'll know."

"I don't think about that."

"You're going to have to. Ask me. I know." Edith flicked an ash, missing the target. "What do you do about sex?"

Marge started to blush and stopped. "I think about it."

"I know what you mean. Listen, Barney's a damn good-looking guy. If you'd like, I'll mention the matter."

Marge laughed abruptly and said, "Don't you dare."

A few moments later Barney Cole opened his office

door, and Edith rose, stubbing out her cigarette and smiling to show him that nothing was desperately wrong, Daisy was not dead, her children were all right, and the only immediate problem was within herself, which he had probably guessed. He kissed her cheek and closed the door behind her. She sank into the worn leather chair near his desk, the seat warm from the previous occupant, who had left by a different door.

"Daisy's giving up his office," she said.

Cole, who had remained standing, peered down at her. "He shouldn't do that. He'll have no place to go."

"Sure he will. Wild Bill's Tavern, the Hibernians, or some other joint."

"Is it the rent?" Cole asked. "I'll pay it. It can't be that much."

"He's in arrears."

"How much?"

"Who the hell knows? He doesn't know himself."

Cole's desktop was a confusion, but he found his personal checkbook without a search. The problem was finding a pen that worked. Sitting down, he tossed two away and came up with a red one that wrote.

Edith said, "Make it out to me." When he gave it to her, she blinked. "This is too much," she said, reexamining it. "I didn't come for money, Barney."

"I know that."

Her voice went stiff and practical. "When's the last time you gave your secretary a raise?"

"I can't remember exactly."

"Give her one," she said, and tore the check in two. "When it comes time to bury Daisy, that's when I'll need your help. I know he'll want all the trimmings."

"You make it sound imminent."

"He was pretty sick last night, but he bounced back

this morning, full of jokes I couldn't listen to." She threw her shoulders back in the chair. "It's not him I'm thinking of. It's me. I've never lived alone in my whole life. The thought is starting to terrify me."

"You still have the kids."

"For a while. Then what? I wouldn't know how to be Edith Pratt again. She walked in right now, I wouldn't know her. And she sure as hell wouldn't know me."

"I'd introduce you."

"I wouldn't like her. She was a silly kid, as I remember, full of mistakes. She made all the wrong choices."

"Would you like coffee?"

"I've already been asked that."

"Then tell me what I can do for you," he said.

"Flatter me."

"That's easy. That's a lovely outfit you're wearing."

"I charged it. God knows when I'll pay for it. You really think it looks good on me?"

"It's you," he said.

"That's not what I asked."

"I can't win," he said with a smile.

"Nobody can, Barney. People aren't happy anymore. Happiness belonged to another era. Back in the Depression people were happy with what little they got. Today expectations are too high. I expected to live in Andover like you. Instead I'm still in Lawrence and working as a waitress. Where's my fine house, Barney? Why isn't Daisy a judge?"

"Why am I not a United States senator?"

"You never wanted to be one. That's the difference. Different snores, different dreams. I never did know what you wanted, Barney, except maybe Louise. Probably a lucky thing you didn't get her."

"I won't ask your reasoning on that."

ANDREW COBURN

"I don't act on reason. I'm pure emotion. Yesterday I read in the paper about a Worcester woman slitting her husband's throat while he slept. I didn't need to know the facts. I could understand it all."

Cole said, "Remind me never to come to you for cheering up."

"But that's exactly why I come to you. I know you'll listen. You think you owe me something, Barney, but the joke's on you. You don't owe me a damn thing."

He rose from his desk. She rose too, with tears she had not seen coming, with more emotion than she had allotted for the situation. She felt his hands on the top of her hard stubborn hips; then his arms went around her and her face edged into his shoulder, her hair a crash helmet of tough wiry curls. She whispered, "That's all I came for Barney. A hug."

"It's what I do best," he said with only slight irony.

"It's a gift," she said. "Don't question it."

His hand was under her elbow when he opened the door and stepped out with her. She was composed now, her old self, and with a gust of exaggerated emotion she swept toward Marge, who was pulling a legal paper out of the typewriter.

"Guess what, Marge? Barney says he'll think about it."

Cole stepped forward. "Why didn't you ask me yourself?" he said, and Marge's face ignited.

Emma Goss sat in the den, at Harold's desk, and began a letter in her neat hand. It was her birthday. "I am sixty years old," she wrote, "and you are not here to wish me many happy returns." She was using his gold Parker pen, which she had just refilled with jet-black ink that gave a keen gloss to her words. "I haven't written you in some time. So much has happened, but it is nothing I want to tell you about. I feel you would blame me." She took a firmer grip on the pen. "Besides, irrational as this may sound, I feel you know most of it, if not all."

Her eyes flickered sideways. She heard a groan from the kitchen, but no approaching footsteps. "I'm using the pen you always feared losing. A few nights ago it could have easily been stolen, but that's something else I won't tell you about, for the same reasons, which perhaps makes no sense to you. Let me assure you that nothing makes sense to me anymore."

She took a breath, for her mouth had been moving as she wrote, and she clenched her jaw in an attempt to think calmly about matters that had to be said. "You always worried about money, Harold, even though we always had enough. I suppose you are thinking to yourself that I should thank you for leaving me well provided for and I do, but you left me with nothing else. For instance, you never encouraged me to learn to drive. In fact, you discouraged me, though I shouldn't blame you for that. I should have had more gumption. And sometime during our life together I should have scratched out one of your eyes."

Her pen came up quick from the paper. She had not meant to say that, but now that it was there she would let it stay. She shuddered a little in the rereading and then went on. "I don't hate you, Harold, I could never hate you, but I don't like you very much, which you shouldn't take too hard because I don't like my mother and father either, though I shall always love them, wherever they are. Perhaps they are near you, and you occasionally run into them. If so, please don't show them this letter. What's done is done."

She had filled the sheet of paper and reached for another, noticing that her handwriting had started small and had grown progressively larger. With the fresh sheet she started off small again. "Mommy and Daddy molded me wrong, and I did not possess the spirit to break out to be somebody bigger. I certainly can't blame you for that, and I don't. I'm trying to be very fair. The problem, Harold, is that I never went deep enough into myself. I never went into my tropic parts to get away from the cold. I bet you don't know what I'm talking about. I'm not sure I know either. The words are coming too fast. I do blame you for some things, Harold. You took advantage of my weaknesses. You meant for me never to have a voice of my own. And worse, never to have a child. For that, I can't forgive you." She paused. "That is how I feel. I can't help it."

She was not sure she cared to go on, but it seemed a waste to stop now, especially since she knew that once she placed the pen aside she would not write to him again. "All this rage I didn't know I had frightens me, and sometimes I wish you were here simply so I could beat my fists against you, but it would not change anything. So much is too late."

From the kitchen came louder groans from Henry, who was soaking his hand in a heavy salt solution. He cursed. She ignored it all and wrote, "If you were to peek in on me this moment, you might not recognize me. My hair is clean but looks a wreck. I'm not wearing stockings because I haven't done a wash in two weeks. I've lost weight, but in a way you would not like. I have less bosom. The house would shock you. It's a mess. Pretty soon I'm going to lie down for a while on the bed, which is unmade. I don't feel all that well today. I'm old, Harold. I wish I had been happier."

She went to a third sheet of paper. "I hope this letter reaches you, I really do, not to settle a score, but to let you know how I feel. It's owed you." She signed her name Emma Robinson Goss and then after some thought added a postscript. "Do you know what I wish with all my heart, Harold? I wish I were Mildred Murphy."

Louise Baker, looking slim and crisp in a linen suit and tan pumps, pulled the plug from the desk phone in her bedroom and then did the same with the two extensions. "I want no calls coming in on my private line," she said to Mrs. Mennick. "Any other calls, you're to simply say I'm away caring for my mother. Any emergencies, you have the number." She took an envelope from her bag. "This is for you," she said. "For the extra bother with Ben."

"I don't need to open it to know it's generous," Mrs. Mennick said in a curiously flat tone. She slipped the envelope into her apron pocket. "Thank you."

"Something's on your mind, Mrs. Mennick. What is it?"

"The bonuses you give me are always appreciated, don't misunderstand me, but I believe I deserve a raise in my basic salary. Mr. Ben has become quite a handful, and I'm not getting any younger."

"Are you saying you're too old for the job?"

"No, no, I'm not saying that," Mrs. Mennick said rapidly. "But I feel I should be getting more for all my responsibilities. Mr. Ben is a big part of them, but there's still this whole house to look after. And you being away so much now, Mrs. Baker, adds to the burden."

"Are you giving me an ultimatum?"

There was a momentary pause by Mrs. Mennick, like that of a poker player with a good hand but unaccustomed to high stakes. "All I'm asking for is fair wages, Mrs. Baker. You can't expect me to work for less."

"I wouldn't expect you to do anything you didn't want to do," Louise said evenly.

Mrs. Mennick's expression changed subtly, as if she found the situation disagreeable but had no choice in laying out her cards. "You'd be hard-pressed to find somebody as good as I am. I might as well tell you I've had offers."

"Are you giving me your notice?"

Mrs. Mennick paused again, longer, too long, and Louise smiled coldly.

"I'll make a few points, Mrs. Mennick. Then we'll consider the matter closed, and you do as you wish. First, your wages are more than adequate. I know professional people who make less. Second, I give you extra money to hire temporary help, but usually you prefer to keep the money and do all the work yourself. That's your business. Third, you pad the grocery expenses. You've done it for years, and your brother overcharges for gardening and lawn care. These are matters I've not mentioned because I've been satisfied with the arrangement. But if you're not satisfied, then I advise you to take one of those offers."

Mrs. Mennick started to speak, but faltered, the wind sailing out of her words.

"I will, by the way, give you excellent references," Louise said, and then seemed to lose all interest. She consulted her watch and snapped her bag shut.

"I don't know what to say, Mrs. Baker."

"You'd better say it quick. I'm leaving."

Mrs. Mennick looked this way and that, as if for a rescue. Then something broke in her face, and her whole jaw sagged, which threatened to bring down the rest of her features. "I'd like to stay," she said.

"Be sure."

Tears showed. "I am, Mrs. Baker."

"Don't cry!"

Louise left the house by the front door and looked back to wave at Ben, who was in a window. She had had a long talk with him about leaving again and had promised to return soon. He had promised to do what he was supposed to, his lips trembling from the kiss she had given him. When she climbed into the Porsche she waved again, but he was gone.

She drove to the bank in the quaint center of town. The president was at the country club playing golf, which did not surprise her, but the treasurer, a mild man with a mustache similar to Ben's, instantly made himself available and ushered her into his office, where she signed a pink withdrawal slip.

"I'll be back in a few moments," he said.

"Please take your time," she replied. "I'd like to use your phone."

He left, bowing a little, not quite scraping.

Seated at his desk, ignoring his confidential papers, she rang up her broker in Boston and, after a short discussion, told him to shift the bulk of her high-yield holdings, which had been doing quite nicely, to safer vehicles. Then she called her lawyer in Springfield and authorized him to handle the sale of her less profitable properties in and around that city.

When the treasurer saw that she was finished, he tapped on the glass door and came in with a small briefcase of simulated leather. "Would you care to count it?" he asked.

She stretched up from his desk with a smile that lightly mingled affection and amusement. She knew from a reading of the town history that the seventeenth-century forebears of this tame little man had lived by their considerable wits in the woods and had found more comfort in warm caves than drafty cabins. She patted his hand, which felt much like Ben's, and said, "Certainly not."

* * *

The offices of Pullman & Gates comprised an upper floor in a historic building in Boston's financial district. Kit Fletcher's office, though hardly grand in comparison with those of the senior partners, had its own distinctive carpet, a window, and enough wall space for a large painting by a local artist whose craftsmanship exceeded his art. Her desk was neat but busy-looking. She was reading a letter when Chandler Gates, whom she had been expecting, peeked in on her. "Glad you're back," he said, a smile evincing perfect teeth. "I missed you."

She tossed aside the letter. "I wasn't away that long."

"Long enough," he said, advancing upon her, fit and tanned in his British tailoring, his hair styled to give his aging face a younger meaning. "I won't ask any embarrassing questions."

There was an answer on the tip of her tongue, but she kept it to herself.

"I've missed you at tennis," he said with sweetness. They were occasional partners in doubles at a private court in Cambridge, where later they usually had drinks at a table overlooking the Charles.

"Yes, I must get back to it," she said.

His eyes dawdled on her, no surprise to her. He lusted for women he saw on the street, in the dining room of the Ritz, behind the steering wheels of open cars, and he had lusted for her since her first day with the firm.

"By the way," he said suddenly, "your new office should be ready in a week. It has a Pollock on the wall."

"I don't like Pollock."

"Clients do. Their eyes widen when they see the signature. Besides, it'll grow on you. It did on me."

"I see. It was the one in your office. What have you replaced it with?"

"An Andy Warhol. Since his death he's become more valuable."

"How nice for him."

"No, dear. How nice for us. We just happened to have one."

She leaned back in her chair. "When do you tell the world I'm now a senior partner?"

"Soon, dear, soon."

"Not having second thoughts, are you?"

"Heavens, no. We plan to do it in style. You'll be the first female senior partner in our esteemed history. Quite an honor, no?"

"It's quid pro quo, Chandler."

"Yes, certainly," he said, his teeth shining. "The firm's grateful, you know."

"I would hope so."

He arched an eyebrow. "You're being a little snippy, Kit. Not nice." Then his smile flew back. "Dinner tonight?"

"Not tonight. I've a lot of work to catch up on." She waited for him to leave. When he did not, she said, "How's Agatha?"

"Fine. Very heavily into aerobics."

"Good for her."

"Yes. Still a fine-looking woman for her age. We're doing Italy in August. Would you like to come?"

She shook her head. "I've never been much interested in that three-in-a-bed business."

"Don't be gross. How about coming along for half the month? I'll pick up the expenses."

"I make quite enough to pick up my own."

"I know that, but I like to do things for people I consider special."

"Yes," she said. "That was some necklace you gave your secretary. Agatha got wind of it, didn't she?"

He nodded with momentary regret. "Impossible for people not to hurt each other. It's the nature of things, Kit."

"Is that what it is?" she said. "I knew it must be something like that." She moved her hands over the papers on her desk. "Forgive me, Chandler, but I must get back to work."

"Yes, work. Some of us do more than others. I've noticed that." He backed off in a little dance as if someone were playfully pulling his strings. "You will at least think about Italy, won't you?"

"No, Chandler, I won't even think about it."

At the door, he said, "Tennis tomorrow?"

"Probably," she said.

Louise Baker sat in Rita O'Dea's immense living room, where the length of one wall was sheer glass and seemed to allow the lush outdoors to creep in. Sheepskin rugs were scattered over the gleaming hardwood floor, which smelled of polish. Rita, her enormous white knees flung apart, reclined in a chair that was a sling of black leather attached to African wood. Louise, whose chair was more conventional, said, "You have a lovely house."

"You haven't seen the latest addition," Rita said, and within seconds an extremely handsome young man in an open shirt and poplin pants appeared with a tray in one hand. He placed two frosted tumblers of fruit punch on the cocktail table. Rita cast her huge eyes on him. "This is Mario. Isn't he lovely? Say hello to Mrs. Baker, Mario."

Mario, no more than nineteen, flashed eyes dark and intense, almost hypnotic in their pretended innocence. "Hello," he said.

"He doesn't speak much English," Rita said.

"I speak a little."

"He's my houseboy," Rita said. "I got him here on a five-month visa. He behaves, maybe he can stay longer. He makes me mad, back he goes. Isn't that right, Mario?"

"That is right, Rita."

Louise said easily, "How do you like the United States?"

"I like," he said in a voice deeper than his age. "People live good here."

"Only the smart ones," Rita said. "Same as in Palermo. What do you think, Louise? You see a family resemblance?"

"Yes, I do," Louise said. "Especially the eyes."

"He's a distant cousin." The leather seat creaked under Rita's weight. "You should see him in shorts. He's got a perfect body. Fact is, you should see him with nothing on. He's the only guy I know with an ass you could call elegant. Look at him smile! He loves compliments, but don't give him too many, he gets aroused. Don't you, Mario?"

"I get what?"

"*Ci verra un caso duro.*" To Louise, she said, "Only thing is, he could be a little taller."

"You can't have everything," Louise said.

"Sure you can. Far as I'm concerned, everything is only just enough, and I'm a big woman. I need more."

Louise had a vision of Rita in bed, the bed full of her, no man able to extend his arms around her. She said, "Is he good in the kitchen?"

"He's learning."

Mario said, "Will you be wishing more?"

"I do, I'll call you. Say good-bye to Mrs. Baker."

"*Ciao.*"

Louise tipped her head. "*Ciao*, Mario."

Alone, the two women tasted their punch. Rita listed the ingredients, which included a heavy dose of St.

Raphael, which had been her brother's favorite aperitif. "The kid reminds me of my brother at that age," she said. "In looks, nothing else. There was only one Tony."

"You loved him very much, didn't you, Rita?"

"Like a woman. He was here, he'd hit me for saying it, but that's the way I felt." She pushed a hand through her heavy hair, the growth luxurious. "With Tony gone I hate holidays, like Christmas and Thanksgiving. I don't like places closing up, people pulling in. That happens, the whole world seems to shrink. I don't mind Sundays because supermarkets stay open now. I go to DeMoula's because the aisles are wide and it takes my mind off things. And now I've got Mario to push the carriage. Only problem is he likes to look at the women. He thinks I don't see." Suddenly she waved her hand. "Enough of me. What's doing with your problem? Have you taken care of it yet?"

"Most of it," Louise said.

"You happy so far?"

"Yes."

"Good. What's left of it?"

"A small matter, which I'll handle."

"I see." Rita rocked her knees. "I got this feeling you want to drop something else on me. What is it?"

"I want to retire. I want to turn my business over to you or whoever you think should have it. I've made good money, it's bought me what I want, and now I just want to enjoy what I've got."

Lines crowded the brow of Rita's otherwise perfectly smooth face. "You just want to walk away?"

"If it's possible."

"Getting shot give you the jitters?"

"That's part of it."

"A friend of my brother's, Louie Feoli, hairy like a

bear, three hundred pounds, got shot twice and never knew it. He thought he had bug bites under his arm. He used to scratch himself there all the time, which drove his wife crazy when they went out to eat. Doctors found the bullets when he died of an unrelated cause, a crowbar across the head. What else is bothering you?"

"The feds are interested in me."

"Only the cocksure get caught by the feds. You're too cautious for that."

"I've had enough, Rita."

Rita heaved a sigh. "So your mind is made up."

"With your permission."

Rita half rose from the huge sag of the chair and then fell back into it with a smile. "First of all, I don't want your business. I don't need it. Second of all, you got it running like a science. Big people in Boston need to finance something fast, they always count on you. Somebody else might not be so reliable. You see the problem? You're too good. You're a fucking whiz kid, that's what you are."

Louise smiled weakly.

"You mentioned a small matter still hanging. Is it more of this?" Rita pounded her right fist into the palm of her other hand.

"Yes."

"Then you'd better take care of it before we get down to serious talk."

"I understand."

Rita picked up her punch glass and drank fully, and Louise closed her eyes to refresh them and to keep her thoughts from getting out of hand. Rita said, "About this time Mario usually gives me a massage. I got a bad back, you know. How's yours?"

"I've not had a problem."

"He hasn't quite got the touch yet, but he's learning. He

can use the practice if you want to join me." Rita threw out a confidential smile. "Might make you feel better."

Louise laughed lightly. "You forget I'm wounded."

"He'll go easy."

The sun fired its last rays through the wall of window. Louise said, "What the hell, why not?"

Rita raised a hand. "Help me up."

"I feel so alone," Ben Baker said, and Mrs. Mennick swiftly turned to him.

"You're not alone, Mr. Ben. I'm right here."

"No, in here," he said, tapping his temple. "In my head. That's where I live every minute of my life."

"We all do, Mr. Ben, every one of us. That's how God made us."

"He made my head different. He put too much of me in there. He had no right."

"He made you special," Mrs. Mennick said, and tried to smooth his hair, the fine gray strands springing up between her blunt fingers. "You'll always have someone to care for you. I've got nobody. My husband died, and my children don't bother with me."

"You have your brother."

"I look out for him same as I do you, Mr. Ben. See how lucky you are?"

"I don't feel lucky," he said, a hint of calamity etched into his face, and she abruptly stepped back to view him better.

"Did you take your medication?"

"You saw me."

She shook a finger. "But you're smart, Mr. Ben. You can fool me."

A little later he went outdoors, where in its final blaze the sun looked like meat. Shadows ran deep, carrying the scent of cut grass. Near a trellis he observed a Japanese beetle boring a perfect hole into an unborn rose, which grieved him. He knew the bud would never blossom. At the far side of the house he saw. Mrs. Mennick's brother, who had finished his work but was hanging around.

"Hello, Howard."

His face in shadow, Howard barely looked up. He was sitting on a marble bench with a beer can in his hand and an empty one beside him. "Hello, sir."

Ben ventured closer. He sometimes suspected that Howard stole things, but he was never sure what they might be, though he knew Mrs. Mennick occasionally deposited loaded grocery bags in the back of Howard's truck, food Ben assumed was going to waste. And once last winter he had seen Howard wearing a scarf much like one he seemed to remember owning. He said, "What are you still doing here?"

"Waiting for her." The voice was gruff. "Taking her to the movies."

Ben stiffened. "I'll be alone."

"Yeah, I guess you will."

"She didn't tell me that," Ben said. In the shadows he could not tell whether Howard was smiling or scowling. "She'll be coming back, won't she?"

Howard swigged beer. "This is where she lives, isn't it?"

"I'd better check just the same," Ben said nervously, turning quickly. He trod on grass that was amber in the dying light, the scarlet sun sinking away. Howard's large lips twisted over the rim of the beer can.

"You little puke."

The words were uttered in hardly more than a whisper, but Ben heard them and spun around as if he had been punctured in the small of the back. A breeze swept across his hot face. "Do you mean me?"

"What's that, sir?"

"What you said. I heard you."

"Couldn't have, sir. I didn't say anything."

"You did!"

Howard crumpled the beer can. "No, sir."

Back inside the house, Ben listened for Mrs. Mennick and heard her in one of the downstairs bathrooms. He crept into the kitchen, ran his finger down the list of numbers she kept next to the wall phone, and dialed the one at the bottom. "Be there!" he said in a desperate whisper, but it was not Louise who answered but her mother, whom he had never met, not his fault, Louise's. She had always made excuses. He asked for her in a shaky voice, and Mrs. Leone, whose mind was obviously elsewhere, answered in Italian. "I can't understand you," he shouted. "What are you saying?"

In English she said, "What do you want?"

He could not hold back the tears. "My wife."

A little after nine in the evening a convenience store on Broadway, near the Methuen line, was the scene of an armed holdup. Shots rang out. Witnesses on the street said they saw a skinny dark-haired man in a warmup jacket, jeans, and red sneakers run from the store into an alley. A woman inside the store, who had flung herself to the floor at the first shot, gave an opposing description. By nine-thirty heavily armed police officers, one with a dog, were searching the side streets. At nine forty-five Captain Chick Ryan arrived at the store and viewed the blood-spattered body of the male clerk, which lay in a heap behind the counter. Turning to the detective in charge, Chick said, "He hasn't moved, has he?"

The detective, a weary-looking man whose partner

had recently died of a heart attack, said, "No, course he ain't moved."

"Then I guess he's dead. What happened?"

"Lone gunman," the detective said. "Woman customer said he demanded money from the register and the clerk refused to open it."

Chick made a face. "Never throw a stickup guy off his rhythm. Otherwise he goes bananas, this is what happens."

"Sometimes he shoots anyway."

"You got more of a chance the other way. Bet he was a spic. Am I right?"

The detective said, "All we know is he had dark hair and some kind of bright jacket. When the clerk wouldn't open the till, the guy pumps four, five shots into him and runs off with no money."

"Had to be a spic," Chick said. "First one I ever busted was maybe twenty years ago, Peter's Sweet Shop, two in the morning. I'm checking doors, there he is inside. You know how many arms he had? One. The other was a stump. You know what he had in his pockets? Cookies."

"This guy had two arms."

"I'm not saying it's the same guy. You being smart with me?"

"No, sir."

"Where's the medical examiner?"

"We're waiting on him."

Chick took a candy bar off the rack and unwrapped it. "You want one? They're free."

"No, thanks," the detective said.

Chick took a bite. "Too chewy," he said, and threw it away. He brushed past an officer dusting for prints and stepped outside the store. The night air was alive with

ANDREW COBURN

whirling lights. Two blocks had been cordoned off, and
officers were rerouting traffic. Crowds had gathered behind the barriers. When a reporter from the Lawrence paper, a young woman provocatively wide-eyed, approached
with a steno pad and asked for a statement, he reeled off
what he knew and added that the suspect was a Hispanic.

"Oh?" she said, scribbling. "That's not what I heard."

"Then get your facts straight." He sighed as if the task
might be hopeless for her. "You want, I'll have lunch
with you, give you the real lowdown what's bringing this
city down."

"That would be nice."

"For both of us," he said with his best smile. Then he
moved off smartly, for the medical examiner had just arrived, a shuffling man with lazy eyelids, whose breath
smelled of an after-dinner mint. Chick said, "Hope we
didn't disturb you, Doc."

"Where's the victim?"

"In there. Good thing you showed up. We were about
to slice him up, sell him as sandwich meat."

"You're quite a guy, Ryan."

"So are you, Doc," he said, and wheeled around, for
there was a flurry among the officers. The radios in the
cruisers were squawking. A young uniform rushed to him.

"I think we got him, Cap'n. He was spotted on Oak
Street, near Jackson. Our guys had to shoot."

"That's what they got guns for. They hit him?"

"They said he was down."

Chick ran to his car, waving to officers to clear a way for
him. The car, unmarked, started up thunderously. He
slammed the portable dome light on the roof, activated the
siren, and rammed the gearshift into Drive. Barriers were
heaved aside. The crowd parted. With the siren wailing and

248

lights flashing, he sped to Oak Street; within minutes, squashing a cat along the way, he made it to the Jackson Street area and skidded to a stop. A crowd had gathered, children were running about. Chick leaped from the car and elbowed his way along the sidewalk, where two young officers, his favorites, were waiting. Each was in riot gear. The stout one, bulldoggish, was trembling, but the other one, knife-thin, was smiling. The suspect lay in the gutter.

The thin one said, "We got him, Cap'n."

"I can see that. He alive?"

"No way."

"Which one of you hit him?"

The stout officer lowered his head and breathed into his shirt. The thin one said, "We both did."

Chick strolled to the gutter, but there was little to see. The body did not seem whole, only approximate. "What the hell did you use?"

"Shotguns, Cap'n."

Chick nodded slowly. "Spic, huh?"

"No, he was white."

"You sure?"

"I saw his face."

"I knew him," the stout officer said in a strained voice. "He worked at Snelling's Car Park. They called him Snooks."

"It must've fit," Chick said, stepping back to the officers. "You guys did good." He slapped the thin one on the shoulder and said to the stout one, "Buck up, for Christ's sake. You're a hero."

The trembling increased. "It's different than I thought, sir."

"Different than what?"

"Shooting rats."

Thirteen

Too many things were falling off the edges of Emma Goss's memory. She could not remember the name of the boy whose family had coerced him into asking her to the senior prom, who on that memorable night had sent a lovely corsage to the house but never showed up himself, the chore too much for him. She remembered the names of all her teachers in her senior year except the name of the one she had admired the most, a kindly man with tousled gray hair who had drawn her aside before graduation and wished her the very best in life. If he could see me now, she thought and leaned her face against a chill window to still the noise in her head.

She looked at her watch, the band loose on her wrist. There were too many long hours in the day now, and she was ready for bed by eight o'clock, sometimes seven, the bed a luxury now that she had it all to herself, her only locus of solitude, which Henry resented. He stayed up most of the night nursing his hand, banging about, hoping to wake her. Sometimes he did, but she merely turned over and went back to sleep, no longer fearing her dreams, in which she now always seemed a spectator, never a player, so that she woke untouched by any unpleasantness her subconscious might have conjured up.

She moved from the window to the bed, which she had left unmade. She began straightening it, her ear tuned to the kitchen, where Henry had begun to stir. She heard him shuffling about, knew he was looking for her, and stood perfectly still as if her heart stopped. All the beating was in her mind. He appeared in the doorway and held out his hand. "Stay out," she said.

"I just want you to look at it." He swayed into the room as if the motions of a boat dictated his step. "I think it's looking better, don't you?"

It looked neither better nor worse to her. She said, "Yes, it looks better."

"And I got less pain in my arm. That's a good sign, right?"

"Yes," she said. "Now get out."

He stared at her with a dismay that turned to anger when she resumed straightening the sheets. "You're not going to bed, are you, for Christ's sake? It's only six-thirty."

"I need my sleep."

"You get too much," he said, aggrieved. "I'm up all damn night. I don't know what to do with myself."

"That's not my problem."

"But you got problems, Mrs. Goss. You got bills piling up. I'd write the checks out for you, but I can't on account of my hand." When she said nothing, he hung his face out. "You don't care if they cut the power off? You going to sit here in the dark?" He raced his good hand through his shaggy hair. His jaws were stubbly. "We got no food in the house. We were supposed to go shopping, remember?"

"Go yourself," she said softly.

"You got to do something. The house is dirty, starting to stink, you know that?"

She fluffed a pillow.

"You don't give a shit, do you?" Something went out of him. "You don't care, why should I?"

She revealed no feelings. Her trick was in pretending she had none.

"My hand gets better, I'll leave," he said.

She turned her back on him. "You're never going to leave, I know that."

He swayed from the room with the same sailor step with which he had entered. She closed the door without clicking it shut, for she knew the sound would rouse him, possible incite him. He did not want to be shut out any more than he was. With a light and almost carefree step, she returned to the bed and gazed down at it, pretending it was smaller, not this bed at all but her childhood bed. She yearned for her pigtails, Girl Scout shoes, innocence. She wanted her coloring book, her cutout dolls, her bedroom with animals on the wallpaper and the sweetness of a cleaner air blowing in on her. She wanted her diary, every page pure. She wanted to split open her Donald Duck bank and rake her fingers through a wealth of pennies, some Indian heads, gifts from her grandfather, who had served in the Spanish-American War and was photographed on a horse. Henry called through the door.

"I'm going for pizza. You want some?"

"No," she said in a clear voice.

Undressing, she heard him back the car out of the garage and pictured him battling the wheel with one hand while protecting the other. In bed she nestled well under the covers and listened to a stiff breeze that mimicked the rush of her breathing, as if there were a connection. For a long while she did her best to remember the name of the tousle-haired teacher who had been so kind to her. It was on the tip of her tongue when she fell asleep and dreamed she was watching a man disrobe in a kind of bathhouse. He made a neat pile of the garments and then took off his legs, shook away his arms, and smiled. The head stays on, he told her. Queer dream. Senseless, she told herself while dreaming it, ridiculous, and woke up. Henry was staring down at her.

"The pain's come back," he said.

She paid no attention and drifted into another dream that made less sense than the first. The nicest part was knowing unequivocally that none of this was real, that should she choose she could easily float away. She woke again, gradually, her head turning. Henry had crawled into bed and lay against her. She pressed a foot against him, but he would not move. "You don't belong here," she said.

He hung his hand near her face and moaned, "Kiss it and make it better, Mrs. Goss."

"Then will you go?"

"Yes," he promised.

Barney Cole spent the afternoon with Arnold Ackerman in Boston, box seats in Fenway Park, a makeup game between the Sox and the Tigers. Five dollars rode on it. Cole had the Sox and lost, which he could not understand. "Clemens pitching, I should've won."

"He's won too many games," Arnold said, accepting the five as if it had been his from the first throw of the game. "Law of averages was pressing on him. It's like ragweed in August. You can't escape it."

Though the hard chairs hurt their haunches, they stayed seated while the crowds pushed toward the exits.

Crews were already on the field smoothing down torn turf, erasing every trace of the contest. Arnold wrinkled his brow from too much sun on his semibald head and loosened his lizard-skin belt: too many hot dogs from a vendor who had borne a startling resemblance to one of the Three Stooges, Moe.

"Looking out at the field, Barney, I remember all the times your father and I sat here, maybe even these same seats. A big game for us was when the Yankees came to town. Williams against DiMaggio, that's the way we saw it. Your father couldn't understand how I could root for the New York Italian over Williams. He thought it was perverse."

"Actually DiMaggio was from San Francisco."

"I'm talking about the team, Barney, not where the hell he was born."

"Excuse me."

"Not your fault. You don't know better. We took your mother to a couple of games, but she didn't enjoy herself, and to be truthful we didn't like having her there. It was like we had to entertain her. But they were close, your mother and father. It was no surprise she passed on so soon after he did."

"No surprise at all," Cole said, "but still a shock." They rose from their chairs, Arnold furling his souvenir program and then pausing to rub his legs. Cole said, "As I remember, you and my father never took me to a game."

"Course not. We didn't figure baseball was for kids."

They followed the last of the crowd out of the park and trekked across Kenmore Square to the lot where Cole had left the Cutlass. A fresh dent in the driver's door was impossible to miss, but Cole ignored it. He opened the door and unlatched Arnold's side.

"We should've taken my car," Arnold said. "I smelled oil all the way from Lawrence."

"Why didn't you say something?"

"Figured you knew." Arnold anchored himself down with a seat belt and lowered his window for air. Cole failed to start the engine with the first try but succeeded with the second. Arnold said, "You don't take care of a car. Your father didn't either."

The air in Kenmore Square was gritty. Arnold raised the window. On Storrow Drive the traffic was a river of noise. On the up-ramp to Interstate 93 Cole said, "There's something I never asked my father. I'd like to ask you, Arnold. Why did he put himself on the take? It wasn't like him."

"Don't judge him, Barney."

"I'm not. I'm just asking."

"It was expected of him," Arnold said flatly. "You know how Lawrence works. A few phantom jobs in a department, a modest kickback from a contractor, that's all considered legitimate. If your old man hadn't done it, no one would've trusted him. They'd have shunned him. And let's face it, he wasn't the sort to rock the boat. So he went along. That answer your question?"

Cole had an unsavory image of his father floating among city hall officials habited in dark overcoats collared with ratty strips of fake fur. "He wasn't very smart about it. Long after he quit taking, the state cops came in and got enough so the D.A. could've indicted."

"That's the irony, Barney. He was never greedy, never brought attention to himself. It was the flagrant guys the cops came after, and when those guys got caught they started finking on everybody. That's how your father got swept into it. If it wasn't for you getting help from Louise, he'd have died a broken man."

"I did what I had to."

"You were his son. What else could you do?"

"When I got married he bought me a house. I knew the money was dirty. I'm still living in it."

"That bothers you?"

"It didn't at the time."

"You had to take it. Otherwise you'd have made him feel lower than he already felt." Arnold dropped the window an inch and enjoyed the breeze, his eye on faster-moving cars that fishtailed into other lanes. "You work at it hard enough, Barney, there's always a way to justify everything you do."

"That's what bothers me the most, Arnold."

Arnold scooched down in his seat, the belt buckle riding up on him. "Do what I do, Barney. Act like the whole world is perfect." He closed his eyes. "Don't mind, do you? I'm not as young as I used to be."

Two or three minutes later Cole pressed down on the accelerator and switched lanes. He thought Arnold was asleep but soon felt a touch on his arm.

"Take your time getting me home, Barney. All I got waiting is a can of Chef Boyardee spaghetti."

Cole made himself a sandwich and plucked a bottle of dark German beer from the refrigerator. In the sun room he flicked on the small television set and, with his feet up, watched highlights of the Red Sox loss on the six o'clock news. When the camera panned the stands he looked for himself and Arnold, but the movement was too swift. During the weather report he thought he heard a car pull into the drive but moments later detected the sound of one puttering away. Then the telephone rang. Taking his bottle of beer with him, he answered it in the kitchen. The caller was Marge, working late, reminding him that he had an early court case in the morning. "Go home," he told her.

"Easy for you to say. A Mr. Cruickshank called, wouldn't tell me what he wanted, said he'd call back sometime."

"I'm sure he will. By the way, Marge, put yourself down for a ten-percent raise, effective next paycheck."

"What? Why?"

"You deserve it. After you do that, go home."

He finished his beer and set the bottle in the sink. He was peeling pages of the calendar, wondering when he and Kit Fletcher might coordinate a vacation, when the phone rang again. He picked it up with a smile, thinking it was Marge with something she had forgotten to tell him.

"It's me." The voice was Louise Baker's. "I'm back."

"I heard you were," he said. "Why?"

"My mother still needs me."

The reply did not entirely wash. Mrs. Leone had always struck him as an independent person even in times of calamity and tragedy. He said, "You're a good daughter."

"Family's important. Friends are too."

"You sound different."

"I am," she said. "I've come to a decision about the rest of my life, nothing I can tell you about on the phone, but I think you'll like it."

He guessed what it was and said, "Tired of working?"

"Yes, Barney. That's it exactly. Time I was the real lady of the manor. What do you think?"

"I think it's a wonderful idea."

"I thought you would. Now I want you to do me a favor—and don't argue, just do it. Go look out your front door, then come back and tell me what you see."

On his way he checked the time, for he wanted to

ANDREW COBURN

watch the network news at seven. Opening the door, he
saw nothing extraordinary until he shifted his gaze. Sitting in the driveway was a brand-new Cutlass Supreme
much like the one West Street Motors had briefly lent
him, except this one had a roof rack and fancier hubcaps.
He returned to the phone.

"Whose is it?"

"Yours, Barney. From me to you. A gift, an apology,
call it what you want, just don't refuse it."

"Are you crazy?"

She spoke passionately. "It's a token of what I owe
you, and I do owe you, Barney, I really do. You're always
there for me. You don't know what that means to me."

"The answer's no, Lou. Definitely no."

"You drive a junk, for God's sake. A man your age
should drive something better. So let me do this, OK?"

"No," he said with an excruciating feeling that there
was something more he should be doing, that there was
some significant precaution he should be taking against
her. The feeling haunted him.

She said, "Keep it for a few days. Drive it around, see
how it goes. If you still don't want it, I'll take it back. I
promise."

"I like my own car, Lou. When I want a new one, I'll
buy it myself."

"But you won't. You'll drive what you've got into the
ground. I know you, Barney. So do this for me."

"How do you think the feds will look at it? Use your
head, Lou."

"With you, Barney, it's my heart. Are you alone?"

"No," he lied.

"Can you get away?"

"Impossible."

"I understand," she said. "I'd never want to mess up your life. But keep the car, Barney. Please."

"No way," he said, but she had already rung off.

He went outside, a tremor of anger tripping his legs. The car in the drive glimmered in a fanciful way, as if breathing its own life. The windows were slightly lowered, and the driver's door opened with a touch, exuding in scent and polish the newness of the interior. He suffered throes of regret when his shoe sullied the paper mat shielding the real one. The seat was a woman's lap. He skimmed the heel of his hand down a slope of leather and experimentally flicked the ignition key into the first notch. Points of fire streaked across the digital panels like the spitting tongues of snakes. Ownership papers carrying his name lay beside him, along with a small vellum envelope, which he opened. The notepaper was scented, the script was Louise's. "You were my first." A lie, but so what? The car started up with all the force and none of the noise of a modern weapon. Then, with scarcely a nudge, it taxied toward the empty half of his garage.

Daisy Shea had a hundred dollars in his pocket, the price he'd gotten for the furniture in his minuscule office, twin file cabinets included. Depression had gripped him when he closed up the office for the last time, but later, downtown, a haircut and shoeshine made him feel right again. He began strolling Essex Street. It was a lovely afternoon, none nicer that he could remember, the sort of day that reinforced his theory that diseases in all stages were negotiable and his own sickness curable with a simple swallow of medicine, the trick being to find the right one.

Plate glass mirrored him and the growing crust of traffic beyond him. The hour was not as early as he would have liked, but nothing in life, he reasoned, was truly perfect. From a women's store lilac-eyed mannequins flirted with him. Pausing, he flirted back. His stomach felt fine, and his barbered white hair gave him, he mused, a distinguished look tainted only by the stain on his tie. Behind him an elderly Hispanic woman dropped a package, which delighted him, a chance to do a good deed, perform a service. He swooped it up with a flourish and was thanked in overwhelming Spanish. Several stores down, he went into Kap's and bought a tie.

At ten after five he was one of a handful in the dining room at Bishop's. A marvelous neatness marked the person and manner of his waitress, whose brown eyes were enormous. Her figure was dainty. As soon as she set down his drink, a double Cutty on the rocks, he felt awash in a tide of good cheer and fond memories. Here, more than two decades ago, family and friends had toasted him and Barney Cole, Lawrence's newest lawyers. Here, over lamb on a stick, Edith had mentioned that she was carrying their first child, which had hastened their marriage. Here he had entertained clients, pals, persons with wit, sportsmen with schemes, secretaries with sad stories, and always he had preempted the check, his pleasure, his nature. Those had been special years, the best, but the speed with which they had vanished astounded him.

At five-thirty the waitress asked whether he was ready to order. Yes, indeed, he told her, and made a show of examining the menu, which he knew by heart. His eyes strayed to her. She was too young, too hale, too alive, with everything ahead of her: heartache, bad luck, suspicious lumps, disappointments of the highest order. Why in the world would he envy her?

"I don't," he said aloud, surprising himself.

"Don't what?" she asked.

"I don't want French fries," he said rapidly, as if she had caught him in a struggle with his diet. "Bad stomach, you know." He reexamined the menu. "Prime rib sounds good. Rare. Very rare. They'll know. Tell them it's for Daisy." He lifted his Cutty glass, weightless in his grip. "And another of this."

At six o'clock many more tables were occupied, which pleased him though the lack of familiar faces disappointed him. The dinner crowd, unlike that at lunch, was mostly from out of town. He cut into a slab of beef that looked gory, as if it had just been plucked from the animal. He savored each bite while chewing carefully on tender teeth and wished now he had gotten the French fries. The waitress, busy at other tables, slipped over to his.

"Everything all right, sir?"

"Please, call me Daisy," he said with immense sympathy for her and a gladness for himself.

The place filled up by seven o'clock, with new arrivals congregating in the lobby or slipping downstairs to the lounge. The wine waiter, energetically busy, flitted from station to station. Daisy missed the ornate costume and tinkling accessories of the previous wine waiter, killed some five years ago in a car crash, but he was elated when he glimpsed the faraway faces of a couple of brother lawyers. Good old Herbie Schultz, a Suffolk grad to boot, with his wife, Carol, a lovely person. At another table blustery but softhearted Ignatius Piscitello, another Suffolk alum, with his wife, Suzanne, who was assistant superintendent of schools. Good God, there was State Senator Pat McGovern and her mother, Phyllis! He knew the whole family, cousins and all. This was his world. The world was right, his life was in sync, and his stomach was strong. His waitress returned.

"It's all perfect," he said.

"Enjoy," she said.

The lilt of her voice, the warmth of the scotch in his chest, the caressing sight of the familiar faces all served to uncork him. He began to cry.

The waitress, startled, said, "What's wrong, Daisy?"

"I'm happy," he said.

Abe Bashara, the restaurant's gentle doe-eyed owner, came over. "What's the matter?" he asked softly.

"He's happy," the waitress said.

"I am, Abe. I'm happier than I've been in years. I'm going to be waked from here, did you know that?"

Abe, without batting an eye said, "No, I didn't."

"Barney Cole should've mentioned it, surprised he didn't. You don't mind, do you?"

"Certainly not," Abe said.

"I've paid my dues."

"You have," Abe said, not mentioning the large uncollectable tab Daisy had run up over the years.

"I love Lawrence," he said through his tears. "I love the house where I was born. I love this restaurant. The whole city passes through it." His face was trembling, his stomach hurting.

Abe whispered to the waitress, "Tell my brother to call Barney Cole."

The sergeant rapped on the frosted glass of the open door and said, "Excuse me, Cap'n, but there's two guys looking to see you."

Chick Ryan glanced up from the newspaper spread out on his desk and tugged the creamy cuffs of his dress shirt a good inch below the sleeves of his fawn summer suit.

His braided captain's uniform, back from the dry cleaner, hung flat against the wall. He said, "Who are they?"

"I don't know, but if I was gonna guess I'd say feds."

"You've been wrong before."

"Bet I'm not this time."

Chick folded the newspaper and tossed it beneath his desk. He did not rise when the two men appeared, one fair and the other black. The door closed behind them. The fair one, Cruickshank, produced identification. "I'm impressed," Chick said.

"This is Agent Blue."

"No shit. Any relation to Agent Orange?" Chick guffawed. "Sorry. I couldn't help that." There were chairs, but he did not ask them to sit. "I might as well tell you, Blue, I've got racial prejudices, but I keep them pretty well hidden."

"That's all right," Blue said. "I have the same sickness."

"No cure, right?"

"None on the horizon."

Cruickshank said, "We tried to get hold of you once before, but you were out of town."

"Was I? When?"

"Must've been a week ago."

"That so?" Chick creaked back in his rotary chair. "Where'd I go?"

"That's your business, Captain. Of course if you want to tell us we'll listen."

Chick did not return Cruickshank's smile. "Why don't you guys tell me what you want, quit beating around the fucking bush?"

"We don't want anything, Captain. Unless you have something you think might interest us?"

"What would I have? You tell me."

"You're overreacting," Cruickshank said mildly. "This

is only a courtesy call to let you know we're in the area. This is an exciting little city you have here."

Chick regarded him with narrow eyes. "We have our ups and downs."

"That was a bit of drama the other night at the convenience store," Cruickshank went on. "Blue and I happened to catch the tail end of it. Glad you got your man."

"It was a clean shoot. I'm proud of my boys. Is that why you guys are here? You think they violated somebody's civil rights?"

"I didn't say that. Did you say that, Blue?"

Blue's gaze was on the uniform hanging against the wall. "I didn't say a word. I know my place."

"You guys are playing patty cake," Chick said, his face sharply alert. "What the hell do you want?"

"Relax, Captain." Cruickshank waved an assuring hand. "We're just nosing around. It's what we do best. Most of the stuff we come up with we don't even use. Just store it in the computer."

"What are you nosing around here for?"

"It's an interesting area. You got some heavy hitters here. That includes Tony Gardella's sister."

"I heard of *him*. He's dead. I don't know her."

"Lives in Andover."

"That's a different world," Chick said with disdain. "Andover, the birds tweet. Here, we only got pigeons. All they do is crap. Put that in your computer."

Blue said, "That's a nifty uniform hanging there. I bet you look good in it."

Cruickshank said, "I like his suit better. Custom-made, isn't it?"

"You only go this way once," Chick said, unfazed, unsmiling. His eyes swept over Cruickshank. "That suit you're wearing didn't come off a rack."

"True, Captain, but the difference is I have only one. I bet you have a closetful."

"That's a good bet. Go find somebody to take your action. You'll win."

"You think so?"

"I know so."

"You're pretty confident."

"I got nothing to hide."

There was a momentary silence as Cruickshank and Blue shared a look that harbored a smile. Blue shifted his weight from one lean leg to the other and said, "I had a uniform like that, I'd wear it."

"I had fingers like yours," Chick said, "I'd play basketball. Where the fuck did you get those fingers?"

"Africa." Blue held up a hand. "White women find them sexy."

The color rose faintly in Chick's face. Also his heart seemed to beat a little faster, as if a bit too much were bearing down on him. He had dealt with feds before, but never this intimately. Cruickshank said to him, "Another heavy hitter is Louise Baker. You probably know her as Leone."

This he had been expecting, and he let it roll off him. "Sure, I used to know her well. So what?"

"In fact, you used to work for her. I mean, a long time ago, right?"

"Where the hell did you come up with that?"

"Computer shoots out a lot of garbage," Cruickshank replied. "Forget I said it."

"I already have."

Cruickshank looked over at Blue. "I think we've taken enough of the captain's time, don't you? He's probably got a lot on his mind."

"I think enough's been said," Blue answered with a final glance at the uniform and a smile that revealed only the tips of his teeth. "He knows we're around if he needs our help."

Both agents turned to leave, and Chick came forward in his chair. "I know what you guys are doing."

Cruickshank swung easily around on his heels and appeared perplexed, an expression also appearing on Blue's face. Cruickshank said, "What are we doing, Captain?"

"You're trying to give me something to think about. Let me tell you something, I've got *nothing* to think about." Chick's color rose. Something in his mind twitched, warned him to say no more, but did not stop him. "You think you're telling me something, but I'm not buying. I don't care what it is."

Cruickshank glanced at Blue. "This is an occasion."

"It sure is," Blue replied from the door.

Chick glared at them. "What's the occasion?"

"You're a man without a worry in the world," Blue said with a smile showing all his teeth. "We've never met one before."

Barney Cole parked the car under the portico at Bishop's restaurant and hustled into the teeming lobby, where a voice sang out to him, "Over here, Barney." Daisy Shea waved his padded hand, which looked too large and floppy for its chicken wrist. He was sitting tentatively on a cushioned bench, with Abe Bashara standing protectively near him. Cole eased his way to them, and Daisy said, "Everybody comes in, they speak to Abe. God, Barney, the whole world knows him."

"I'm not surprised," Cole said, and, sotto voce, thanked Abe, who discreetly melted away. Cole placed a hand on Daisy's shoulder. "How are you doing?"

"I had a little spell, but I'm better now."

"Can you stand?"

"In a minute. I don't want to take things too fast."
Daisy flung his face up. "You're tall, Barney. I never realized how tall you are. Sit down."

Cole sat beside him, and together they viewed the eager and expectant faces of the crowd, the happy young
man whose hand grazed the seat of his girlfriend's dress,
the chattering Japanese businessmen in identical suits,
the array of wives with pearls and poolside tans, the well-
dressed aging woman with the beauty-parlor hair who
unexpectedly broke from the man beside her and came
to Cole with a smile.

"We seem to meet only here," she said, her voice and
face instantly familiar to him, but her name eluding him.
"You forgot it the last time too," she said divining his difficulty as he bounced to his feet.

"You're wrong," he said, and, nudging the name off the
tip of his tongue, introduced her to Daisy, who had not
yet mustered the energy to rise but made a polite attempt.

"Yes, and I remember you," she said with no break in
her smile, which she quickly returned to Cole. "I believe
I told you my daughter graduated from Merrimack. Now
she's got a job in Boston. Honeywell Bull."

"That's wonderful," Cole said.

"My oldest boy's at Merrimack," Daisy interjected, but
she did not hear him.

"And I have a friend now," she said to Cole in a tone
that told him that more than friendship was at stake.
"My daughter can't believe it. Nor can I. You were right,
Mr. Cole, things do, sometimes, have a way of working
out." She gave Cole's hand an awkward squeeze. "I'd better scoot back before he gets too jealous."

She slid away as if on a high school dance floor, a dee-
jay providing the music. Daisy, tugging Cole's sleeve,

said, "What did she mean she remembered me? I don't know her from Adam."

"But everybody knows you," Cole said.

The crowd thickened around them, and Daisy, breathing audibly, yielded himself up from the bench. Cole grabbed his arm. "Little shaky on my feet," Daisy said, "but I'll make it." Cole made a path, and together they slipped carefully through the double set of doors and halted just beyond the outer ones. The night air was a balm. The starry sky, more spectacular than usual, seemed to have drawn closer to the city. A calm worked its way into Daisy's flushed features and settled in his eyes. Pointing, he said, "Is that Venus?"

"I don't know."

"I don't either, but they tell me there's an open bar in Heaven. You think that's true?"

Cole smiled unwillingly. "Is that your idea of the place?"

"No, Barney. My idea of heaven is starting all over again and doing everything right this time." He shook his head with regret. "I had a talent, but I slathered it. Christ, you and I, Barney, we could've built a big practice together, but I was in the bag too much, I don't deny it. You were right to kick me out."

"I didn't want to."

"I'm not whining. You gave me a hundred chances. But if you're feeling guilty, I'll absolve you, the least I can do."

Cole angled him out of the way of groups of people leaving and arriving. Cole's eyes followed the departure of a woman with a luxuriant mane of hair and a young unsurpassable figure. Daisy peered at two priests descending the stone steps.

"I'm a good Catholic, Barney. I confess everything.

Last time I went, Father Flaherty asked me if it was the same old stuff, and I said yes, and he saved time by just giving me the penance. Everything's quicker today, like at McDonald's."

Cole stared at him.

"I'm sober, Barney, in case you're wondering. It's my stomach. It's always my stomach."

Cole said, "It's time you went home. Edith will be worried."

"Look at me, Barney. Look me straight in the eye and tell me the truth. You think Edith loves me?"

"I know she does."

"What about my kids?"

"Without question."

"Then that's all that's important," he said, and began descending the steps, Cole trailing him. At the bottom he wheeled around and said, "Will you look where some jerk parked his car! It's blocking everything. You oughta run back in and tell Abe."

"No need."

Daisy placed his hands on his hips and admired it. "Brand-new Cutlass Supreme. How much do those go for? No, don't tell me. It'll hurt my stomach." He walked around to the front of it, with Cole following. "All my life, I've never had a new car, always had to buy iron." He tapped the shiny hood with his fingers. "I was twenty years younger, you know what I'd do? I'd steal it."

"You don't have to," Cole said, and dangled keys in front of him. "It's yours."

A secretary at Pullman & Gates typed out the press release announcing attorney Katherine Fletcher's elevation to senior partner. In her vast new office Kit contemplated the Pollock on the wall and decided to keep it. The vase of long-stemmed roses on her desk was from Chandler Gates. At seven o'clock, in celebration, he took her to Maison Robert, where they dined sumptuously and killed a two-hundred-dollar bottle of wine. Former mayor Kevin White stopped by their table, as did a woman editor from Houghton Mifflin who had edited a biography of Chandler's grandfather. At ten o'clock Chandler accompanied Kit to the harborside tower where she lived, rode the elevator with her to the upper reaches, and invited himself in for a nightcap.

Her place was minimally but aesthetically furnished and had much window space overlooking the waters of the harbor, whose daytime murk shifted into an iridescent magic under starlight. She served Chandler a brandy, none for herself, which disappointed him. He did, however, coax her to a place beside him on the sofa. In a tone that was a shade accusatory, he said, "You won't be in tomorrow."

"I'm afraid not."

"Duty calls?"

"If you want to call it that."

Opening his gray pinstripe knees, he took a swallow of brandy and placed the snifter on a low lacquered table. Usually he wore a regimental necktie, but tonight he sported an absurd little bow tie under his vulpine face. He took her hand, which she withdrew when he began spreading her fingers.

"Behave," she said, their eyes engaging.

"I was hoping you'd sit on my lap," he murmured, closing his knees.

"I'm too big a girl for that."

He retrieved his snifter and stared at the amber light it cast on the silk cuff of his shirt. His wrist was no wider than hers. "You're not thinking of marrying this fellow of yours, are you?"

"It's a possibility," she said.

"I never thought I'd hear you say that."

"I didn't say it was likely, just a possibility that I might want my life to be more than a yellow legal pad."

"Ah, but think about it for a minute," he said, his voice carving a warm place for itself in front of her face. "A small-time lawyer. He'd be out of his element in your life."

"You've never met him."

"I'd be happy to."

"You wouldn't like him."

"See what I mean?" he said triumphantly.

"That's too subjective an argument, Chandler, and specious to boot." She shored up her smile before going on. "What would you do if I did marry him?"

"I wouldn't do anything. But I'd be very disappointed."

"You wouldn't take away my promotion, would you?"

He moistened his lips with brandy. "Certainly not. A deal's a deal."

"That's reassuring."

"You should trust me more."

"That's not always easy," she said.

"But you can handle any situation," he said, placing his hand on her knee. "You're a cool customer. It's what I've always admired about you."

His hand, as if it could shape her future more than it already had, moved with force into her skirts. She stood up. "It's getting late, Chandler."

"Yes, I know." He raised up the empty snifter. "Another one, please."

"That wouldn't be wise."

"Don't be so sure." He rose slowly, his eyes stretching

over her. "When I drink too much, I can't get it up. That would suit you, no?"

She took the glass. "I'll get you another."

When she returned, she saw that he had slipped off his jacket and shoes and was padding about on his black-stockinged feet, inspecting potted plants, pictures on the wall, though every item in the room was familiar to him. The Japanese vase that adorned a corner was a gift from him.

"Don't settle in," she said. The fresh brandy she gave him was a small one. Though at the moment his smile was merely mischievous, she had on occasion watched him drink himself into a condition of ugliness.

He pointed. "The vase would look much better somewhere near the windows."

"Yes, you're right," she agreed. "My mistake."

"You don't make many." His eyes went cruel only for a second. The he gazed through a wide window at the pulsing red signals of a jetliner sailing into Logan. Turning, he said, "Yes, it is late. Would you mind terribly if I stayed the night? On the sofa, of course."

"Your wife," she reminded him.

"Darling, she's at the Cape."

Kit tipped her head. "She has a nice life."

"She adores it," he said, sipping. "And I adore mine. I also adore you."

He stepped toward her, but she kept him at bay, his drink between them. Without his shoes, he was shorter than she, which was the reason he immediately went up on his toes. Standing that way, his pointed jaw raised, his feminine hands clutching the snifter, he looked like a small public monument.

"May I tell you a secret?" he asked. "It may embarrass you."

"Perhaps I'd better not take the chance."

"When I pleasure myself, it's always with you in my mind."

"That's nice to know," she said.

"You mean it?"

"Yes. I'm flattered."

"May I stay?"

"No," she said. "I wouldn't want you to stain my sofa."

After he tossed off the last of his brandy, she prodded him back into his jacket and placed his shoes at his slender feet, which were as shapely as a ballet dancer's, the toes straining the silk of his hose. He wanted help putting on his shoes, and to speed him along she obliged. While she tied the laces, he stroked her hair. "I deserve more than this," he said with an edge, but before he could act she was on her feet, maneuvering him along. At the door, he said, "What if I were not who I am? What if I'd had a different grandfather? Would you have ever looked at me?"

She leaned toward him, kissed his cheek, and whispered, "Never put that question to your wife, Chandler." Then she eased him out the door.

The night turned muggy in the small hours, and the dawn broke watery and shimmered with impending heat. Emma Goss slept badly, rose from clammy sheets, and peeked into the front room, where Henry Witlo lay without covers on the couch, sleeping with his mouth open as if dead. She withdrew, hoping he would sleep late, but he began banging about while she was in the bathroom and was waiting to get in when she came out. He said, "It's going to be a hot one, Mrs. Goss. I heard it on the TV." She tried to edge by him, but he stayed firm. "I slept pretty good last night . . . and I didn't bother you, did I?"

She said, "Go brush your teeth."

She made coffee, enough for both of them, and carried her cup outside to the back lawn, where she settled in an aluminum chair, disturbing a finch in the birdbath. The morning had a sparkle unlike that of any other morning of the year, the scent of green at its freshest, its burning best. Her eye lit on flares of scarlet lilies, simmering balls of matricaria, flashes of butter daisies, all planted by Harold in his prime, some now struggling with weeds. Bending forward, she pulled a few. Henry called from the window, but she did not reply. Over in the Whipples' yard a mother robin noisily fought back a squirrel that had trespassed too near her nest. Henry came out favoring an arm.

"I'm going for groceries," he said. He had slicked back his long yellow hair but had not shaved. "You want anything special?"

"No," she said.

He rattled the keys to the Plymouth. "I thought I might get some strawberries so we can have a shortcake."

"Not for me," she said.

"How about something cold to drink? What do you like best?"

"Anything," she said.

He shuffled off in Harold's loafers, which had been resoled once and reheeled twice. Emma plucked a few more weeds before sitting back with her coffee to watch the Plymouth roll out of the garage. "He's driving your car, your baby," she said to Harold as if he were not dead but just offstage and not quite ready to speak his lines. "He's not doing it with my permission, so it must be with yours," she said, feeling the growing heat. When a muggy breeze licked over her, she drew her dress above her knees and examined her legs under a critical eye. They were not at all bad-looking. She should never have been ashamed of them. "All of those ocean vacations, I never wore a bathing suit," she said. "You shouldn't have let me be such a fool, Harold. But it pleased you that I was, made you feel safer."

The sun gushed golden through the young trees in the Whipples' yard and gilded the bordering shrubbery. Mrs. Whipple appeared on the back step in a sleeveless jersey and bright shorts. Stretching her neck, she gazed over at Emma, who pretended not to see her, a fruitless ploy.

"You won't be sitting there long, Mrs. Goss. The weatherman says nineties."

Emma did not lower her dress. She was not ashamed. With little difficulty, she visualized herself taking a place on the beach in a one-piece bathing suit.

"How's that nephew of yours?" Mrs. Whipple called out.

"He's gone grocery shopping," Emma said.

"You're a lucky woman, Mrs. Goss. I wish I had a nephew like that."

Speaking into the sunshine in a low voice, Emma said, "Did you hear her, Harold? I'm a lucky woman."

When the heat threatened to clamp her down, she dumped out the remains of her coffee and shifted the chair into the shade, from which she watched a monarch bouncing between the golden clusters of daisies. She closed her eyes and dozed off as the heat sneaked up on her. She woke when she heard the Plymouth rumble into the garage. Carrying one bag at a time in his good arm, he made several trips through the breezeway into the kitchen. On his last trip, he smiled out at her. She smiled back bitterly and murmured, "You're in cahoots with him, aren't you, Harold?"

Resettling herself, she again shut her eyes. Despite

ANDREW COBURN

Henry's banging about in the kitchen, all his noisy movements audible through the screen of the window, she drifted back to sleep. She slept through the revving of a motorcycle across the street, the honking of a taxi a few houses away, and the insistent bell of a Good Humor truck. She stirred when the shade she was in vanished and the sun threatened to cook her. Henry hovered over her.

"You ought to come in," he said.

She needed help from his good hand to get up. Her hair curled against the wet of her brow, her dress clung. "I'm all right," she said, and after a few seconds she was.

"Cool in the house," he said, and she followed him in. He had put away the groceries, loaded the dishwasher, and cleaned the kitchen, which smelled of Lestoil and ammonia. He smiled proudly. "Looks nice, huh? I'm going to clean one room at a time so the house will be like it used to. It was looking like a pigpen, Mrs. Goss. Half my fault, maybe more."

"Yes," she said, "maybe more."

He was staring at her. "You've still got those circles," he said suddenly, "but, I'm not kidding, you look younger every day." He sprang back for a better perspective. All her underwear was in the wash, and she was wearing nothing under her dress, which was still adhering to her damp skin. "My God, you're beautiful."

She said, not to him, "I could have been."

He was on her heels when she went into the bathroom to freshen up. He forced her to the mirror and rammed his hip against hers. "You don't believe me, look at us! You're getting younger, I'm getting older. Not fair, Mrs. Goss, but that's the way it is. In the supermarket I felt like a bum, people gawking at me." He stripped off his T-shirt, loosened the top of his jeans to relieve pressure, and snatched up an aerosol can missing its cap. "Shave me," he said, foaming his face.

The razor was Harold's, the blade double-edged, the last in the packet. She ran it under hot water and seemed resigned to the job until Henry plunked himself down on the closed toilet seat and lifted his face, hanging it out sacrificially. "Come on," he said. "I'm not afraid."

She made a razor road into the foam, taking away some of his hairline and more of it when he touched her knee. When his hand ventured higher, she cut him. Blood stained the foam like strawberries in cream. When he began raising her dress inches at a time, she cut him again. And again. He never flinched. "You can't hurt me, Mrs. Goss. Women have tried, but they can't do it." He caressed a sprawl of bared flesh. "And never fight a man who's got nothing to lose," he said, and drew her over his lap.

Barney Cole, planning to leave the office early, still had a couple of phone calls to make. The first was to the Andover Inn, a dinner reservation for two. The second was to a woman who had brought an indecent assault charge against her boss for goosing her as she was serving him coffee, which she had promptly thrown in his face. He had filed a countersuit. Cole said, "He wants to settle."

"How much?"

"I got him up to five thousand," Cole said, and she laughed. "Do you want money or revenge?" he asked.

"I want both," she said with steel in her voice. "Tell him to double it."

Cole smiled. "I thought that's what you'd say. He's thinking about it."

When he hung up, Marge came in with an overdue

bill to a client. "Should I just resubmit it," Marge asked, "or give her a call?"

Cole looked at it. "This isn't like her," he said. "Let me call her. I'll try to be subtle so she won't die of embarrassment."

He tapped out the number and began clearing his desk while waiting for an answer. A pen dropped to the floor. As he leaned over to retrieve it a man's voice came on the line, surprising him. "Is this Mrs. Goss's residence?" he asked.

"Yes, it is."

"Who is this?" he asked, for the voice was familiar in a haunting way.

"Her nephew. Who's this?"

Cole sat erect. "What the hell are you doing there, Henry?"

There was a short silence, and then Henry said, "I thought it was you, Mr. Cole, but I wasn't sure. I'm doing odd jobs for Mrs. Goss, like I did for you. She's a real nice lady."

"Let me speak to her."

"She can't come to the phone right now. She was out in the sun and the heat got her."

Cole shot to his feet. "I'm coming over!"

FOURTEEN

Henry Witlo swung open the front door and gave Barney Cole a chill. Gory bits of toilet tissue hung from his face. When he smiled, a thread of blood unraveled at the corner of his mouth. His whole head seemed uneven until Cole realized that one of the sideburns was gone. "I hurt my hand," Henry said, and exhibited the dark deep wound in the palm. The wound looked both fresh and old at the same time. "I sliced it on glass fixing something for Mrs. Goss," he said with an air of martyrdom. "I don't think it's healing right, do you?"

"I'm not a doctor, Henry." Overhead, birds were piping in the heat, their notes shrill like warnings. "What happened to your face?"

"Shaving with my left hand—a hard thing to do, Mr. Cole. I wouldn't advise it for everybody."

"Are you going to let me in?"

"Sure." He jerked to one side, waited, and then closed the door after Cole. "But like I told you, she's not feeling good. If you don't have to disturb her, it'd be better you don't." He smiled again. "Something you want to know, maybe I can tell you."

Cole said, "You're bleeding at the mouth."

"Yeah, I can feel it. Guess I've sprung a leak."

"Why did you say you were her nephew?"

"She treats me like one."

"I don't think I understand, Henry."

"I don't think you should try, Mr. Cole. No offense."

Cole strained his eyes for a deeper look into the house, for clues of mayhem. "Do you work anywhere else or just here?"

"Just here."

"I want to see Mrs. Goss."

"If you think you should, OK," Henry said. "This way, Mr. Cole."

Cole hesitated, his head fuming with a fearsome image of a deathblow, of his own body lying limp on the floor. "No, after you," he said and followed Henry into the kitchen, where for a split second he did not recognize the woman sitting at the far end of the table. Her cinnamon hair was brushed back hard, her violet eyes were circled, and her face, slimmer than he remembered, had a scrubbed look, as if a layer of skin had been removed. He pegged her smile. "How are you, Mrs. Goss?"

"Pretty good." Her voice was dull. Her head tilted out of a nondescript housedress that was too loose for her. He looked for marks on her and saw none. "Is there something I didn't sign?" she asked.

"No," he said, still scrutinizing her. "I just stopped by to see how you are."

A folded newspaper lay on the table. She fumbled with it. "Would you like a cold drink?"

"Maybe he'd like some of those fresh strawberries we

got," Henry said, drawing closer to Cole. "We got all the fixings for a shortcake."

Cole stood still, his eyes planted on Mrs. Goss. "I understand Henry's doing odd jobs for you."

Her answer came slowly. "He does little things."

"Not so little," Henry protested, experimenting with his posture, loose-limbed and unconcerned in one pose, commanding in another. "Remember how I got cut?"

"He hasn't fixed the screens yet."

"I told you, Mrs. Goss, they can't be fixed. They got to be replaced. She's talking about the breezeway, Mr. Cole. We had some vandalism."

"Did you report it?" Cole asked.

"I wanted to, Mr. Cole, but she said no. That's the way she is. Doesn't like to cause a fuss."

Cole's eyes were flitting from one to the other. He said to Henry, "Where are you living now?"

"Here."

Cole peered at Mrs. Goss, whose face took on a faint blush. "It's temporary," she said.

"Is there anything you'd like to tell me?" Cole asked, stepping nearer, leaving Henry behind him.

"I can't think of anything," she said as if the effort exhausted her. She drew the newspaper closer to her.

"Would you prefer to talk to me alone?" he asked.

"You want me to leave, I'll leave," Henry said helpfully. "I got work to do anyway."

Mrs. Goss shook her head wearily, as if choosing between the lesser of discomforts. Cole, leaning toward her, had the distinct impression that she was scattered and unable or unwilling to pull the pieces back together. When he reached for her hand, she withdrew it. "Things aren't the same with Harold gone," she said. "You understand."

Henry walked him to the door, more of a strut now in Henry's stride, though his right shoulder listed. Cole dropped easily back as Henry opened the door, letting in heat and sound from the street. "Heat doesn't bother me like it does her, Mr. Cole. I got used to it in Nam." Children scampered by on the sidewalk. "You're welcome back, you know. Anytime."

Cole lingered. "Nothing bothers you, does it, Henry?"

"I don't know what you mean."

"You prey on people. That's unforgivable."

"Make you feel better, Mr. Cole, send a policeman over. I got nothing to hide." The voice was assured and somewhat aggressive. "Lot of people live together now for different reasons. Mrs. Goss needs a man, I need a home. It works. There's nothing more to it than that."

Cole's eyes smarted from looking at him so hard. "Is it that simple?"

"The woman likes me, no surprise, lot of women do." Henry leaned forward confidentially. "Want to hear the kicker, Mr. Cole? I like her. What do you think of that?"

Cole stepped out into the heat and glanced back a last time. "You'd better do something about your face."

"It'll heal."

"How about your hand? It looks infected."

Henry, with effort, turned over his palm and examined it. "That's the only thing that worries me."

"Pretend you're in Nam, no medics available."

"That's what I do, Mr. Cole, when I can't sleep."

John Rozzi was summoned to the Springfield police station for questioning. While being escorted to an interrogation room, he noticed two well-groomed men, one black, standing near a desk, and guessed right away that they were either state or federal, certainly not local. He ignored them and they ignored him. The detective in the interrogation room was bald and had a plump jovial face that looked as if it might easily be baked and served with the tongue out. He said, "Sit down, John. Make yourself at home."

John sat at a small table, and the detective sat away from it. A small two-way mirror was in one of the walls, and John stared at it lazily, without concern. He said, "Who are those two guys I saw—feds?"

"Could be, John."

He jerked a thumb at the mirror. "Where are they now—there?"

"I wouldn't discount it."

For nearly a half hour the detective questioned John on the disappearance of his friend Sal Botello. The air conditioner was operating only at half speed, and both men were sweating. John loosened his necktie and finally removed his jacket. The detective ran a pudgy finger inside the throat of his collared polo shirt. The blunt points of the collar stood straight up. John said, "How about some water?"

"You don't want any water. Sweating's good for us. You and me, we'll lose some weight." The detective sat back with his knees spread, the top of his fly unzipped. "So you got no idea where Sal is?"

"I'm not his keeper."

"But you're his pal."

"I know him."

"Know him, or *knew* him?"

"What's that supposed to mean?"

"We think he's dead."

John laughed in a kind of grunt. "Sal ain't around, it's

because he don't want to be. Check Atlantic City. Vegas. Check the golf course at Palm Springs. He ain't there, he's somewhere else, probably with a broad."

"What broad? Anybody I know?"

"He's got all kinds of broads. The guy spends four-fifths of his time pumping."

"Yeah, Sal had a good life. You and me, John, we're lucky we can find our socks in the morning. We got too much in common. Have you noticed, we both got pig noses."

John said, "Yeah, I noticed."

"Me, I'm never going to make sergeant. Years ago I didn't make the right moves, politically speaking. Guys give me good advice, I don't take it. Shit comes flying my way, I don't know enough to duck."

"You got an interesting life history," John said.

"You too, John. We're two pigs in a pod."

"Peas is the expression."

"Peas is what we got for brains." The detective scratched the flab of his upper arm. "But you were right about those two guys. They're feds. They're after big people, but the kind of net they use scoops up the little ones too. Know what I'm saying, John?"

"I got a little brain. What are you saying?"

"I'm giving you good advice. You talk nice to these guys, maybe you can cut a deal."

"I'd rather cut my mother up, eat her for supper," John said.

The detective hefted himself out of his chair and tugged at his polo shirt, which had risen over his paunch. "Better get yourself a lot of napkins, John."

John stayed seated, his gaze shifting to the mirror and then back to the detective. "That it?"

"That's it," the detective said in a way that seemed to

tighten the air between them. "You change your mind, it ain't too late, come back and see me."

John's car was parked a block from the station. Before climbing in, he stripped off his tie and jacket and glanced around. After sealing the windows and flicking on the air conditioner, he eased into traffic with an eye glued to the rearview. He drove through city streets for a good twenty minutes, making random turns, timing traffic signals and shooting through them. When satisfied that no one was on his tail, he sped to a gasoline station in a derelict neighborhood. The mechanic, a monkey of a man with dirt on his nose, hoisted the car on a lift and checked it for a tracking device.

"It's clean, John," the man pronounced, lowering the lift.

"Good," John said. "Gimme gas."

As the man filled the tank, John switched the license plate and breathed deeply. He enjoyed the red reek of gasoline as much as he savored the aroma of his mother's tomato sauce. The man racked up the hose, wiped his hands on his coveralls, and said, "That'll be twelve-fifty." John paid him with a fifty-dollar bill, no change expected, and climbed back into his car. "Going on a little trip, John?"

John looked out at him. "What did you say?"

"I didn't say nothing," the man said, and quickly closed the door for him.

Louise Baker and Chick Ryan met at Memorial Hall Library in Andover. Louise arrived first, picked up a magazine, and sat at a corner reading table, under which she placed a briefcase. It was a time of day when few other tables were taken. Chick arrived minutes later, hairy arms bulging out of a yellow jersey, sunglasses hooked to the breast pocket. He sat across from her, dropping his elbows on the table. The chunk of gray in his hair stood out like a block of granite. "I was just a little worried," he said with a smile. "I hadn't heard from you for so long, I was afraid you were holding out on me."

"Foolish fear," she said.

"I agree." They were keeping their voices low, and Chick leaned forward on his elbows to hear better. He said, "Is that it under the table?"

"That's it," she said. "Before you take it we've got more business to do."

His eyes glittered. "More money?"

"No, just more business." Her voice was strangely flat, though there was heat in her heart, a vibration in her chest. "I know it was you who set me up," she said.

Chick's jaw dropped slightly. Then a smile took up too much of his face. "You're crazy."

"You want to argue?"

Each went silent as a patron of the library, an elderly man with dimples and a book in his hand, approached a nearby table and then suddenly, because of a look Chick gave him, veered off to a cushioned chair much farther away. The silence grew as Chick seemed to mull much over and come to a decision. The lines in his brow were deep and ugly, as if he had dug them himself. He said, "That slob Rozzi been telling you stories?"

"I figured it out for myself. Wasn't hard."

He slid back a little on his elbows. "What are you going to do about it?"

"Nothing, Chick." She turned a page of her magazine and scanned the pictures. "You're lucking out for a couple of reasons. The first is I'm getting out of the business, retiring." She lifted her eyes. "That means you're ceasing to be a factor in my life."

"All's forgiven, I'm supposed to believe that?"

"Nothing's forgiven," she said in a voice free of emotion. "And you can believe what you want."

He viewed her closely with wondering eyes. "What's the other reason?"

"A negligible one. For better or worse, you're part of my childhood. It wasn't a particularly great one, but it's the only one I've got."

He grinned slowly. "I'm sitting here, I'm supposed to be scared, right?"

"No, Chick, what you're supposed to be is smart. You're getting a break from me; I don't think you even know it."

"Is that what I'm getting?"

"Depends on you."

Raising an elbow, he kneaded the back of his neck and then gave the end of his nose a pull. "Like they say in the movies, Lou, it wasn't personal. Sal made an offer I couldn't refuse."

"Said he'd bring you into the business, right?"

"It was an offer you never made."

"With reason," she said. "I never trusted you."

"But you trusted Sal."

"I paid the price, didn't I?"

They fell silent again when a library worker, a pretty blond woman with a flimsy authoritative air ready to blow away, returned newspapers to their rightful places on a rack. Louise peeled the magazine to a color spread of summer finery worn by high-hipped fashion models. Chick whispered, "Nice to know I'm off the hook."

"You're not off it yet," she whispered back, admiring the cut and fall of a dinner gown. "I want the hitter."

The blond woman finished racking the newspapers, cast a curious eye in their direction, and melted away. Chick said, "What are you talking about?"

"The one who put the hole in me. Your boy. Don't tell me it wasn't."

He shifted restlessly in his chair, resettling his elbows. "I don't get it. You don't want me, but you want him. He's a Puerto Rican, a punk. What I'm saying is he's a nothing."

"He's the one who came at me with a gun in his hand. He's the one I see when I can't sleep. I don't want him walking around anymore."

"You're serious," he said, and did not wait for a response. After glancing quickly around, he lowered his head and toughened his voice. "What if I don't want to do it? You're asking for a freebie on this one, am I right?"

"You're absolutely right," she said. "And if you don't do it, all bets are off."

His grin was instantaneous. "You're in luck, Lou. The punk's name is Rafael. After he screwed up the job, he blew town, but I heard he's back. So there's no problem. The truth is I was going to do him anyway."

"I thought as much," she said.

"I should've figured that. You know there are feds in town. They ever squeeze him, they get me. They get me, they get you. We don't want that to happen, do we?"

She said coldly, "When are you going to do it?"

"Soon."

She said, "I want to be there."

Two adolescent girls came in and sat down at a nearby table, dropping down books. Their heads together, they began whispering and giggling. Louise closed the magazine, swished her hair back, and with her foot nudged the briefcase between Chick's knees. He reached down and drew it into his lap. "This thing going to explode on me when I get home?"

"If you're worried, open it now," she said.

He did, just enough to peek in at the money.

* * *

Barney Cole and Kit Fletcher dined at the Andover Inn in celebration of her promotion, which came as a surprise to Cole. Over shallow bowls of spicy soup he asked why she had not warned him. "I didn't want to jinx it," she said. "Besides, it came as a sort of surprise to me."

"You must've settled the *Globe* case for a big amount."

"I settled it, but not for money."

"You got a retraction."

"Only an agreement that the *Globe* wouldn't press for their legal expenses, which my client thinks is a victory."

Cole looked at her askance. "You never had a case."

"Only my client's ego."

"So how did you get the promotion?" he asked. "You threaten to quit?"

"If I had done that, I'd have been out on my fancy bottom. No, Barney. My boss gave me a push. He likes me. He likes me very much."

"Should I be jealous?"

"Why not?" she said, "He is of you."

Cole frowned.

"I'm only joking." She smiled warmly. "If I didn't have you in my life, I'd go crazy, believe me."

"With my clients," he said, "I believe everything they say, then wait to be deceived. How about yourself?"

"I'm a little different."

Between their salads and their entrees, people Cole knew came into the dining room, and he proudly introduced them to Kit. There were Jim Doherty, who was the town moderator, and his wife, who was in real estate. Moments later there were Bill Dalton and his wife. Bill was a lawyer and a former selectman. Then came the Tuckers. Mike was in publishing, and Sue, whose big-boned beauty rivaled Kit's, was a state representative.

The two women chatted briefly, each oblivious of the attention they drew.

Later Kit said, "I have the distinct impression you're showing me off. Am I a prize?"

"You make my stock go up," Cole said.

Her knee touched his under the table. "I want to be valuable to you."

He said, "Have you ever considered kissing my ear in public?"

The table was small. Holding on to her wineglass, she leaned over and did it. "Your stock just soared."

Their dinner was veal Oscar, which they ate leisurely over a second bottle of wine. Dessert was cake soaked in brandy, topped with exotic nuts and dabbed with whipped cream. Kit ate hers and most of his. Then they each had Irish coffee. She gazed at him through her lashes. "You don't mind living high, do you?"

"Occasionally," he said. "Then it's nice to float back down to earth."

She ran a foot up his calf. "I'm a little tight."

"I guessed."

"I could give you trouble tonight," she said suggestively.

"Perfectly all right. I'm a troubleshooter."

She squinted. "You're the only man whose bad jokes I laugh at. It must be love."

They stepped out of the inn a little after eleven. The heat of the day had carried into the night, and the air was rich with dark grass smells. She tossed her hair loose and took his arm. They kissed in the parking lot and again in the car. She pressed fingers against his cheek. "Do I want too much, Barney, or do you want too little?"

"How should I interpret that?"

"It's something we can talk about in bed. I might even forget the question."

"Good," he said, "because I probably don't have an answer."

She slumped her blond head against his shoulder as they drove home and was slow to get out when he pulled into the garage next to her car. She climbed out, but instead of proceeding into the house, she wandered out to the driveway and listened to the night chant of a bird. Bugs beat their way to her through the dark. Cole called to her from the garage.

"The phone's ringing."

"Answer it."

"What if it's for you?"

"I'm asleep. Tell my boss I'm in your arms."

The night heat was defiant. She let it bathe her. She batted mosquitoes from her hair and in the secrecy of the dark listened to the chant of the bird, the ring of peepers, the whistle of crickets, gather into a single summer sound. The sky, afire with stars, seemed grander and greater than ever, as if it too had a season for growing lush. When the mosquitoes became too much, she made her way through the garage into the house.

Cole, his head lowered, was on the phone in the seldom-used family room, where the clock on the wall was an hour off. She moved near him, but his voice was too soft for her to distinguish words. After standing still for a number of moments, she said, "Who is it?"

He whispered quickly, "My friend."

She threw out her hand. "Let me talk to her."

The heat lessened in the early hours of the morning but returned in force with the rising sun. Henry shaved the lawn, back and front, with Harold's Toro mower, maneuvering it with one hand. The sun roasted his bare back. Mrs. Whipple peeked through the shrubbery with a mind for conversation, but the roar of the mower allowed her only a long, curious look. Without meaning to, Henry obliterated an abundance of butter daisies glowing from a great clump of foliage and, in another miscarried effort, shredded a burst of marigolds. From some mysterious will, stacks of lilies seemed to retreat out of harm's way. When he finished, he slaked his thirst at the outside spigot, though the water had a nasty taste, full of treatment. He went into the house smelling of sweat and grass and the perfume of flowers.

Emma Goss was at the kitchen table reading yesterday's newspaper and glanced up at him as she might have done with Harold coming in from the yard or the garage. "Don't mess up the bathroom," she said.

He smiled, the cuts in his face brightly scabbed. "You ought to look out the window, see what a good job I did. I was a kid, I used to cut ten lawns a week. I had a regular route."

"Where did you go wrong?" she said quietly, and turned her attention to an article about next week's Fourth of July celebration at the Lawrence High School stadium, an evening of festivities and fireworks that she and Harold, away at the beach, had always missed. Henry suddenly swept over her and gave her a fast affectionate kiss that left her mouth shiny with saliva. She immediately swabbed her lips. "Don't do that!"

She read the rest of the article while Henry took a fast shower, and pushed the paper aside when she heard him padding about in the bedroom, opening drawers, making enough noise to disorder her thoughts. Presently he returned in a white T-shirt and Harold's old chinos and joined her at the table, laying out his good hand like an offering and leaving his other one to lie lame in his lap.

"It was getting real hot out there," he told her. "Supposed to be worse than yesterday."

"It's cool in here," she said automatically.

"Won't be later on," he predicted. "If it gets too bad, we can go to Cinema Showcase. That would be nice, huh? Something to look forward to."

She considered it, far away in the deep part of her brain, which produced a long-forgotten image of the last movie she had seen in a theater, a comedy with a worn woman doing a jig on her husband's grave. She remembered how hard Harold had laughed, his hand slapping his knee when the woman dropped to all fours to tell the dead man exactly what she thought of him.

"Last movie I saw," Henry said, "was *Deerhunter*. Actors playing Polacks going to Nam to get blown up. I saw it and cried. I identified with Christopher Walken, the guy who wouldn't come home. He even looks a little like me, don't you think?"

"Nobody looks like you," she said, with no knowledge of Christopher Walken. Heat was beginning to seep into the kitchen, and she tugged at the front of her dress, beneath which her parted breasts were loose and lolling.

Henry said, "You go to war, you make the supreme sacrifice, what's it mean to average slobs on the street? Like it never happened. They live, what do they care about you?"

"What do you care about them?" she asked in a voice that even a ghost would not have heard. Her face was clicking shut on him.

"Fourth of July," he said, "I want to go to that memorial in Washington. I want to find the names of black guys I knew got killed. I've forgotten some of them."

"Go," she said.

"I don't want to go if you won't come with me."

"Then you don't go," she said.

"There are things you don't understand," he said in a mild reproach. "I haven't been lucky, Mrs. Goss. No time in my life have I been lucky till now. You know who I used to think was lucky? It was this guy in Chicopee who scrapped his car for a Winnebago and lived in it. I thought that was a damn good idea. Anywhere he went, he was home soon as he stopped. Now I'm not jealous anymore. I got something better."

She was not listening to him. He was there the way the furniture was, his voice no more obtrusive than the hum of the refrigerator. When he raised himself in his chair, her eye glanced over him as if he were the sort she would pay a dollar to roll out the trash barrel.

"Something's mine, I protect it," he said. "In Nam all I had was myself, so I protected me. Now I'm protecting you in ways you don't even know about. The woman next door, Mrs. Whipple, she's got the hots for me, but I don't give her a second look. I got too much respect for you, Mrs. Goss."

A line of sweat glistened from her temple to the no-longer soft curve of her jaw. In the intervals that her ear opened to him, she felt she was listening to the voice of a child from the mouth of a man. It gave her a disquieting sense of her own early and pampered beginnings.

His good hand rested gently on her wrist. "I don't want to embarrass you, but if we go the movies you should wear a bra."

"I don't want to go to the movies," she said.

"It's all right. We don't have to."

"And I don't want to go to any memorial next week." Suddenly she thought of herself as a child, not yet civilized, with a fussing face and grabby hands. She said, "I want to go to the fireworks."

* * *

They met at the Andover Inn for breakfast. Each arrived in a simple silk dress of elegantly clinging cut. Kit Fletcher's was cerulean, which illuminated her blondness and the authenticity of her figure; Louise Baker's was creamy beige, which set off the black gloss of her hair and dramatized the slender length of her limbs. The reservation was in Kit's name. They were seated near a window, white linen and fresh flowers on the table. Checking the menu in the waiter's presence, each gave the same light order of coffee, juice, and oatmeal toast. Louise's smile was distant.

"Kit, you said. Is that your real name?"

"It's Katherine."

"Katherine Fletcher of Boston. Are you from wealth?"

"Hardly. My father worked for a printing company."

"You could fool people."

"That's my job. I'm a lawyer."

"I'm an investor of sorts," Louise said with a tincture of irony. "Call me Lou if you like."

"Why, do you think we'll become friends?" Kit asked, her smile friendlier and looser.

"Stranger things have happened."

The waiter served juice and toast and poured their coffee, the aroma standing rich between them. The breakfast crowd was predominantly male. A heavy man, comfortably unwieldy in his suit only because his tailor was doubtless a genius, flashed them a shrewd businessman's smile that quickly faltered and died, as if he had first thought he could add them up on a pocket calculator. Louise powdered her coffee with Sweet 'n' Low and stirred it with a weighty spoon.

"Does Barney take you here?"

"We were here last night."

"This is my first time."

Kit showed mild surprise. "But you're from around here. Originally, I mean."

"Lawrence. That's a million miles away. I fool people too."

A beeper went off in the midst of the dining room, and a well-known doctor rose with only a slight sign of irritation and threaded his way to the door. Kit added jelly to her toast.

"You must be wondering why I wanted to meet you."

"I can think of a couple of reasons. Barney's the obvious one. Is the relationship serious?"

"It seems to be heading in that direction," Kit said with a forthright smile meant to be trusted. "He's the only man I'd consider marrying."

"You could do worse."

"No, I could do better, but it wouldn't please me."

"Should that be a consideration?" Louise asked with another touch of irony. She drained her juice glass with easy swallows. "Women like us usually put pleasure in its proper place. Maybe you should rethink your position."

Kit viewed her with fresh eyes, as if a window had been slightly raised in her mind. "Are we alike?"

"I try not to size up people too fast, so I'll let you answer that."

In an unsettling way Kit felt she was dealing with another lawyer, one with a stronger case and more trial experience. "You could very easily intimidate me," she said. "Are you asking me to back off on Barney?"

"Why would I do that?" Louise glanced at the jelly. "Is that strawberry?"

"Yes."

She spread a generous amount on her toast and said, "I don't think I intimidate you, Kit. At least not very much. So maybe you'd better tell me exactly what's on your mind, unless you just wanted to get a look at me. I'm supposed to be Mafia, you know, did Barney tell you?"

"Not in so many words." Kit smiled archly. "But all Italians are, aren't they?"

"No," Louise said, chewing easily. "Some are pretenders."

Kit lifted her coffee cup. "Shall I get to it?"

"Please. I don't have that much time."

"There's something between you and Barney I know nothing about," Kit said with quiet concern. "Maybe it's none of my business, but as a lawyer I don't like unknown factors. As a woman in this situation, I like them even less."

"You want to know what Barney is to me. He's a buddy. I call him when I need him. On occasion he calls me. What we have is private and too basic to explain. It wouldn't come out right in the telling."

"If you give me the chance, maybe I can make sense of it."

"I wouldn't worry about it if I were you."

"But I do," Kit persisted gently. "Is it sex?"

"A man and a woman, it's always sex. Barney might deny it, but I won't. Does that bother you?"

"It's the emotional attachment that bothers me. Besides, it's impossible not to be jealous. You're a beautiful woman."

"You have an edge. You're younger."

"I don't think too many people would guess that," Kit said over the rim of her cup. "I noticed something when we walked in. It was you the men looked at first."

"That's not necessarily a compliment, is it?"

"But it's a proof of strength. That's your edge."

Both women finished their toast and shook the crumbs

from their fingers. The waiter poured more coffee, Louise's move to cover her cup coming too late. Her hand, Kit noticed for the third or fourth time, was as smooth and slender as a girl's, the jeweled wedding ring exquisitely demure. The doctor had returned and shot glances at them over his *Wall Street Journal*. The heavy man who had failed to add them up stared shamelessly, his attention evenly divided, as if each were a creature to whom the gods had blown a kiss. Louise cast aside her napkin.

"If it'll make you feel better, I've always been jealous of blondes."

"I've always been jealous of women who look like Sophia Loren."

"We're full of compliments, aren't we? What you don't understand is we're not competing. You want to marry Barney, fine. You get a man who happens to be my friend. The only catch comes from statistics. Marriages break up every day. Friendships seem to survive."

"There's another catch," Kit said. "I couldn't bear not to have all his loyalty."

"Nobody gets all of anything. Even in the best of marriages people hold back. It's the same with business deals. Somebody always fudges a little."

"Did you know his wife?"

"She was like us, but she lacked direction. If Barney marries you, he'll gladly be making the same mistake all over again, which is why I won't bother to tell him." Louise checked her watch, which was as exquisitely demure as her ring and the ice impaling her earlobes. "I'm afraid I can't stay any longer."

"If I thought you were leaving for good, maybe I'd breathe easier."

Louise looked at her keenly. "Somehow I feel that's all

298

you really wanted to know, how long am I going to be around. So far I've been lucky."

The check paid, with Kit's gold card, the two women rose in silky unison. As they angled between tables, the heavy man quivered inside the fine cloth of his suit, as if in disguise he were Bacchus, god of the grape answering to the flesh. Neither gave him a glance.

Outside the heat of the morning rushed over them. Each sought her dark glasses against the blinding circle of sun. They descended into the small basin of the parking lot, where their cars squatted in the glare. They halted near Louise's and faced each other, their eyes hidden behind their glasses. Something remained on Kit's mind.

"Make it fast," Louise said.

"I think Barney and I would be good for each other, but I have something else at stake. You wouldn't hurt the marriage, Lou, I would see to that, but you could jeopardize my career. Any breath of scandal on Barney would taint me."

Louise's smile was slow, the irony returning to it. "You're not worried about me, only the business you think I might be in."

"It comes down to that."

Hot sunlight slanted through trees majestic and dauntless against the brilliant sky. In some ways the two women seemed miniatures of the trees. Louise said, "I'll put your mind at rest. Whether I'm in the business or not won't matter much longer. I've had enough. I've also got enough."

Kit extended a hand. "Thank you for telling me."

Louise gripped the hand. "Have a long marriage and a spectacular career."

It was three in the afternoon. The heat was brutal, swarming over John Rozzi like bees as soon as he stepped out of his cool car, attacking him as he huffed up the graded walk toward a house that, to his mind, had too much glass and glare, no protection against people peeking in. He rang the bell and was surprised by the young man in the open shirt and tight poplin pants who let him in with a smile. John glanced around quickly and said, "I'm expected."

"You John?"

"Yes."

"I am Mario," the young man said in precise tones. "Hot out there, huh?"

"Yeah, hot. Cool in here." John ran a voluminous handkerchief over the fat of his neck, which cascaded over his wilted collar. Mario fluttered a hand.

"You come, OK?"

John followed him over hardwood floors and sheepskin rugs, up some steps to another level, and into a skylit room shadowed by the overhang of trees. A mammoth television was tuned to a soap. Rita O'Dea sat deep in the sag of a canvas chair that looked on the verge of collapse.

"He is here," Mario said in stilted English, and retreated.

John started to speak but Rita put a finger to her lips and continued to watch the soap until it surrendered to a commercial. She killed the picture with a click of the remote-control device and stared up at him with mild curiosity, her sleeveless frock revealing the shapely heft of her arms and legs. "You're John."

"Yes." He had phoned her earlier from the motel where he was staying. She did not ask him to sit down, so he remained standing. "Thank you for seeing me," he said.

"You're Rozzi from Springfield."

"Yes. You probably don't remember me, but I went to your brother's funeral."

"Did you know Tony?"

"I didn't have the privilege."

"That's what it was, John, exactly what it was. A privilege. Sit down."

He pulled up a bulky hassock and came down on it with a squishing of air. He placed his hands gravely on his knees. "I don't want to step on toes, Mrs. O'Dea. I don't want to do anything out of line."

"Nobody if he's smart wants to do that. Suppose you tell me the problem, John."

He glanced around to reassure himself that Mario had left and then leaned forward with his large face sprung out, though a part of it seemed to hang back in deference. In a voice low and raspy, his throat in need of clearing, he explained his problem. Afterward, he drew his hands from his knees and laced his fingers together.

For too many moments, her eyes resting upon him, Rita did not respond, which disquieted him. Finally she said, "You remind me of somebody, same face, same big build. He worked for my brother and then for me. Ralph Roselli."

"I know the name," John said. "He's dead, isn't he?"

"He died of a heart attack shoveling snow off my walk. Good man." She clicked the television back on. "About the other thing, John, some things *have* to be done. So I got no objections."

He nodded and rose.

"But," she said, her attention on the screen, "you were smart to ask."

He drove back to his motel, which was a few miles outside of Lawrence on Route 114. The manager sold beer from a cooler, and John bought a six-pack. In his room he ripped open a can and took a long swig, belching when he lowered the can. The room was air conditioned, yet seemed unaired. He was sweating. After stripping down to his underwear and burying his weapon beneath a pillow, he finished off the can of beer and stretched out on the bed.

An hour later the telephone woke him, the ring reverberating in his ear, his bladder in need of relief. He fumbled for the receiver.

The voice said, "John?"

"Yeah."

"We on?"

"We're on."

FIFTEEN

The neighborhood was noisy, tenement houses full of commotion, too many families stuffed inside, hanging out of unscreened windows, overloading rickety porches. Graffiti blazed from a concrete abutment, blubbery block letters of red and gold, painted one-word shouts of defiance in Spanish. The humidity hung heavy in the darkening air. A woman crossing the street looked as if she would relinquish her soul for a breeze. A boy of four or five opened his short pants and relieved himself on the sidewalk. Louise Baker said, "How long do we have to wait?"

"I told him eight-thirty," Chick Ryan said. "I don't want to surprise him."

They were seated in Chick's car, which was parked in front of a boarded-up superette, the back of which was burned out. The neighborhood was a block or so away from the one in which she had grown up, a fact that pressed upon her.

Chick said, "Could you live here today, Lou? Could you survive?"

"If I were Hispanic, yes," she said with certainty. "I'd work, I'd learn, I'd get out."

Chick disagreed with a dark look. "You were a spic, you wouldn't have the values we had. We had pride. We had morals, for Christ's sake. These people got nothing. There're women on this street grandmothers before they're thirty. Gives you an idea what's going on here, no upbringing, no nothing. Did you see the kid piss on the sidewalk?"

Louise said, "Sugar O'Toole used to take dumps in the hallway, remember? Hot weather like this, his mother Millie sat on the stoop in her slip, and the guys would come around to look at her. Your father was one of them. And your sister, I remember, got pregnant in high school."

"You trying to make me mad?"

"No, just trying to remember how it was."

"Not like this. Can you smell that coming into the car? These people aren't clean."

"That's the Spickett River, Chick. It blows rank every summer."

"I'm not going to argue with you," he said. "You want to believe these people are like us, that's your business. I deal with them every night, so I know better." He shoved a hand inside his shirt and scratched his stomach. "I'll tell you what I think of spics. I got more respect for the real niggers, I mean the ones born here."

"You're right, Chick. You shouldn't argue."

"And now that I think about it, your father never held a steady job in his life." He laughed. "You people were on handouts."

"You got it, Chick."

He checked his watch.

"What time is it?" she asked.

"Time," he said.

He started up the car, flicked on the headlights, and cruised down the street through opposing blasts of stereo music, the tires crunching broken glass, which produced a music more tonal than the other. Faint hues of silver glinting through the ripening darkness proved to be the shirts of youths contemptuously handsome. Spindles of light became the legs of girls.

"Dopers," Chick told her with satisfaction.

"We live off them," Louise replied carelessly.

"You maybe, not me."

"You don't take a cut along the line?"

"Only what's due me."

He took a turn onto a side street, the buildings low-lying and commercial, windowless and roughcast, a solemn loneliness about them all. Turning the wheel with a light finger, he nosed the car into an alley that led to an auto-repair garage with a bare bulb burning over the door next to a stall. Graffiti of the filthy variety marked the facade. Louise said, "You sure you know what you're doing?"

"You're putting your life in my hands," Chick said smugly. "You want to change your mind, now's the time."

"I trust you," she said. "Up to a point, of course."

He drew up in front of the garage, killed the motor and the lights, and listened to vague sounds in the sultry uneasy air. "You know, it'd be better you weren't here. Something goes wrong I could say I was apprehending him in the commission of a crime."

"What could go wrong?" she said flatly.

"OK, we'll do it your way." He yanked the keys from the ignition. When he started to push open his door, Louise dropped a hand on his arm.

"Tell me about him."

"Rafael? What's there to tell? He's a degenerate. He was younger, he was a hitter, street-gang stuff in New York. He came to Lawrence, became a pusher. I busted him two, three years ago, but made a deal with him when I found out how much business he was doing. What I didn't know till recently is he was using."

"Was he high when he came at me?"

"He must've been."

"He's scared, you said. He ran, right?"

"Yeah, he's scared," Chick said. "That't why we're meeting on his ground."

"What makes you think he'll be alone?" she asked suspiciously.

"He's got no friends, I've seen to that."

"How'd you get him to agree to meet with you?"

"I told him I want him back in business. I miss the money."

"OK," she said. "Let's get to it."

Now it was he who held her arm, gripping it tight enough to hurt. His eyes seemed to advance beyond their lids. "This is over, you going to send somebody after me, Lou? I mean, one thing could easily follow another, right?"

"I explained myself once. I'm not going to do it again."

"You're a cool lady." His grin was all over her. "It's why I've always had a thing for you."

"This is over, I don't ever want to see your face again."

They opened their doors. He was still grinning. "Don't be so sure," he said. "How many heavyweights can you find like me?"

It was a small garage, without cars, without a lift or a pit, with a few workbenches but no tools. Tires, worn out or blown out, had been thrown into corners. Odors of motor oil, rubbish, and cats permeated the shadows. The light came from a fluorescent fixture dangling precariously from the ceiling, illuminating an old overstuffed chair that might have been rescued from a dump. Magazine photographs of naked women clung to the far wall, sexless against the dank concrete, resembling inmates more than models. Louise, hanging back, murmured, "He's not here."

"He's here. He's in the toilet." Chick laughed. "Come on out, Rafael."

The toilet was a cubicle without a door. The man who emerged surprised her. She had expected somebody shabby and shaped like a frog, pop-eyed and cold-blooded, but he was as slender as she, clean-shaven, sinewy in an immaculate white T-shirt, his full mustache worn with formality. His neat nappy hair was African, his face Indian, and his nose, thin-walled, was Spanish. He was almost beautiful.

He said, singsong, "You s'posed to come alone."

Chick slung a glance back at Louise. "He's dancing on a cloud."

"What you say?"

"Look at the lady, Rafael. Smile your prettiest."

Brilliant teeth made the smile audacious. "What you bring her for? Fun?"

Louise had been gazing at him without emotion, but suddenly the moment outside the funeral home spun back at her, not Rafael's hypnotic face, for she had failed to freeze it in her mind, but the scrape of his shoe, the sound and stink of the gunshots, the chill in her soul as Barney Cole rushed to hold her up.

She advanced with a shaky step. "Remember me?"

He did not, but something seemed to alert him. His glazed eyes leaped from her to Chick. "We s'posed to talk business. What we doing this for?"

"Tell him, Louise."

"You tell him," she said.

Rafael said, "What she want? A snort? I got crack, that's all."

"Don't tell me, tell her," Chick said, and drew a small-caliber pistol from the back of his pants under his shirt. He fired it. Louise staggered backward, and Rafael dropped to his knees, a spot bubbling up on his T-shirt. It was as if a tick with blood had burst. No more than that. Then Chick shot him in the head.

Louise stood with a hand over her mouth and sweat cooling on her forehead. "I'm going to be sick."

"I thought you were tough," Chick said with cold disdain, every line in his face mocking her. "Why the fuck have I been scared of you? All you got are connections." His eyes glued to her, he seemed to mull something over. Then he tucked the pistol away. "Go on, get out of here. I got to spread some crack around, make it look like a dope deal gone bad."

She wheeled around. The plock of her heels rang louder than the reports of the pistol had, the stench of which she carried with her. He called after her, "Hey, Lou. Barney Cole could see us now, wonder what he'd think of you."

She made it to the door, her heart in her throat.

"Hey, Lou, you know what's one step from a spic? A Lawrence wop. That's all you'll ever be."

She stepped out into the heated night air, letting the door fall shut behind her. With a hand pressed to her chest, she took a deep breath. From the shadows a raspy voice said, "You all right?"

"Perfectly all right," she replied, straightening her shoulders. "Where's your car?"

"On the street."

I'll wait for you there," she said.

John Rozzi reached up through a blizzard of moths and extinguished the burning bulb above the door.

"Don't miss," she said.

"I never do," he answered.

Edith Shea rose early, the first tentacles of sun stealing through watery mists, the morning a gift not yet unwrapped. Her hands on the sill of the open window, she breathed in air not yet tainted by the heaves of the city. The lilac bush stood empty, the great clumps of blossoms gone, either snipped off or withered away, but her mind retained the ghost of the scent. Gone from the dirt driveway was Daisy's clunker, sold for fifty dollars, which paid for shifting the plates to the new car already scratched by children in the neighborhood and anointed by pigeons. With a twinge, she looked back at Daisy, sprawled on the bed with the top sheet snagged between his naked legs, and hoped that he would sleep late, for the heat had kept him tossing. The small fan, still whirring, had not helped much. She bent over the bed, listened to his heavy breathing, and drew the tortured sheet over his sunken chest. Then, purposely allowing no time for feelings, she tiptoed out.

She tapped lightly on the bathroom door. "Are you going to be long?"

Her second daughter, who had a summer job at Raytheon and an unexpected scholarship to Merrimack, came out wrapped in a rose robe. She had Edith's eyes, bones, cap of curly hair, even Edith's voice, and little of Daisy. Of all the children she was the closest to him. "How's Dad?" she asked.

Edith gave a little shrug. "Sleeping. Try not to wake him."

"I was talking with him last night."

"I heard you."

The girl pulled at her robe, drew the top tight around her throat. "I wish he wouldn't joke about it. You know what I mean."

"It's his way of dealing with it," Edith said simply.

"He told me a story about a man who was given only weeks to live but found a way to delay his death indefinitely. He boarded airplanes and constantly shifted through the world's time zones, so it was always yesterday, never today, which is how he avoided tomorrow."

Edith said nothing.

The girl said, "He's worse, isn't he?"

"He's not better," Edith said simply. The girl's narrow face was glum, and Edith slipped an arm around her, which was partly a way to confirm her own existence. "Don't let yourself think about it too much, honey."

"How can anybody be happy in the house? Knowing?"

"Happiness isn't important right not. Later maybe."

"If there was just something I could do, Ma, but there isn't. I can't even laugh at his jokes."

"That's the injustice of it," Edith said with sympathy. "That's what the dying do to us. They make us helpless, then they flatten us with guilt. We have to pick it up and carry it, worst baggage of all. Three years after my mother died, my father told me the grief had eased, but not the guilt."

The girl, silent, suddenly squirmed free. "He won't even be serious about the new car. Where did he get it?"

"It's his secret. He deserves one."

"He wants me to believe he bought it himself. Why?"

Edith said gently, "Why do you think?"

Her waitress's uniform, which she had washed out last night, was hanging in the bathroom. She felt it to make sure it was dry and then took a fast shower, time pressing upon her. She needed to be at the coffee shop within the hour and was running late. In the kitchen, gulping instant coffee, she heard the tail end of a news report on the radio, which was tuned to the local station. "Double shooting" were the only words she caught. She placed her coffee cup in the sink, threw a pack of cigarettes into her bag, and then, for some reason feeling more protective than usual, looked in on Daisy.

He was in exactly the same position, but something was different. Something rigid about the set of his legs, something off in his color. She stepped to the bed, listened for his breathing, and heard none. His face was shut, his head tipped as if a prop had been pulled from the back of it. Viewing him numbly, she said in a hollow voice, "You're never going to open your eyes again, are you Daisy?"

An eye jittered. It winked at her. "Fooled you," he said.

"You bastard!" she said through a rush of tears.

Barney Cole drank his coffee fast. Kit Fletcher took her time. She was leaving later, after the commuter rush. She sat at the kitchen table with her bare feet tossed up on the chair Cole had just vacated. He looked at her from the kitchen sink, where he was rinsing out his cup. "I wish I had your hours," he said.

"No, you don't. Sometimes I'm in the office till midnight. When I'm in litigation I don't sleep."

"Ever consider taking things a little easier?" he asked, moving to her and standing neat and tall in a cord suit back from the cleaner's. She lifted a foot, angling it at his pant legs.

"No, I've been thinking of increasing my schedule," she said. Her foot was playful.

"You're in a terrific mood."

"I feel good, Barney. My life is going right, and I know where I want it to take me."

"Am I included in the journey?"

She swept the hair out of her face. "In a very vital way, but we can talk about it tonight."

"That's not fair," he said. "Give me a clue."

"My biological clock is ticking loud, Barney." She retracted her foot, its effect obvious. "I think it's telling me something."

"I see."

"I thought you would. It's worth discussing, no?"

He smiled down upon her. Smiling back, she seemed to give off her own golden light. "What would you want, a boy or girl?" he asked.

"I'd prefer a girl."

We don't always get what we want."

"I understand there are ways now."

"I wouldn't want anything scientific."

"We can discuss everything tonight." She brought her foot up again, a soft jab. "Kiss me and get out of here."

"One last question," he said. "Would this be with or without a wedding ring?"

She lifted her face for the kiss, took it, and said, "In some ways I'm a very conventional gal."

A couple of minutes later Cole backed the Cutlass out of the garage. Despite the unquestionable promise of more heat and humidity, it was one of those splendid summer days when he felt zestful, irrepressible, immeasurable, but when he turned onto Wildwood Road the car stalled. He let it roll to the shoulder and twisted the key. It started up again, gasped, and gave out for good. The motor, the battery, or something was dead.

Cutting across a neighbor's lawn, admiring towers of Shasta daisies, he made his way back toward the house.

He paused once to tie a shoe, propping his foot on a white wooden post serving as a property marker. He entered the house through the sun room. He did not see Kit and thought she might be showering. Then he heard her voice and stopped short.

"No, I can't do that," she said in a tone of exasperation. She was on the phone, the cord stretched to the sink and wrapped half around her waist. She had a hand on her hip. "Listen," she said, "there's a limit to what I can do."

He smiled, guessing she was talking to a partner no longer a level above her, and moved into the dining room. Again her voice stopped him. It was cold and direct.

"Quit pushing, Cruickshank. I've had dinner with her, I've told you everything she said, I've done my bit. . . . What? . . . No, he's told me nothing." Then she turned slightly to free herself of the cord and saw Cole.

"Keep talking," he said.

She killed the connection.

"Silly world, isn't it?" he said, gazing at her from the archway of the dining room. "Full of weird surprises."

Collecting herself, she said, "Would you like an explanation?"

"I'm sure it's a good one," he said, his smile bittersweet.

Louise Baker slept as if drugged until her mother shook her, shouted over her, raised the shade and let the sun hit her. Louise pulled the sheet tighter around her, and her mother yanked it off. She was naked. "I don't see you that way since you be a baby," her mother said, staring hard. "I don't know you. Whose child are you?"

"Yours, Mama. Never anybody else's."

"Those not my bazooms. They my sister Rosa's. You get up."

She rose sluggishly and sat on the side of the bed, ma-

ANDREW COBURN

nipulating her arms into a robe. She yawned, rubbed a
bare foot with the other, and said, "What time is it?"

"Eight."

"Oh, my God." She had wanted to sleep till noon. Her
mother aimed a finger.

"You promise you take me to the cemetery."

"So early?"

"Before it gets too hot. You hurry."

Bathed and dressed, her feet fitted into white pumps,
she drank her coffee in the kitchen, where her mother
rambled in Italian, stories about her father she did not
wish to hear, revelations she did not want to know, certain suspicions she did not want confirmed. When her
mother's mind wandered into fantasy, she said in an in-
terrupting voice, "Were you listening to the radio at all?"

"What radio?"

"Any radio at all, Mama. I thought you might've had
on the news."

"What kind of news?"

"Any kind."

"I don't listen," her mother said with sudden impatience. "You get ready now. Put some lipstick on."

"Papa wouldn't like that," she said dryly.

"Papa won't see."

She was doing her face in the bathroom mirror when
the telephone rang, the shrillness startling her. Quickly,
resorting to an old trick learned as a child, she ran warm
water over her wrists to calm herself. She was using the
towel when her mother appeared.

"The woman who works for you says it's very important."

She folded the towel and hung it neatly. "Mrs. Mennick?"

"Something like that."

"Why don't you wait for me in the car, Mama? I'll be right there."

"Yes, you talk your business."

"It's not business. It's personal." She held the phone loosely until her mother left and then spoke into it, her voice clear and precise. "Yes, what is it?"

"Mr. Ben's gone out of his mind," Mrs. Mennick said.

She stared at gilt-framed religious pictures her mother kept on the wall, one Madonna and two Christs, one as an infant and the other nailed to the cross.

"It wasn't my fault, Mrs. Baker."

"Nobody's blaming you."

"Nothing I could do. Even Howard couldn't handle him. He ran off, and we had to look for him in the dark."

"Nobody's fault, Mrs. Mennick, except maybe nature's. Where is he?"

"Back in the hospital. Somebody had to sign him in. I signed your name, Mrs. Baker. I didn't know what else to do."

"You did right. How bad is he?"

Mrs. Mennick sobbed. "He's catatonic."

"Like the last time he went in?"

"Worse."

The telephone cord was snarled. Louise straightened it and asked for the number of the hospital, which she presently jotted on the face of her mother's electric bill, along with the office number of the doctor who had previously treated Ben.

"There's something else, Mrs. Baker. Nothing to do with Mr. Ben, but I think I should mention it."

Louise waited.

"Two men came to the house, one black. They showed me identification and asked questions."

"What kind of questions?" Louise asked.

"About you, Mrs. Baker. I told them nothing."

Louise folded the electric bill in half and slipped it into the side pocket of her bag. "Anything else, Mrs. Mennick?"

"I might give my brother a few groceries now and then, but I'm loyal to you." There was another sob. "And to Mr. Ben."

Louise's mother was waiting in the shade of a red maple that throbbed with birds. Together they walked toward the Porsche, which was baking in the sun. "That call bring you problems?" her mother asked.

"No, Mama, no problems." She slipped an arm around the old woman's frail shoulders.

"Too hot for that," Mrs. Leone said, and shrugged her off.

Kit Fletcher still held the dead phone. Deliberately she hung it up with a bittersweetness that matched his. "Pullman and Gates is a big firm, Barney. It has a chummy relationship with the government. Several members have held high positions in the Justice Department."

"Yes, I know."

"No, you don't. In their world, everything's hardball."

"I know that too. The big leagues. Curves and sliders." His smile had turned rigidly polite and eerily understanding. "The feds wanted you to do them a favor. I assume that after some quick thought you said no, but your bosses put pressure on you. Of course they didn't want to make it seem they were forcing you into anything, so they added a sweetener. Senior partnership, which you deserved anyway, should've been yours a long time ago. Am I in the ballpark?"

"More or less," she said negligently, as if details did not matter, only intentions. "But in no way did I agree to hurt you. Information on your friend was all they wanted, and after all, I am an officer of the court."

"Yes, I've heard the argument."

"I always went out of my way to protect you, and there was little enough I could pass on about her. You saw to that."

"But every little bit helps. A piece that doesn't fit now can fit later. We lawyers know that, don't we?"

"You're a good lawyer, Barney, but I'm a bigger one. With the stakes involved, I had no choice."

"Sure you did."

"No, I didn't. My life's on a course." Her eyes were a deepening blue and declarative. "Your friend's on a course too. She's a smart lady. She'll be all right."

Cole altered his voice, make it slightly more responsive. "Nobody's that smart. Enough people want you, they get you." He stepped into the kitchen, past her, to the telephone. "I think she's had it, Kit. With a little bit of help from me and you." He called the Mobil station on South Main and asked for a tow truck. Then he began flipping through the directory.

"Don't call a taxi," she said. "I can give you a ride."

"You have your own schedule." He rustled through the Yellow Pages. "By the way, you played your part well."

"I didn't want you to know. I hoped you wouldn't."

"Blame my automobile. I should've traded it in months ago."

"Barney." Her voice took on a softer quality. "Before you come to any final judgments, any decision, I want you to know I still feel we can have something fine together. For what it's worth, I love you."

"It's worth a lot," he said.

"But?"

"But your terms are too high. Too much fine print I didn't know about."

"Why don't we wait and talk about it tonight? As we planned."

"Why don't we give it a rest?" he said.

"You don't want to see me tonight?"

They gazed at each other affectionately. He said, "Not tonight."

"What are you telling me, Barney? You might as well say it straight."

He lifted the receiver and called for a taxi.

He was riding the elevator to his office when he learned from two other lawyers that Chick Ryan had been shot to death. He went pale and pressed for details, but they knew only what they had heard on the radio, a sparse report of a double killing off Park Street, the other victim a male Hispanic. "You knew Ryan pretty well, didn't you, Barney?" one of the lawyers said, and Cole nodded. His stomach turned. When the doors wheezed open, he stepped out like a pallbearer in need of directions.

Later, at Dolce's, he learned more. Arnold Ackerman, who had friends throughout the police department, said in a near whisper, "Something's funny about it. He wasn't on duty. Told his wife he was going to the Hibernian Club. That's where she thought he was, tipping a few. The question is, what the hell was he doing alone in a Spanish neighborhood with a known pusher. Rafael Somebody?"

Cole took a chew of a doughnut and cast it aside, no appetite. "Maybe he was undercover."

"Captains don't do undercover. Certainly not Chick."

"Maybe the guy was his snitch."

"Look me straight in the eye, Barney, tell me you believe that."

"He could've been trying to bust him."

"Sure. Alone? That sound like Chick?"

"You tell me, Arnold."

Arnold picked up the doughnut Cole did not want and nibbled on it. "We both know the reputation he had. Some guys at the station speculate he went in with his hand out, something went wrong. He got too greedy, is what they think."

"What do you think, Arnold?"

"I think it was a shame, whatever it was." He abandoned the doughnut, not to his liking, not a honeydip.

Cole said, "Any idea how his wife's doing?"

"How would you be doing, situation like this?"

Cole drew himself erect, feeling another turn in his stomach. "Can I borrow your car?" he asked.

"Where's yours?"

"Towed, I hope."

Arnold produced a mass of keys. "It's got no dents. Bring it back that way."

"Where's it parked?"

"Judge's spot. I do it to get his ass."

It was a ten-year-old Cadillac, mint condition, the radio tuned to the classical music station. Cole listened to Mendelssohn as he drove up Common Street. He crossed Broadway and maneuvered up rising streets to Chick's house, where he saw a cruiser parked in the drive, a uniformed officer behind the wheel. Unmarked cars, official-looking because of their sameness, were parked in front. He pulled into the first free space and walked back. The district attorney emerged from the house.

"What are you doing here, Barney?"

It was too hot to stand in the sun. They sidled into the shade. Cole said, "I thought I'd talk to Chick's wife, see if there's anything I could do."

"I wouldn't disturb her right now," the district attorney advised. "Too many people in there as it is."

ANDREW COBURN

"How is she, Chugger?"

"Nothing's hit her yet. She still thinks he's coming home. Christ, I didn't know Chick had nine children." He shook his head sadly. "Doesn't look good. We found a briefcase hidden in the attic. Fifty grand in it, used bills. If it was up to me, I'd have left it there for the family, but too many people are involved now. State police narcotics squad have come into it, and those two feds have taken an interest. You just missed them."

"Any conclusions yet?" Cole asked warily.

"Theories. Narcotics guys think he was taking drug money and got involved in a shoot-out. They don't know yet, but they think it was Chick shot the other guy. The feds got their own theory, I don't know what it is."

"Can you guess?"

"I'm not even going to try. I gotta go, Barney."

They walked along the sidewalk together. Each passing car, even dirty ones, blazed with sunlight. Neighbors looked out their windows. The district attorney, stopping, stripped off his suit jacket and rolled up his sleeves.

"What a dumb way to die. He had no business doing that to his family, Barney. What the hell kind of cop was he, anyway?"

"He considered himself one of the best."

The district attorney tossed his jacket through the open window of his car and pulled open the door. "You know what the greatest pleasure in life is? Bet you think it's sex. That's second maybe, but not first."

"I'll bite," Cole said. "What's first?"

"Lying to yourself."

Two Springfield police officers, one a woman, rousted John Rozzi from bed in the fleabag hotel where he maintained a permanent residence. It was two in the afternoon. A fan whirred from the ceiling, agitating the heat of the room. The room was threadbare but surprisingly neat; the only clutter was dirty laundry heaped in a corner and empty beer bottles on the bureau. The male officer, gazing about, said, "Guy with your money, I'd think you'd live better."

John, whose boxer shorts hung to his knees, held a hand over his crotch. "You busting me or what?"

"Or what," the officer said. "Come on, get dressed!"

John groped for his clothes. "Tell the cunt cop to turn her head."

The woman, a bit of a thing who wore her cap at an angle, stepped forward as he struggled into his trousers. "I'm Officer Mary Finn," she said smartly, and with a quick swing laid a baton against his knees. He doubled up with a yelp.

"One thing you never do is talk smart to Mary," the other officer said.

John reeled to one side, gripping and rubbing his knees, cursing foully under his breath. "I can't walk."

"You'll learn."

They threw the rest of his clothes at him, dumped his shoes in front of him. "I got to go to the toilet," he said.

The male officer, again gazing about, said, "I don't see one."

"It's down the hall."

"You want Mary or me to go with you?"

"Not her."

Mary Finn said, "Piss your pants."

They drove him to the station, escorted him in through a side door, and left him in the interrogation room where he had been questioned before. He hobbled painfully to a chair and sat at the bare table. He was soon joined by the detective with the plump and jovial face. The detective was wearing, he noticed, the same knit shirt with the scruffy little collar curled at the points and the same pants with the defective fly zipper. The only difference he observed was the detective's manner. It reminded him of a cardplayer who had filled an inside straight.

"I got bad news for you, John. It's about your buddy Botello. We found the body."

He had no comment, no reaction other than a glance at the suspect mirror on the wall.

"Nobody's behind that glass, John. It's just you and me. In case you think I'm bluffing about the body, I'll tell you where we found it. That piece of swamp behind the place used to be a tannery, then was a plastics factory, now is nothing. Nobody goes there because everybody thinks it's loaded with toxic waste. Except kids go there. Kids go everywhere." The detective smiled. "You slipped up, John."

John reached under the table and massaged his knees. The left one hurt the worst, though not as bad as his bladder.

"I know what you're thinking," the detective said. "You think we can't identify it. What did you use besides lime? Acid? The face and fingers are gone, but the teeth are there. You'd be surprised what we can do with teeth."

John said, "Seems to me Sal had false teeth."

"Caps and crowns is what he had. Three minutes ago I was talking to his dentist. See how easy this is going to be?"

"If that's Sal you dug out of the swamp, I'm sorry to hear it. He was a pal."

"You saying you don't know anything about it?"

"That's what I'm saying."

The detective regarded him with a display of disappointment and regret. "Sorry to say I got more bad news for you. Day Sal disappeared a lady friend of his, Mrs. Reynolds from across the lake, was strolling over to see him. What she saw instead was somebody stuffing something into the trunk of Sal's Lincoln. Something big in a blanket, she said. She took her time coming forward because she's a married woman, but her conscience got the best of her. Plus she thought a lot of Sal. Pretty woman, wouldn't you say, John? We got her in protective custody, which she didn't like at first. Now she finds it exciting."

"Sounds like a flake," John said. "That the same woman Sal and her used to swim bare-ass in the lake?"

"Could be."

"Yeah, she's a flake."

"I'd be more worried, I was you, John. No matter how you cut it, we got you."

"You got me, bust me."

"I got to ID Sal first, then I'll bust you. And then I'll go all the way with it. No deals. Only deal you might get is from the feds. If they're still willing." The detective pawed his shirt and produced a slip of paper from the shapeless breast pocket. "I got a number here, you want to call them."

"Guess you didn't hear me the other time," John said. "I don't deal."

The detective suddenly looked bored. "It's your life."

Barney Cole got home a little after six. On the table was a note from Kit Fletcher. Warm and touching. He read it twice and then tossed it away. With no appetite for supper, he drank a bottle of German beer in the sun room, shady at that hour, the bare suggestion of a breeze traveling through the screens. The early evening was painted bright, but he viewed it with a drab eye. Across the way a young woman and her daughter cavorted on their lawn. The child, golden-haired, did a cartwheel, and the mother, lemon legs flying out of white shorts, did a better one. The sight, which should have stirred him, dug at him in a spiteful way. Moments later he phoned Louise Baker.

They met in the downstairs lounge of a restaurant in Andover Square and sat in low comfortable swivel chairs at a tiny table. They talked of Chick Ryan as if his body were laid out on the bar in full uniform. Cole, gripping a glass of Harvey's, said, "I can't get him out of my mind."

"I can." She swiveled in her chair, her legs thrown to one side. "I'm sorry he's dead, but I never liked him, not even when we were kids. No honor, no loyalty, no class, and he was the worst kind of cop. I'll cry when I see him in the casket, but that won't change what he was."

Cole pressed his drink glass against his hot brow. "A crazy question keeps ripping through my head."

"One I'm supposed to answer?"

"Yes." He spoke fast. "Did you have anything to do with it?"

"Nothing," she retorted with the same speed. "Nothing whatsoever. Maybe you think you had reason to ask, but I don't appreciate it. What do you think I am, Barney?"

He lowered the glass, spoke over the rim. "I had to get it out of the way."

"Now you have, let's forget it." She leaned forward, revealing pale cleavage, and sipped Chablis without seeming to taste it. She was without makeup, lipstick, which made her face more daring, much more her own personal belonging.

"Where's your lady tonight?"

He shook his head. "We won't talk about Chick, and we won't talk about her, OK?"

Her hand came across the table. "I'm glad you called, Barney. If you hadn't, I would've."

"I was afraid you might've gone back," he said. "Your husband must be anxious."

"He's in the hospital. God knows how long this time. We won't talk about him either."

Their fingers interlaced, her wedding finger glistening. Two women in fashionable summer plumage took a table nearby. They looked at Louise first, at Cole by the way, and then studied the limited but delectable supper menu chalked on the wall. Cole whispered, "Are you hungry?"

"No," she said.

Each gazed at the other more intently than ever. Her unadorned face gave her eyes a greater depth, and he wondered whether she knew everything in his mind and decided she did. "How wonderful that we know each other so well," he said.

"Do we?" She directed her eyes away from him, then back to him as if to burn him. "It might spoil things if we did." Their fingers tightened. Her voice was guttural. "What do you want, Barney?"

The two women were staring at them. "Every single bit of you," he heard himself say.

He drove her Porsche, the first time he had ever been behind the wheel of one. She did not ask where his car was, either the old one or the one she had given him. The headlights poured through the early darkness as they glided through the choice part of town, the grounds of Phillips Academy on each side of the divided road, the misty buildings lurking like ships in dim-lit waters, a fleet manned by ghosts, here and there a porthole of light, as if alumni from another era were back at their books. "It's magical," she said.

"Yes," he said, gazing at the spectral shape of the bell tower.

"I mean us."

His house was pitch black, surrounded by choruses of

peepers, the signals of fireflies. He unlocked the front door and she stepped in. She had been inside his house only a few times through the years but easily found her way through the dark. She turned on only the necessary lights, then waited for him in the passage beyond the kitchen. She stood straight and still, as if someone had turned her into sculpture.

"Hot in here, Barney. Don't you have air?"

"Only in the master bedroom."

"I should've remembered."

The words touched a nerve in him. They were what she had said the last time, much too long ago. Their hands went out to each other, and he kissed her, lingering on her full lips. In the dim bedroom her elbows rose like a butterfly lifting its wings as she came out of her bra. He remembered the first time he had seen her naked, a wallop to his senses. It was no less now.

He reached her in two clean strides.

On the bed she said, "Do you love me, Barney?"

"When have I not?"

His head sank. She tasted rich, nutty, of long-vanished days yanked out whole from his memory. Her head twisted above full bright breasts. "I can smell her in the sheets, Barney. Your other lady. Doesn't matter," she said with vigor. "It goes with the territory." Their naked legs coiled, hers softer in strength but superior in suppleness. They were nose to nose when the telephone rang in their ears. "It's her, isn't it? Are you going to answer it?" she asked needlessly and drew him into her. The bed pitched.

Within the hour, the plug pulled from the phone, they made love again, with no less abandon but perhaps with deeper feeling, and then collapsed in the disarray of sheets. The pillow that had been under her looked as if it had been punched to death. A framed picture above the headboard hung cockeyed against the wall. Her voice was a whisper. "You're better, Barney."

"Better than I used to be or better than others?"

"Both."

They caressed each other indolently, murmured playfully, and drifted off to sleep. He slept soundly, six and a half hours of death, from which he woke with a start. His hand reached out, but she was gone.

It was eight o'clock in the morning, downtown Springfield. A shrimp of a woman punched coins into the slot of an outdoor pay phone. When her call went through, she tipped her cap back and asked for Mrs. Baker.

"She just come in," said an elderly voice full of reproach. "You wait a minute."

The woman waited impatiently, tapping her foot. "You got reason for concern," she said tonelessly when Louise came on the line.

There was a small pause. "Pretty sure of that, are you?"

"Would I call if I weren't?"

"Thank you, Mary."

The line went dead. The woman walked back to the waiting cruiser and plunked herself in. The male officer behind the wheel gave her an inquiring look. "Did you get through to her?"

"Yes," she said, and removed her cap, placing it on her stiff knees.

"How much do you think it was worth?" he asked with a glitter in his eye.

"Plenty," she said.

Sixteen

It was the first Sunday of July, the air spicy and warm. There were a few streaks of heat lightning and smashes of thunder, but no rain. Cole was mowing the lawn. He took a rest when the blade threw up a grass snake in three pieces, the head the highest, the forked tongue spitting. Kit Fletcher was in the house gathering her things. She came out presently, husky and athletic-looking in khaki culottes. Her smile was loose, her voice droll.

"Somebody's been sleeping in my bed."

He mopped his brow with his forearm. "Me."

"Besides you," she said, stepping to a rosebush beset with Japanese beetles, mostly three to a leaf, two mating and one waiting. Instinctively she seemed to choose the right place to stand, where the sunlight played most effectively in her blond hair. She glanced back at him. "Change your mind about anything?"

He said something light and noncommittal while toying with a lever on the mower. She gazed off at lush summer trees that seemed taller than they were, birds stationed high in them.

"I'll miss this place."

"You're welcome anytime."

"As what? Friend, sweetheart, overnight guest? Could we just be chums, you and I?"

"Doesn't seem likely, does it?"

"Nothing seems too likely anymore, Barney. We were planning an August vacation. Should I forget it?"

"Plenty of time to talk about it," he said.

She turned to him with a wry look. "Know anything about spiders?"

"Not really."

"I'm reminded of the one that spins a web in the evening and destroys it at dawn. Our relationship wasn't unlike that."

"First I've heard of such a spider."

"One is standing right here," she said, "but I'm not sure whether it's you or me."

He accompanied her to her car, which was crammed in back with cartons and garment bags. His old coppery Cutlass squatted nearby, operational once more. Kit held out a hand, and he gripped it.

"We might not see each other again," she said.

"What's to prevent it?"

"Our egos." She pushed herself into her little car with a girlish ungainliness that always touched a thread in him. After strapping herself in, she smiled out the open window. "You know something, Barney? We would have had a beautiful kid."

He finished cutting the grass and stowed the mower in the garage. A little later, his back to the sun, he sat in a lawn chair with a bottle of beer and listened to the birds uttering their sounds. Stretching his legs out, he gazed at the shorn grass and wondered what the property had looked like a couple of centuries ago, what untamed trees had soared overhead, which red men had eaten off the berry bushes. He had, his father had told him, a touch of Indian blood, a Canadian tribe, and he wondered whether a brave remotely resembling him had ever ventured down this far. His eyes closed, he heard a car turn in at the driveway and recognized it by the sound, as if it were a peculiar breed of animal.

Louise Baker appeared through a torpid veil of sunlight as he erected another lawn chair. She waved it aside. "I can't stay," she said, an otherworldliness in the float of her voice, faint signs of fatigue in her face. She took a thirsty swig of his beer and wiped her mouth with the back of her slender hand. Light flooded through her dress. "My sister and I are taking my mother to dinner. That's what I came to tell you. I can't see you tonight."

He composed his lips into an expression of understanding. "How is your mother?"

"Getting on my nerves." She took another swig and gave another wipe. "All she does is pray and talk to the dead. Last night she claims my father materialized, but all he wanted was quick sex. Then he left. She's mad she didn't deny him. She's sure forty years ago he fooled around with my Aunt Rosa. I'm supposed to look like Rosa, which doesn't help matters."

"What can I say?"

"Nothing. You asked, I told you." She dug a vivid red fingernail into the Beck's label on the bottle. "I promised my mother I'd take her to the fireworks on the Fourth. After that, I'm going home. I've had enough around here."

"I'll miss you," he said. "I'll also worry about you," he added in a slower voice.

"Why?"

"The feds."

"I always cover my ass. Scampy taught me that."

"Let's forget good old Scampy."

"He worshiped the ground I walked on, but he was a jealous prick. He hated you."

"I hated him."

"Now it comes out." Her smile effectively covered him. "You've never seen my place in Mallard Junction. Would you like to? You could stay awhile, a long while if you like."

"I don't think I'd be comfortable."

"As my lawyer, not just my lover. I told you I'm retiring, and I meant it. I'll be strictly legitimate." A silence fell, a strain on each. She said abruptly, "I have many investments that would keep you busy."

"Not my line, Lou. I'm lousy about money."

"What I'm saying," she said with a throb of color, "is I don't want any more garbage in my life, no more Henrys. I want you, Barney."

"You have a husband."

"At his best he's baby talk. He's my child. You understand?"

"Only that I'd make a lousy stepfather."

"We could work around it," she said with supreme confidence. "Nothing's impossible."

"That is," he said.

She lifted the bottle and drank the dregs, the sun blazing on her diamonded ears. She placed the empty on the seat of the chair he had set up for her. "One last question, Barney. Is the reason her? Your other lady?"

He was silent.

"Is it none of my business?"

"It's not a factor," he said in a way that revealed more than he had intended.

He walked beside her to her car with the same lope and finality with which he had accompanied Kit, but with a great sense of aloneness, as if an old chill in his soul were making itself felt again. He opened the driver's door for her, but she stepped back and peered into his garage.

"Where is it?"

At first he pretended he did not know what she meant, but her eyes rolled too hard at him. "I gave it to Daisy."

"I should've known," she said, and kissed him.

They met in DeMoula's Supermarket at Shawsheen Plaza in Andover. With her young man, Mario, steering the overburdened cart, Rita O'Dea in a flouncy floral sundress rounded an aisle like a big Bo Peep exploding into a personification of summer. She halted after a few steps into the next aisle, motioned to Mario, and with one hand began fitting cans of Bumble Bee Tuna into the pyramid of the cart. Her other hand clutched a wad of grocery coupons, Mario's job to snip them from magazines and newspapers, a good way to learn to read English, she had told him. Slowly she lifted her eyes and said, "I was wondering when you were going to show up."

Louise Baker carried a plastic basket containing a loaf of bread. Her jaw was set rather tight.

"You look a little haggard," Rita said. "The weather or what?"

Both women edged aside, Rita the slower, as other shoppers sought passage, some casting curious glances as they might have at the zoo in nearby Stoneham.

"You certainly remember Mario," Rita said, and Louise nodded. Mario, no less a curious object than his patron, was wearing a fishnet top, running shorts, and sandals. His smile was dazzling. "You go pick out some treats for yourself," Rita said, and watched him maneuver the heavy cart down the aisle. "Look at that beautiful ass," she said with wonderment. "Be truthful, you ever see a sweeter one?"

Louise tilted toward a shelf stacked with pound cans of coffee, as if some inner rhythm had pushed her into an unexpected place. "I need a bailout," she said.

"I thought it might be something like that." Rita riffled the wad of coupons. "You use these? You'd be surprised how much you save. Place I go sometimes in New Hampshire they count for double, once triple, but that was a special time."

Louise shifted her basket to her other hand.

"Go ahead, tell me about it," Rita said, and listened with a cool ear, once throwing a punch with her eyes at a woman who stared too hard. When Louise finished, Rita said, "This is going to cost you."

"I expected that."

"I told the people in Boston about you wanting to retire. They asked me if there was a way to convince you it'd be better you didn't. I guess this is it."

The traces of fatigue in Louise's face sharpened noticeably and spread to her voice. "I guess it is," she said with resignation. She reached behind her and dropped a can of Maxwell House into her basket.

"I got a coupon for it," Rita said quickly. Her fingers flew. "Here."

They moved down the aisle, Rita with an amble, rocking from side to side. They spotted Mario at the cookie shelves. He saw them coming and, with a swing of his boyish hips, tossed up a package of chocolate-covered graham crackers.

"You want, you can borrow him sometime," Rita said.

Louise said, "Who knows, maybe I will."

* * *

"Hold my hand," Daisy Shea shouted to his wife. "Don't lose me." They were in the maw of the crowd storming the stadium for seats at the fireworks. Edith grabbed his wrist. Their two younger children had accompanied them but, armed with pocket money from Edith, had soon bounded off to an ice-cream truck with their friends. An hour remained until sunset, but the bleachers were filling fast. Families with folding chairs and blankets were camping on the grass girding the field, where Daisy had once made a spectacular run before a crowd nearly as large. His heart leaped as he remembered every detail, which made him shiver.

"You all right?"

"I'm fine," he said as they mounted the concrete steps of the bleachers. The higher seats were choice and taken, and they contented themselves with lower ones on an aisle, though the rubbish beneath the seats disturbed Edith. Daisy's heart continued to race, and the heat of cherished memories raised his color. Edith gave him a quick look.

"Did you take your pill?"

"I took it," he said, stretching his neck, seeking familiar faces in the swarm. Policemen roamed the fringes, the young ones stiff-backed and martial, the others shapeless in their soggy shirts. The air was heated and humid. He spotted a vendor setting up a food cart, laying out hot-dog rolls, and he prodded Edith. "You want something to eat?"

"We just had supper," she reminded him sharply.

He was restless. He wanted the darkness to descend immediately, fireworks to spray the sky. Suddenly he struck Edith's knee and pointed straight out. "There's

Barney Cole. He's with Arnold Ackerman, see him?" As she strained her eyes, Daisy jumped up. "Barney!"

"Christ, Daisy, he's clear across the field. He couldn't hear you in a hundred years." She pulled him down, but he bounced back up. "Stay in your seat," she said with another pull.

"I can't."

He was up and away, sliding on one foot, dropping abruptly onto the grass, where he squirmed into a crowd that carried him to the smell of boiled hot dogs, but the queue was too long, too many young healthy fathers carrying children on their shoulders. Veering away, he cut through the ranks of lolling youths and a flurry of children waving toy American flags. Real ones blazoned the distant end of the stadium. He scanned the opposing bleachers but could no longer see Barney.

Mosquitoes bit him. He slapped away several and pushed toward another vendor, this one hawking popcorn, but again the line was too long and, he noticed, too rowdy. Youths were shoving one another while off to one side a middle-aged bull of a man in a khaki shirt waited for one of them to wave a red flag in his face.

"Daisy!"

He spun around, uncertain where the voice came from, and nearly stepped on the shapely foot of an Hispanic girl. His eyes darted randomly, then lit on a man and a woman standing with video equipment next to a panel truck. The man waved, and Daisy forged ahead. The fellow was a long-ago drinking buddy named Ed. They had grown up together in the project. Ed had gone to work for the city and now was with the local cable channel.

Daisy embraced him. "How'd you spot me?"

Ed pushed him away. "I see a white-haired old drunk stumbling around, I figure it's Daisy Shea."

"I'm not drunk, Ed. I'm ill."

Ed laughed. "You mean you got the shakes?"

"I'm dying."

"No kidding." Ed's eyes were minnows in his big face. "You let me know when, maybe we can get it on camera."

The woman said, "You really dying?"

"Yes, I am."

Ed said, "This is my tootsie."

The woman, young and plain, had on a white dress that brought to mind the purity of an Easter lily. Daisy, bathing her with his stare, suddenly stroked her head. "I wish I could be around to watch you grow up."

"Shit," said Ed with disgust. "I got a kidney stone, two raw ulcers, and a heart murmur. You'll see *me* buried!"

"You were always a braggart," Daisy murmured.

Mosquitoes got to him again. He slapped an arm, aware of the shadows lengthening on the field, his ghost galloping through them for a touchdown, but the roar he heard was not for him. A fight had broken out near the popcorn vendor. The big man in khaki was beating a youth senseless while warding off his friends. The woman reached down for the video camera, but then changed her mind. Ed nudged her.

"Tell him what your father does."

"He's a funeral director," she said, rising on her toes to watch the ruckus, which two policemen were now trying to break up. Daisy gazed at her with respect.

"When they put your hands together, do they put the right over the left or vice versa? I'm concerned because I've got a deformed finger on the right. I broke it playing football."

"One lucky game you got into," Ed said. "Rest of the time you were a bench potato."

The police officers swung their clubs. The man in khaki took a glancing blow on the head from the first officer and a solid one at the base of the skull from the other. The woman again contemplated the camera, but it was all over, the first violence of the evening.

Louise Baker espied Henry Witlo moments after she and her mother entered the stadium. The shock of yellow hair was immediately recognizable. His gait, however, was different, which at first she attributed to the spin of the crowd but then to the fact that he was favoring an arm. Also, though his clothes were clean, he looked unwashed and unkempt. The improbable woman at his side was fiftyish, maybe even sixty, with cinnamon hair scraped back as if by a wire brush and with lipstick fastened to her face like a holiday decoration dug out of the attic. Her dress was dowdy and a size too large.

Then they vanished.

But Louise could not get them out of her mind. She unfolded lightweight aluminum chairs and placed them on the grass. Her mother was glad to sit down but grew uncomfortable when a lively Hispanic family spread a blanket nearby. The smaller children waved little flags. With a prod, her mother whispered, "That's not their flag."

"Yes, it is, Mama." Mrs. Leone, unconvinced, settled in warily, opened a small bag she had brought from home, and offered up a *torrone*, which Louise declined with a shake of her head. "It's not American, Mama."

"You being fresh." The old woman ate cheerfully of the candy, her teeth strong enough to relish the almonds. "All the time you looking over that way. What for?"

"Just looking, Mama."

"Somebody there?"

"Nobody."

A few minutes later some sort of disturbance broke out across the field, but was soon quelled, which raised both cheers and boos. Girls pink and fleshy, playfully shameless, paraded by, precipitating censure from Mrs. Leone. Louise came up from her chair.

"I'm going for a cold drink, Mama. You want one?"

"No, but you hurry. They begin soon."

Somehow she knew she would run into him again. He was waiting his turn at an ice-cream wagon and finally came away with two Fudgsicles in one hand. He seemed to feel her eyes on him and immediately squared his shoulders and pulled in his gut. He would have strode past her had she not stepped in his way.

"What's your hurry, Henry?"

Her voice took him back, and all at once he seemed uncomfortable, somewhat ashamed, his body full of strain. She stared at him hard and cold. The only aspect of him that seemed the same was his eyes, blue studs that might have been scratched at birth. "I want to apologize for what I did to your car, Mrs. Baker. It was an accident."

She ignored the apology. "What happened to your face? When's the last time you got a haircut? You look a mess."

He ignored the questions. "I've stayed away like you asked. I haven't bothered you at all, have I?"

"Far as I know you haven't." She felt she was talking to the wind, to another child, like Ben. "Who's the woman I saw you with?"

"Don't say anything against her, Mrs. Baker."

"I was merely asking."

People forged by in the fading light. Behind them, the

whine of a child imitated the pule of a dog. Waves of excitement washed through the crowd as the pyrotechnician and city officials made their way to the middle of the field, where they circled guarded stores of fireworks like Pentagon people ogling the latest weapons of war.

Henry said, "I've made a new life for myself, Mrs. Baker. I've got a woman that needs me."

"A lot of women have needed you, Henry, but not for long. I probably put up with you longer than most, but that's because I've got a soft spot."

"This is different, Mrs. Baker. This is love."

She gave him a searching gaze. "The gal's no spring chicken. What else is it?"

"You wouldn't understand," he said.

"You'd be surprised how smart I am."

In the middle of the field someone was blowing into a microphone, priming it for the mayor, who was ready to make a speech. The crowd began to chant.

"I got to get back to her, Mrs. Baker."

"She'll go crazy if you don't?"

"Don't make a joke about it. She's not like you and me."

Louise recoiled as if he had slapped her. She felt all of her roots tugging at her. She felt the draft from a tenement window, the dead of winter. She heard the drip from a corroded faucet and heard a rat in the woodwork. She said, "Looks like I did you a favor sending you to this little shithouse of a city."

The Fudgsicles were melting. "I got to go."

She took hold of herself. "Best of luck to you and your lady," she said, proffering her right hand.

He tried but could not raise his.

The mayor's amplified voice, scratchy and at times unintelligible, boomed through the stadium. His jokes, those the crowd could hear, bordered on stupidity. In the bleachers on the visiting-team side, Arnold Ackerman dozed off, slumped hard against Barney Cole, and woke with a jolt, his back hurting. He rubbed the small of it and said, "That's the damn trouble getting old. You start sleeping sitting up. You know, Barney, there's not a chair in my house I haven't dropped off in." The mayor's voice vibrated, accompanied by mechanical reverberations. "What's he saying?"

"He's telling Pat and Mike jokes," Cole said.

"Oh, my God, somebody tell him we've heard them all."

"He's young."

"He's that young, he should have his mouth washed out." Arnold yawned, his rubbery mouth expanding to the fullest, his eyes watering. "Christ, I could be home right now watching old movies. You know something, Barney, all the ones I saw as a kid I'm seeing again. Like living my life over. All the funny little feelings I had back then, I get again. I even got a pimple." He touched his chin. "Look, right here."

"That's what modern technology does, Arnold. Intrudes even into your past."

Arnold swallowed and grimaced, as if his mouth tasted of something deep within himself. "I ask myself where all the years have gone, and then I realize they're all inside me, every damn one, the good and the bad." He belched softly. "Queer, but it's the good ones that come up on me."

"You OK?"

"I wouldn't mind a Pepsi. You wouldn't think it would, but it always settles my stomach."

"You want me to get you one?"

"I wouldn't want to be a pain in the ass."

Cole picked his way out of the bleachers and onto the edge of the field, where an air of expectancy and carnival was growing. The mayor, done with jokes, concluded his speech, and the crowd, which had been hooting, cheered. Cole looked for a vendor and found Daisy Shea.

Daisy tottered one way and then another, torn in opposing directions. He grabbed on to Cole. "You got to show me the way, Barney. I've lost my bearings. I must be in the final stages."

"Do you want to sit down first?"

"No, I've got to get back to Edith. To my woman. A man doesn't have a woman, he's got nothing. I'm lucky, Barney. I'm the luckiest man on earth. Lou Gehrig said that to thousands at Yankee Stadium. My father heard him say it. My father wasn't there, but he heard it on the radio."

Cole drew him out of the path of a throng of children.

He said, "Do you think the mayor would let me use the microphone? Just for a minute?"

"I don't think so. The fireworks will be starting soon."

Daisy smiled his brightest. "I got to thank you again for the car. It drives like a dream. My father used to say wheels make the man. I feel like a bigger person already," he said, and rose on his toes, his bare arms smeary from slapping mosquitoes. He slapped another. "Am I the only one they're biting, Barney? Seems that way."

Cole batted the darkening air. "No, Arnold was whacking a few."

"I didn't see you at Chick's funeral. I looked for you."

"I was there," Cole said quietly.

"Police came from all over, far away as Connecticut. One of the biggest funerals in the city's history, the paper said. Mine won't be that big," he said with a shrinking voice and a misplaced smile. "That's why I wanted to use the mike."

"Where did you leave Edith?"

"Let me think," he said, stooping to pull up a sock that had lapsed into his shoe. "Which bleachers are you in?"

Cole pointed.

"Then it's got to be the other one."

"You want me to walk you there?"

"Would you, Barney? I'd appreciate it."

As they trekked through the dark the first rocket soared into the sky, exploded high up, and luminesced the night. The crowd, caught in the brilliance, responded with a concert of oohs and aahs.

One of the Fudgsicles fell from Henry's grasp. Furiously he licked the other one under its paper wrap, but it was melting too fast and messing his fingers. He tossed it away, and a dog dragging a leash pounced upon it. Somebody in the crowd bumped him. Somebody else pushed him. Then they pressed in upon him, an overwhelming presence holding him in place, a black man in scholarly gold-rimmed glasses and a blond man with a face so flawless he looked unnatural. The blond one flashed identification he did not properly see, though he caught a glimpse of silver, which reminded him of the crossing-guard badge he had worn in grade school, a proud possession until a misdeed in the boys' lavatory took it away forever. The blond man spoke. "What's your name?"

"Henry," he said, and thought the worst. "She's an old lady. You going to believe her?" They wanted his wallet. Both examined it, the black man with the longest fingers he had ever seen. Fear scrambled his brain. He considered bolting, but his buttocks tightened. "That money's mine," he said. "I sold my car."

The blond man returned the wallet intact. "Chicopee. You from Chicopee? What are you doing here?"

He had answers, but in his head none of them sounded right. "What have I done?"

"We're more interested in what you might do. How long have you known the woman you were talking to?"

Something clicked. "You mean Mrs. Baker. Year." A load was lifted from him. He wanted to sing. "You guys got something on your mind, better you say it straight out."

"We're interested in Mrs. Baker's friends. You act like one."

"You harassing me?" His voice rose, drawing stares from a hot press of faces. Children giggled. A woman burped her baby. A half-dozen Hispanic men stood straight and small, brightly painted against the approaching darkness. They had been chittering like birds but now were silent. Henry relished the audience and played to it. "Name, rank, and serial number is all I got to give. The rest, you'd better talk to my lawyer. He's local, name's Cole."

The blond man smiled easily. "My name's Cruickshank, his is Blue, in case you want to file any complaints."

"That depends on you guys," he said, his eyes now fully on Blue, who fascinated him for reasons not yet fathomed. Something about the eyes, the remote manner; he was not sure. Then it hit him, and he trembled. "Do I know you?"

"We tend to look alike," Blue said.

"Nam."

"A lot of us were there."

"This guy had fingers like you, but every bit of him went up. Nothing I could do. I took cover."

"I'd have done the same."

343

"The rest of them, your guys, got theirs later. Got caught in a crossfire." Henry wanted to shut up, but it was as if someone had tripped the mechanism that set him talking. "They done what I did, they wouldn't have got killed."

"What's a few more niggers more or less," Blue said.

"Wasn't my fault."

"It never is."

Someone was competing with him, an amplified voice from the middle of the field. The crowd was hissing. His audience was dwindling. He said, "Christ, I was just a kid. Just turned seventeen. Some of them were old as twenty."

"You had your whole life ahead of you."

"You think I came back whole? I got no use in my right arm." He raised his other arm and swabbed his face hard as if he feared his darker secrets were showing. His voice swept away from him, and he breathed it back, inflating his lungs. "I got to get back to my aunt. She's an old lady. She's waiting for me."

"It's all right," Blue said. "I've got your name."

Cruickshank said, "I got his number."

He slipped away from them, threaded into the crowd between the bright shirts of Hispanic men whose lacquered faces opened into smiles, all of which he ignored. The darkness was falling too fast for his step, and he stumbled against a child wearing a plastic space helmet. The eyes, the button nose, which were all he could make out, reminded him of a boyhood pal, Felix Stanky, with whom he had pitched a neighbor's dog off a roof. When the cops came, Felix, motherless, took the blame and a social worker assigned him to a home for wayward youth, where, according to rumor, a Franciscan brother buggered him and beat him to death. Henry never doubted the rumor.

Somebody brushed his arm. It was his bad arm, and he stiffened. In the light emanating from a hot-dog wagon he scowled into the face of a middle-aged man with a patch over one eye, something familiar about him, but then everybody was beginning to look familiar. A woman scooping popcorn into her mouth reminded him of his mother, and the amplified voice of the mayor had a haunting ring, as if he had been hearing it all his life. When he moved into the dark, a smaller voice shot after him.

"I forgive you."

He spun on his heels, suddenly enraged, partly because he did not know where it came from. "Who the fuck are you to forgive me?" he shouted. And then he remembered.

He groped his way into the bleachers, followed his instincts, and found Emma Goss where he had left her. A floodlight from the top of the bleachers revealed her disappointment when she realized he had brought back no ice cream, nothing on a stick, only his own overly emphatic self. Squeezed in next to her, he pawed through his wallet and tugged out a grimy business card that had gone soft at the edges. He forced it upon her.

"The guy's name printed there, you know him?"

She glanced at the card in the half light. "Pothier," she said through too much lipstick. "Harold bought the china closet from his father."

"He says he forgives me."

She returned the card dismissively, with no curiosity. Henry said, "I don't believe him."

* * *

It was an hour of polytechnics, a splendid display in the hot iridescent night, the explosions ear-popping, the air full of flare and smoke. Roman candles shrieked up one after the other in high arching trajectories, streaking, bursting, and blitzing. Streamers festooned the sky and burnt holes in it. Rockets burst into chunks of gold, spirals of silver, gigantic pinwheels of brilliance, so that the earth now seemed heavenly. Henry grabbed Emma's hand. "This is what war should be like, Mrs. Goss. Not the other stuff." He jerked his hand away and whistled through two fingers. He relished the noise, the smoldering smells, the blizzard of sparks. When someone set off a cannon cracker under the bleachers, he savored that too, though Emma clutched her heart. When it was over, he shouted for more. Emma gathered herself together and prodded him.

The crowds herded toward the open gates in a sluggish mood of anticlimax marked by random bursts of disembodied laughter. Henry's letdown was keen. He felt there should have been more, certainly a brass band, a final salute, the added drama of a volley. Here and there he viewed an isolated shape in the crowd and viewed it with challenge.

"Stay near me," he said with bravado, as if her safety depended upon him. "You see him, let me know." She did not know what he was talking about and did not ask. "Pothier," he informed her theatrically. "He's wearing a patch." She glanced at him as if he were crazy. When she stumbled over a discarded soda can, he said, "Don't worry, I got more strength in one hand than he's got in his whole body." He was itching for a confrontation, angry as one seemed less likely with each step closer to the main gate, which was flanked by policemen, but that was where it happened.

Emma saw them first, five or six of them, recognized one, and said nothing.

They came out of the crowd without missing a step, Hispanics who had been part of the half-seen audience he had played to earlier and now were performing for him with grins too big for their lacquered faces, with low catcalls in Spanish, with elaborate hand waves. As they swept by, he focused on the wrong one, fingers in splints, and never had a chance. The knife went in and out like lightning. He felt no pain until he tripped over his own feet and knew what they had done. Clutching himself below the heart, he let out a sigh of relief when he saw no blood. Then it came.

The crowd swerved when he fell; he lay on the grass as if every face in the world were aimed down at him. He looked for Emma, but it was a policeman who crouched over him and asked something he did not hear. "I want my aunt," he told the officer, who was soon replaced by a leaner figure whose face was black and framed by gold-rimmed glasses. "Am I going to make it?" he asked.

"There's always a chance," Agent Blue murmured.

"Hold my hand," he pleaded.

"Like you held theirs?" Blue asked, and a second later gripped Henry's hand, the right one, which suddenly had gathered strength, as if Henry were in the process of becoming whole again. "Anything you want to tell me?" Blue asked.

"Cops killed my mother."

"Anything you want to tell me about Mrs. Baker?"

Henry's eyes rolled back. "Where's my aunt?"

Blue rose and, with a glance at Agent Cruickshank, shook his head.

Emma Goss, unladylike, hunkered down beside him.

It seemed that she was trying to kiss him, especially when his face twitched her way, but it was his ear she sought, not his cheek. "When you get to hell," she whispered through painted lips, "tell Harold everything." Then she tugged at his shoes. A policeman stopped her.

"What the hell are you doing?"

"They're not his," she explained.

The policeman pulled her up, and a woman who smelled of the baby she had been holding kept her on her feet. A siren wailed in the distance as a team of officers held the crowd back at one place and pushed it along at another. In the welter Daisy Shea's face burned. He shouted, "I know that guy, Edith. I forget his name, but I know him." Edith was ahead of him, ignoring him. He caught up with her. "Jesus Christ, everybody's dying but me."

"Maybe you're not," Edith said. "Did you ever think of that?"

The attendant's name was Clarence, a fastidious fellow who changed his work whites twice a day and carried a piece of chalk in his pocket for scuff marks on his white shoes. He had the plump clean face of a master baker, with cornflower eyes that might have been colored by crayon. His two dumpling chins added a third when he smiled, revealing little teeth better suited to the head of a baby. He did not look especially strong or agile, but he lifted Ben Baker from the bed with scarcely any effort and deposited him in a comfortable chair at the open French windows. "About time you saw the sunshine," he mandated, and patted Ben's head. "I've missed my little man."

"I missed you too," Ben said, as if he had not, or not as much.

"Do you want your slippers or would you rather wiggle your toes?"

"I want my slippers," Ben said peevishly, and stretched his pale feet out of his silk pajama trousers. The pajamas were monogrammed, one of several sets Mrs. Mennick had packed for him. Clarence fetched the slippers of soft tan-faced leather and sniffed them.

"Nice," he said, and, crouching, counted toes. "Remind me to clip those nails," he said, and worked Ben's pliant feet into the slippers. "I knew you'd snap out of it, Mr. Baker. You're a fighter."

Ben agreed. "It's bred into me. My people helped settle this country."

Clarence stayed in his crouch to massage Ben's ankles. Showing his little teeth, he said, "Your lovely wife phones every day. I talked to her yesterday. I told her you'd be coming out of it. I could tell."

Ben said negligently, "She worries about me."

"She should worry more about what she's paying for you here. I know for a fact they're soaking her."

Ben pulled at the front of his pajama top. "She can afford it. She's Mafia, you know."

"Yes, you told me that the last time. That must be very exciting."

Ben gazed out at rolling hills not unlike those viewed from his bedroom windows at home. With cold petulance, he said, "She thinks because she has my name she has my breeding, my bloodline. But she's just an Italian. I'd never use her toothbrush."

Clarence, kneading Ben's calves under the silk, said, "Would you use mine?"

Ben said, "I cringe when she sits in my mother's chair. She thinks she belongs there. My nanny and I know better."

"But her money's nice," Clarence said. "Yum, yum."

"She's not like us," Ben replied suavely. "Different smell."

"Seems to me something doesn't smell right here," Clarence said, wrinkling his pink nose. Then abruptly he slapped Ben on the wrist. "Damn you, Mr. Baker, did you do dirty in your pants?"

Ben smiled prettily. "Change me," he said.

The first bullet missed John Rozzi by a foot, the second grazed his shoulder. Instinct, premonition, natural wariness: he had instantly gone on the alert when he stepped out of his room.

Somebody was waiting to use the toilet. A young guy with his back to him, wearing a girlish kind of jacket with the sleeves hiked to the elbows like a movie star or a sport. When the guy whirled around with a piece in his hand and fired, John was already charging like a bull. He slammed into him full force and knocked him ass over teakettle, took all the wind out of him, stomped his gun hand, and grabbed his throat. He would have strangled him then and there, but other lodgers were popping out of their rooms, people were shouting from other floors. A woman with the back of her dress caught in her underpants ran shrieking from the bathroom. Also, he recognized the sweet Sicilian face.

He lifted Mario to his feet, shook him, banged his head against the wall, and an inch from his nose said, "You go back. You go back, you tell the fat woman you missed." With a violent twist, he threw him down the stairs. Then he unloaded the pistol and hurled it after him. "While you're at it, tell Mrs. Baker too."

An hour later, after some deep thought and a double shot of rye whiskey at the Italo-American Social Club, where he and Sal Botello had often played forty-fives, he drove to a pay phone on the highway. He dialed a number from a scrap of paper, and when a voice came on the line he said, "This is John Rozzi."

After a slight pause, the voice said, "Yes, John, what can we do for you?"

John went silent.

"Do you have something for us, John?"

"You the white guy or the black guy?"

"I'm the black guy," the voice said. "Name's Blue."

"Let me talk to the other guy."

"Whatever makes you happy," Agent Blue said, and a moment later Agent Cruickshank came on the line.

"What do you want, John?"

"I want that witness protection program, that's what I want."

All of July was hot, no rain except for a few brief thunderstorms, one violent enough to tear off a large limb from the tree next to Emma Goss's house. The limb landed on the roof but did no damage according to the man who removed it for her. Despite the heat, Emma spent much time in her yard. Every day she watered the lawn, and twice she mowed it, avoiding the milkweed. The monarchs needed it. Once, while she was reading the newspaper in the shade, a monarch gently worked its way over the humid air and lit on her arm, where it stayed until she turned a page.

Several times, from her side of the shrubbery, Mrs. Whipple tried to get into conversation with Emma, but each time Emma cut her short. Finally Mrs. Whipple beat a path through the boundary bushes and confronted her. "About your poor nephew, Mrs.—"

"You know he was not my nephew," Emma interrupted, superimposing her words on Mrs. Whipple's. "You know that very well."

"I was only being polite, Mrs. Goss. After all, it was not *my* fiction, was it?"

Emma heard her words quite clearly but felt her presence only obliquely and was beginning to dismiss it altogether.

"My husband treated it as a joke," Mrs. Whipple said, "but I said more power to you. Romance isn't just for the young. And at any age, I said to him, what's worse than living alone?"

"Living a lie," Emma said coldly, and turned away.

A little later she sat at the desk in the den with Harold's gold pen. After some hesitation, she wrote a letter to Mildred Murphy in Florida and told her exactly what she thought of her, but upon reading it over she tore the deckle-edge notepaper into bits. It no longer seemed important.

Doing housework, she stopped short when she thought she glimpsed Henry in the glare of the china closet and grimaced at her foolishness when closer inspection revealed only the dishes that had been her mother's. She did her housework in a pair of striped shorts, which she did not yet dare wear outside or in front of the two young men from Sears, Roebuck who maneuvered a new mattress into the house and took away the old. She also stuffed Harold's clothing into cartons and placed them in the driveway, knowing the rubbish man would sort through them. In one carton were Harold's Florsheims and loafers and Henry's ripple-soled construction boots. That evening she took a long bath, went to bed early, and savored the crispness of the fresh sheets and the hardness of the mattress. She had her best sleep in years, not unlike that of a child exhausted by a day of play.

During the second week of July she made an appointment with the Lawrence Driving School. She had never been behind the wheel of a car in her life, and her first lesson was a disaster, though the instructor assured her that he had seen worse. Her second lesson was no better. Her hands gripping the wheel, her nose dripping sweat, she proclaimed, "I'll get it if it kills me."

The perfect repartee died on the instructor's lips. Something about the intensity of her determination made him say instead, "I'm sure you will, Mrs. Goss."

It was the first week of August. Stealthy storm clouds appeared in the midnight sky like sailing ships from another time, bringing hours of howling rain that lasted into the late morning and left the landscape smashed and drowned. Then came sudden sunlight, prismatic puddles, quaking lilac leaves. "Everything's beautiful," Daisy Shea said, greeting the world with a smile and failing to notice that someone had stolen the hubcaps from the Cutlass Supreme. Edith pointed it out. "It's OK," he said with irrepressible optimism. "I'll file a claim."

"You've got a three-hundred-dollar deductible," she said with a long face. "How much do you think you're going to get?" She waited poignantly for an answer and then said, "You should've sold it like I wanted. The only kind of car you can keep in this neighborhood is a junk." She viewed him with a critical eye and softened her voice. "You shouldn't wear short sleeves, Daisy. You haven't got the arms anymore. And you're wearing your pants too high. You look like a pear."

"But I feel good," he said. "That's what's important. How do you feel, Edith?"

"Tired. Come on, let's go."

She was late for work. He drove her. Within a few minutes he slid into the clatter of downtown traffic with two fingers on the wheel, which was how he had driven when courting her, impressing her then, annoying her now. When he pulled up at the coffee shop, she took a ten-dollar bill from her bag and gave it to him.

"Have a good lunch," she said. "Not here. The food's poison."

He tucked the bill in his breast pocket and thrust his smiling face at her. "Give the old man a smacker," he said, and puckered his lips. In a hurry, she placed her fingers against her own mouth and then pressed them against his.

"Don't spend that money on booze."

He drove to Bishop's, got there before the full lunch crowd, and was seated at a good table in the middle of the dining room where he could see everybody coming in. Brushing aside the menu, he ordered lamb on a stick. "No fries," he told the waitress. "And nothing to drink. I'm being a good boy."

He knew none of the faces at the surrounding tables, mostly women from downtown offices, but he smiled jauntily whenever he caught an eye. He liked the slipshod way one woman tore her bread and the vigorous way another chewed her food as if life were to be enjoyed to the fullest, no compromises. When the waitress brought his order, the lamb as succulent-looking as anticipated, he prepared to eat in the same zestful fashion, but never took a bite.

A pain shot through his head, lasting only seconds but so excruciating he felt something had been torn from him. His whole head ballooned, which impaired his hearing. Everyone in the restaurant was carrying on as before, but now without him. It was as though he were watching a mute movie in which all looks, gestures, and movements were sudden and sharp, in many ways sinister, and in all ways exaggerated. Slowly he pushed aside his plate and cradled his head in his arms on the table. The women around him stopped eating and stared. The waitress bent over him. Without raising his head, he whispered, "I'm quite sick." The next moment he was dead.

A federal grand jury handed down secret indictments against Louise Leone Baker, 5 Baker's Meadow, Mallard Junction, and Rita Gardella O'Dea, Farrwood Drive, Andover. Both women, along with Mario Paolino of Palermo, Sicily, were arraigned in Boston, where they had been in deep consultation with their lawyers, the indictments not as secret as supposed. Later, outside the courthouse, they faced a welter of reporters and television cameras. Rita's lawyer told her to say nothing, but she ignored him and positioned herself for the cameras. "They hounded my brother, now they're hounding me," she said in a rich voice, and paused dramatically. "I'll tell you something, ladies and gentlemen, my brother was tough, but I'm tougher."

Louise, averting her head, referred all questions to her lawyer. Mario, who pretended he knew no English, posed. Later he asked Rita whether it would be on Italian television. She grabbed his wrist and nearly broke it.

Ben Baker was released from the hospital on that same day. Clarence, blinding in his freshly laundered work whites, walked Ben down the flower-lined path to the pickup truck, where Mrs. Mennick and her brother, Howard, were waiting. Clarence handed over Ben's old leather suitcase to Howard, who unceremoniously tossed it into the back of the truck. Clarence stuck out his large placid face, which looked as if a little of everything were kneaded into it. "You take care of yourself, Mr. Baker."

But Ben had forgotten him. He was gazing wildly about. "Where's Lou?" he whined.

Mrs. Mennick opened the passenger door of the truck. "Get in, Mr. Ben."

When he failed to move, Howard gave him a push.

Aged aunts and forgotten cousins shed tears in the central viewing room of John Breen's Funeral Home. The mother who had borne him was dry-eyed until she approached the casket, and then she broke down. Old drinking buddies reached in for a final touch. A flicker of light on the dead man's face softened the features, and for an amazing moment the eyelids seemed ready to twitch open, as if the deceased were moved by all the attention and grief.

Barney Cole moved from the casket to Edith Shea, who immediately gripped his upper arms. Her eyes were liquid, like oil. She said, "His left hand should be over his right. Could you tell Mr. Breen?"

"Yes," Cole said, "I'll tell him."

"Barney, I didn't even give him a proper kiss good-bye. I had the chance, I didn't take it." For a moment her mouth was all muscle. "If I could have him back for one more minute, that would do it. But Mr. Breen can't do that for me, can he?"

A while later Cole left the funeral home, stood beside his car, and immersed himself in the dark air, his eyes reaching upward. The night sky was a jewelry box thrown open. Kit Fletcher climbed out of the old Cutlass and joined him, slinging an arm inside his.

"What do you see up there?"

"Too many stars to count," he said, and took a breath. "I don't get it. A guy dies, the sky stays bright."

"The world goes on, Barney, with or without us." She pressed closer. "How are you doing?"

"Good. Fine. I'm OK." He looked at her. "Thanks for coming with me."

"Thanks for calling."

"You've got that wrong," he said. "I didn't call, you did."

Her smile was mysterious. "Are you sure of that?"

"Absolutely."

"Could I persuade you otherwise?"

Heated smells of the city drifted through the lot. Across the way were low brick buildings for the elderly, where the only signs of life were from Sonys and Zeniths, their colors fluttering in the windows like flowers no more comforting than the bouquets girding Daisy Shea's casket. "Why would I want to fool myself?" he asked.

"So I won't have to beg."

"I wouldn't want you ever to do that."

The night murmured. People trickled out of the funeral home, a couple of the men heaving around to look at Kit, whose arm had tightened against Cole's. "We had something, Barney. Do we really want to say good-bye to it?"

Cole had no answer, only a sensation of heat lurking in the ashes. Loosening his arm, he opened the Cutlass door for her and then moved around to the other side and slipped in behind the wheel. She had taken the key from the ignition.

"I know what's going on in your mind," she said. "You're wondering to what extent I'm dishonest. If my word's good for anything, I can promise you I'll never do anything again behind your back." She smiled into his face. "Scout's honor."

Lights from a turning car swept over them and made them stark. Cole returned the smile but stayed within himself. The moon was radiant, like a sort of cake. At that moment he could no more believe that men had walked on the moon than he could that he and Daisy Shea had once been nineteen years old, with everything ahead of them. He was still smiling.

"What's the joke?" she asked.

"You're not a Girl Scout."

"That's right. Just an attractive and intelligent person like you." She handed over the ignition key. "Let's go home and have that kid. A damn waste of nature if we don't."

Leaning into the windshield, he took a final look at the stars and said, "Most of us can't come anywhere near predicting the future, but the guy lying in there knew exactly what his was."

"We can predict a little of ours," she said with confidence as more headlights poured over them. Her voice, turning husky and playful, touched his cheek. "By the way, I'm giving up a lot for you. A trip to Italy."

He said, "I think you'd better take it."

ANDREW COBURN

ON THE LOOSE

By the time he was twelve years old, young Bobby Sawhill had killed two people, brutally and with no remorse. He was tried as a juvenile and sentenced to a youth detention center, where he refused counseling. All he seems to care about is bodybuilding, getting bigger. Stronger. Soon he'll be twenty-one. He'll be released— and then Bobby's coming home. Home to a small town that will live in fear, certain that Bobby will kill again, unable to do anything but wait for him to strike.

AMERICA'S LAST DAYS

DOUGLAS MACKINNON

Is the United States of America the nation our Founding Fathers intended it to be? Or has the government lost sight of our ideals? To some of the most powerful men and women in the country—including a former Chairman of the Joint Chiefs of Staff and a former Director of the FBI—the answer is growing increasingly obvious, and so is the only possible solution: The time has come to revolt. Their daring plans will not only drive a government to its knees, they will change the course of history.
